Praise for *Elinor*

Being long intrigued by th[illegible] [illegible]read *Elinor*, Shannon McNear'[illegible] [illegible]tery. I wasn't disappointed! The [illegible] [illegible]ally painted. The characters, Elinor and Sees Far in particular, were vivid and sympathetic in their courage to adapt to challenging circumstances and new ideas. To call the research behind this story thorough is an understatement. By the end, I couldn't turn pages fast enough yet didn't want the story to end. Readers of *Elinor* will be glad there's more to look forward to in this series.

—Lori Benton, Christy Award-winning author of *Mountain Laurel* and *Shiloh*

A riveting, romantic, and redemptive story that shines hopeful light on what might have happened to the Lost Colony of Roanoke. *Elinor* is beautifully told, and Shannon McNear is sure to win historical hearts with this stirring, well-researched tale of early America.

—Laura Frantz, Christy Award-winning author of *A Heart Adrift*

A haunting tale of the New World that doesn't merely tug at the heartstrings. . . . It wraps around and squeezes until the story becomes part of you—and you part of the story. Elinor is a complex character of strength and weakness, courage and fear, the sort of woman who is truly an everyday hero.

—Michelle Griep, Christy Award-winning author of *Once Upon a Dickens Christmas*

Tender and terrifying, beautiful and raw. Shannon McNear's *Elinor* offers a gripping depiction of what might have been the fate of the Lost Colony of Roanoke in a story as haunting as the mysterious mist-shrouded isles and inlets of its setting. McNear brings to vivid life a world populated by intriguing, realistically portrayed characters who draw the reader ever deeper into this compelling and, at times, unsettling story. Despite the tragedy and heartache the colonists endure, the ending brings tears with its vision of a hopeful future for those left behind on that fateful shore. Though it is not the outcome they desired, they choose to trust in the Lord who led them to that land and to believe in the faithful fulfillment of his promises. In *Elinor*, McNear encourages readers to do the same.

—J. M. Hochstetler, author of The American Patriot Series and coauthor of the Northkill Amish Series

She's done it again! Shannon McNear sweeps readers into a world our society barely remembers—much less understands—this time taking up the longstanding mystery of the Lost Colony. Her pen brings to life not only Elinor Dare, her young family, her father—the governor of the colony, and the native people of the New World, but the majestic forests and undiscovered wilds of the land itself. Painstaking research provides a sound explanation for what happened to the citizens of Roanoke, then, in mid-story, you're snatched away on a nail-biting adventure that doesn't slow down until its unexpected ending.

—Denise Weimer, historical editor and multi-published author of *Bent Tree Bride* and other Early American frontier fiction

Shannon McNear blends a believable tale from documented history, accepted lore, hours of research, and vivid imagination that will pull the reader back in time. Meet the brave men and women who set out to start a colony in the New World even before the Pilgrims. Also meet the Native Americans who befriended and opposed them. *Elinor* is a compelling and thoughtful story of what might have been.

—Pegg Thomas, award-winning Author of *Sarah's Choice*

The haunting story of the Lost Colony of Roanoke is richly reimagined and hard to put down in Shannon McNear's *Elinor*. With a deep regard for historical detail and a voice that brings to life the dangerous and beguiling wilderness of the New World, the author spins a fascinating tale of redemption and possibilities. *Elinor's* compelling story is sure to linger long in my memory.

—Naomi Musch, author of 2019 Selah finalist and Book-of-the-Year nominee *Mist O'er the Voyageur, Song for the Hunter,* and *The Lumberjacks and Ladies* collection.

A Riveting Story Based on the Lost Colony of Roanoke

SHANNON MCNEAR

Print ISBN 978-1-64352-954-7

eBook Editions:
Adobe Digital Edition (.epub) 978-1-64352-956-1

All scripture quotations are taken from the Great Bible (1539). Public domain. Spellings have been updated.

This book is a work of fiction. Names, characters, places, and incidents are either products of the author's imagination or used fictitiously. Any similarity to actual people, organizations, and/or events is purely coincidental.

Cover Design: Kirk DouPonce, DogEared Design

Published by Barbour Publishing, Inc., 1810 Barbour Drive, Uhrichsville, Ohio 44683, www.barbourbooks.com

Our mission is to inspire the world with the life-changing message of the Bible.

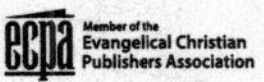

Printed in the United States of America

For all of you who believed
I really could do this

O Lord, thou hast searched me out, and known me. Thou knowest my down sitting and mine uprising: thou understandest my thoughts long before. Thou are about my path, and about my bed: and spyest out all my ways. For lo, there is not a word on my tongue, but thou, O Lord, knowest it all together. . . .

Try me, O God, and seek the ground of mine heart: prove me and examine my thoughts. Look well if there be any way of wickedness in me, and lead me in the way everlasting. (Psalm 139: 1–4, 23–24)

Dear Reader,

Few droplets of history have captured the imagination and curiosity so firmly as the "Lost" Colony of Roanoke Island. Subsequent explorers to the region have sought word of them, with only the barest rumors and scraps of evidence to mark their existence. Both weather and local politics have prevented serious pursuit of verifying those clues, almost as if God Himself intended them to vanish into the mists of time. But historians and storytellers, shysters and honest businessmen alike have fallen under the spell of the question: Who were the Lost Colony and where did they go?

At some point, all historical fiction becomes speculative fiction. This story especially so, because there is so little we know for certain about the fate of these people, or of those with whom they sought to build community. I can only hope my own attempt at exploring the possibilities in some small way does justice to their faith and courage, on all sides.

A note about names: though standardized spelling did not exist until the advent of Noah Webster's great work, and language has changed greatly over the past four hundred years, I have used contemporary terms and spellings as much as possible. Sir Walter Raleigh spelled his own name in various ways, but the most common in his time was *Ralegh*. I also call Roanoke Island by what seems to be the closest phonetically to the Carolina Algonquian name, *Roanoac*, giving the word four syllables and not the modern three. More about this later in my notes at the end of the book, but many Algonquian place names carry the *oh-ock* suffix, transliterated to English as *oac*, *oak*, or *ooc* but spoken as two distinct syllables.

In the same way, the actual spelling of Elinor's name varied between *Elyoner* and *Eleanor*, both of which lead me to believe the pronunciation of the time gave two syllables in the middle of the name: *ELL-ee-oh-nor* or, more likely, *Ell-EE-oh-nor*. I chose the simpler *Elinor* because it is one of the spellings recorded in her father's own accounts (strangely enough, not even he was consistent), and it seems easier for the modern reader—the alternate pronunciation would probably be lost in translation, with the printed word.

I have also spelled native words more or less phonetically. More on this later, and a glossary and cast of characters are included at the end.

A last note on words that carry negative cultural connotation. I personally hold great respect and appreciation for indigenous peoples—but an author often finds herself needing to use terms that while accurate to history are, frankly, very loaded in our time. The word *savage* in this story is one of those. It was used universally by Europeans—the English, Spanish, French, etc.—for the indigenous peoples of the Americas, whom they viewed as less refined, less educated, and less informed on true religion than themselves. Sometimes it was a reflection of their own personal attitudes toward such people, but in some cases it was considered just a word—a colloquial term of the time. It will no doubt offend some of my readers or at least cause discomfort—as did my use of the word *Negro* in *The Rebel Bride*—but it is an accurate reflection of the terminology of the era. While I do attempt in this story to explore the implied meaning of the term *savage*, please understand that mostly I am attempting to portray people in their own historical and cultural context, and no personal offense is intended, nor does it reflect my own views.

Thank you for venturing on this journey with me!

My most earnest regards,
Shannon

Part One

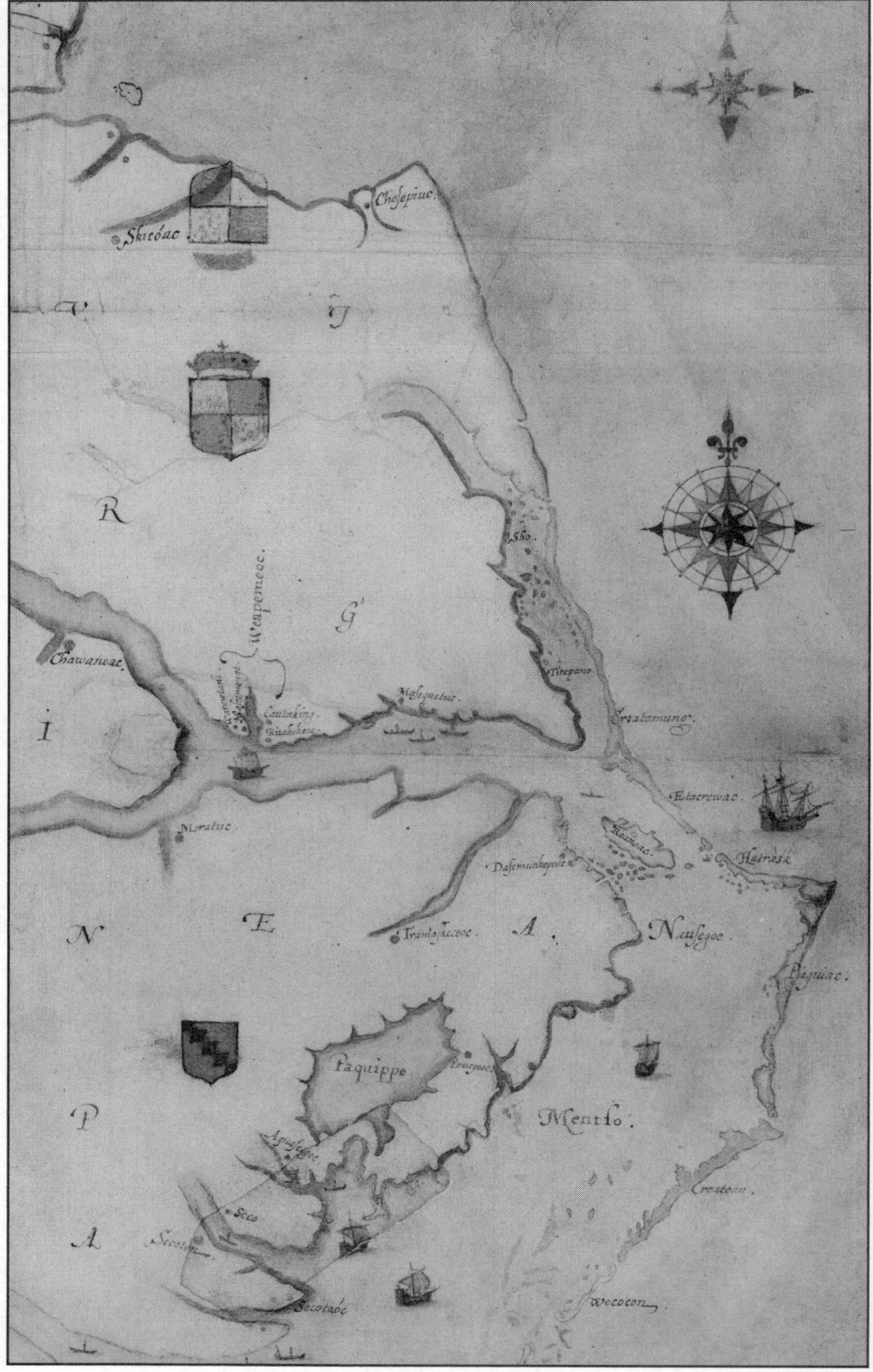

Skicóac
Chesepiuc
Weapemeoc
Chawanoac
Masequetuc
Cautaking
Sho.
Titepano
Croatamung
Etacrewac
Roanoac
Hatrask
Dasemunkepeuc
Moratuc
Tramaskecooc
Nausegoc
Paquiac
Paquippe
Pomeiooc
Mentso
Croatoan
Seco
Secotan
Secotaoc
Wococon

Prologue

August 1590

Three years.

Three long years. But soon, please God, he would hold his daughter and granddaughter again.

This close, it seemed impossible to contain either longing or hope. Yet he must. He knew, with every shred of his being, how unlikely it was that the colonists had stayed on Roanoac Island beyond that first autumn. But the anticipation of stepping upon this shore once more—of gaining at least a hint of what had become of them—

He could hardly breathe.

Green and grey and blue were the waters around and behind him, but he had no eye for the dancing splendor of the waves. Only for the blinding brightness of the strand before him, the dunes clothed with grasses bending in the unrelenting sea winds, and the smudgy dark green of the forest rising beyond.

God had, despite much peril and many months of privateering, brought them safely through the storm. Would that He'd now hold back the tides long enough for him to find them.

Days of longing. Days of hope. He was near to exhausted with it. In their slow sail past the islands to the south, he'd expected some sign of life, of habitation, but—nothing. Not even a signal fire. Then, drawn by smoke to the north, they'd passed on without any attempt to go ashore. Smoke to the south led to the decision to go ashore nearer rather than farther, leading to a long, hot trek only to find. . .an unattended, burned-out fire. An entire day lost. One delay after another, even that morning.

Now, however, they readied the boats for launch while the ship sat at anchor alongside—but not too close to—that brilliant shoreline, within sight of the inlet he recalled too well.

Please, gracious God.

Chapter One

July 1587, three years earlier

In the beginning was the sea," she murmured.

Face turned to the wind, Elinor Dare clutched the ship's rail with one hand, her coif with the other. Salt spray drove up over the rail, cooling her cheeks.

The scripture reading earlier in the week had been from the first chapter of Genesis, describing how God—who, aye, had created the heavens and the earth—hovered over the face of the deep before dividing the waters from each other and then dry land from ocean.

And so the sea had been, from the very start. Staring out over the stormy blue, with towering clouds rising in the distance, white and all shades of grey, Elinor could feel its ancientness to her bones.

Surely the sea would be either her deliverance or her doom. Mayhap both.

Inside her, the babe kicked. Elinor smoothed a hand across the roundness of her belly, which increased with each passing day. Soon, and the little one would be clamoring to make his appearance.

Would they reach land in time?

Please, gracious Lord. . .

'Twas a selfish request, mayhap, but she wished most heartily to be on dry land to give birth—not on this crowded sea vessel.

With the creak of the ship and its rigging, the snap of the sails and the shouts of the crew filling her ears, only the scuff of a shoe warned her a mere moment before strong arms closed about her and a man's body settled against her back. The briefest alarm shot through her, then a laugh broke from her throat as she snuggled into the embrace of her husband. "La, Ananias! You are far too fond of catching me unawares."

His answering chuckle vibrated through her shoulders. "Guilty as charged, milady."

She crooked her neck to peer up at him. Beneath his soft hat, fair hair, streaked with gold, blew free in the sea wind, and eyes reflecting the color of the sky narrowed against the sunlight, the corners crinkling with a grin. "And what if," she went on, in her best scathing tones, "I were to become so used to your rude ways that one of these times I mistake the embrace of another for yours?"

"You are so fierce, Goodwife, that none other would dare," he said evenly, and she had to laugh at his play on words.

"Oh, is that it? Only you would dare because. . .only you are Dare?" And another peal of mirth shook her.

His reply was to snug her in closer, his bearded cheek against hers. She closed her eyes, savoring his strength and, aye, warmth as well, even in the full hot sun, not caring that they were in view of the crew and anyone else who might be strolling the decks.

Here, just for a moment, she could pretend the hardships of the last months had never happened.

The long anticipation of the voyage itself, when she'd hardly believed it would truly take place.

The days they'd lain at anchor before leaving England's shores.

The long, circuitous trek around the wide sea, whereby they passed Spain and Morocco and sailed on to the West Indies, taking advantage of sea currents, drawing their voyage from an expectation of weeks to a duration of three months.

Their most discomfortable accommodations, little more than a blanket upon the floor in the ship's hold, women with women and men with men, and married couples separated for the duration of the voyage and thus denied conjugal comforts.

The disappointment of visits to exquisitely beautiful islands where they were promised revictualing, then denied for reasons Elinor still did not comprehend.

The delight and relief of actually going ashore turning to dismay and horror, as many suffered burning and swelling from fruit they were assured was good to eat—and blindness for some who washed with unclean waters.

Inexplicable delay and, aye, mayhap even betrayal from those tasked with protecting and guiding them to safety. And then, after all else, to hear rumors that they'd not be finally put ashore at their intended location, but far to the south. A place whose very mention carved furrows in Papa's brow.

They'd seen wonders, verily—tropical waters bluer than the sky above, verdant forests, creatures passing all imagination—but there were too many things it would please her to forget.

She pressed more deeply into Ananias's embrace. "Tell me again we've done the right thing."

His beard brushed her ear, crisp-soft. "We've done the right thing, love. I swear it. There was no staying in London, crowded as it is."

She vented a sigh. Too true. The clamor, the filth, the murders and robberies, and pressing mobs on every street. . . Elinor popped her eyes open again and drew in a breath of the salty but fresh wind. Where they were bound, they were promised houses and land enough for each man to have a planting of his own.

At the moment, the prospect even of her own garden, to grow herbs and flowers, seemed almost too fantastical to believe.

"Granted, we expected to have arrived long before now," Ananias said.

"It matters not. Although I own I'd rather your son not be racing to make his appearance before we're landward."

His arms tightened a bit. "My brave girl. I'd rather that as well."

"I simply. . ."

She let her voice trail off. The words felt too silly for her, a woman now grown, to voice.

"You what?"

Ananias's voice was but a breath against her ear.

"I simply wish a place to call home."

There. She'd said it.

John White turned his head as he crossed the ship's deck, pretending not to notice his daughter and her husband embracing over against the starboard rail. After such a long and arduous journey, it was good to see them enjoying each other's company. Although, with the knowledge he held, it might be the only moment of idyll they enjoyed.

He stepped from the main deck to the tiny compartment designated as his office, shut the door despite the day's warmth, then tossed his hat into a corner and sank into the chair. With a sigh, he leaned his elbows on the table and shoved both hands through his hair.

God—most gracious God—

His trust in the Lord of heaven and earth was not the thing floundering. It was his surety that they as a people still had any favor with Him.

The cry yet echoed through his head. *"Christ our victory!"* And then the screams of the savages as Lane and his soldiers fell upon them.

The terror congealing in his own limbs as he stood, rapier in hand, unable to move.

Dear God in heaven, the utter wrongness of it all.

A sharp rap sounded on the door. Suppressing a groan, he straightened and cleared his throat. "Come."

The door swung open, and the lean form of the ship's master and navigator, Simon Ferdinando, stood outlined against the daylight.

The very last person he wanted to see, or speak with, in this moment.

The Portuguese navigator—not only shipmaster but also one of the colony's Assistants, despite a former career of piracy, which the Queen had pardoned—shut the portal behind him and crossed the floor in a single stride. His braided sailor's tail swung across his shoulders. "We're but two days out of the West Indies. You've need to tell your people of the change in plans."

Mingled annoyance and dread surged through him, as if he'd the sea itself sloshing about inside him. 'Twas not his own change of plans, but—John unclenched his teeth. "And tell them I shall."

Ferdinando stared at him, blue eyes dark beneath the brim of his sailor's cap. "Sooner rather than later best befits your state."

White tugged at the point of his short beard. "See here, I'm not yet convinced—"

"Do you wish your colonists to be slaughtered by the Spanish? Or worse, tortured and enslaved as papists?"

He fought the urge to swallow. "You know I do not."

Ferdinando leaned his fists on the edge of the table. Teeth bared behind a yellow beard gone mostly grey, his breath gusting foul in the small space. "Then—tell them. You are the one appointed governor of this colony. It is your duty."

White found himself seized of a nearly irresistible urge to glance away or to fidget—anything to avoid the weight of that stare—but he forced himself to hold the unblinking gaze. A dozen questions and accusations came to his lips, but he could find voice for none of them.

"In my own time and way," he said at last. "Do not press me."

The Portuguese shoved upward, still glaring. "You've not much time left. Mind that at least."

"Aye," White snapped, and with a nod, Ferdinando quit the chamber.

John hissed softly in the man's wake. The entire affair gave him no small vexation—that "the Swine," so called for his vile manner and lack of proper reverence to God, presumed to dictate to White where the colony should go, and for what reason? His superior knowledge of the New World? Or was it rather revenge for John's insistence they spend the voyage in such industry as benefited the planters, rather than the crew collecting prizes of the Spanish as they willed? And then to pretend concern for the planters' well-being, when time and again on the voyage he had arranged hap for his own benefit, the harm of the innocent, or his own apparent entertainment.

He sank his head into his hands. "Merciful, gracious Father, grant me strength—and wisdom. Remember that You are the One who called us to come out from among them. Do not forsake us now!"

When he had composed his spirit and a semblance of peace had returned to his heart, he stood, straightened his doublet, and stepped to the door. Ferdinando was right, at least in this one thing. It would serve nothing to delay sharing the news, at least with his closest officials.

He emerged once more into the brilliant day, where sailors worked the rigging and snapping canvas, and Elinor and Ananias had moved to a different portion of the rail. A dozen or more other passengers likewise tried to take in the sight of sunlight on heaving waves while not getting in anyone's way—a near impossible feat, with conditions on the vessel.

He angled toward the boys clustered at the foot of the midship rigging. "Ho, Georgie!"

Eyes rounding, the boy broke from the group and trotted toward White. "Aye, Gov'nor?"

"A favor, dear lad, if you will."

Young George Howe was something of a ringleader with the lads on board, the cabin boy included, but eagerness stretched the broad, freckled features. "Of course, Gov'nor! That is, if I can."

White allowed himself a smile. "You and your cronies—take word to my Assistants and tell them to come to the deck as soon as they may."

Georgie darted back to the others, the chatter of their efforts rising over the clank and creak of the ship and its crew. Just as they darted off to accomplish their mission, however, a cry came from the crow's nest.

"Land ho!"

Elinor pressed her way between the shoulders of others as they jostled along the gunwale, two and three deep, to catch a glimpse of Virginia, the first English colony in the New World. This—this was the land they'd been promised, still but the barest smudge on the horizon. Although landing would not yet take place, not until they'd stopped to look in on the fort at Roanoac Island, to see how the men left there the previous year were faring. Just a day or two, and then the ship would carry them up the coast to a place at Chesepiok, called Jacán by the Spanish.

Or would it? With the way talk had spread like wildfire amongst their fellow settlers, it was anyone's guess what might happen.

Ananias had been called away on an errand before the crowd gathered. Elinor thought herself safe enough to linger abovedecks, but now the press grew so deep that someone elbowed her in the belly, and she lurched backward, in turn thumping the person behind her. Tightness seized her entire middle, nearly doubling her over. Air—she needed air, just to breathe—and something firm on which to lean, just for a few moments.

"Excuse me—please—"

Doubtless hungry for their own look at the nearing coastline, folk resisted her nudging them aside, and none too gently. Not one took note of her distress.

At least, she thought none took note, but just as the sway of the ship and the crush of the crowd knocked her off her feet, a pair of hands plucked her by the shoulders and set her aright. Elinor glanced up into the round, tanned countenance of Manteo, the savage who was just completing his own second voyage to England and back, and whose homeland they were in all likelihood gazing upon now.

The man dressed so thoroughly in English clothing—shirt and doublet and characteristically baggy trunkhose, with a jaunty cap covering hair tied back at his nape—that only the indelible markings across cheeks and beardless chin gave him away as being of another nation altogether. He flashed a grin, his brown eyes crinkling. "Careful, Mistress Dare. Come sit aside until the others tire of looking."

The words were heavily accented, but clear. She expelled a hard breath, then summoned a smile. "Thank you kindly."

She took the perch he offered, a barrel lashed to one of the masts, where one of the boys had been standing before Manteo shooed him off in favor of Elinor. When she peeked up at him, his pleasant expression had not altered, despite the press about them. How would the rest of his people appear, and would they receive the English settlers with as much openness and generosity as Manteo evinced, and Papa insisted they possessed?

"You must be very glad to see your own country again," she ventured to add.

He nodded once. "It will indeed be good."

"And—your family too, mayhap?"

Though present for many a conversation with the quiet but cheerful savage, she'd never yet engaged him directly in talk before now. Her curiosity had been much aroused, however, and it seemed a most opportune time—if not strange, with all others vying to see the approach of land while the two of them hung back.

His expression became more thoughtful. "Aye, my family as well."

Was that now sadness in his eyes? She thought of kin to their own party who remained in England. "And what family did you leave behind?"

He crouched beside her, and she wasn't sure at first that he'd reply. "A people is all family," he said, so softly she had to lean to catch the words. "But my mother is there, an older brother and his woman and children, and younger sisters."

He looked as if he'd say more, but he had no time to do so, and she'd likewise none to respond, for the strident, accented voice of their Portuguese pilot rose above the din of the crowd. "Ho! Patience, good folk. Back from the rails and return belowdecks. 'Tis but a first sighting and we'll not be putting ashore for several days yet."

The cargo hold was no place for a council meeting, with a dozen men, eight of them his Assistants, packed in amongst crates and barrels and furniture. But it would have to do. "Hush," John warned them all sternly. "This must not be noised about."

His words had the intended effect. Thankfully. The other men's eyes were instantly on him, sharp and curious. A single lantern gave just enough light to discern faces.

That scourge of a Portuguese navigator was nowhere among them. Also thankfully.

"We must ourselves keep calm, and we must do our best to calm the rest of our planters as well. I cannot emphasize this enough. But you have heard it whispered that we are to disembark at Roanoac Island and not farther up the main at Chesepiok. I have gathered you to say that, aye, those whispers are true."

As expected, a murmur arose as the men turned to each other, but John held up his hands for renewed silence. "All is not yet settled, and the situation may yet change."

"Pardon us, Governor," said Roger Prat, one of the older colonists, the lamplight catching his bald forehead and the silver in his dark hair, "but was this your decision? Or that of another?"

John shifted to address him. "It most emphatically was not. I have outlined before my reservations regarding a settlement on Roanoac Island—that the island itself is insufficient to sustain a full colony, including its attendant plantings, and that the harbor cannot accommodate anything but the smallest of ships. We will be stopping to look in on the men that Greenville left, and to be advised by them, but Lord willing, no more. Our esteemed pilot, however, is of the opinion that we should settle there, if only temporarily, because of the threat of the Spanish. With Darby Gland's departure from our company—" John forced a deep breath, in and out. What he wished to say about that matter was much stronger. "Well, let us just say, it is probable that the Spanish may be informed of our intent to settle the Chesepiok. And we have women and children to think of on this journey, where we had not before."

The sound of shuffling and harrumphing filled the close space. "Do you mean to tell us you favor us being left where we choose not?" This time the voice was of Christopher Cooper, nephew to John's own Thomasyn, God rest her soul. A young man of good courage, if overbold to speak his mind at times.

"Most assuredly, nay. I am, however, compelled to inform you good sirs that there is that possibility. I will continue in conversation with Ferdinando. And perhaps plans may unfold as originally laid out, but we must consider the alternatives."

Dread already pooled heavy in his gut, and the other men's palpable shock and anger were helping it not a whit.

"We were promised the Chesepiok," Prat said slowly. "It makes no sense to—" He stopped and shook his head. "When was this suggestion first made to you, that we might be landed upon Roanoac instead?"

"Just after the West Indies. Ferdinando and I have been hotly debating it ever since."

More mutters and head shaking.

If they only knew the full of it. . .

"Christ our victory!"

John gritted his teeth. *Please, God, no! You are our victory, aye, but our shame in misusing those words is more than I can bear. Abandon us not to our past folly, I beg You!*

"None are happy about this, and I blame you not for it. I only ask that you remain steadfast, no matter what may befall us. We launched this endeavor in submission and trust of our God—let us not falter now."

The murmur turned more assenting, but still, he knew they liked the news not. He shared that sentiment, but better to forewarn than to surprise them on Roanoac's shores.

"Mum's the word, now, until we know for sure. No sense in raising a panic among the others."

As the men quietly dispersed, a bare handful lingered, questions in their gazes. "And you," John said, meeting their eyes, "accompany me back to my office. I mean to question Ferdinando here and now about this."

While he had the impetus to do so. Before the Portuguese swine could squirrel out of it.

A short while later, he sat on the edge of his desk, facing the half dozen assembled—or crammed, more like—in the office. Ferdinando's blue eyes remained flinty. So did those of Sir Kendryck, once-corpulent jowls hanging more loosely than their wont, betraying the rigors of the sea journey on a man unused to such privations.

"Are you honestly looking to be slain by the Spanish?" Ferdinando said after a moment.

That tired argument again. 'Twas not insignificant, but he was beyond weary of hearing it used to overrule other concerns. "Of course not," he snapped.

"Then I do not understand. What does it matter where your colony settles, so long as you have resources and access to an inlet?"

"Resources." John snorted. "You cared nothing for our resources when you refused to let us go ashore and get salt or mutton. When you assured us those greenish fruits were edible—"

"Now, now, my good men." Kendryck's voice was a study in boredom. "Ferdinando, of course White wishes for the most felicitous setting for his colony. And of course you have only their best interest at heart. Surely we will reconsider the matter and give it our best answer, anon."

"And now," the Portuguese said, pushing away from the wall, "if you will excuse me, gentlemen, I have a ship to navigate. These waters are too treacherous for inattention."

Chapter Two

July 22

The hours crawled by, and the distant shore neared, then receded. Elinor had barely ventured on deck yet again before the cry went up that the ship was in peril from the shoals that abounded along this coast. She thought to tuck herself into a corner, out of the way, but one of the crew snarled at her to get below and pray, if she valued her life.

Ananias was nowhere in sight. With the barest hesitation, Elinor hied herself back belowdecks.

In the women's section, partitioned off from the rest of the hold, she lowered herself to her pallet and fought back tears. Rose Payne scooted across from the next space over, setting one arm about Elinor's shoulders. The other women huddled similarly around them. Would they perish now, within sight of land, after all the tribulations they'd endured on the passage over?

The ship pitched and rolled. That itself was a familiar enough sensation. Shouts rang out abovedecks. Elinor closed her eyes and let the tears flow.

Gracious God, You are Lord of heaven and earth. It is for Your name and for zeal for Your Word that we embarked on this voyage. We are Yours. Save us!

The vessel yawed again, sending all the women grappling for each other and nearby beams. A sob bubbled up from her chest.

Will You not save us, oh God?

A shout, and then the ship righted itself and steadied. Cheers and whistling ensued. Elinor covered her face with her apron and wept without restraint.

Hours later, the announcement was made that they'd found the right inlet, and preparations began in earnest for the men to go ashore. Ananias rolled and tied his pallet before tossing it next to the knapsack on the floor and turning to gather Elinor into his arms. "We shall return as soon as we can."

She laid her head on his chest. Beneath her ear, his heart thudded, strong and sure. "I know." There was no room for tears now, nor show of fright.

"That's my brave girl."

A smile curled her lips. How well she knew him, even in the short time they'd been wed. He valued strength.

"Now then." A long, lingering kiss, then another, and he released her, bending to retrieve his knapsack and bedding. "It'll be but a few days."

"Aye."

She followed him abovedecks so as to watch him and the others depart. They emerged into the open air, the wind nearly taking her coif, and Papa turned from speaking with a group of his Assistants to catch her in a quick embrace. "Today is the day!" he called out over the crowd, stilling their voices. "Let us give thanks to our Maker and Savior for safe passage."

The *Sunne*, a full-rigged pinnace, was drawn up next to the *Lyon*, with but a plank connecting the two. After Papa led them in prayer, the men hefted their baggage and filed across. Ananias easily traversed the space, dropping lightly onto the deck of the *Sunne*. Quickly enough they all crossed and the plank was withdrawn. Once the windlass holding the *Sunne*'s anchor began to turn, the pinnace slid past the *Lyon*.

Elinor tucked herself against the rail, lifting an arm to wave at Ananias, who caught her eye with a jaunty grin and waved back. As the swells and wind lifted the smaller ship and carried it farther away, he blew her a kiss.

A man called out over the waves from his place at the rail of the *Lyon*, and Elinor realized with a jolt that it was the older gentleman, Kendryck, whom Papa and Ananias told her had helped fund the voyage and then had come along for who knew what reason.

"—charge thee, do not bring any of the planters back again, but leave them on the island, save the governor and two or three such as he approves!"

A murmur went up from the crowd on the *Lyon*'s deck. At the rail of the *Sunne*, Papa pushed between two of the other men, his bearded face pale beneath the tan he'd acquired on the journey.

"The summer is far spent, and we can go no further," Ferdinando called out. "We will land all the planters in no other place."

"What means this mischief?" demanded one of the men near Elinor.

"Aye, aye," one of the sailors on the *Sunne* replied, and others echoed him.

Not a single sailor said him nay, nor even Captain Stafford, master of the *Sunne*, despite the outcry among those left upon the *Lyon* and the mutterings and protesting among Papa's Assistants, all milling about him on the pinnace's deck.

Elinor marked it well, the slackness of Papa's expression in obvious shock at first, then the tightening of his features, the clenching of his jaw and the grimace. He shook his head, said something aside to Ananias, then turned and was lost to her sight amongst the crowd on the deck.

"What is he saying? We are to be left upon Hatorask? Or another of the islands? What about Chesepiok?"

Mutterings around her became an uproar. She found her hands clenching the rail, her throat dry as her mouth hung open and lungs heaved for breath. A terrible tightness gripped her belly and buckled her knees.

"Hie now!" Ferdinando's accented command rang above the commotion. "Disperse and back belowdecks!"

Some obeyed, but Elinor could not move. Nearby, Margery Harvie, as great with child as Elinor, was helped toward the ladder by her husband.

"Mistress Dare, are you well?"

The soft voice of Rose Payne broke through the babel around her, but she remained unable to respond.

"Mistress Dare? Elinor. . . ?"

The woman's hands took hold of her shoulders, and the round, plain, but earnest face swam into view.

"Is it your time?"

Elinor shook her head, slowly, then more sharply. "I—know not. I think not, but—" The tightness about her middle eased, and sucking in a deep breath, she drew herself upright. "I earnestly hope not."

Rose slipped one arm around Elinor's shoulders and drew her toward the belowdecks ladder. "Well. I'll stay with you until we know for certain."

His heart beat double-time with the rise and fall of the bow in the swells. *We will land the planters in no other place. No other place. No other place.* The words echoed in his head like the wind soughing through the rigging, punctuated by the snap of the sails.

This must have been their plan all along. They'd likely only made a show of being persuaded to consider otherwise. And he, the governor, so-called by Sir Walter Ralegh and endorsed by Her Majesty Queen Elizabeth herself, had no say in the matter. None whatsoever.

What kind of governor could he be if robbed of his will even in regard to where they were to settle?

He pushed through the press of men until he found Captain Stafford. "Are Kendryck and the Portuguese in earnest? Surely they cannot contradict the order of Ralegh and Her Majesty the Queen that we be settled on the Chesepiok."

The captain's lips firmed, but he refused to meet John's eye. "It is their command that we bear you to Roanoac and settle you there. I can do naught else."

Stafford might as well have punched John in the gut. He fought for breath. "Surely not. I am the Governor of Virginia, and our plans were clear—"

At that, Stafford did turn, his gaze colliding with John's, and he gave a single hard shake of his head. "I am most regretful, Governor, but—nay."

Aghast, John swiveled, and found every sailor aboard the vessel pointedly looking away. Howe, Ananias, and the others all stood shaking their heads, scrubbing hands across mouths, gripping sword hilts, or clenching fists.

What madness was afoot, that they behaved thus?

"Very well. For now. We will land at Roanoac Island as planned and see to the state of our men left there last, and then we will talk of this again."

How quickly the thrill of adventure turned to something much darker. Not that Ananias was terribly surprised.

One moment he was waving farewell to Elinor, and the next their foppish sponsor Kendryck was bawling nonsense across the water between them. Leave the planters at Roanoac, indeed. The Spanish notwithstanding—were Kendryck and Ferdinando trying to ensure they all perished?

He looked over at his father-in-law. Still white-lipped and tight-jawed, squinting out over the water, though composed. The governor had, in fact, been muttering his suspicions regarding their navigator for weeks now. And how they were expected to explain this development to the rest of the company—

And how Elinor must be awash with confusion and anxiety. He'd caught but the barest glimpse of shock on her sweet face before his view of her was lost as the pinnace sailed on. His darling wife, left to deal alone with the wake of the Swine's evil pronouncement. How patiently she'd borne this voyage, with all its privations. How cheerfully she looked forward to landing at last, and helping build a home for their family to come.

And now—this, after the insults they'd already borne. First the series of disasters on the journey. The delay leaving Plymouth. The abandonment of the flyboat off Portugal. The debacle over the mysterious green fruit—which Ferdinando avowed were good to eat—on the island in the Caribbean where they'd gone ashore for water and found only a bitter and poisonous pond. The promise to put ashore later for victualling, and the failure to deliver on that promise. No salt to replenish their stores, and no fresh meat.

Elinor's father quietly assured them that their savages, Manteo and his kinsman Towaye, knew well the ways of living off the land. They'd not starve, at least, which was more than could be said of Lane's ill-fated journey upriver in the New World last year, though by all accounts, the brash stubbornness of Lane himself was at fault there. It was the fervent wish of White and his friend Thomas Harriot, both of whom had been sent to explore and record all the wonders of the New World for the benefit of England, that they, the planters, treat far differently the peoples here than Lane and others of a more martial mind—and so might in turn fare better.

With such ill hap met thus far, Ananias prayed it would be so. In this moment, prayer seemed all they had.

He hoped, however, to also be a practical part of that endeavor, with his skills in bricklaying and tile. A quick mind and strong body surely could be nothing but an advantage.

After passing through the inlet, a fairly simple if tedious affair due to the need for close navigation every yard of the way, they sailed across a remarkably smooth stretch of open water and neared land again—one large island, White told them, surrounded by several small ones—rounding a reedy-looking shoreline and approaching from the west.

Roanoac Island at last.

"The sun sits low in the sky. Should we go a-land just yet?" Captain Stafford asked.

"We should not delay any longer," White answered. "We'll camp ashore if need be."

The men were divided according to who would stay and who would go, the boat was let down, and White beckoned Ananias forward.

As he climbed down into the craft, elation rose within his breast. Despite the trials and hardships, despite the shock of Ferdinando's announcement and the scramble to grasp that this would be their landing place, Ananias could not deny the sudden beating of his heart nor the eagerness to set foot at last upon the ground now within their sight.

He grasped an oar and set to, taking his turn even though a handful of the sailors from the pinnace accompanied them. The task kept his thoughts busy, but at last he looked over his shoulder. The shore loomed close, reeds or grasses rippling in the breeze like the water itself. The smell of the salt marsh, so like and yet unlike marshlands in England. The cry of both seagulls and other shore birds startled away at their approach.

Was this it? Was the island truly to be their home? Please God, if so, that they would flourish here.

His father-in-law and Manteo directed them toward the mouth of a creek, and the boat entered a stretch flanked by clumps of thick grasses—he could see that now, some greenish but some a dark brownish grey—and edged with a narrow strip of pale sand. Scrubby trees, which minded Ananias of oaks, lay just beyond, their shade beckoning as they neared the shore. As one, they slowed their rowing and glided into the creek's channel under the strange trees' branches. He breathed a sigh at the respite from the sun's heat.

"The town where we left the soldiers last year lies up this stream," White said, his voice low against the warbling birdsong and throbbing buzz of insects.

No one else spoke, except in murmurs to point out this or that. Beneath the canopy of the scrubby, gnarled oaks, interspersed now with impossibly tall pines, squirrels scampered from tree to tree and leaped from limb to limb. A pair of deer lifted their heads to stare but remained unmoving as the men guided their craft past.

The creek narrowed until the boat scraped bottom. White directed them toward the bank, and they disembarked and tied the boat to a nearby tree. Ananias's gut tightened as he looked around, one hand on the pistol at his belt and the other on his rapier. Nothing to be seen in the underbrush, but that meant naught, all things considered. The others felt the same, gauging by how they similarly gripped their weapons and peered about.

Governor White indicated a direction then set off into the maritime forest, roughly parallel to the stream. He'd not gone more than twenty or so steps, though, before he stopped with a grunt, staring at the ground.

Ananias edged closer, the others crowding about as well. A skeleton lay there, still clothed in remnants of unmistakably English garb, the skull rent by a jagged gash. An arrow still lay across the neck.

A chill seized him scalp to toe. Others sucked in their breath, and one or two cried out.

"Long dead," White muttered. He looked about. "And—it is sunset. We must needs make camp for the night then continue tomorrow to Lane's fort."

"Not here, we will not," one of the men said, too emphatically to brook argument. The others murmured their assent.

"Well then, back to the ship's boat," the captain said, and they retreated the way they'd come, to the creek's edge.

Elinor stayed belowdecks as long as she could, but as the light waned outside, she could bear it no longer. Thankfully she had suffered no more recurrence of the terrible tightness around her belly, so Rose had gone above with some of the other women. Elinor was glad at first for the quiet, but now she simply craved open air, despite the prospect of having it spoiled by the sailors' rough talk.

The sea breeze swept over her, sweet and clean, as she poked her head abovedecks. Her hips protested the climb—not an uncommon thing, these days—but the vivid blue of the sky beckoned her on as she trudged up each step with her skirts gathered in one hand.

At the top, she paused to catch her breath and acknowledge the nod of greeting from a passing sailor. The sweetness of the breeze—oh, she could not help the wetness springing to her eyes! Carefully she made her way to the port rail, facing the sun as it sank in the west, turning the waves to fire and casting the rough outline of Hatorask in silhouette. Where was her strong, darling Ananias this eve? And Papa? They'd warned her not to expect them back for a few days at least. She understood the necessity of staying aboard while they explored, but she longed for solid ground beneath her aching feet.

Someone was tucked up in the sterncastle playing a lute or bandora, with the crew singing along—not the usual sea shanty but "Greensleeves." Elinor shook her head at the song's theme of a man longing after a woman who would not be true to him. 'Twas but frivolity, yet she could not resist humming along.

A flock of water birds left one side of the inlet and flew, their wings fluttering against the brilliant sunset, to the other side. Their cries filled the air, audible even above the shush of waves, the sailors' song and calls one to another, and the clink and snap of rigging and fittings. It was a lovely moment, and Elinor drank it in.

Evenings for the *Sukwoten*—for all the *Tunapewak*, the People—were meant for enjoyment. Food and the company of one's family and people. Song and dance, leaving aside labor, celebrating the day and its accomplishments and joys. A savoring of peace and contentment in what the land and water offered in their care of them, and a thankfulness to Montóac for it all.

Sees Far's anticipation of that approaching peace was shattered by the huffing, pattering approach of young Owlet.

"The white-skinned men from across the water," he panted. "They—they have returned."

Sees Far stopped in the act of binding an arrowhead to the hard shaft of a reed with a length of seagrass and lifted his eyes to the boy. "Speak that once more."

"The—the white-skinned ones. From across the water. The—*Inqutish. Wutahshuntas.*"

English. Foreigners. The tremor began deep in his belly, and seeking to still it, Sees Far rose swiftly. "They have returned? You know this for certain?"

A flurry of memories assailed him—ugly faces half covered in hair, bodies said to be men but clothed in strangely crafted garb, harsh voices, weapons whispered to throw spirit arrows. They'd proved, to the intense relief of all, that they were indeed men who could both bleed and die, but the power they wielded—

At the least, sickness had swept through their peoples in the strangers' wake, many of whom had no contact with them. And this, despite the strangers' insistence that they wished only for their people's good, unlike the dreaded *Spanish* who also roamed the coast in their giant *kanoes*, and even ventured inland.

This sickness had claimed some of Sees Far's own family, including his father Granganimeo, a sister, and the girl intended to become his wife.

And then, in an act of horrible treachery, his uncle Wyngyno was cruelly murdered by these strangers.

The tremors spread from his gut to all his limbs. And with them, a white-hot fire.

Once more he affixed his gaze on Owlet, who was leaning, hands on knees, to regain his breath. "Where did you see them?"

Owlet straightened, with effort, and pointed toward the bay. "Out—there. Just this side of Roanoac. A big kanoe, like before, with a smaller making its way toward the island."

Seeking the small company they'd left behind the year past, then. "How many?"

"Many tens. Hard to count."

Sees Far pulled in a long, slow breath. "Wanchese must be told."

Early the next morning they rose and soberly made their way northward. Ananias could still scarce believe the wild beauty of the oaks—for so White assured them they were—and such impossibly tall pines. A spicy fragrance hung heavy in the air, presumably from the pines.

After making camp the night before, they'd done their best to give the bones of that hapless soldier a fitting burial. Elinor's father remained grave, almost withdrawn, and the rest of them fared no better. Their first night ashore in the New World and—this did not bode well. No sign of habitation at all where they lay for the night. None as far as they could see through the forest.

There was none as they walked, either, until a cluster of two-storied cottages came into view through the trees. The shabbiness of those dwellings became readily apparent as they neared, with melon vines growing up the walls, in the midst of which grazed a herd of deer, nibbling at the melons. At their approach, heads went up, ears flicked, and away the deer bounded.

Once more the company hefted weapons and looked about, but no threat appeared, at least any worse than the deer startling away.

"A year," White muttered. "No more than one year and look at the height of those melon vines. The houses in such disrepair. And the fort itself razed. The men we seek are, I fear, long gone."

Indeed it was so. "Was this the work of savages, do you think?" George Howe asked, as the others spread out, searching more carefully for any sign of the men who'd dwelt there.

White shook his head, but thoughtfully. Manteo made no reply at all, only walked round with Towaye, both men observing intently. At last, all dripping from the heat and humidity, they gathered in the midst of the fort's ruins, its star-shaped outline still rimmed in earthenworks, if flattened somewhat. Ananias removed his hat and dragged one hand through his hair, grimacing at its lank, oily feel.

"I am afraid for their fate, but I think we will see no more of those Greenville left here," White said quietly. He straightened, scanning the treetops as if they held some clue to the men's fate, and drew in a long breath. "Now begins the task of determining where first to begin the work of settling our own planters."

"If it please you, sir," John Sampson spoke up, "should we not see to the repairing of these cottages? So our women at least have shelter?"

Others murmured their assent, and White nodded. "First we return to the pinnace to let the others know what we have found."

It was decided, with none dissenting, that most of the planters who had accompanied John on the pinnace would return to the island and begin work making the cottages habitable again. This included Ananias, who among others possessed skills necessary for the task.

That left John to return to the *Lyon*, along with Chris Cooper and Roger Bailie, and arrange passage for the rest of the colony.

The Lord had brought them thus far, and He'd not abandon them now. Although the reminder fell flat against John's heart, it was all he had—the very thing he must offer to those still on the *Lyon*, to declare truth and comfort in the face of such severe insult. For insult it was, no matter how prettily Simon Ferdinando might say it, or how skillfully he defended his foul actions.

They made the passage back across the sound and through the inlet without event. Back on board the *Lyon*, John was fairly mobbed by the other settlers. Elinor he embraced heartily, reassuring her of Ananias's safety, then told everyone to gather once supper had been served.

In the meantime, he prayed he could answer all their questions to everyone's satisfaction.

The babe lay especially heavy in her belly tonight. With a great sigh, Elinor shifted from one side to the other, scooting her hip this way and that until she found some measure of comfort. Squirms and kicks within, as if her unborn infant were protesting his confinement as much as she wished to protest hers. And that dratted tightness which came and went from the moment she espied Papa at the bow of the *Sunne*, returning, but without Ananias, through the hurried supper and meeting thereafter.

Please, God. . . She could not finish the prayer, only repeat the opening plea. *Please, God. Thou knowest.*

On the pallet next to hers, Rose pushed up on her elbow. "You aren't sleeping?"

Elinor huffed and sat up as well. "This little one won't let me. He is as impatient with the wait as we are."

"Well, Lord be thanked, at least ours is ending." Rose scooted closer so they could whisper without waking the others. "Even if it does mean shoring upon an island where we never intended to stay."

"Aye." And even if the mere thought of all that needed now to be packed and moved from galley to pinnace wearied her. Or the thought of setting up housekeeping once ashore. . . "Papa says there are cottages, at least. So we have shelter, the Lord also be thanked."

"And we have been too long at sea to protest overmuch, methinks." Rose clasped her hands and set them in her lap. "Regardless of the danger."

"There is danger no matter which course we are given." Elinor yawned. She craved sleep, despite her spinning thoughts and the babe dancing within. "We must simply take the one God hands us and see it through, trusting Him with the outcome." When Rose blinked at her, she realized with a hiccupping giggle how like Papa she must sound. "Well. Just because my father said it first in no wise renders it untrue."

Her friend smirked. "I forget at times that you are daughter to our governor."

"Oh, I hope I do not make myself insufferable because of it." True, Ananias was appointed one of his Assistants—but it was among her worst fears to be one of those females who leaned only upon her position and pedigree, with no usefulness in her own right.

Rose's smile went wistful. "Elinor, you are sweetness itself. You could not be insufferable if you tried."

Heat washed across her face—and not because of the closeness of belowdecks. "Oh, Rose. Surely you flatter me."

"Never," Rose said, suddenly sober. "You are loved, and for good reason. Those who say otherwise are merely envious."

Elinor found herself tongue-tied, caught between pleasure and distress. If only Rose knew how often Elinor warred within herself, vexation beating inside her breast. . .

"I am not as good as you think," she murmured at last.

Chapter Three

July 24

The next day was spent packing, inventorying supplies and foodstuffs, and hauling crates and baggage up out of the *Lyon*'s hold and over onto the *Sunne*, tethered at anchor beside the larger ship. John busied himself from before sunup, directing those who were able in carrying crates and chests and bundles, answering the same inquiries a dozen times over. And in between—

"Ho, Georgie, look sharp there!" He beckoned to the boy, who wore an abashed expression at being nearly clunked in the head by a sailor hefting a chest. "I've an especial favor for you, my boy, if you will?"

"Aye, Gov'nor?"

"Go find my daughter Elinor and help her tend to whatever she needs. Assist her in packing, carry her baggage, that sort of thing."

"Aye, aye, sirrah!" And away the boy went, in a flash.

John grinned in his wake and went on to the next task. Things were, predictably, taking far longer than he'd like.

They'd debated where to actually land the colonists and had settled on approaching from the north end of the island. The sand beach, combined with the proximity to the fort and village, would make it easier to unload and transport their goods.

It would take the pinnace at least two trips. The first load was nearly ready, and he'd decided that they'd rest the remainder of the day and start again bright and early tomorrow morning.

'Twould be easier to send the women and children first, they'd also decided, especially Margery Harvie and Elinor and those with nursing babes. Poultry and swine were already onboard the *Sunne*. Part of the orders to the men left on Roanoac Island were to create enclosures for livestock.

Could they get everything, and everyone, in just two trips? Despite the distress of the change of plans, how gladsome to be finally shot of Simon Ferdinando, who lurked about, seemingly everywhere at once, as if to make sure they took only their due and not a single bit more.

Elinor found a place at the rail of the pinnace that seemed least in the way of the crew, and determined not to give it up.

She wanted her first sight of their new home etched on her memory forever.

For all its shallow draught, the pinnace sat low in the water. She knew this only because of the sailors' worry about the depth of the sound, their voices barely distinguishable against the squeals of the pigs being herded into a corner of the deck. The chickens made a similar outcry, protesting the move from ship to ship. Poor creatures. If only she could reassure them that they'd soon all be ashore.

The weather could not be more perfect. The sailors exclaimed over that as well, and agreed that the passage through the inlet was as calm as anyone would wish for. Elinor only marveled at mile upon mile of pale beaches on either side of the inlet, edged by seagrass adorning the dunes, with dark smudges beyond that resolved into scrubby trees. Then the land slid by on either side, and they emerged into a wide sound, where land was the barest shadow on the horizon ahead of them and not visible at all to the left and southward.

To the north, however, lay small islands edged in rippling seagrasses with a tall forest rising on what appeared to be a larger island beyond.

Their island. Her island. *Home.*

Elinor drew a deep breath, then another. She could not get enough of the sea air blowing fresh off the water, sweeping away the stink of livestock and people too long cooped up on board the *Lyon*.

They sailed on into the sound, swinging about so that Roanoac Island was now on their left, past the marshes edging its southern end and circling round from the east, until they'd brought the pinnace around to the north where she spied more beach—a narrow strand, but unmistakably sand. A shout went up from the shore, and figures emerged from the trees, arms waving.

Gladness surged through Elinor, and she felt not a whit of the ache in her feet and legs from standing so long at the rail.

The pinnace drew near—closer than she'd have guessed possible. They put down the anchor, set out the gangplank, and just like that, folk gathered up their things and began to go ashore.

Young Georgie Howe, whom her father had tasked with aiding her, was suddenly at her elbow after being who knew where for the duration of the short final journey landward. He went ahead of her down the gangplank, offering his hand despite the two bulging satchels slung across his thin shoulders, but she shooed him on. Just ahead, waiting where gentle waves eddied against the plank, just short of the beach, stood Ananias, grinning broadly.

Encumbered as he was, Georgie scampered down the plank and hopped across the short space onto the sand. Ananias reached out a hand to steady him before turning to aid Elinor.

She gathered her skirts in one hand, resettled her satchel across her shoulder and hip, then minced her way down the plank. Ananias caught her elbow as she neared him. "There, now!" And before her shoes touched water, he swept her up into his arms and lifted her onto the beach.

They embraced, exchanging a long kiss. Ananias tasted of salt and smelled of hard labor, but oh, his strong arms felt wonderful about her. "I missed you," she murmured, riffling the edge of his beard with her fingertips.

"And I, you," he said, swooping in for another kiss.

"Ho, none of that here!" someone called out, laughing. "It's barely been three days."

Elinor's giggle effectively broke the embrace, and they stepped back, Ananias chuckling as well, but only to take her hand and lead her the short space up the beach, toward a narrow path that disappeared between gnarled shrubs. Her shoes slid in the loose sand, but Ananias's grip remained firm, steadying her and half lifting her up the incline into the trees.

Just past the rise, she found herself surrounded by forest: tall, straight pines such as she had never seen, and oaks with long, twisting limbs, festooned with feathery streamers of some grey material, swaying gently in what sea breeze could penetrate the canopy above. The ground was more open than she expected, sandy earth strewn with an abundance of pine needles, but the treetops were what brought her gaze back—the oaks gnarled and grave in the shadow of the stately and dignified pine.

"Is it not beautiful?" Ananias asked, breathlessness edging his voice.

She turned to meet his shining gaze. "It is, that."

"This place"—he pushed a branch out of the way—"we can make a living here, I feel it. Mayhap not on this island, but here in the New World, aye."

They emerged from the forest into a sandy clearing where the earthenworks of the fort rose with a cluster of cottages just visible beyond. And all was a hive of activity, as everyone made their way off the pinnace, or assisted with those arriving.

"And here we are," Ananias said. "The City of Ralegh—or at least its beginnings."

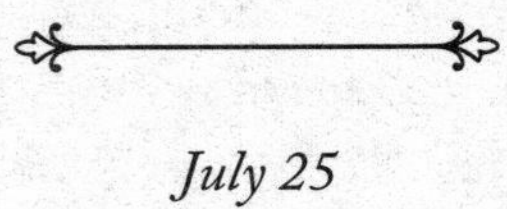

July 25

Come morning of the second day, the *Sunne* lay alongside the *Lyon*, waiting to be loaded for its second trip to the isle of Roanoac. As the sun made its slow ascent from the eastward waves, the glories of its rise fading into the light of another clear day, John conferred with Stafford on how the first trip had gone and what, if anything, they should do differently this time. The *Sunne*'s decks had been scoured already from the livestock taking temporary residence there, and on the *Lyon*, crates and bundles lay waiting beside stacks of furniture and building supplies.

"Ho! Another ship!" The cry from above broke across all other discussion and brought them to the rails to look.

"It is Captain Spicer and the flyboat!" came another voice, jubilant.

John's heartbeat quickened. The flyboat! After Ferdinando's abandonment of their companion vessel in Portugal—among his most egregious offenses, with no more explanation but that they should be on their way and had no more time to wait on the smaller ship's recovery—John had expected Spicer to turn about and head back to England. But here she was, safely arrived in the New World!

He could not wait to hear Spicer's account of the whole affair. And judging by the sullen pout on Simon Ferdinando's face, that one had much to answer for.

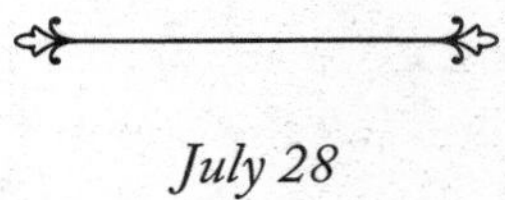

July 28

Setting up housekeeping had never been a more gladsome task. Despite the heaviness of her belly and the ache that plagued her entire body, Elinor embraced the sweeping and arranging and unpacking with a whole heart. The other women did the same, the entire company possessed of a festive spirit, especially since the safe arrival of the flyboat. All had been removed from the *Lyon* and brought ashore in the three days since she'd first made landing.

Even Papa was in a fine mood, laughing and talking more than she'd seen in, well, forever.

It was a wonder and a marvel, what they'd accomplished in just those few days. Trees cut, more houses built. Furniture and provisions apportioned out according to the endless lists now carried about by Ananias and the other Assistants to the new city.

Manteo had helped a group of the men build fishing weirs as his people did, and the wonderful fragrance of the smoked and grilled fish still lingered in the air from the night before. They'd gone back out this morning for yet more, and some mentioned combing the marshes for crabs and other shellfish. In that as well, Manteo had been enormously helpful, explaining what was in season when, and how best to gather it.

The house she and Ananias were given as their own was small, and not one of those with an upper story, but after enduring the cramped hold of the *Lyon* and the press of London, Elinor minded not. 'Twas a veritable paradise compared to throngs of people always roaming the streets and greasy smoke hanging perpetually in the air, where the windows in their stuffy, cramped apartments had let in only clamor and stench. Here, nothing but the friendly chatter of the town reached her ears, with the sweetest of breezes wafting in, scented by the pine trees surrounding them and the salt of the ocean beyond.

Oh Lord God, we thank Thee!

At the moment, it mattered not that they'd intended to land somewhere else. She was just so happy to be off that crowded ship, to walk upon solid ground, to breathe clean air for the first time in recent memory.

She stood in the middle of the room, hands set upon her hips, and surveyed her handiwork. In one corner, the bedstead which Ananias had set up, properly made with a freshly filled tick and aired linens. They'd gathered the lacy moss hanging in abundance from oak trees to stuff their ticks—Manteo had warned them to dip all in boiling water and dry in the sun before using as bedding. A kettle, a skillet, and other cooking implements beside the fireplace. A small table and chairs—luxuries afforded her as daughter of the new colony's governor—and pitchers and crockery stacked neatly against one wall. Incredibly, all had survived the voyage, packed carefully into hers and Ananias's chests, wrapped about with linens and various items of clothing, as well as extra lengths of fabric for sewing more garments as needed.

Some of which she'd been busy with on board the *Lyon*, and now lay folded in one of said chests, near the bed—a collection of baby gowns, clouts, and various other articles awaiting her little one to make his appearance.

As if he knew the bend of her thoughts, a strong kick came from within, then a wriggle. Elinor chuckled, smoothing both hands over the taut curve of her belly. "Soon, my sweet. Very soon now, and I'll hold you in my arms."

The last word was hardly out of her mouth before a scream from outside, not too distant, shattered the day's peace. Elinor's heartbeat stuttered, then pounded with near pain in its suddenness, and that awful ache of days ago seized her middle.

What in heaven's name now?

She scurried to the open door and peered out. Folk were running toward the edge of the village, where a cluster of men surrounded a pair of others bearing a bloodied form on a makeshift litter.

For a moment she could not move. Was it Ananias? But nay—his sturdy form was one of those carrying the litter, she could see now as he bent to set his burden on the ground. His shirt and hose, however, bore testament to close handling of the poor soul on that litter.

Or was that his own blood?

Hands gripping her belly, her feet carried her forward of their own will. She came to a halt beside Rose, who stood covering her mouth. Little enough could be seen through the crowd, and though a bloodstained doublet draped the form—the garment looked like Ananias's own—there was no clue to who the man might be.

One of the men turned, her cousin Chris Cooper, his gaze sweeping the crowd. " 'Tis George Howe. We found him murdered out in the marsh, a full two miles from here, alone."

The cry that burst from Elinor's throat was echoed by the dozens around her. And then, when she believed the moment could get no worse, a cluster of the boys ran up and pushed their way into the crowd, young Georgie at the forefront.

Without thought, Elinor reached out and snatched him to her, turning his face into her shoulder. "Don't look," she whispered into his sweat-soaked hair. "Pray do not look."

They ran from the place of the deed with all the fleetness they could summon, huddled low in the bushes along the shoreline until reaching their kanoes, and then with swift, hard strokes were away between the reeds. They angled southward, away from the English and their hated white skins, away from the one they'd come upon, catching crabs in the reeds with a forked stick, his pale skin ridiculous and reddening under the sun in what little clothing he'd not shed. He died so easily, without the armor of cunningly wrought *wassador* to protect him.

Sees Far cast a glance back at Wanchese. The visage of his old friend was still etched in hard, angry lines. The death of this one only served to inflame, it seemed, rather than satisfy.

It was just he and Wanchese in one kanoe and four in the other, but they kept apace with each other and got away into the small islands to the south. There they drew up, still breathing hard.

"Perhaps"—Sees Far kept his voice quiet, but looked around to include them all—"perhaps the pale ones will now get back into their large kanoes and go elsewhere."

Wanchese's features hardened even further, if that were possible. "They will not. You do not know them. You have not seen that which I have seen, while spending more than a full turn of the seasons with them. They will not be discouraged. They will come after us, and we must be prepared."

"What then shall we do?"

"We return to our towns and warn them. We must leave, go farther inland, and hide, then wait for the right time to strike from the shadows. It is the only way."

The others nodded, eyes bright and eager.

Georgie's wails of grief reverberated inside John's own chest like a volley from the ship's guns. Despite Elinor's attempt to shield him, the lad's response upon realizing that the slain man was his own father came swift and hard, weeping mingled with protests that this could not be. At last, Elinor and some of the other women drew him away, still sobbing, no doubt with the intent to ply him with tea and something to eat.

Since George Howe was among those who had come without a wife or anyone else who might attend such things, Ananias and the other men began the task of preparing his body for burial, as much as was possible, given his injuries. John could only watch, still catching his breath from the brutality wreaked upon the man. Sixteen wounds from arrows, and his head beaten to an unrecognizable pulp. This was no accident, of a surety.

With the burial yet to be accomplished, he gathered aside for questioning those involved in the discovery of Howe's body.

Even then he struggled to compose his thoughts. The men surrounding him appeared to suffer similarly. Ananias scrubbed at his beard, staring off to the side as if lost in thought. The others looked back at John, or at the ground, with a mixture of lingering shock, fear, and ire. Only Manteo appeared calm and composed, almost without emotion.

John swept a hand over his face and adjusted his hat. He was governor here. He must lead accordingly. "This has been asked once already, but how is it Master Howe came to be so far from the rest of his company?"

Henry and Richard Berrye, Dyonis Harvie, and the others who'd gone hunting and foraging all exchanged sheepish glances. "We know not," Harvie said at last, his voice low. "He said only that he was going to gather crabs and other such shellfish as might be found."

They'd no idea of the dangers, however often John had warned them to be watchful, to go about in pairs at least—

He pinched the bridge of his nose and then, with a sharp shake of his head, leveled his gaze upon them. "It is, without doubt, the work of savages. I know too well the look of it." And perhaps such were not to be blamed, but—they'd yet to discover who had indeed done it.

"Can you hazard a guess as to which ones?" Ananias asked.

John shifted from foot to foot. How much could he admit to these men about the wrongs he'd witnessed the year prior? He shook his head. "Likely whoever now dwells at Dasemonguepeuk, as they are nearest. 'Twas the Secotan, when last I was here."

Manteo stirred, the expression in his features so fleeting that John could not name it before it was gone again. "May I speak?"

"Of course," John said with a nod.

The savage turned slowly to include the others. "We should go now to my people, at *Kurawoten*. Ask them what they have heard of this matter, as well as the others who were here."

"Dare we do such a thing," Cooper asked, "not knowing who slew Howe?"

"Nay, it is a good plan," John said, "and something we should soon have done, regardless."

"We should make sure the village is adequately guarded," another chimed in.

"And so shall we," John said, more firmly.

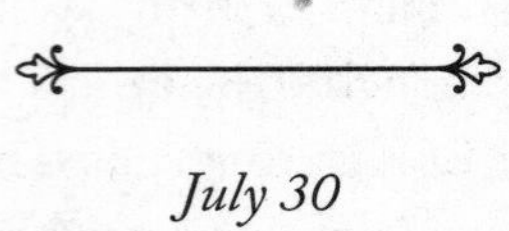

July 30

Two days later, John and twenty of his best men were back on board the *Sunne*, with a heading south through the sound for Croatoan, or Kurawoten as Manteo said. It was a visit perhaps overdue, but given that they'd intended only the briefest stop on Roanoac before sailing on to Chesepiok, their delay could not be helped.

Breathing hurt, and his gut churned. *God, be with us. . .go before us. Grant us Thy favor and blessing on this venture. And above all, grant us discovery of what happened here, in truth, and let us be well received.*

The sea wind blew over him, at once warm but refreshing as it dried the sweat on his face and neck—for every one of them wore armor and carried a musket or arquebus.

Tall clouds gathered on the eastern horizon but the sky above remained clear, and they made steady progress. Fifty miles it was to Croatoan, less than a day's journey if the weather held. Standing at the bow, John glanced over at Manteo, similarly stationed, his face set into the wind. What thoughts coursed through the savage's mind? Though one could look at him and call him savage no longer, at least in regard to its description of a method of living and depth of understanding of God. In the latter, Manteo was well schooled, now able to recite much scripture and give account of its meaning. He'd not yet presented himself for baptism, but it had been the subject of conversation between them on more than one occasion.

Already, however, if truth be told, Manteo comported himself more a Christian than many of those baptized and reared in the Church. Which was part of the very reason John and others had quietly, or in some cases not so quietly, dissented from the Church of England in recent years.

Rafe Lane's despicable behavior over the disappearance of a mere communion cup, silver notwithstanding, was part of John's own determination to distance himself from such.

Please, Lord, give us favor with the peoples here. Let the friendship between us be renewed, as we all desire.

He couldn't help repeating that prayer.

Father, also guard our planters left this day on Roanoac. The women, the little ones. And—oh Lord, give my daughter and Margery safe delivery of their babes, in the fullness of their time!

After much debate, he'd left Ananias behind—Dyonis Harvie too, though both be Assistants—reasoning that if he and the other men were delayed in their mission to Manteo's mother and kinsmen, their interests lay most strongly with wives and unborn babes, and thus they were most suited to defense of the village. Beyond that, Ananias's occupation as a carpenter and bricklayer meant his skills were needed more urgently in the ongoing repair and building efforts than on a diplomatic mission to neighboring peoples.

Meeting Manteo's people would come in due course for the rest, of that he was confident—at least, if all went well.

With the barrier islands to their left and the open sound to their right, beyond which the mainland lay out of sight, the inlet marking the northern edge of Manteo's home island came into view before the sun was at its highest. Manteo straightened at the rail, his arm outflung with the first strong emotion John had witnessed from him in a long while. The savage gave a cry that was lost in the wind, but the sailors must have heard it for what it was meant to be, because the order was given to heel about and put down anchor.

John gathered those who were to go ashore with him. "I beseech you all to remember that these people were our friends in time past. Be on guard, aye, but shoot only at the last extremity. If they cannot provide us with news of our missing countrymen, then we are without any other help, so tread gently."

Those going ashore hastened into the boat. By the time they reached the shore, movement flickered at the edge of the forest, and as the first of them set foot to the sand, figures dressed in deerskin stepped from the trees, bows and arrows at the ready.

Determination, if not menace, etched every line of their lithe bodies. No wonder, for how John and the others had left the New World last year.

All around him, John could hear the intake of breath as their company scrambled ashore, matchlocks and crossbows already lifted. "Do not yet shoot," he said, keeping his voice low but clear enough to be heard over the splash of waves and clank of boat fittings. "March forward, but do not fire."

In the next moment, those facing them at the forest's edge turned and dove back under cover. A cry split the air—Manteo, calling out to them in words John had not heard in more than a year. Motion ceased, then as Manteo yanked off his hat and called again, a few brave souls turned back and reemerged from the forest.

Manteo's voice was quieter now but no less urgent. John waved to the company to lower their weapons, and of a sudden, bows were flung down and those come to greet them crowded about Manteo, touching his face, gripping his arms and shoulders, and flinging their arms around him, murmuring and exclaiming all the while. As John and the rest of the company looked on, the surge of Manteo's people included them, embracing and patting them with fervor, an unmistakable joy in the dark eyes. Some even greeted Captain Stafford by name, having recognized him as well.

More exchange of conversation between Manteo and his people, and then with a broad grin creasing his face, he turned to John and the others. "I have told them who we are. They are most earnestly desirous that you not spill or spoil any of their corn, of which they have but little."

"Please," John said, "hasten to assure them that we have no such intention. Neither corn, nor any other thing of theirs, shall be diminished. Our coming is only to renew old love, which was between us and them at the first, and to live with them as brethren and friends."

Manteo relayed the speech to them, and exclamations, nods, and cries of joy issued from his people. They spoke then amongst themselves and with Manteo, and at length he turned again to relate what had been said.

"They wish you to come up to their town, so we may speak more at length."

"God be thanked," Stafford muttered, and the boat was drawn up forthwith, out of reach of the tide, and they prepared to follow Manteo's people.

John's limbs trembled with nothing more than undisguised relief. Their walk through the maritime forest minded him of similar events in days past, when he'd accompanied Lane and others, and the savages still welcomed them with all friendliness.

Please, God, that we not spoil it this time!

Chapter Four

They were seated with much fanfare, John himself given a place of honor across from none other than Manteo's mother, a *weroansqua* of the Croatoan. A deerskin mantle adorned her slight but dignified form, her grey-streaked black hair lying loose across shoulders adorned with strings of pearls and copper beads. Copper ornaments hung from her earlobes, a narrow band of the same circled her brow, and strings of pearls, her wrists. Bright, dark eyes studied them all, intent despite the easy smile tugging at her wide mouth. In her mannerisms, she was so like Manteo, seated beside him, that it was all he could do not to gape like a small child.

She spoke to Manteo, her voice musical, and he turned to John. "We will eat first, and after that, talk. But it pleases her that we have sought her out to find news of our situation."

John nodded gravely. "Tell her that she honors us. We are pleased to sit at meat with her and your kinsmen."

Manteo repeated the speech in his own tongue, and her lips parted to reveal small but strong white teeth. The effect was entirely charming, despite the fearsome painted designs tracing her features.

Oh, how he loved these people. He was here at last. To stay, please God.

And please God he could begin to right the wrongs done them.

His men, roughly assembled around him, were restless, most openly staring at the savages, men and women alike. John chuckled inwardly. The novelty would wear off in time, but he'd warned them of the initial shock of witnessing such casual nakedness, while emphasizing their extreme innocence. Perhaps in time they could be brought to Christian faith, and thus to proper civilized attire, but until then—

Manteo's mother spoke again, and Manteo turned again to translate, his smile now rueful. "She says it has been so long since she has seen me. She wishes to know what has brought us, for surely this is no mere visit of courtesy."

John let himself smile in return. "Would, alas, that it were." He cleared his throat, pulse quickening again. "I will say again, however, that we do come with earnest desire to renew the old ties between my people and yours."

Manteo relayed the speech, and she sat back, clearly considering his words before replying.

"She wishes to be given some token or badge, that our people not be mistaken for enemies when we meet outside this town or island. They have suffered much from the lack thereof when Master Lane found them at Dasemonguepeuk last year, and many of them still bear the hurt. Although they hold you at no fault of that."

John bowed his head. Aye, too well he recalled. Did she know he had been at that fateful conflict?

She spoke again, shortly. "Come, walk with me," Manteo translated.

They left the longhouse and went out into the sunlight, where the smells of food cooking drew a growl from John's middle. He followed steadfastly after Manteo and his mother, her retinue and his own trailing after. She led them to one of the smaller huts and, beckoning, ducked inside.

The smells here were sharply different—of illness and bodies in quarters too close. A man lay on an upraised pallet, draped across his privities with a deerskin but otherwise unclothed. After a flurry of conversation between Manteo, his mother, and the man lying prostrate, with Manteo greeting him as some long-unseen kin, Manteo's mother lifted a hand and addressed John. "This man lies lame, and has been so from hurt he took from Master Lane's men. But we know your men mistook ours for Wyngyno's men."

"What is this?" Berrye asked, at John's elbow.

"Later," John murmured. "I shall explain all anon. But not here." He eyed the prone man's withered legs, one more so than the other, and gave another bow. "I greatly regret your injury, sir. May God bring healing, sooner rather than late."

And perhaps he could bring their physick to examine the poor soul's leg, to see if aught could be done.

Manteo's mother nodded, her smile returning, beckoning again. "Let us away, for the feast is surely almost ready, and you and your men must be famished."

And famished they were. All gladly partook of grilled and smoked fish, goodly fruits, cucumbers, nuts, and shellfish stewed with root vegetables that had always and still minded John of chowder, with a wilder flavor than wont, but still toothsome. Some of his men hesitated at the fare presented them, but all ate, as John had warned them to do otherwise would sorely offend their hosts and bring hurt to their cause.

Afterward, the chiefest men of Croatoan gathered around with Manteo's mother and shared what they knew of the surrounding peoples. They had heard already of the colonists' arrival, and of the killing of Master Howe. After their ships had passed by Croatoan weeks ago, several young men in their ranging had observed their anchoring off Hatorask, and the pinnace's passage to Roanoac. They'd afterward witnessed the furtive passage over the sound by a remnant of Wyngyno's men who kept company with Wanchese, crossing from their dwelling place at Dasemonguepeuk over to Roanoac the day the killing had occurred, and from afar marked their passage to the marsh where Howe was slain.

"We have also heard stories told, from the people of Secota, Aquascogoc, and Dasemonguepeuk, that they waged a cunning and brave battle against the ten and five your chief men left behind last year."

By this time, John had drawn out a slate and pencil and was scribbling hasty notes so to better remember all the details.

"They took twice the number of your people in their own, a score and ten, and finding four of your Englishmen away, two of them showed themselves to the one and ten remaining, gesturing by friendly signs that the English send two of their own, unarmed, to speak with them. Two of the chiefest went to them with gladness, but whilst one of their men traitorously embraced one of yours, the other drew his wooden sword, which he had hidden beneath his mantle, and struck the Englishman on the head and slew him.

"The rest of the company came out of hiding, and the other Englishman fled to his town as they pursued with bows and arrows. The English took shelter in their houses but their assailants set the houses on fire, so the English sallied forth with such weapons as they could to defend themselves. The skirmish lasted about an hour, and at least one was shot in the mouth with an arrow and died. One of those from the mainland was shot in the side and also died.

"At last the remaining English were able to retreat, fighting all the way, to the water side, where lay their boat. They fled toward Hatorask but on the way saw their four fellows coming from a creek, where they had been to fetch oysters. Once they had taken these four into their boat, they left Roanoac and took shelter on one of the little islands near the entrance of the harbor of Hatorask. They remained there a little while but afterward departed, to whence we know not, but they were never seen again in this place."

John set down his pencil and examined the grave expressions surrounding him. "How is it you are privy to this account? Has Croatoan been more friendly with Secota, Aquascogoc, and Dasemonguepeuk than in times past?"

Manteo translated, and one older man leaned forward, elbow on his knee. "Wanchese makes no secret of his ill will toward your people. He has been heard boasting that he drove the men of your people out of Roanoac, and has vowed to do similarly if you were ever to return. Our younger men range about and do trade and speak with the other peoples. It was widely noised about that these ten and a score made attack upon the town on Roanoac, and the particular deeds of their bravery much vaunted."

"I. . .see." It was something about which he would question Manteo in a more private moment. With all the intrigues back in England, whether in the Queen's court or elsewhere, boasting of one's exploits, particularly in such a way that one's enemies might catch wind of it, had never played a part. At least not in John's own experience.

It was a curious thing to contemplate.

Elinor lay in the hot darkness, listening to the sound of Ananias breathing within the cottage, and of village life without.

Grateful she was for a real bed—although she missed the motion of the ship more than she'd dreamed possible—but between the babe going kickety-kick, his father's soft snoring, and the unaccustomed heat of this new country, sleep had fled far away.

A cramp rippled across her hips. Muting a sigh, she levered herself up, very carefully, and crept from the bed, so as not to disturb Ananias. He had labored enough this day and needed his sleep.

She paced the floor, hands smoothing across her belly as she circled the cottage. How good it felt to wear only her shift under cover of darkness, rather than having the heavy, boned kirtle laced over all, and her hair loosely braided rather than pinned up. She stopped at a window, peeking past the thin linen curtain. Nothing stirred but a hound nosing about outside a nearby cottage, an owl hooting somewhere off in the trees, and the constant chirring of insects. Fireflies swarmed in the trees and all the spaces in between, like living, moving starlight. She watched them for a little while, then mindful not to let in more mosquitoes than necessary, dropped the curtain and resumed pacing.

She'd not even circled once before the low voice of Ananias came out of the shadows, edged in anxiousness. "Is it your time?"

"Nay. Go back to sleep. I am merely walking about."

"You are having no pains?"

"Besides being weary? Nay." She padded over to stand by the bed. Ananias reached out a hand, his eyes but darker shadows against the paleness of his features, and she clasped it a moment before laying his palm against her belly. "Your son is restless tonight. And I cannot sleep for thinking of Papa and where he might be."

Ananias gave a thin smile. "I'm sure your father is well able to handle whatever may come. Would that I'd been able to go along, although I do not begrudge remaining behind for your sake." His hand moved across her belly, hesitating as the babe responded with a firm kick. "Ah, so strong. And not long, eh, little one?" He sat halfway up and leaned to kiss her belly.

"Very strong. And aye, I'd as lief hold your son in my arms sooner rather than late."

Ananias's gaze came to hers. "Why are you so intent upon referring to the babe as a lad? Could be a maid child, you know."

"Of course, but—" Why did he ask that? The unspoken reminder that she was not the first to bear him a child, that he indeed had a son already back in England, unexpectedly stung and snarled her tongue. "But a—a son—in the New World, to carry on your name—is a fine and honorable thing."

He lay back, mouth curving. "Any child of ours will be a fine and honorable thing, Goodwife. And a sweet girl who looks like her mama would be a joy and delight."

She laced her fingers more firmly with his. "If you say so, my husband."

He blew out a long breath. "I do. And you'd best believe me when I also say that I love you, my dearest and best."

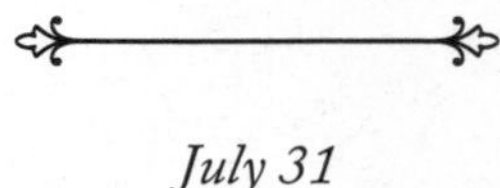

July 31

The morning dawned clear and fine, and after they'd broken fast, John and his men gathered once more with Manteo's mother and her chiefest men. "Of the surrounding peoples, then," John began, "all those of Secota, Aquascogoc, Pomeiooc, if they would accept our friendship, we would willingly receive them again and all past hurts and offenses will be utterly forgotten. Would your people be willing to convey them this word, and make certain to us their answer?"

"We will gladly do our best," one aged man said, and the others assented. "Within seven days, we will bring the weroances and chiefest governors of their towns to your town and to you the Governor of Roanoac, or we will bring their answer."

All gestures of friendliness and respect were again exchanged. John and his men bowed, and the Croatoan nodded and embraced them, both by grasping their forearms and encircling them about the shoulders. As they assembled to make their way back through the forest to the boat, Manteo embraced not only his mother but two other women and a young girl whose features, to John's eye, mirrored his.

Another curious thing to inquire after. The previous evening had afforded no quiet moment for John to ask Manteo about the account of the attack on the town at Roanoac the year past, so closely did the Croatoan attend upon them both last night and again that morning. But it remained uppermost in John's mind.

They returned to the boat and offered final farewells to the Croatoan who had accompanied them, including Towaye, whom Manteo had released to stay with their people. As they rowed back out to the *Sunne*, some of Manteo's kin paddled out with them in their own *kanoes*, curiously carved from sections of tree trunks. John tipped his face to the midday sky and breathed a prayer of thanksgiving. They had not merely discharged their business here but also escaped further harm themselves.

Please God the next seven days would bring further marvels.

Back aboard the *Sunne*, having returned there himself the previous evening, Captain Stafford met them with hearty gladness. "We should rejoin the fleet at the inlet of Hatorask, Governor, and hear what news they might have, as well as discover when indeed they intend to return to England. Unless you have some reason to go straightaway back to Roanoac?"

John shook his head slowly. "No, we have time to revisit the *Lyon* and flyboat. I should like to speak with Spicer and hear more of his adventure coming here."

As long as they were back on Roanoac within a day or so.

Visiting the fleet proved as vexing and counterproductive as John feared. Simon Ferdinando lurked everywhere, damping free conversation with the usual supercilious expression carved forever upon his features, and Spicer declined to speak in the presence of the hated Portuguese navigator. John could not blame him. They spent the night aboard the flyboat but at first light sailed back through the inlet and for Roanoac.

Just as John felt he might breathe more easily again, the old doubts and cares assailed him. What if it were not the Secotan and others, old followers of Wyngyno, but their friends the Croatoan who were responsible for Master Howe's slaying, not to mention the assault on their fifteen soldiers from the year before? And regardless of who truly had done the deed. . .could John truly fault them for their anger?

Oh great, gracious God, have mercy on us. . . .

Manteo leaned as was his wont against the rail, and John stepped up next to him, assuming a casual pose with elbows against the wood. The wind ruffled his beard and the edges of his hat, yet was not so strong as to threaten to tear it away. "I saw the young girl you were bidding farewell to," he said without preamble. He'd learned well enough over the past two years that Manteo appreciated directness.

Manteo let out a long breath, which John might have missed had he not been watching for it. At last he said, "She is my daughter."

John nodded slowly. "And—one of the young women is your wife?"

"Nay. My wife died before your people first came. My daughter is under care of my mother and sisters now."

"But—why did you never say so before? We might have gone sooner to Croatoan for you to see them."

"There was no time," Manteo said evenly. "Ferdinando said so, and often. Besides, I had a duty first to you, and the planters." He shifted to face John. "When first the elders chose me, and charged me with being whatever help I could to your people, I knew it meant I might never again see my own people. But it was a choice I made gladly, for I felt it, here"—he placed a fist over his heart— "that it was a path I was meant to take."

For a long moment—several breaths in fact—John could not speak past the sudden thickness of his throat. He'd never considered what Manteo might have left behind. Not even with the knowledge of his mother being *weroansqua* to their people. But in this moment, knowing so intimately what it felt like to sail away and leave a daughter—one freshly bereaved of her mother as well—and for that matter, how difficult had that been for his Elinor? Had John himself been so lost in grief and busied with adventure that he could not think properly of the hurt to his own child?

And yet so often men left family behind as a matter of course, in the pursuit of new ventures or simply to provide for them. Especially seafaring men.

"My daughter has lacked nothing in my absence," Manteo went on, as if he knew the bend of John's thoughts. "My mother and sisters would not allow her to suffer in that regard. My part in all this has rather given her a place of honor, and indeed the entire town looks after her. I cannot say that would be the case had I stayed."

"I am happy to hear that." John cleared his throat, stretched his back and shoulders. "Please God you may see her again very soon, regardless."

Manteo gave a grave nod.

"I have also desired to ask you—what think you, truly, of this account your people gave of our fifteen Englishmen left on Roanoac last year? There was so much of the attack that—forgive me, I mean not to question your people's integrity, but how could they have known, without having been present as well?"

Another long silence issued from Manteo, but John knew better than to think he'd not taken in every word and was considering them most carefully.

"It is indeed the way of our people," he said at last, "as the elder chief men have already affirmed, to speak boldly of one's exploits in battle. Wanchese and the others would have had no cause to hold back on the telling. They would rather—what is the word—add adornment with each piece of the story."

"Embellish?"

Manteo's smooth brow creased, a rare enough occurrence. "Aye. Mayhap."

"But that would imply there were details related to the event which were not strictly true, and—" John drew a deep breath of his own. "I would not fault your people's truthtelling."

The dark eyes of Manteo had gone strangely shuttered, his visage once more void of expression.

John's heart beat hard and painful. Not for the first time did he feel as though the ground beneath him had simply dropped away, leaving him to tumble into nothingness.

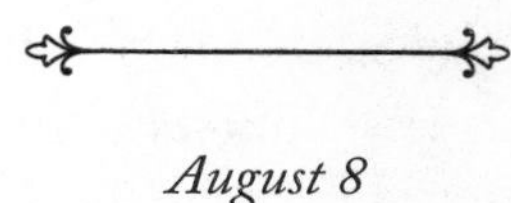

August 8

Shellfish and venison. Elinor was fast becoming skilled in presenting both as the most savory dishes, though she herself had little enough appetite these past days, between the weather's unrelenting heat and the burgeoning weight of the babe.

As the sun dipped low, she carried a bowl of the pottage she'd made, half crab and half venison, to Papa as he labored inside his own small house not far from the one she and Ananias occupied. They'd talked of sharing a house with Papa, but he insisted his presence would be an intrusion, with his needing to tend colony business, and her babe expected any day. Elinor included him, however, and most gladly, when she prepared meals.

She found him alone, a rare enough hap as governor, seated at a small table and leaning a little with quill in hand, doublet cast aside and shirtsleeves rolled above the elbow. Cheekbones and forehead gleaming with sweat in the light from the nearby window, he looked up as she entered and offered a weary smile. "What have you for me tonight, Daughter?"

She gave a short laugh. "Very same as yesterday, Papa. Provender does not change, so neither does the menu." A sigh escaped her. "But I miss bread, I do."

"As do we all." Papa's tone belied the gravity of his expression as he moved aside his vellum and set his quill back in the inkwell, making room for the covered bowl she carried. Once she'd put it before him, he lifted the cloth and breathed deeply of the aroma. "This smells wonderful, however. I thank you."

As he bent his head, recited a soft prayer over the food, then sampled the first bite, she stood back, arms folded. "What are you writing today?"

He slurped the broth, chewed the bit of meat he'd taken on the spoon, and sucked air into the side of his mouth to ease the heat of it. "Oh, working on my daily accounts. Thinking that it has been a week since we returned from Croatoan, and thus we should have heard from the weroances on the matter of Master Howe's death."

A chill skimmed her spine, but she shook it off. Naught else amiss had taken place since that awful day. Still, none of them could rest quite easy until the matter was resolved, or at least until they had heard back from Manteo's people about their venture to go round and speak to the other tribes.

She eyed the half-written document now resting on the other side of the table. "Do you ever miss your painting and drawing?"

He shot her a half smile, strands of grey-streaked hair framing his angular features, then laid down the spoon and riffled through the stack of papers. He hesitated between a few, then drew out a sheet and handed it to her.

A girl of Croatoan, the caption read. It was but a rough sketch, but in the utterly realistic style she knew and loved as her father's own. A young girl, she had to be, in clothing so sparse it could hardly be called decent despite her obviously yet-immature body, recognizable as female only by the wisps of long hair trailing across her shoulders in the manner Elinor was familiar with from Papa's previous artwork. Shorter wisps feathered across her forehead, accenting a round face with the sweetest expression, eyes bright despite the crude penciling.

Elinor lifted her gaze to Papa's. "From your recent journey?"

He chewed a bite, nodding. Blew out a breath as if considering. "Manteo's daughter, by his own admission."

"Truly?" She peered closer, seeing now the resemblance to their beloved savage's features. "How enchanting," she murmured, then looked up again. "I hope to meet her someday."

He nodded, once more grave. "I've no doubt that you shall, perhaps sooner rather than late."

Elinor handed back the sketch, and he tucked it into the stack.

"So he left behind a wife as well?"

Papa shook his head. "She died some time ago, like your mother. I better understand his willingness to leave his people, though, for the venture of coming to England. 'Tis not easy to lose one's spouse."

Elinor did not miss the heavy swallow following his words, though he tucked his head and applied himself anew to the pottage. "Nay. I can imagine 'tis not."

Papa's blue eyes were upon her again, sharply. " 'Twas not with perfect willingness that I left you behind, either, my sweet daughter. I realize now how you must have suffered, to be separated from us both, though for different circumstances. I am—I regret that, except for the fact that it allowed me to make provision for you and Ananias to have your own place here—your own land."

She laid her hand on his shoulder. It had been a trial indeed, but she would not admit that, not with him already so obviously distressed. "All is well, Papa. I understand. And we are glad—I am glad—to be here to share the adventure with you at last."

He sniffed. "Some adventure, with a man slain so foully already."

The chill returned. "Please God we might hear from Manteo's people soon."

"Please God, indeed."

Did his words hold rancor, or were they a sincere plea for the Almighty's attentions? Elinor hoped the latter. It would be a thing of utmost terror if in the face of such hardship her father had himself lost faith.

"And how is Georgie faring?"

Elinor shifted and stretched, easing the sudden cramp down one thigh. "Well enough, I suppose. Ananias and I offered to keep him, but he'd rather be with the other boys, so Joyce Archard took him in."

Papa nodded, chewing another bite as he scraped up the last of the pottage in the bowl. "Understandable. 'Tis best for him to have a companion, I would think. Especially here."

" 'Twas Ananias's thought, and mine as well." How lost and alone Elinor would feel had she not the friendship of Rose Payne and Jane Jones.

He finished the pottage and handed back the bowl and spoon. "Thank you kindly, Daughter. If you could let Ananias know, as soon as you might see him, that I've need to call a council tonight, I would appreciate that as well."

"Of course, Papa." She gave him a one-armed embrace and kissed his forehead.

The house was quiet again after Elinor had gone, taking bowl and spoon with her. And blessedly so—it seemed as though everyone in the new colony continually needed him for something or other the past week.

Aye, he missed drawing and painting—and the days when the weightiest thing he had to bear was to observe and sketch, so to offer a glimpse of these people, so curious but carefree, to the Queen and her court and any of the masses with whom she saw fit to share such knowledge.

He was in no wise unmindful of the honor she'd granted him, to be appointed governor of this colony, under Ralegh. Nay, not at all. But that even for a moment he'd honestly believed they might escape the awfulness handed him by Lane's actions—and now it had cost at least one innocent man's life.

Most gracious God, make me strong enough, wise enough, for this.

He'd prayed that prayer so many times over the past months, he'd lost count. Did the Almighty even still hear him?

Elbows on the tabletop, he covered his face with both hands.

"Governor White, are you well?"

He straightened and composed himself, meeting the gaze of his Assistant Roger Prat. "Oh aye, merely a bit weary."

If governor they had chosen him to be, then it behooved him to behave as one.

Chapter Five

August 9

They sailed across the sound around midnight, coming ashore a little south of where John remembered Wyngyno's town lay. Stealthily, as silently as possible, rapiers and muskets at the ready—the glow of the fuse on an arquebus would give them away—they crept through the darkness. Dawn had not quite begun to lighten the eastern sky.

Twenty-four of them there were, twenty-five including Captain Stafford. Manteo led the party, with John close behind, making their approach so that the houses of the town were between them and the water. A fire flickered up ahead, and as they neared, the forms and movement of human bodies became visible.

The moment had come. All the indignation of the past days, mingled with the dread of past hours, swirled through John's belly. The memory of George Howe's bloodied and mutilated form fueled his resolve, and with a whisper to Manteo, answered by his nod, he motioned to the others. Nearly as one, they gave a shout and dashed forward.

The figures gathered about the fire surged to their feet, shrieking, and fled toward the reeds. John and his company gave pursuit.

At the edge of the marsh, they halted, shoes sinking into the mud. Three or four of the soldiers lifted their muskets and fired. One of the savages fell with a cry, and yanking off his shoes and flinging them onto the bank behind him, John waded into the reeds. "Hold your fire! Hold, I say! Apprehend them all and bring them back and we will see what they have to say for themselves."

One by one they dragged them, flailing, slippery, eyes and mouths stretched wide in terror, through the reeds and to dry land once more, where some scrambled to escape. But then another kind of cry—dear, merciful Lord in heaven, there were women here, one with a babe clinging to her back in the way of this people.

One man called out, "Stafford! Stafford!"

Over all came Manteo's shout: "Cease! Do not fire, do not strike! They are friends! Friends, I say."

Dropping his rapier, John fell to his hands and knees, breaths heaving. *Gracious God. . .oh Lord in heaven, no. . . .*

Nearby, the woman huddled with the child in her lap now, rocking and weeping. Manteo muttered furiously in a manner that sounded to John like cursing.

To his knowledge, he had never heard Manteo curse before. The temptation was strong to do the same.

"They are friends," Manteo repeated. "They are Kurawoten."

"And what the devil do they here, in what is formerly Wyngyno's town?" Cooper asked the question rimming John's own thoughts.

John reached for his rapier and struggled to his feet. His legs protested the task of holding him upright.

"We will find that out," Manteo said, and rattled away in his native tongue. Slowly his countrymen—and -women—stirred from their moaning and shock and, as he beckoned, followed him, straggling, back to the fire.

John looked about, making sure the wounded man was brought along, then shambled along in Manteo's wake as well. As others stoked the fire, John slumped to the ground, close enough to feel the warmth—but no fire could burn away the terrible chill seeping from his heart outward. *Oh God, forgive us. . . .*

Still standing, Manteo was already engaged in earnest conversation with a handful of the men. Not until he'd heard a lengthy explanation, with many gestures and their voices yet tinged with anxiousness, did he turn to John and translate. "They came here and found Wanchese and the others gone, and the town abandoned with such haste as to leave behind all corn, tobacco, and pumpkins. They could not refuse such provender, for so the birds and deer would eat and spoil it all, were it not gathered in."

"Why, though, in heaven's name, did they not send to us first, to let us know what they had found?"

Manteo fired off another round of questions, sharply, waited for the reply, then turned back again. Sorrow and anger hardened his features in the growing light of dawn. "Menatoan says they did not think of it. Only that the harvest of our enemies must be gathered in before it was too late."

"And what of the peoples who lived here? The Secotan, the Aquascogoc, others? What word of them?"

Another exchange of conversation, and Manteo shook his head soberly. "No word, or else refusal to come and treat with us."

John felt a strong desire to do as those around him, to huddle on the ground and cover his face in his hands. "God have mercy on us all," he muttered at last.

Gatherings always took place in the open area between the fort and the village, where, as it was said, they could run into the fort if there was an attack or something else amiss. For her own part, Elinor simply appreciated the open air where a breeze could reach them and she could let her gaze roam across the towering pines and arching oaks. Their majesty provided a welcome distraction from the tediousness of the business at hand, and often she'd come back to the moment, realizing she'd no idea what had been discussed.

Today 'twas not merely diversion but outright distraction, in the form of Manteo's kinsmen, loosely huddled in the center of the gathering, seated on the ground or crouching before Papa and Manteo. She listened with half an ear, though not without interest, as Papa recited the events of the past night and morning, his tone and expression heavy with the tragedy that had nearly taken place. Beside him, Manteo stood, uncharacteristically stern, shocking in itself.

How like, and yet unlike, were his kinsmen! Elinor's gaze went back time and again to the manner of dress and arranging of hair, both strange and yet familiar from Papa's drawings. And what a marvel to see these people in life, when they were until now only sketches and paintings. The soft, supple deerskins that comprised their clothing, often merely as a skirt draped about their hips, with the pelt of some other animal covering the men's privities where deerskin did not. Ornaments of copper and—were those strings of pearls? She had not been prepared for how they glittered and shone, just from their various adornments. And then the wonder of such lean, muscled bodies, men and women alike, so strong and graceful in their movements. The curious designs on their skin, whether around their upper arms or on their legs or faces, or the mark some shared on their upper back—forsooth, their skin itself, of such a rich shade as to seem not skin at all, except for the occasional flash of a bare breast or buttock.

Papa had spoken of this over and over, but it still caught her by surprise.

The woman with the small child in her lap turned and met Elinor's gaze, then glanced down at Elinor's rounded belly and back up again before offering a shy smile. Elinor let her own mouth curve, and the other woman nodded, once, very quickly.

It was agreed at last that all which could be related about the past night and day's events had been, and the men were done speaking, at least formally. Manteo's kinsmen rose, looking about in a way that seemed both shy and curious. The woman slung her child around to her back, holding one of the child's arms over one shoulder and his opposite leg beneath the other, then hesitated, glancing this way and that before taking a few steps toward Elinor.

Her heart pounded suddenly—but why was she afraid? Was this not what they'd all looked forward to? Were these not the people Papa had told her about and described with such affection?

She stepped toward the woman, offering another smile and lifting one hand, palm upward. Delight lit the woman's dark eyes with an answering smile, and as she moved closer, she shifted the child on her back and tapped her own chest with her free hand. "*Wesnah.*" She tapped again. "Wes-nah."

Elinor dipped her head. Was that the woman's name? "Wes-nah," she repeated, then patted her own chest. "Elinor. El-in-or."

The woman repeated the syllables, or attempted to—it came out as something like *Ettinor*—then laughed shyly. She said more words, pointing at Elinor's belly, then indicating her own child, and it was Elinor's turn to laugh. "We are about to prepare supper for everyone. Would you like to help?"

Of course the words of Elinor's invitation could not be understood, but when she beckoned and made to walk away, the woman followed—and others after. Once they saw the food preparation taking place, they understood right away. Many exclamations of "Ah!" and chattering in their own tongue accompanied their immediate efforts to assist the Englishwomen.

And though the meal took longer to prepare and cook than it otherwise might, it was accomplished with much amazement and far more goodwill than Elinor had dreamed it could.

After a meal of broiled fish, roasted pumpkin, and corn cakes—they'd brought as much food back from Dasemonguepeuk as was ripe enough to harvest—John retreated to his cottage and table again. While the ink dried on the day's account, he tugged toward him the curling parchment bearing the words *Charter of the Cittie of Ralegh in Virginia.*

Fingertips brushing the edges of the document, he read there again the names of the twelve Assistants, three of whom had stayed behind in England, and his own name among them, appointed as governor.

With this business of Master Howe's death resolved as best as they could under the circumstances, they must now give attention to choosing who would return to England and take word of their situation to Ralegh himself. 'Twould be best to send a pair of men who had not brought wives along, which shortened the list considerably. And they'd need to be well spoken. John sniffed. Christopher Cooper would be a likely enough choice because of the family connection, though he tended to act first and think later.

Such a trait was more of a hindrance here in the New World than not.

He scrubbed a hand across his face. This line of thinking would not do.

A sharp double knock sounded from the door. "Come," he called, and the woven reed panel, more a screen than a proper door, swung open to reveal Manteo, who stepped into the circle of light cast by his lamp. John sat back in his chair with a smile. "I've not commended you for all your help this past day and night. We are indebted to you."

Manteo tucked his head, accepting the praise without a word.

John could feel his smile becoming rueful. "You did indeed comport yourself as a perfect Englishman." He sniffed. "Would that others showed half as much honor."

The savage's dark eyes met his. "When will you tell the others of what took place before, with Rafe Lane?"

A sigh escaped him. "Soon."

"You should not delay. They need to know."

If it was not Ferdinando hounding him, then it was his own savage Assistant. He made a dismissive gesture. "Have we done enough to mend this latest rift with your people, do you think?"

Manteo's expression went thoughtful. "Aye. It grieves me still, although it was their own fault, not coming to us once the seven days had passed."

John shook his head. "I am just grateful beyond words that nothing more terrible happened, and that the man who was shot is recovering."

Manteo gave a distracted nod.

Did he have more to say? John waited.

At last Manteo looked up again, drawing himself straight. "I have made a decision. I know already that Ralegh commanded such to happen, but on my own will and not for his sake, I wish forthwith to be baptized as a Christian and be counted as truly one of your people."

John caught the sag of his jaw just in time. For all that he'd hoped for this day, longed for it, yet it caught him by surprise. The grin tugging at his mouth, however, he could not deny, and he pushed back his chair and rose to grasp Manteo's shoulders. "God be praised! This gives me much joy to hear it."

And so the following Sunday, August 13, Manteo received the sacrament of baptism.

Nicholas Johnson, who served as minister, stood before the assembly and read from the leather-bound volume of scripture. " 'For if thou acknowledge with thy mouth that Jesus is the Lord, and believe in thine heart, that God raised him up from death, thou shalt be safe. For to believe with the heart justifieth: and to acknowledge with the mouth maketh a man safe.' "

He straightened and fastened a firm glance upon the congregation. "These words from the epistle to the Romans cannot be more clear on what is needful to make us safe in Christ. With our heart we believe Jesus was raised from death, and with our mouth we acknowledge His lordship. There are some who would have us think we may do or say what we will, as long as we pay lip service to the Church, or give alms or do other good deeds, or carry out sundry traditions as taught by men. Alms and other good deeds are needful, in their place, but what is required is not mere lip service. It is the deep belief of the heart, and the giving of the entirety of our lives to Jesus as our Lord.

"Our place here in the New World means nothing if we do not both believe and live out that lordship. Our community will be for naught if we are not, first and foremost, a community of God, under God, believing what He has told us in His Word." He bent again to the great book. " 'For the scripture sayeth: whosoever believeth on him, shall not be confounded. There is no difference between the Jew and the Gentile. For one is Lord of all, which is rich unto all that call upon him.' "

Master Johnson again addressed the congregation. "We are not, being English, any different than those we seek to live among. While we have, many of us, professed Christ, the same Lord who has richly granted us salvation will richly grant the same to any of other peoples who similarly call upon Him. And today, we joyously receive one who has decided indeed to call upon God, and receive the holy sacrament of baptism.

"The Candidate for Holy Baptism will now be presented."

John stepped forward. "I present Manteo of Croatoan Island for the Sacrament of Baptism."

Johnson turned to Manteo, who had likewise approached the front of the gathering. "Do you desire to be baptized?"

He nodded. "I do."

"Do you renounce Satan and all the spiritual forces of wickedness that rebel against God?"

"I renounce them."

"Do you renounce the evil powers of this world which corrupt and destroy the creatures of God? Do you renounce all sinful desires that draw you from the love of God?"

"I renounce them."

"Do you turn to Jesus Christ and accept Him as your Savior? Do you put your whole trust in His grace and love?"

"I do."

"Do you promise to follow and obey Him as your Lord?"

"I do."

Though the words were drawn from the *Book of Common Prayer*, as the Anglican Church was wont to use, they sought to imbue the service with all the sincerity it ought to have. It was not, after all, the words that were the problem, but men's hearts, speaking from rote and never letting the truth saturate, cleanse, and change them. And if any indeed evinced fruit worthy of baptism, it was Manteo.

Johnson continued, facing the gathering. "Will you who witness these vows do all in your power to support this person in his life in Christ?"

They answered as one, "We will."

"Let us join with this one who is committing himself to Christ and renew our own baptismal covenant.

"Do you believe in God the Father?"

"I believe in God, the Father almighty, creator of heaven and earth."

"Do you believe in Jesus Christ, the Son of God?"

"I believe in Jesus Christ, His only Son, our Lord, who was conceived by the power of the Holy Spirit and born of the Virgin Mary. He suffered under Pontius Pilate, was crucified, died, and was buried. He descended to the dead. On the third day he rose again. He ascended into heaven, and is seated at the right hand of the Father. He will come again to judge the living and the dead."

"Do you believe in God the Holy Spirit?"

"I believe in the Holy Spirit, the holy Christian Church, the communion of saints, the forgiveness of sins, the resurrection of the body, and the life everlasting."

"Will you continue in the apostles' teaching and fellowship, in the breaking of the bread, and in the prayers?"

"I will, with God's help."

"Will you persevere in resisting evil, and, whenever you fall into sin, repent and return to the Lord?"

"I will, with God's help."

The solemnity of the service, and the weight of the words themselves, swelled within Elinor's breast, and the babe kicked as if affirming the truth as well.

Nicholas Johnson led the assembly through the questions and answers, whereby they promised to uphold God's good news in Christ, to seek and serve Christ in all persons, loving their neighbors as themselves, and finally to strive for justice and peace with all people, respecting the dignity of all people. She thought the words especially appropriate, given their new home and Manteo's identity as a savage, and their mutual pledge to live in love and brotherhood with his people.

"Let us now pray for this man who is to receive the sacrament of new birth. Deliver him, oh Lord, from the way of sin and death."

"Lord, hear our prayer."

How did the words, so familiar to Elinor and the others, fall upon Manteo's ear? Did he find them strange?

"Open his heart to Your grace and truth. Fill him with Your holy and life-giving Spirit. Keep him in the faith and communion of Your holy Church. Teach him to love others in the power of the Spirit. Send him into the world in witness to Your love. Bring him to the fullness of Your peace and glory."

"Lord, hear our prayer."

"Grant, oh Lord, that all who are baptized into the death of Jesus Christ Your Son may live in the power of His resurrection and look for Him to come again in glory; who lives and reigns now and forever. Amen."

What a curious thing indeed, for mere mortals to truly live in the power of Christ's resurrection. Did any of them accomplish that?

The minister moved to where a basin of water stood upon a table they'd set out for the occasion. Lifting a hand, he prayed over and blessed it, then the oil used for consecration. He and the other men had debated long and hard over whether to trek down to the creek or beach and actually immerse Manteo, but at last decided that the traditional washing from a basin would suffice. Upon being beckoned forward, Manteo bent over the basin and Johnson scooped a handful of water and poured it over the top of Manteo's head, three times in turn. "Manteo, I baptize you in the name of the Father, and of the Son, and of the Holy Spirit. Amen."

They both straightened, Manteo letting the lingering drops fall across his face with a look of such sweetness and joy that it brought tears to Elinor's own eyes and a thickness to her throat.

The anointing with oil came next, as the minister applied it to Manteo's forehead in the sign of the cross. "Manteo, you are sealed by the Holy Spirit in baptism and marked as Christ's own forever. Amen."

Nicholas Johnson lifted a hand again and gave the closing prayer and formal welcome to the newly baptized. Elinor knew she should close her eyes in proper reverence, but she could not tear her gaze away from the wonder still shining in Manteo's eyes.

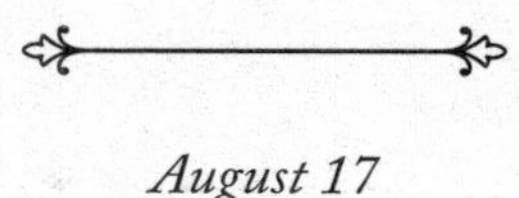

August 17

Three long days they'd planned, and labored, and debated. What notes and tokens did each of them wish to send back to England? And whom should they choose to make that return voyage, and speak upon their behalf?

They were no closer to deciding that than they ever were.

Ananias tramped the short distance to his house from the gathering area between fort and town, his father-in-law the governor keeping pace with him. He could see the distress still etched on White's face, deepening the lines already there, though the prospect of supper had lightened him somewhat.

That, and seeing Elinor's sweet face. It always cheered both her father and himself.

The smell of freshly baked corn cake wafted on the breeze as they neared the cottage—no wonder, since it was nearly evening and the entire town was preparing supper—but when he stepped inside, he was not disappointed to see an iron pan cooling on the table, full of this country's stand-in for bread. Beside it were laid roasted pumpkin on one platter and broiled fish on another.

Elinor straightened from some task over by the fireplace and greeted them with a smile. "Well that you've come! I despaired of serving you while the food was yet warm."

He crossed the room in two strides, catching her into his arms and kissing her soundly. "You know that matters not to me, long as there is food and plenty of it."

She laughed and nodded toward the table. "There is that. Although"—she sighed—"I do wish we'd butter. What I'd not trade for a fresh cow to provide milk and cheese."

"They'd only room for swine and fowl on this voyage," he reminded her as she broke free and went to embrace her father. "Kine to come later."

"Of course," she said, and then, stepping back, set her fists on her hips and stretched this way and that, her belly now impossibly round beneath her kirtle and apron. "Go, then, do you sit down, both of you."

White grinned. "You are certain there is enough? I know my son-in-law's appetite."

Elinor flapped a hand in his direction, waddling to fetch a stool from the corner so they might all have seats. "Always. And you've saved me the need of bringing you a portion, by joining us this eve."

Ananias hesitated only a moment, watching the ponderousness of her gait, before claiming a chair and setting to. His father-in-law took the other. Elinor shortly had scooted herself up to the side of the table, perched on the stool.

"I still say," White said, continuing the line of conversation from the end of the meeting, "that Chris Cooper should go. And possibly Thomas Harris with him."

Ananias chewed, a chunk of fish upon a slice of corn cake—and Elinor was right, it might have been improved with butter but was toothsome enough after a day's labor intermingled with vexing talk that went nowhere. He shook his head. He'd his own idea of who should return, but he'd not say so to White. Not yet. Not without the others, especially those more seasoned than he, in agreement.

But White, as usual, was too observant. "You say not, Ananias?"

"I am reserving opinion for now," he said blandly. "Of greater concern to me is the time. The *Lyon* and the flyboat are done with unloading our supplies and victuals, are they not? And have trimming and new calking for the voyage back."

"Aye." His father-in-law's eyes were steady upon him, measuring.

But Ananias deflected his gaze with a nod toward Elinor. " 'Twould be good to send back word of the babe's safe arrival."

His wife's head did not come up at those words, as if the meager bits she'd portioned herself drew all her thought and attention. Ananias knew better, although come to think, she'd been eating sparsely enough these past several days. She'd claimed it was merely the unrelenting heat of each day, but—he wondered.

"Aye, they've said they hope to sail within the week." White sniffed. "All the more reason we should choose who will speak for us, and soon."

"Aye," Ananias said. Elinor fidgeted on her stool, poking at her roasted pumpkin with the tip of her spoon. "Are you well, Goodwife?"

She flashed him a quick smile, but it appeared strained. "Well enough, Husband." Under his lingering gaze, she huffed. "It is—not so comfortable to sit, these days. The babe seems lower than wont."

Now she had the attention of both him and her father. "I'd have thought," her papa said slowly, "that you were expected to have been delivered by now."

Her smile thinned decidedly at that as she scooped up a morsel of fish. "A week or more ago, aye." A bite of pumpkin followed the fish, and she swallowed, but with difficulty. "I am determined I shall be the first woman in history to carry. . .forever."

White chuckled. "Oh, hardly. He's simply biding his time, I expect."

"Well—" She shifted again, stretching. "He seems as impatient with the tightness of his quarters as I."

"Soon, dear daughter." His father-in-law's eyes crinkled. "Very soon. I've yet to see a woman what did not birth sooner rather than late."

Papa's words did nothing to soothe the restlessness gnawing at the edge of her consciousness this eve.

Elinor nibbled at the corn cake. Oh, how she longed for a simple loaf of bread. Or a scone. Anything with flour.

And butter. Of course she knew it was not possible, and Ananias's reminder only made her feel like a scolded child, but—just as with Papa's reassurances of the babe coming soon, knowing did nothing to take away the longing.

She suppressed a sigh and turned her attention to the roasted pumpkin. The rich sweetness was a flavor unlike anything back in England, and almost made up for the absence of butter.

By best calculations, as she had said, she should have delivered at least a week past, if not two. She'd jested over it, but perhaps it truly was so, and she would never deliver at all. Elinor imagined the weeks turning into months, and her extended body never giving up its burden, so that she remained big and cumbersome forever—

Her lips twisted, and she tucked her head so that Ananias and Papa might not see and make note again. But what folly, to let herself think such things! Papa was right, and neither had she known a woman to carry a child indefinitely. Her worst fear ought to be of the babe's safe delivery, for herself and the little one both to be healthy and well—and that concern lurked in the shadows as well, but for now—to say she was uncomfortable beggared the state she was in.

Thoroughly miserable she was, though she'd never own it.

At last Papa and Ananias were finished, and they wandered away to once more take up their everlasting debate over who would return to England. Speaking of a thing that had no end in sight—!

She gathered the food left by into a single trencher and set it in the middle of the table for later, with a cloth laid over to keep the flies off. Ananias was often fond of a bite just before bedtime, so it would not go to waste. If all else failed, she could feed it to the small cur that her cousin had brought along.

After came the washing up of pots and dishes, and setting them back in their places near the hearth. Then, seeing the untidiness of the earthen floor, she took up her broom and swept until satisfied no more dirt would come up under its bristles.

That done, she straightened the bed linens, folded up the clothing items she'd laundered the day before but left in their basket, put them away in their chest, then opened a second chest where all lay ready for the babe's arrival. A great sigh escaped her, and she slid a hand across the expanse of her belly. "Please come soon, little one."

That night she tossed and turned, never fully asleep but not fully awake either, with scattered dreams in which the faces of Manteo and his kin figured as strongly as the more familiar ones of England. At last the aches and discomfort of the past days resolved into a definite cramping across her belly, almost as if her customary woman's time had come.

Except those had ceased nine long months ago.

She came full awake, rolling to one side, which helped but little. A deep breath, then another, in and out, until the pang had eased.

When she could, she crept from the bed and began the now-habitual pacing around the cottage. She'd not completed a circuit before the next pang hit, and she went on but slowly, then made three more rounds before the next after that.

Another three pangs, and she had to stop and lean on the wall—or more properly, one of the posts on which the wall depended—and breathe through it. Another two after that and mid-pang, a low moan escaped her throat.

It was time to wake Ananias.

Chapter Six

The babe made her appearance as the first rays of dawn broke over the horizon, attended by Jane Mannering, the midwife, and three other women, wives and mothers all, who in their excitement could not bear staying away. And in the end, Elinor minded not, for the encouragement and help they were during the long night's labor.

She should not have been surprised, after all else they'd endured, to hear Jane exclaim, "You have a fine daughter!"

"A daughter?" Elinor promptly broke into weeping as the other women helped her turn from her knees to settle back onto the bed. Jane laid the tiny, wriggling, wet form into her arms. Dark eyes opened wide, and between plump cheeks, a tiny mouth pursed. "Oh," Elinor squealed, between quiet sobs, "you are the sweetest thing!"

A daughter, and not a son! For all that she'd been so sure. . .

By the end of the day, news came of Margery Harvie being delivered of a son herself. Such joy—and how strange, both of them giving birth in the same day.

Elinor could feel no disappointment, after all, that she'd given Ananias a daughter, and Papa a granddaughter. Certainly the joy of both remained undimmed at her failing to birth a son. Papa suggested that as the first Christian child to be born in the New World, she be named Virginia after the colony itself, and their dear Virgin Queen, although Elinor had wanted Thomasyn for her own mother, watching from heaven.

In the end, they chose both.

And so on the following Sunday, John had the joy of witnessing the christening of his own granddaughter, Virginia Dare. The Harvie lad's would take place the week after, since his mother Margery was still very much recovering from her delivery. Elinor, however, had insisted she was well enough to walk out to the gathering space, if someone would but place a chair for her to use during the service.

After, regardless of it being the Sabbath, it was necessary to meet in order to further discuss who would be making the journey back to England. The afternoon dragged on with nothing but arguments and controversies, as they debated without resolution which two of the Assistants would share the task of serving as factors for the colony in England. Christopher Cooper agreed at last, after much persuasion on John's part, but no one else would agree.

Exhausted, they all retired to their beds as thunder rumbled in the distance.

They woke the next morning to clouds scudding low before a gusty wind, and all discussion had to be moved indoors. A hasty message was sent to John via one of the sailors from the *Lyon* that with a storm moving in, both the admiral and the flyboat would be moving out of harbor to open waters, and all preparation for departure would be forestalled until the tempest had passed.

The seven Assistants who remained were gathered at John's house, passing around mugsful of watered ale and sharing from a platter of corn cake that someone's wife had been kind enough to prepare.

"Well," John began, "now that Master Cooper has agreed to go as one of our factors, we must needs choose another."

"Aye, well . . ." The younger man shifted and tucked his head for a moment. John's heart sank. When Chris looked up, he would not meet John's eye. "I do not believe I am fitted for the task. My word would have no weight with Sir Ralegh, much less the Queen, and—" He cleared his throat, casting a glance about the room. "Too many of my close friends have thrown their all into this venture at my behest, and I cannot abandon them."

John found his hands clenching into fists and had to force himself to breathe. What madness, that they were back to this! "And who then do you suggest, my dear nephew?"

But Chris had no reply. The other men likewise merely looked at each other, and into their cups, and ate and drank in silence.

John huffed. "Rubbish. Let us go round again, and each of you explain to me why you cannot be one of those to go."

After barely half an hour of hearing their excuses yet again, head aching, the storm worsening outside as well as in their midst, he sent them home.

The wind and rain beat relentlessly upon the town throughout the day and into the night. While Ananias made fast the shutter on one of the windows which had come loose in the gale, and then went about the house to look at this or that, Elinor lay on her side in the bed, curled around the tiny, beautiful bundle that was her daughter.

A girl! She could still scarce believe it. And yet little Virginia Thomasyn was real enough, her tiny limbs moving just as Elinor had felt from inside her belly, the delicate lashes rising and falling over eyes Elinor was already sure would be blue like her husband's, the sweet rosebud mouth opening and closing. "Just look at you, my wee maid," she murmured. "My own darling babe."

Virginia turned her head at the sound of her mama's voice, setting askew the infant cap Elinor had so carefully tied in place. Elinor tsked and straightened it, drawing a mewl of protest from her little one and more squirming, further twisting the cap.

"Does she truly need that?" Ananias asked, coming back to the bed and stretching himself upon it, facing Elinor with the babe between them.

" 'Twas my thought that the wind was too strong, and the damp too thick in the air, to chance the babe catching cold."

"Were it wintertime, or were we still in England, I'd say aye. But here, I'd think snugged in the bed with you, she's warm enough. Not like you've need yet to tuck her into basket or cradle, alone."

"Ah, true enough." Elinor untied the cap ribbons, now off under the babe's ear, and removed the offending cap altogether. Virginia seemed immediately happier, and Elinor cupped a hand around her head, smoothing the downy golden strands sticking up every which way, and pressed a kiss into the velvety-soft cheek. The infant responded by turning her face toward Elinor's, the tiny questing mouth grazing Elinor's chin. "Well, then!" Elinor laughed.

Ananias's low chuckle joined her. "Always ready to nurse at this age, as I recall."

Elinor's smile thinned at the reminder—again—that she was not the first to present him with a child—but to be fair, she could not fault his delight in the tiny girl. And it was not Elinor's fault if he'd loved already, but lost.

As she arranged herself to suckle the babe, a task that seemed amazingly natural and familiar already, he settled and sighed, elbow bent over his face.

"What thoughts this night, Husband?"

He rolled his head from side to side in a slow shake and remained silent for several breaths. At last, with another heavy sigh, he shifted his arm and peered at her through the gloom. "I'm not sure I can admit where my thoughts take me of late."

A chill brushed her, but she disregarded it. 'Twas only the uncertainty of this new country. "Is it. . .this matter of choosing factors to return to England?"

"Aye." The arm bent over his eyes again. A third sigh escaped him, long and slow. "I am afraid of what our choice must be, under the circumstances."

In the pause, her own thoughts scrambled now to anticipate who he meant.

"I am more afraid, however, that you should be warned before such a choice is made evident—which, on the morrow, I am certain it must be."

Elinor's heart beat with painful suddenness. "Mercy, Husband. Do just say it and spare me the agony."

He unbent his arm but stared upward at the ceiling. "I fear, dear Goodwife, that. . .it is the governor himself who must return."

The governor himself did not receive the news well.

Ananias held his ground, having gone to the entire company, Assistants and planters alike, some while the storm yet raged the previous evening, even before he'd broken the news to Elinor, and some the morning after. The wind had lessened, but the rain held steady. Where in the town could they meet, that would accommodate them all? Perhaps they, the Assistants, would need to just take word of the colony's collective will to Governor White, but several of the other men insisted on coming along so that White would be convinced of the severity of their opinion.

And so they all crowded into his father-in-law's house, dripping quietly onto his floor, with White himself looking from face to face, struck to dumbness at first by the gravity of their expressions before ever a word was spoken.

He slowly drained the ink from his quill against the inside neck of the bottle and laid the writing implement down. "I presume I am not to like what you have to speak this fine morn."

"Nay." Ananias drew a deep breath. Truth be told, it felt harder to face the man's daughter the night before. "We have all agreed on who our choice should be for returning to England on our behalf. That choice, Governor White, is yourself."

The flaring of his eyes, the slow wag of his head increasing to a firm shake, the paleness of his cheek—all betrayed the governor's deep dismay. His mouth thinned to a hard line for a moment, then, "Well, first the ships must needs come safely through the storm or we've no way to send anyone back."

Ananias folded his arms and did not reply.

His father-in-law scrubbed his fingertips through his beard. "I—cannot. Do you not realize what great discredit this would be to me, to suddenly return back again, leaving this action and so many whom I partly procured through my persuasions to leave their native country and undertake the voyage here? Christopher, you alleged that as your greatest reason for refusing to go as well. How could it hold any less true for me—nay, even more true." He shot out of his chair, fair knocking it back and nearly tipping it, but he heeded it not. Both hands went to his head. "Indeed, certain of my enemies would spare not to slander falsely both me and this venture—'Oh, he went to Virginia, but only politically, and for no other end but to lead so many into a country where he never meant to stay himself, and there to leave them behind.' Dear Lord in heaven, spare me! But I can hear them already."

"Speak such they might, but we will provide you letters and a statement proving it most false," Ananias said. "But the word of none other but you will hold such weight with Ralegh and the Queen."

Shaking his head again, White let his hands fall to his sides, and he turned as if to pace, but the press within the house afforded him no room for it. "And—my stuff and goods. I have brought all with me. With your present plans to remove fifty miles farther up into the main, all I own might be spoiled or pilfered away during transport. And then what? Either I am forced to provide myself of all such things again, or else at my return find myself utterly unfurnished. You've already seen some proof of what I say, being but once from the town for three days! Nay. I cannot. I will not, myself, go."

Silence stretched yet again, broken only by the shuffling of too many men in a closed space, and the rain on the roof. Ananias cleared his throat. "Father mine. . ."

White turned on him, eyes glossy and red-rimmed. "Do—not—ask of me—again. Are you yourself willing to leave your wife and newborn daughter, to go in my stead? Nay. And I'd not require it of you. Do not require it of me, to leave all my own flesh and blood behind as well."

And with that, he yanked his chair back toward the table and planted himself most firmly therein, once more taking up the quill, elbow on the table and head on his hand.

Well. His father-in-law was right in one thing, that naught could be done until the tempest passed and they had word of how the ships had weathered. Ananias turned and gestured the others toward the door.

Outside, he tucked his hat farther over his eyes and beckoned them to follow. Thankfully the rain had slackened somewhat. When they'd proceeded far enough that his words would not be distinguishable inside the governor's house, he gathered them about. "Let me go speak again to Elinor, and all of you with wives do likewise. If she herself agrees to entreat her father to go, and if we all with one will and voice promise to provide anything he lacks, should indeed his goods be lost—" He stopped, shaking his head. "We all agree that none else can argue for our cause and assure that we are properly supplied. Especially with the way Ferdinando has used us."

"And pray," Nicholas Johnson chimed in, his deep voice muffled by the rain. "Let us spend a goodly portion of the day in prayer, for only God Himself can prevail on our account. It is our colony's very future at stake, and we must not fail to acknowledge His hand in it, regardless of the schemes of the Portuguese navigator—or anyone else—to see us ruined."

"Aye, most fervent prayer," Cooper said, and thus agreed, they all dispersed to their own homes.

How unfair of Ananias to expect her to be the one to persuade Papa that he must go back to England for the colony. Or did he think because of the years she'd already been deprived of his company, it mattered not to her whether he went or stayed?

Nay, it was not that, she knew.

"If none go back," Ananias said, "it means trusting Simon Ferdinando, God forbid, with whatever letters and tokens we send. And you know very well yourself what folly that is." He paced the length of their house and back, hand tangled in his hair. "And none others are willing. All resist even constraint, as did your cousin Chris." He huffed. "Not that I blame them."

Unable to stem the flow of her tears, Elinor cuddled the sleeping form of little Virginia against her shoulder.

"I could almost wish we'd never come," she murmured at last. "Almost."

"Aye," Ananias said, barely above a breath. He stopped at the window to push the shutter open a bit and look out. "The wind has lessened more, or at least 'tis changed directions."

And once the storm had passed, and the ship returned. . .she must say farewell to her beloved papa yet again.

As if he'd heard her thought, Ananias turned and gazed across at her, pleadingly. "You have me yet, dear Goodwife. Is that worth so little to you?"

"Nay," she said through the fresh wave of tears. "And I am grateful for you, beyond words. It is only—he was gone for so many years, and that freshly after my own mother flew away to heaven—and now, just when we at last have the hope of dwelling at least in the same town with each other—" She shook her head and could not finish.

Ananias crossed the floor to her once more and took her shoulders gently in his hands. "If none go back," he said very softly, " 'twill mean certain ruin of us and our town, for we need supplies, and soon. And your father has the best chance of having Ralegh's ear, and thus the Queen's. You know this. You. . .agreed, even, last night."

"Aye," she sobbed. " 'Tis just. . .so dreadfully bitter."

His arms came around her then, embracing both her and the babe, not even shushing her but simply letting her weep against his strong shoulder.

"He will be back as soon as he can," Ananias whispered, once she had quieted.

She could only nod against him. She knew 'twas true—if they could persuade Papa to go for them, he would go to any lengths to return. She'd heard him speak of his affection for the people of this country, of the country itself, and 'twould wound him sore to leave it.

But why was her heart so very leaden at the thought of his departure, however temporary?

'Twas unfair of them to demand this of him. 'Twas. . .wrong. That they could even think of sending him away—not only the damage to his good name and that of the colony, but— *Oh Lord in heaven, that sweet infant granddaughter—and Elinor!*

How could he even begin to entertain the notion of being parted from them?

John sat there, eyes open but unseeing, long after the men had left—and then, once the shock had begun to wear away, he slid from the chair and fell to his knees. A sob, half of anger and half of grief, tore itself from his chest.

God in heaven, how could You do this to me? To us? Were we not led here of You? Is it not to worship You, free of the constraints and corruptions of either the Anglican or Roman churches? Why then would You bring us, let us be cast off in the wrong place, without proper supplies and under threat of attack from those who hate us, whether the Spanish or the Secotan or Powhatan or—whosoever. And now this—not one man has the heart to go, so they ask me. Will it not appear that I've abandoned them? That I seek only my own comfort and interests in this?

The rain eased to a drizzle by the next morning. Ananias was up and gone early, but Elinor had barely risen and laced her kirtle over her shift before Jane Jones and Joyce and even Margery came a-calling. "Gracious! If you wish anything to drink, you'll have to wait until I've fed and changed Virginia."

"Please, do not go to any bother for us," Jane said, and they all took chairs and stools while Elinor tended the babe.

While Virginia's fussing rose in pitch to a full cry, she finished wrapping a clean nappy in place, with a wool soaker over to protect her swaddling and Elinor's own gown, then perched on the side of the bed, facing the others as she prepared to nurse the babe.

"I know why you are here," she said, once the child's cries were hushed with the sating of her hunger.

Jane dipped her head, coif a bit rain spattered beneath the jaunty hat she wore. "The men have been talking—and praying—for several days over the need to persuade your father the governor that he must be the one to go back to England and factor for us. We women also agree it must be so, and are prepared to go to him to say so ourselves."

Elinor considered them for a long moment. Jane and Joyce sat quiet and composed, while Margery similarly arranged her own babe.

"I am in agreement," she said softly. "Not happily of course—I so recently gained him again after a long year away—but even I see the sense in him going back on our behalf."

The three women breathed nearly as one in a sigh of relief. "Oh, I am so glad," Joyce said. "We were so afraid—that is—"

"I understand," Elinor murmured. "Ananias already spoke with me, however, and—I am well prepared to accompany him and throw my attempts at persuasion in with his on the matter."

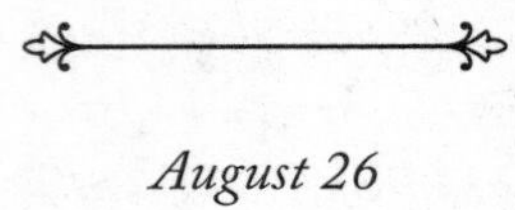

August 26

By the time the storm abated completely and the sky cleared to sun while a fresh, cool breeze blew across the sodden island, John knew what he had to do.

The knowledge of it, however, didn't mean he had to like it.

His heart lay shredded and broken, its final shattering from the clear grey eyes of his own daughter, cradling his firstborn grandchild in her arms, begging him to reconsider his stubborn stance on returning to England.

Begging, even with tears standing in those eyes and her voice catching with the strength of her feeling.

Merciful, gracious God in heaven. How could he refuse?

"I relent," he said, his own throat thick with tears. "For nothing but the prospering of this colony, and with hope of seeing my daughter and granddaughter again, I will go."

Amidst the cheering and exclamations of relief from the assembled planters and Assistants alike, Roger Bailie stepped forward. "We do promise to make you all our bond with our hands and seals for the safe preserving of your goods for you, at your return to Virginia."

Indeed, in just a day or so, they'd written it up, complete with signatures and seals, and delivered it into his hands:

> *May it please you, her Majesties subjects of England, we your friends and countrey-men, the planters in Virginia, doe by these presents let you and every of you to understand, that for the present and speedy supply of certain our knowen*

> *and apparent lackes and needes, most requisite and necessary for the good and happy planting of us, or any other in this land of Virginia, wee all of one minde and consent, have most earnestly intreated, and uncessantly requested John White, Governour of the planters in Virginia, to passe into England, for the better and more assured help, and setting forward of the foresayd supplies: and knowing assuredly that he both can best, and will labour and take paines in that behalfe for us all, and he not once, but often refusing it, for our sakes, and for the honour and maintenance of the action, hath at last, though much against his will, through our importunacie, yeelded to leave his governement, and all his goods among us, and himselfe in all our behalfes to passe into England, of whose knowledge and fidelitie in handling this matter, as all others, we doe assure ourselves by these presents, and will you to give all credite thereunto, the 25 of August 1587.*

And thus he was left without any reason to object. But oh, the heaviness of such a task!

They'd received word that both flyboat and admiral had come through the storm—not without much peril, that—and that they planned to weigh anchor and set sail for England on Sunday the 27th, just two days after the planters had delivered him their written bond.

Which left John only half a day to prepare, with the time it took the sailors to go back and forth between Roanoac and the ships.

Oh, the wretchedness. Oh, the inequity! But if God had fitted him for the task and none other, who was he to protest? It was his only to obey, and forthwith, trusting that God would give him the ear of Ralegh, and that he could return to Virginia in a few short months with supplies and the goodwill of the Queen.

He planned to carry with him two satchels, one for his journals and sketches and paints, the other for clothing and other such personal items as he could not be without for the next several months. All else he packed into three chests—books and maps, paintings and sketches, which he had brought to furnish his house and for the betterment of the colony. After much deliberation, he also packed away his armor, layered among spare shoes and boots and other articles of clothing, while planning to carry rapier and pistol.

And once he'd divided up his goods and had all prepared, there was one last act he must carry out, if the colony were to survive at all.

Evening had fallen, the feast they'd prepared for Papa's departure was mostly eaten, and with someone still playing lute and viol in the background, they all gathered in their usual space, slapping at mosquitoes and waiting for Papa to compose himself to speak. They'd learned to set torches around the perimeter, the smoke serving as a discouragement to the mosquitoes, and the evening breeze helped as well, but the creatures remained a menace.

A longboat had come from the *Lyon*, ready to take Papa away at first light. He'd insisted upon this last meeting—and they upon a last meal together. But now it seemed he could not bring himself to begin. Even in the torchlight, Elinor could see the glimmer of his eyes, the tightness of mouth and cheek as he struggled to remain composed.

At last, when a song had just ended, he gestured for attention. "You all must know how difficult this is for me, to leave not only daughter and grandchild, but all of you and this place which has become so dear. But—I will endeavor, inasmuch as it is within my power to do so, to return in a few months. In the meantime, there is something of what took place before, that you must know the fullness of."

He took a deep breath, almost a gulp, his gaze sweeping their faces. He lingered on Elinor's for but an instant, then squared his shoulders and went on.

"Much has been whispered of Sir Greenville's and Rafe Lane's expeditions here, the most recent of which ended last year with Lane's return to England. I was part of those ventures, charged with painting to life this land and the peoples thereon, to assist in recording all that was seen and done. And indeed, many of you have seen my portraits of Wyngyno and others, of the Secotan and Croatoan and such."

Nodding heads dotted the crowd. Indeed, it was how any of them had familiarized themselves with this land and its people before venturing here. Elinor had so loved Papa's excitement upon returning from the New World, his eagerness to show her his paintings from what had been seen and done—not only the peoples but various flowers and fruits, and wondrous creatures.

It still struck her with awe that here they stood for themselves, on this very land.

"Lane in particular was fresh from the wars in Ireland, and you all know the horrors wreaked there. But Greenville and Lane both are much vaunted as great explorers and bold adventurers." Papa grimaced. "Unfortunately, such traits tend them to roughness in dealings with the peoples of this land, and indeed, both charge the other with being prideful and high-handed, utterly unable to be contradicted in their wills. I saw it for my own eyes with Greenville, when a silver cup disappeared from our possession at Aquascogoc, and he charged the savages with its theft. I do not know whether it truly was stolen, but the people of that town promised to find and return it, and when they failed to do so, Greenville sent a company back there, who proceeded to spoil and burn the town and its corn. The people all fled. I do not know whether any were hurt."

Papa paused again with another deep breath, pain etched on his own countenance.

"After Greenville and his men departed, and Lane and his company had settled in here at the fort, I accompanied Thomas Harriot on his surveys north and westward, up the coastlands as far as the Chesepiok, and inland. The savages were very friendly and gave us much help. Not only were they in great awe of us because of our divers weapons and instruments of navigation, but the appearance of a comet in the sky had, in their opinion, been of great portent. And then—everywhere Harriot and I and our company passed, a great sickness spread among the peoples. It was whispered that we English had invisible bullets"—Papa offered a weak, fleeting smile—"or that the spirits were with us in ways that they were not with them. Later they did say, despite their former interest in our teaching as the only true religion, that our God, the Lord, could be no god at all if He suffered us to starve and be in want."

Several in the crowd murmured. " 'Tis not an uncommon hap," Master Johnson said.

"Nay, and Harriot oft explained to them that God moves by His own good pleasure, not always by our wishes and prayers, but they were not to be swayed by any argument we offered to that. And after his brother Granganimeo died, as well as so many others, the weroance Wyngyno became suspicious mostly of Lane and his doings, and changed his name to Pemisapan, which I'm told means 'wolf who watches from afar.' I cannot fault him for those suspicions, not after such rash actions on the part of Greenville over a silver cup."

Papa sighed, rubbing his neck. "Lane and Greenville both said, at the time, that they must make an example. That rule is worth nothing if your subjects do not respect your power to punish. And Lane argued that once mistrust entered Wyngyno's heart and the stage was set for them to be ambushed and killed, Lane had no choice but to strike back. And strike they did. Wyngyno himself was slain by one of Lane's men, and his head cut off. Others, even some innocent of wrongdoing, were hurt in the affair—the man you saw at Croatoan, lame."

"This is why the Croatoan were so quick to beg our favor and for a token of our friendship when we asked them to go to the neighboring peoples," Chris said.

"Aye. And why Master Howe lost his life in such a foul and horrible manner. I'd no doubt that it was vengeance for Lane's actions. And then when all nearly turned to an even worse tragedy two weeks ago, at Dasemonguepeuk. . ."

Papa's eyes were shadowed, positively haunted now.

"We never intended to cause hurt. We never intended to *be* on Roanoac to begin with, not to stay. The risks of settling here seemed greater than what we might face at Chesepiok. And now—now I must leave you to whatever might befall—"

His voice thickened and faltered. He dropped his head, while the others murmured but waited for him to compose himself.

At last he looked up again. "It is all my intent, as I have already told you, to be back in a few months. But if anything should happen before I return, then promise me—you must promise me—to leave a sign of where you've gone. And add a cross, like so"—he bent and sketched on the ground a cross pattée, with arms of equal length, the ends flaring—"beneath such sign, to indicate if you departed in distress."

"We can and shall do so," Chris said, with the other men agreeing.

Elinor said nothing as she dandled little Ginny on her shoulder, soothed mostly to sleep at this point. The burn in her eyes and throat was too much to try to speak past, regardless.

They rose the next morning before first light to say their farewells. After making sure his satchels were stowed in the longboat, John looked each of the planters and Assistants in the eye, last of all clasping Ananias's hand and briefly embracing him before turning to take Elinor in his arms. She nestled against him, the babe between them, and after several long, tear-filled moments, he drew back and lifted the tiny maid-child—oh, his heart!—to peer into her face. She blinked, squeaking a little, and he cradled her in the crook of his arm, bringing her up so he could nuzzle her soft cheek. Elinor's arms surrounded them both. "I will so miss you, Papa."

"And I, you, darling daughter." Not even bothering to wipe his eyes, he passed the infant back to her. "Take care of my granddaughter. And you"—he fastened a blurry gaze on Ananias—"you look well both to my daughter and yours."

"Of course," Ananias rumbled.

John hesitated, and turned at the very last to Manteo, who watched as he always did, steadfast and strong. Was it John's imagination, or did the savage's dark eyes hold a depth of peace they previously had not?

Truth be told, Manteo was savage no longer, and shame bit John deeply that he should continue to think of him in those terms. "Lead them well, my friend, Lord of Roanoac and Dasemonguepeuk."

Manteo nodded gravely. "And may God speed your journey over the waters."

Before he could unman himself completely before them all, John climbed into the boat, seating himself in the stern. As the rising sun turned the sky and water to the colors of the pearls that Rafe Lane coveted so greatly, John waved and watched his daughter and granddaughter, Ananias tall behind them, hands resting on Elinor's shoulders, all standing on the narrow shore that grew farther away with each stroke of the oars.

The fire was warm and comforting against the cool of the evening, even as the smoke kept the mosquitoes at bay. Sees Far took his turn at the pipe, savoring the sweet earthiness of the *uppowoc*'s smoke before passing it on to Wanchese. Across from them sat Okisco, accompanied by Okisco's chief wife, and by Sees Far's mother, who had been wife to Granganimeo, along with the woman who had been wife to Pemisapan.

The pipe made its first round. Okisco drew upon it, blew out a stream of smoke, then passed it to Sees Far's mother. With this, she spoke. "While our men were out hunting, I myself welcomed the English. My women and I fed them, washed their stinking clothing and feet, and made a great show of allaying their fears when the returning hunters gave them cause for alarm. And how then did they repay us? With treachery, and the taking of our warriors and weroance from us by the most brutal means. They have left our children orphans." Eyes wet, she drew in a long breath through her nostrils. "We have given them mercy after mercy, which they met with lies and cruelty. I say we do all we can to drive them away, as we did with those who were left before."

"And if we fail in that?" Okisco said.

"Then we will go further westward. The land will receive us as it has before, and Montóac will protect, though it grieves me to leave our dead."

Okisco turned to Sees Far. "Wanchese has spoken but you have been silent thus far. Tell me what you see, since I know you have been gifted with long vision concerning these foreigners."

Sees Far wished he could deny it. In his boyhood, at the turning of manhood when they were all sent on *huskanaw* to hear from Montóac and find their true names, he had dreamed, not once but many times, of a man walking—in the far distance yet somehow visible in great detail, hence his name—upon the outer shore of Ossomocomuck, wrapped in a mantle but casting light upon the sand and the waves. Sometimes it was Sees Far himself who followed the man down the beach, but in that very first dream, it had been a man and a woman, whose hair was the color of the pale sand. He had seen men with hair that light, among the *wuhtah-shuntas*, but of women matching the one in his dream, he had seen none.

As to the meaning of that dream, none could tell him, not even their most honored priests. And Sees Far had found only silence and frustration in fastings and prayers when he had sought its meaning for himself.

"I think," he said slowly, "we should make war upon them. For the sake of my father and sister and her who was to be my woman."

He did not say it just to please Wanchese, though his old friend smiled with obvious satisfaction at the words.

Okisco nodded slowly. "Then I release you to do what you must."

Part Two

Chapter Seven

England, November 20, 1587

The winter wind blew bitterly indeed, buffeting John as he stepped from the carriage and crossed to the entrance of the grand estate—both owned by none other than Sir Walter Ralegh himself, who had upon John's return speedily granted him audience and sent his own conveyance to bring John hither.

He gave himself the barest moment to examine the face of the estate house—a lovely work of art it was, with sculpted stonework and paned windows of glass—before hurrying up the steps and through the oaken door, already opened to him by the footmen. He caught his breath at the sudden warmth within after the brutal wash of cold without.

"Welcome, Master White," a servant said, bowing. "May I take your cloak?"

John doffed the knee-length outer garment, and while the servant was hanging it up, he straightened the shorter, arm-length black velvet cape over the matching doublet and trunkhose.

"Very good. Right this way," the servant said, and led John down the hallway and into a paneled chamber warmed by hanging lamps and a crackling blaze on the hearth.

Two chairs stood before said hearth, unoccupied. On the far side of the room stood a man, looking out a long window, silhouetted against the dying light of a day that had already begun as grey.

"Sir, Master White, as you requested."

The servant bowed and slipped out. The man turned from the window and came forward, arms extended and a smile playing about the too-handsome face. But however aware of his own charms Walter Ralegh might be, and however ruthlessly he wielded them at court, in private the man was artless and sincere in his enthusiasm for the New World.

Or so John remembered from his interview with the man months ago, and so he hoped Ralegh had remained.

"Forsooth, let me look at you." Ralegh set his hands on John's shoulders, the smile dimming to a squinted scrutiny. "Aye. You appear little the worse for wear. But how fare you, in all honesty? And how fares my colony?"

John could not suppress the sigh that escaped him. "What a long, weary three months it has been since I've last seen my family. But they were well when I left them."

"Come, sit. I could scarce believe the report you'd written me after your recent landing."

"I am sure." John removed his hat and cape, and set the former on a small table nearby, and the cape over the back of the chair. "Especially after hearing that the other ship had arrived long before us. I've heard a bit of the gossip bandied about over us and can only imagine the fullness of it."

Ralegh's expression turned rueful. "Not for nothing is Ferdinando called the Swine." His voice dropped to a conspiratorial tone. "We all know him to be in the employ of Walsingham. I should not have appointed him navigator for this voyage. But—" He spoke more brightly now, blue eyes alight, nodding toward the satchel John still carried over one shoulder. "You've sketches for me?"

Settling into his chair, John set down his satchel and untied the clasp. "I've but a few. Mostly I've a letter from the planters for your perusal, and my written account of the entire action."

He handed Ralegh the rolled vellum, and while he waited for him to read the entire script, he mused on the comment about Walsingham.

The Queen's spymaster had long been at odds with Ralegh, and 'twould certainly explain the navigator's high-handedness and outright animosity toward John and the planters, at least in part.

"Hmm." Ralegh sat back more comfortably in his chair. His gaze went to the fire, then flicked to John. "Ferdinando of course reported that your planters arrived safely at the destination of their choosing, and thus he had discharged his duty most honorably. That all was well with them upon his departure. This, however—this gives me the sense of urgency and no little crisis, as you have written me already."

"Aye," John said. "I thought it expedient to notify you as soon as we landed. I am working on a more lengthy account of it all, of course. But I am happy to relate anything you wish to hear, or to explain more fully what I wrote before."

Ralegh nodded slowly, looking over the missive a second time. At last he rested the hand holding the letter in his lap, and fixed John with a sharp eye once more.

There was the Ralegh he had been waiting for.

"Tell me all, then. Your return journey—how was it? How did your ships come to be separated?"

John unclenched his teeth at the thought of what lies the Portuguese navigator must have already spread. "Aye. We set sail from Hatorask on the morning of the 28th of August, after near disaster involving the anchor capstone. They had to cut the cable, after everything, and a full ten men were so injured by the capstone bar breaking that many are yet to recover. Despite our troubles with the anchor, however, our flyboat kept pace with the admiral for twenty days, all the way to Corvo. Then with Ferdinando being in no hurry to continue on to England, we on the flyboat left them."

A maid entered, bringing a tray of hot punch and an array of cakes and meat. John waited to continue until he and Ralegh were each furnished with a tankard and plate, thanking the young woman with a smile and nod.

"So Ferdinando wanted to linger. . . ?" Ralegh prompted him.

"Aye. He claimed to intend to stay at the island of Tercera and make purchase. The crew of the flyboat was reduced to but five of fifteen who could stand at duty, and we were eager to complete our journey. By the time we had continued our course homeward for another twenty days, met with variable winds at best, there arose a northeast tempest that blew for six days. Our master saw neither sun nor stars for four of those days, together. And our fresh water had already mostly leaked away, so that by the time the storm died down, we had scarce three gallons of terrible beverage between all of us, and the sailors further sickened." John sipped the hot punch and peered into the cup, then lifted it, meeting Ralegh's gaze again. "Such a luxury as this we could but dream of. We'd fully reconciled ourselves to perishing at sea. Two of our sailors did indeed perish before we saw land."

He played with a bite of cake, then set it back on the plate.

"We made land at last on the 16th of October, but knew not where. We put into a harbor, where we found a hulk of Dublin and a pinnace of Hampton riding, but we hadn't even a boat to go ashore in, ourselves. The pinnace sent out their boat to us with a handful of men, who gave us to know that we were in Smerwicke of western Ireland. And they soon relieved us with fresh water, meat, and wine.

"On the 18th, then, the ship's master and I rode to Dingen a Cushe, to see about the relief of our sick and hurt. Unfortunately, our boatswain, the boatswain's mate, and the steward all died within the next four days. Others were brought ashore to Dingen and, as far as I know, recovered—the master's mate and two others—but shortly after, I took passage on the *Monkey*. On November the first we departed Dingle and then on the fifth arrived at Martasew.

"The eighth we arrived at Hampton, where I discovered that our consort the admiral had been there three weeks already. Not only had Ferdinando returned without purchase, but they were in such weakness themselves, both by sickness and the death of their chiefest men, they were scarce able to bring their ship into harbor. No doubt they were caught in the same tempest as we."

Ralegh nodded. He'd listened with perfect attention, having eaten but little. "That is much the report I had from them." He sniffed, lifting a chunk of beef from his plate with thumb and first two fingers. "I confess I wondered whether Ferdinando had the right of it this time, claiming that you'd exerted your will on the master of the flyboat to abandon them at Corvo. With all else you've related of the journey, however—" He shook his head and popped the meat into his mouth.

John set his tankard upon his knee, then swiped the other hand across his face and beard.

"Oh, fear not, White. I would be more inclined to believe you than that Portuguese pirate, even did I not know already of your sense of honor." The corner of Ralegh's mouth turned upward in a slight smirk, then faded. "The way you protested the rough use of those Indians brought back from Frobisher's voyage to Newfoundland. . ." Another sharp shake of the head. "When I read your account of the voyage to Roanoac, and how Ferdinando hemmed and hawed and so obviously sabotaged the colony—well, to say I am unhappy with him beggars my feeling in the matter. To so lewdly endanger the lives of so many is unconscionable."

John released a breath, the tightness of his chest easing at last. To celebrate, he took a bite of the cake he'd been worrying with his fingers.

"Others may not be so gracious as yourself," he ventured after a moment.

"Others whose necks are not also on the line in this action," Ralegh retorted, eyes glittering. He scraped together crumbs and devoured those as well. "As you may already know, the Queen has recalled the entire fleet, for threat of the Spanish. None may go out again without her express permission. However, I will endeavor to find you a ship or three with which to return this spring."

"I had heard that, aye." He studied Ralegh for a moment, so off-handed in his manner and yet— "Have you such influence, then, with her Majesty the Queen?"

Ralegh smirked. "Let us say, she gives less notice to my personal affairs than to others."

Please God in this case it would be so. News of the Queen's stay on shipping had very nearly been his undoing when they'd first landed—that, and hearing how Ferdinando had arrived before him. Who knew yet what damage that one's sly tongue had worked in John's absence. John was sure the man had prayed that he'd perish altogether—if indeed the man prayed at all.

"A pinnace to begin with, methinks," Ralegh went on, offering John the last of the cakes, "and then a fleet after, fitted with all supplies. I will write a letter to reassure your planters of its soon arrival. Think you that will suit?"

For the first time since leaving Roanoac, John could draw a full breath. "Aye, and with all my gratitude."

Okisco lounged, pipe in hand, lazily blowing out a stream of smoke. "What news of the Inqutish?"

Sees Far and Wanchese settled into a crouch across the fire from the weroance. Wanchese spoke. "They held firm through two attacks. They have built a palisade around their town, and it was harder to take them by surprise this last time."

"And what of our allies?"

"Those who were at Aquascogoc steadfastly refuse to oppose the Kurawoten, who themselves hold fast to befriending the Inqutish. Others are willing to join us in driving the Inqutish away, but they must speak to their people. Menantonan also now hesitates, though he agrees the Inqutish must be resisted." He shifted, his chin lifting. "I would venture to the Powhatan and seek their aid."

Okisco's hand lowered in the act of bringing the pipe back to his mouth, and his eyes widened. "You would do such a thing? Risk your own life?"

Wanchese's hand curled into a fist upon his knee. "You have met the Inqutish. You know they are relentless, and how little mercy they have upon their enemies. However, they speak of the love of their Christ." He spat to the side.

Okisco hummed. "It is a strange thing, is it not, this belief in a God who became man and died to atone for the sins of all?"

A burning kindled within Sees Far's breast at hearing such blasphemy spoken aloud, though it was not for the first time. Wanchese replied with a huff. "Would be less strange and more wondrous indeed if this God's followers walked as if they truly believed it. But their mouths are full of the words while their hearts remain black."

Okisco lifted one shoulder. "So it is among our own people at times. Are there none of the English who you would say did truly believe and walk the path?"

"If there are," Wanchese muttered, his face set in sullen lines, "I know not of them."

An unwonted thoughtfulness still held Okisco's features. At last he grunted and lifted the pipe. "Go, make your oblations to Montóac and seek the guidance of the priests. If they say the venture will succeed, you may go to the Powhatan. But if you go, do so with discretion and care."

Some days she loved the fog the best for how it reminded her of England.

Of Papa.

Lord God, protect him. Give him favor, and the ear of Ralegh and Her Majesty the Queen. Silence any slander he might encounter.

The prayer wound its way through her, like a path worn by many feet over the dunes to the shore.

Little Ginny slept in her cradle as Elinor swept the floor. Passing by the window, she stopped to peer out. The next house over was shadowed and ghostly, and the new palisade walls not visible at all, so thick did lay the late autumn mist.

Other days the fog pressed in on her like a living, breathing thing, the embodiment of all her fears. The reminder that any safety they felt in this new land was but an illusion—like the day Master Howe had been found so brutally slain. Or the day, barely two weeks after Papa's departure, that the savages had come screaming out of the forest to attack the town. Were it not for the sharp eyes of their watchmen, and the quick response by Ananias and the others—well, she shuddered to think what the outcome would have been. The crack of gunshots and counter-cries of their own soldiers were terrifying enough, and although the savages had retreated, it was soon decided that the town needed more protection.

Construction on the palisade walls began shortly thereafter.

Elinor kept sweeping, then stopped at the cradle. Ginny's tiny lips moved as if nursing, her fists outstretched against the coverlet on either side of her head, where her cap lay askew as always. Elinor smiled. Weeks later and the babe liked the covering no better than before, but with the weather cooling at last, it was best she wear it.

Truth be told, Elinor was much in sympathy with her child. After witnessing how little the native-born women of this country wore, especially during summer, she'd begun to wonder whether the layers of shift and kirtle and all were really necessary.

Elinor shook her head and returned to her sweeping with much vigor. What heathenish thoughts. Of course a proper and Christian Englishwoman must cover herself with all modesty.

But on the other hand. . .there was no immodesty in the way the Croatoan women comported themselves. They did what was necessary with unconscious grace, and though a part of her found such state of dress—or as it were, undress—off-putting, she longed to spend more time with them, to learn their tongue and converse as ordinary women.

She gathered into a pile all the dirt, twigs, and leaves she'd swept up, then with small strokes of her broom pushed it toward the open door. Oftentimes it felt like an exercise in futility to sweep a dirt floor, but this was her dirt floor, after all, and she was grateful.

At the threshold, she again peered into the mist. The sounds of life came from all around, but muffled. Ananias was doubtless off overseeing. . .something. The men were always planning some new project, and she thought they were still putting the finishing touches on the blacksmith's forge. Manteo and the others had arranged with the Croatoan people to bring clay so brick could be made, and Ananias had been busy with that for many weeks.

In many ways it was no different from when they were England—the long days of keeping busy about the house while he worked. In others, vastly different. How strange the weather here, which did cool somewhat with the autumn months yet rarely became chilly. She was assured that colder days would come, but they'd yet to see those days, even though December bore down upon them.

"Governor White knew we'd have need to move from here," Roger Bailie said. "The two attacks by savages are proof—even though they seem to have been discouraged of late by our superior weapons and the palisade. 'Tis but a matter of time before they try again, so in regard to a move, the only question is when. We've been able to build weirs and catch fish and hunt deer. We have seeds for planting, but do we plant this year or wait until we are settled elsewhere?"

"I say to go sooner is more to be preferred than late," Chris Cooper rumbled.

"And if we go sooner, then whence?" Bailie said. "We discussed removing fifty miles into the main, but methinks the savages to the west of us are not so amenable to that, if they are still going to the trouble of breaking our weirs every week or so." He accompanied the words with an exaggerated eye roll.

Ananias turned to Manteo, who as always sat listening to all that was said. "What think you?"

"I will take a company," he said slowly, "and go speak with my people at Kurawoten. They will tell us what is best."

"We must wait until the weather clears," Bailie said.

"Mayhap." He smiled faintly. "Sailing across the sound is far less dangerous than trying to navigate the inlets."

"How many do you wish to accompany you?" Ananias asked.

Manteo thought for a moment, pursing his lips. "Ten should be sufficient."

It was agreed that three of the seven remaining Assistants should go and the other four should stay to help watch over the town. Ananias found it a frank relief to have plans in motion, but felt torn about whether he'd prefer to go or to stay. Elinor would almost certainly wish him to stay, but—deep within there was a craving to go along, to visit Manteo's home island and town. They'd visitors often enough of the Croatoan people, but 'twas long past time they returned the favor.

"We shall go tomorrow, or the next day," Manteo said. "Soon enough that our enemies shall have little time to prepare an attack, either on us or the town."

In the end, Ananias was indeed chosen to go. With a little sigh over the necessity of breaking the news to Elinor, he gave his next thought to the actual preparations.

He returned home to Elinor tending the babe, in full cry of protest at having her wrappings disturbed. Elinor received word of Ananias's soon departure more quietly than expected, if a little subdued. He packed quickly while she nursed Ginny, then took the baby to dandle and burp her while Elinor went to hang the wet wrapping over the windowsill to air and dry.

She paced back across the room. "I suppose there's no asking when you expect to return."

Ginny wiggled against his shoulder. He steadied her, bouncing a little, and met the clear grey of his wife's eyes. "Nay. We expect no trouble, if that comforts you, but—"

"But we expected no trouble when we first arrived on Roanoac," she finished for him.

"Aye." He reached out and fingered the strands of gold escaping her coif. "But then, you are brave and will hold fast regardless. And do not go outside the town walls, at least not without an escort."

Her lips flattened, and a spark lit her gaze. "I've not—"

He smiled, fingertips brushing her cheek and chin. "I know. I also know how it chafes for you to remain shut up here. And I'd not blame you for sneaking out for a bit every now and then."

Grey turned to silver as her eyes sheened. "I'd not so risk our infant's life and well-being."

He leaned closer for a kiss, but even as he lingered, Ginny squeaked and squirmed again. He broke away with a low chuckle. "She's jealous of her mama already. And I'm glad of it. If aught befell you—well, I am not sure I could bear such ill hap."

A smirk twisted her lips. "I've also no plans to make you a widower a second time."

Another kiss, then he handed little Ginny off and went to gather up his pistols and shot.

She intended to do as he'd requested and not venture out alone, but there were foods and herbs to be foraged in the woods. She and the other women reasoned that they'd be safe enough together. If they did not go far. If they were out for but a short time.

The men, after all, went out both to hunt and fish and returned unmolested.

They would be careful. They would keep watch.

The weather remained cool and misty. After changing the babe's swaddling, Elinor bundled Ginny onto her front with a length of cloth, then tucked her own hair into a coif and settled a hat over that. Though by all rights she ought to be terrified, she could not help her excitement at stepping outside the town walls for the first time in a long while.

Margery's baby boy was fretful, so she decided to stay behind, but two others, Alis Chapman and Wenefrid Powell, joined Jane Mannering, Rose, and Elinor in their foray. Rose's husband was also gone to Croatoan with Ananias, Manteo, and the others, but they spoke to the guard on their way out and reassured them that they'd not go far nor be long. At the last minute Georgie Howe and Thomas Archard tagged along as well.

Little enough they could glean in this season, but they must try. At the least there might be nuts and some roots.

They set out into the forest, huddling together at first, but it soon became apparent that to make best use of their search, they must needs spread out. As Alis and Wenefrid fell to bickering about how best to forage and where, Elinor took the opportunity to wander out of immediate earshot. She was beyond weary of the contention between those two.

Georgie stuck by Elinor, his sharp gaze finding the acorns hiding beneath the carpet of pine needles, and he happily picked them up to spare her bending with little Ginny tied to her chest. Then they found themselves diverted by the presence of three or four deer hiding out in an oak thicket. Georgie unslung the bow at his back and nocked an arrow, but even with the sound-damping effect of the mist, the creatures became wise to his movement and fled.

Georgie likewise scampered ahead, then slowed, bow lifted. Elinor watched his bent, deliberate paces for a few moments, until he was but half visible through the low-growing trees, then turned her attention to the ground and foliage again. Rumor had it that sassafras grew here, amongst all else, but she'd not seen it for herself.

She ventured a few steps into the forest. Without the constant chatter and noise of Georgie, the quiet closed suddenly around her, where only the drip of the fog could be heard, accompanied by occasional faint birdsong and rustle of a squirrel.

Elinor stopped, breathing deeply. Depending upon where one stood on the island, the shush of the waves could be heard, but not here. The faintest salt tinged the air, and the aroma of the pines mingled with the sandy loam made moist by the fog. Such perfect stillness had been rare enough in England, and impossible in London no matter the time of day or night. Here, in this moment, it was easy to forget there had ever been trouble in this place—

A chill touched her, slid down her scalp. Ginny stirred, squeaking. Opening her eyes, Elinor shushed her, rearranging the wrap in the event the babe had grown uncomfortable, and her little one sighed and settled—

A movement, a shape, caught the corner of her eye. With much effort Elinor suppressed the gasp rising in her throat, but she could not quite contain the flinch that shook her body. A savage stood there—a warrior, if his muscled proportions and sternness of manner were anything to judge by, and tall. Bow in hand, as tall as he was, held upright but lightly resting on the ground, arrows all still sheathed. His other arm hung relaxed, yet Elinor felt he might spring into action at any instant. Glossy black hair lay neatly pulled back across one side of his head, the other shaved clean, only a short center crest rising between, with the ends knotted behind his ears and adorned with the usual single feather on each side. Dark eyes glittered in the morning light, fog notwithstanding, and the lines of his face bespoke an intentness that brought a wave of prickling heat across her skin.

A band of iron seemed to bind her chest. Was he Croatoan? Secotan? Or—something else entirely? They carried their identifying marks on the upper back, which she could not see, since he faced her. His visage and body, above and below his deerskin apron, bore both the usual permanent markings in dark blue, with thicker shapes traced in red paint. Ornaments of copper hung from his ears, and strings of what appeared to be dark pearls graced his chest. Leather bracers encircled his wrists.

She drew in a breath, straightening a little, smoothing her hands over little Ginny's form, snug inside her wrap. "*Wingapo*," she said, endeavoring to keep the warble from her voice while yet speaking clearly. *Hello.* If he were of a near people, he should understand the greeting used by both Croatoan and Secotan.

He did not move, but something in his features shifted. A widening of the eye, or a flaring of the nostrils, perhaps? Surprise that she knew the word and offered such, instead of running and screaming? She knew not how to interpret what she was seeing.

She said it again, more softly and insistently. An answering wave of panic beat inside her breast, but with another breath, as measured as she was able, she pushed it down and waited.

His hand opened and closed upon the bow, one finger at a time, while the other flexed and once more slackened. Still he remained there, his gaze flicking over her person and lingering on the bundled form against her chest.

Elinor tried to keep her own expression open and mild, but as if she sensed something amiss, Ginny cried out. Elinor patted and shushed, bouncing a little, and the babe subsided. The savage's gaze went even more intent, with another flare of what looked like interest. Elinor lifted a hand and pointed to the bundled child. "Baby. Infant."

A muted crashing came from a short distance off, and Georgie called out, "Mistress Dare! Mistress Dare!"

Elinor turned only slightly to glance behind her. "I am here, Georgie!"

But when she looked again, the warrior had vanished, with the merest whisper of rustling in his wake.

Georgie came running out of the mist, panting, his own bow still in hand, and a squirrel in the other. "I—I could not get the deer, but here—here is something at least."

A trembling began in Elinor's limbs, which she could suppress no longer. "Why, thank you! No matter about the deer. Let us go see what the others have found."

" 'Twould have fed more of us," Georgie groused, falling into step beside her.

She kept her steps slow and measured, but her shoulder blades itched. The other women came into view through the trees, their voices carrying before them. Still Elinor kept herself from hurrying. She'd not feel completely easy until they were back inside the town walls, but if the unknown warrior yet lingered and watched, she'd not send the others into a panic. Not if there was no immediate threat.

And she'd certainly not give Georgie more cause for fear from savages than the boy already suffered.

Elinor glanced about and saw nothing. As she and Georgie rejoined the others, their chatter continued, with no one except young Thomas Archard so much as noticing she and Georgie had been absent—and only then because Georgie showed the other boy his prize. Elinor pressed her lips together and trailed at the edge of the company, casting looks this way and that as they went, not even attempting to forage anymore.

At last, however, she could bear it no longer and blurted, in between the others' conversation, "Is it not midday? Should we not return for refreshment?"

Rose turned and regarded her curiously. "We've been about for barely an hour. And there—little Ginny is still slumbering, is she not?"

Elinor slid a hand over the babe's form. "Indeed. But I—I confess myself in need of a rest."

"Well, sit yourself down on yon log—"

Elinor breathed out, tucking her chin with a pointed look at her friend. Rose stopped, mouth open then suddenly shut as she seemed to comprehend that Elinor had something she could not say directly.

"I pray thee, let us return to the town," she said very softly.

Eyes rounded, the other women nodded and set off in that direction. Conversation resumed, but more quietly. Elinor continued to keep watch and did not draw a full breath until they passed through the opening of the palisade.

They'd barely gotten inside before Rose rounded on her. "What on earth, Elinor—"

"Shh." She held up a hand, then bent a smile upon Georgie. "Go, you and Thomas, take your squirrel and dress it for Mistress Archard. If she decides she wants it not, then I'd be glad to stew it for you."

The boys dashed away, and only then did she dare speak. "There was a savage in the woods," she said, keeping her voice low. "Not, I think, one we know."

The other women gasped almost as one.

"Georgie and I had wandered a little away, and then he went off in pursuit of a deer—and suddenly there he was, a lone warrior. He only stood and looked at me, and the moment Georgie returned he was away again, but—" Elinor inhaled deeply. "Perhaps now you will understand my insistence we return. Although"—she sought to forestall an outburst with a raised hand again—"it is in my mind that if any meant us ill, they'd have done so."

The outburst did come then, with all four of the other women talking at once.

"We should tell—"

"What if we—"

"However are we to—"

Elinor held up both hands, but then they turned upon her. "We must needs tell the men about this," Jane said. "What if we fail to do so, and there is another attack?"

And so they went to the guards, where Elinor related the entire thing again, and a hasty council was called. By this time Ginny was awake and crying lustily, so she begged leave to run back to her house and change and feed the babe. Rose accompanied her, unwilling to leave her unattended after the morning's fright. Not that Elinor minded greatly, although a few moments to shed tears in private might be welcomed eventually.

Presently they all gathered, and more slowly this time Elinor told the story. They considered the matter, faces grave. "It is evident that we cannot shut ourselves up in the walls of the town and survive," John Sampson said. "And yet we cannot avoid being spied upon either. The savages are stealthy and cunning in their watchfulness."

"Shall we sally forth another attack?" Dyonis Harvie asked.

" 'Tis best not, I think, until the others return from Croatoan. And then we shall see what they say."

"It is a reminder, is it not," Nicholas Johnson said, "that we remain, as we always are, in the hands of God? And it is only by His good pleasure that we continue here and prosper." He scrubbed a hand across one bent knee. "We must trust Him as never before."

"Aye, but our women—" Master Harvie fixed Elinor with a long look. "If aught happened to you, Elinor, how could we ever face Ananias? Or, God forbid, your father, once he returns."

Chapter Eight

It was still odd, even after a few months of visiting back and forth with both the Croatoan and Pomeiooc, to spend time in the presence of a people whose practice was to go about half clothed. Ananias considered himself a righteous man, well satisfied by his wife, and yet it was an effort to turn his eye away and not stare at the nakedness of the women of this land. Or of the men either, for that matter, although he was well enough used to that when he and the others would go down to the edge of the sound to wash.

But even so, he could not deny the pure sincerity of these people, their simplicity and joy and earnest hospitality. It was a glad enough task, then, to seek their counsel on the matter of a move.

Already the differences of dress and appearance were becoming less strange, he found, as they drew their boat up on the narrow strip of beach and were greeted by Manteo's people. Ananias even recognized a few, to his own surprise—Towaye, Manteo's mother, and some of the other men.

They were gathered into the longhouse and made to sit down. A fragrant pipe was passed around, and at last the signal was given and Manteo began to speak, ostensibly explaining their dilemma. Slowly, back and forth, as he stopped to translate, the discussion spooled out.

"It was our plan from the beginning to move. We thought to remove to the mainland, but all agree that is unsafe. We know not where the Secotan make their dwellings, yet it must be close enough they still make attack. Last week they once again broke our weirs. We have built a palisade around our town, but before the next planting season comes, we must make a decision whether to go or to stay. You all know that Roanoac has always been meant by the Secotan as merely a summer dwelling, at best, and we know not whether it can support our entire colony."

The Croatoan weroances nodded, and Manteo's mother spoke. "We have been considering this matter ourselves. Strength lies in numbers, and in sharing a common dwelling place. As we have been pleased to aid and assist your people, we have been speaking of how it would please us to have you live here on Croatoan Island with us."

A collective *whoosh* went out from the entire company, Ananias included, and they all looked at each other. This was a possibility some of them had whispered amongst themselves but not seriously discussed. And to have the Croatoan be the ones to broach it—could this be anything but the providence of God Himself?

"And we would not be a burden upon your own people?"

"The island is rich, and there are resources enough for all, if your people help plant more fields, and hunt and fish as well."

They agreed to discuss it more, and while some of the men decided to accompany a group of Croatoan setting out to hunt, Ananias and others went for a walk into the high ground of the island. They followed the hunting party but loosely, keeping far enough back not to scare off the deer.

As they walked, the low roar of ocean waves came to their ears. The hunting party veered off to their left, but Manteo led them steadfastly on, uphill, weaving between the undergrowth and sometimes stooping beneath the boughs of the maritime oaks. They followed a narrow path around the edge of a boggy pond, then turned sharply upward again and emerged on a ridge where the wind cooled their faces. Beyond the forest stretched creamy sand, where waves whitened and crashed.

He could live here, aye. It was too soon to let his heart hope, but he knew how much Elinor longed for a lasting place of their own. That might not come to pass until they finally did remove to the main and set up a permanent homestead, but for now—verily this would do. And the presence of the Croatoan would lend them all strength, as they'd already said.

Manteo pointed. "Over yon is the fort that Stafford and his men built when Rafe Lane sent them here two years ago. It would be a good place to keep watch for ships, both English and Spanish, and await the return of John White."

"I see that," Ananias said. "And where do you suppose your people would have us set up our town?"

Manteo turned. From their current vantage point, they could see much of the sound-side of the island, at least of the eastern half. "My people have towns there, and there." He pointed this time at the north-eastern corner from whence they had just come, and then a point jutting out a few miles westward. "And one on the far end of the island."

Tendrils of smoke rose from the two farther locations he'd indicated, presumably from cooking fires.

"It is my thought—the weroances will have to approve it, of course—that you could set up between towns, either on this side or the other. Perhaps just over the ridge from the fort, and then it would be an easy passage back and forth."

Ananias had not hoped to be so heartened on this journey.

"And yet. . .why?" he found himself asking.

Manteo swung to gaze at him.

"Why are your people so willing to help us, after all the ill the English have done in this place?"

Manteo's expression became thoughtful, and he took his time giving answer. "The English are a different people, true, and very warlike. My people see it as—how would you say it, an advantage?—to be joined with yours. This is where Wanchese and I disagreed. He came to hate English ways and believed your people should be resisted at any cost from making your home upon these shores." Manteo's gaze remained on Ananias, mild yet with a glint of some strong feeling. "I wish better for my people than endless war with yours. And as it was the wish of John White that we dwell together with all love and friendship, so that is my wish as well."

"Well spoken, Manteo," Roger Bailie said, while Ananias was yet mulling Manteo's words.

Although the savage admitted to more cunning than Ananias had credited him with, he could not fault Manteo's desire to arrange for the best future possible for both their peoples.

Later they were feasted, and more talk took place. Manteo, Ananias, and the other Assistants agreed with the Croatoan weroances that an English town on this island would be more than acceptable, but they would need to secure the approval of all the planters, and then the process would likely be a long and laborious one. But they were eager to explore the possibilities in such a move.

It was even ventured at one point that the English and Croatoan together might make more towns in Dasemonguepeuk and beyond, since Manteo had been given dominion over that region, at least in name. Another intriguing possibility, and practical as well, since no clay for brickmaking was to be found on the islands, and they were already forced to go to the main with the help of the Croatoan. Making bricks and then building with the same would be accomplished much more easily at one location.

They slept that night in the Croatoan longhouses, then took their leave the next morning, piling back into two boats. A delegation of the Croatoan accompanied them, paddling their narrow but sturdy canoes, each made of a single tree, with sure strength and a speed that still amazed Ananias. Others went west, seeking news.

They returned about evening, and while some of the men talked of setting out to hunt and fish for supper, Ananias went in search of Elinor.

The guards at the gate stopped him. "Your wife is well, but she'll want to tell you what took place yestermorn."

His gut clenched at the mere suggestion that his Elinor had been in peril of any sort. He glared at the guard, whose name he thought he recalled as Thomas Phevens. "What mean you?"

The man smiled slightly. "Just get thee home."

He found her at the house, folding linens while the babe lay cooing on the bed. She looked up, flew to him, and clung with uncharacteristic fervor. "Oh—I am so glad—you are home!"

He folded her into his embrace. Her sweetness was certainly welcome and to be savored, but—"Are you weeping, dear one?"

She drew back, dashing away definite tears. "Oh, 'tis nothing but motherhood that makes me overwrought. We are well enough."

Ananias peered at her more closely. Perhaps 'twould be wiser to pretend he knew nothing. "Did anything happen while we were gone?"

Did her cheek pale, then flush more darkly in the shadows of the house? Or was it only his imagination?

"N–nay. All is well."

The quaver of her voice struck sourness into his belly. "Goodwife," he said softly, "think you so smally of me that you cannot even trust me with an accounting of your adventures in my absence? Come now. The guard at the gate mentioned there was some hap. And I can see you are still discomfited by it."

Why did he always see right through her?

Elinor turned away before swallowing hard. She'd not wanted to set him instantly at worry, and yet that had already been done. So what held her back from spilling the tale? What tied her tongue? Was her husband not worthy of trust in this matter?

She watched him out of the corner of her eye as he slid his satchel to the floor and reached for little Ginny. "Look how you have grown in the space of but two days!" he crooned, lifting her, and the babe's eyes lit, her mouth opening wide in a grin, arms waving and legs kicking in delight.

Elinor chuckled, but even to her own ear it sounded shaky. "She changes every day, it seems."

With his own breathless laugh, Ananias put the baby to his shoulder and bounced her. "I've so much to tell you, my darling—but prithee, what is it?"

She couldn't help it. The relief of having him home, and the tears simply welled up straightaway. "I—" He gathered her against him once more with one arm, holding Virginia with the other. A breath or two, savoring the freshness of woods and sea still upon him, and then she forced herself to speak. "Aye, I've something to tell you as well."

He drew back, peering into her face. Ginny squawked, and without thought, Elinor offered to take her, but Ananias held fast. "Nay. First tell me."

She inhaled again, then plunged ahead. "I—saw a savage in the woods yesterday. We'd gone gathering, the other women and I. We intended to stay close, but I was separated from the others—"

Ananias went completely white, and very still. "Go on."

"Georgie was with me. Then he went off in pursuit of a deer, and suddenly, there he was. A man, arrayed as a warrior to my eye—but of course it is hard to tell, and I knew not whether he was Croatoan or another—"

Her husband's hand was upon her shoulder. "Are you well? Did he harm you?"

She swallowed again. "I—am indeed well. 'Twasn't like that. He only stood—and looked at me. I tried to speak to him, but he made no reply, and then Georgie came running back and the savage disappeared."

"And why did the other men allow you to roam without protection?"

She offered a halfhearted shrug. "We didn't intend to go far. You and the others had just departed, so we felt it safe to go out soon after, that if any were watching for occasion to attack, they'd no time to prepare for it. And"—her gaze came to his with a bit of challenge—"you know well that we cannot eat if we cannot hunt and gather."

"Aye. That is so." He relented a bit in his sternness, glancing into Ginny's small, sweet face as he dandled her on his shoulder. Then his gaze came back to her, and he grasped Elinor gently by the shoulder and shook her. "Regardless, all will be well. We are making plans, God willing and the remainder of the town agreeing, to remove to Croatoan. No more long days journeying back and forth to visit with them and consult about the best ways to feed ourselves. And certainly no more of sending you women out alone to find victuals."

A thrill of both fear and anticipation wove through her breast at his words. "Truly?"

How would it be to live beside these wild but gentle people? And to finally, thoroughly learn their tongue as she longed to? Manteo had been far too busy to add more than a few words to what Papa had already taught her.

And then, if caught in the same situation as yesterday, she'd have the wherewithal to speak—and understand—rather than standing there dumbly. Although—God forbid she should be in that predicament a second time.

They ran easily through the forest, single file, following a path older than the trees towering on either side. Sees Far savored the cool wind sliding over body and limbs, the warm pockets of sunlight dappling the forest floor, the chirp and twitter of the birds as they took their own flight through the trees.

Just ahead of him ran Turtle Claws, with Wanchese taking the lead. With skin bronzed under the sun and hair grown out and properly cut—short on one side, a crest across the top, the ends knotted behind his ears, and an additional fringe edging the forehead—Wanchese no longer bore any trace of the many moons spent with the Inqutish.

Unless, of course, one counted the deep bitterness that flowed from him, like water where cypress grew. And Sees Far could not fault him for that. He could remember, however, when they both had greeted the white strangers with eagerness, when Wanchese had celebrated being one of two chosen to accompany them back across the great water to their land while Sees Far burned with jealousy at being left behind. When his friend returned nearly a year later, he was a changed man—nearly unrecognizable as a Sukwoten, let alone as a warrior. Hair unkempt, skin pale from moons of wearing Inqutish clothing—apparently the sun did not shine in that land—hands and feet softened by the wearing of shoes and gloves. He'd even allowed a small beard to grow, rather than plucking out the hairs as they emerged sparsely from cheek and chin.

Worst, however, were the shadows in his eyes, and the harsh set of his mouth where once his countenance had shone with courage and the fierce joy of life. It had taken many suns, many prayers and sacrifices, much cleansing of the soul and body, for Wanchese to begin resembling the man they once knew. The elders had even talked of sending him out for a second huskanaw, an unheard-of happenstance, for Wanchese to once again connect with his true self and the spirits of the land and their people. But while that was yet being discussed, the Inqutish warriors fumbled their way through negotiations with Wyngyno and others, only to prove their selfishness and brutality time and again. At last Wyngyno understood the danger of their presence in their land, but only after his own brother, weroance Granganimeo, perished of the strange sickness that went out from the Inqutish. At that time Wyngyno changed his name to indicate his new stance of caution and watchfulness, and Wanchese himself seemed to reawaken, with a fresh fire few others possessed.

Thereafter, Wanchese put himself at the forefront of every action against the Inqutish and in the midst of any spying effort. Careful painting of his face and body beforehand, and the cutting and arranging of his hair in Sukwoten custom once more, ensured that none of the Inqutish so much as gave him a second glance in all their encounters.

Wanchese did, however, avoid Manteo as much as possible, fearing that one's sharp eyes would see him for who he truly was.

In all other respects, his exploits were admired by all, even if the elders thought him foolhardy. This time was no exception. And yet, after much thought and discussion while sharing a pipe, they agreed to let him try, if reluctantly.

And here was Sees Far, keeping pace with him on this path pointed northward into the heart of Powhatan lands, with Turtle Claws along for his knowledge of the Powhatan tongue, whether they needed him or not.

They were curious, these Inqutish. It was one thing to encounter the man alone, hunting crabs in the marshes, a sure threat if caught in different circumstances and with others of his kind, and then to meet them in battle. Another thing entirely to find a woman alone—for *crenepo* she surely was, despite the strange shape and manner of her clothing, identifiable by the child she carried and the softness of her voice. Sees Far had stepped out of hiding with the intent to frighten, at the least to test her reaction. Though initially startled, she held her ground, even going so far as to offer a greeting. Did she understand the significance of it? How his people extended such a welcome to hers when they first appeared on Ossomocomuck, with Wyngyno eventually ceding the island itself to them? And now Sees Far appearing as an adversary, only to have her welcome him as if he were not? Whether or not she comprehended it to its fullness, she comported herself with bravery. And the curiosity in those eyes that seemed to reflect the mist was arresting, to say the least, even though nothing in her features, from the strong, rounded cheekbones and slightly upturned nose, appealed to him as a woman should to a man.

Only after the encounter did he realize that from what he could see of her hair beneath the coverings, its color matched that of the woman in his dreams.

The sun had sunk halfway down the sky when four warriors stepped into view, blocking their path. They wore no face paint, but the arranging of their hair proclaimed them of the Powhatan people.

At last. Sees Far's heart beat fast as Wanchese motioned them to a walk. They approached, keeping their hands low, with bows and clubs still slung in place, to show their intentions as peaceful. Such a move was full of risk, but Wanchese insisted it was necessary, and Turtle Claws agreed.

The other warriors showed no such inclination, but lifted their cudgels in warning. "We are friends," Wanchese called out. "We wish to speak with your weroance."

"Friends?" The leader's mouth curled as his gaze flicked over them. "Since when did we treat with Sukwoten? And what are you?" he demanded, addressing Turtle Claws.

"The people of my birth were Mandoag, of the hills, but I was adopted into Sukwoten before my huskanaw."

The glittering dark eyes remained cold. "You will understand, then, if we take you bound."

Wanchese gave a single, hard nod, and Sees Far found himself shoved to his knees, his hands roughly forced behind his back and bound with cords of a hard, scratchy weave. Then they yanked him to his feet and shoved him farther along down the path.

He submitted to it all, feigning disaffection. This was no time for his courage to fail.

They were hustled along the main path for a good long while; then, just as the sun neared the rim of the sky, they turned off on a narrower path that roughly followed a flowing stream downhill until the sounds of town life, and the flickering of its fires, could be discerned. Here their captors grasped them even more firmly and pushed them along to the largest longhouse. There, Sees Far and his companions were forced to their knees once more as one of the Powhatan warriors went before them into the longhouse.

He reemerged, accompanied by three other men, the status of the chiefest evident in the lines and sharpness of his face and the substantial strands of wassador and pearls draping the mighty shoulders. The two flanking him wore finely made capes of rabbit skin, one bearing the marks of even greater age and stature, and the other with a dried blackbird fastened above one ear, proclaiming his position of priest.

The weroance regarded him with eyes as hard as the warriors who had taken them. His voice was equally harsh, and Sees Far understood most of the words even before Turtle Claws translated. "Why are you here?"

"We have come to pay honor to your great renown, oh chief of the Powhatan," Wanchese said.

Turtle Claws translated again, and the weroance stood a little straighter, if that were possible.

"We seek your help with a worthy enemy," Wanchese continued. "The white skins who murdered Pemisapan and Granganimeo, as well as many of our people, have returned and in treachery once more think to claim our land."

The weroance sneered. "Tell me why I should join forces with Sukwoten, and who was this Pemisapan?"

Wanchese spoke more urgently. "Pemisapan is he who was called before Wyngyno. He called himself thus, the Watcher, after his brother Granganimeo fell to the strange sickness. Before that was the matter of the town of Aquascogoc being burned merely for the absence of a cup of white wassador belonging to the Inqutish. And then the white ones went to Okisco and Menatonon but dealt only in treachery, again. Upon their return, having become sorry that he'd lent Roanoac to the Inqutish, Pemisapan determined to remove them. But the Inqutish grew wise to his plan and struck first. Pemisapan was shot cruelly from behind, then hunted into the forest by one of the Inqutish devils and brought down as no better than a deer, with his head even being cut off by one of their long knives."

"Treachery indeed," the Powhatan weroance spat, and looked a little less unfriendly.

"So they have returned, to live again in the town they left during the summer before last. We crossed over to espy what they were doing and happened upon one of their men, searching alone for crabs in the sea marsh. We thought to give them warning, and also repay their sorrow unto themselves, and so we slew the man. They returned by hunting us again, and now they resist our every effort to drive them out."

The weroance lifted his chin. "So you come to us, because our strength is superior to yours."

Wanchese's head came up as well. "You have ever been a worthy enemy. These foreigners, however, are of a different kind altogether and without honor. Like the Spanish before them."

The weroance seemed to consider this. By the glitter of his eyes, Sees Far thought he was pleased by Wanchese's words.

He spoke again, gesturing at Sees Far. "What about that one?" Turtle Claws translated.

Sees Far composed himself. "These people do not belong to this land. Their presence alone sickened our people. I have lost family, including the woman who would have been mine. I desire that these English be pushed back into the sea from whence they came. We are determined to see this done, with your help or without it. But we believe it can be accomplished more quickly with your help."

The weroance pulled in a deep breath. "We will consider this matter and send word."

Wanchese nodded, and Sees Far followed suit. It was enough, indeed.

Their hands were unbound for a token meal, then they were prodded to their feet, hands tied again, and herded back the way they had come. Sees Far still half expected at any moment for a blow to fall and to be beaten or killed, or both. Yet when they arrived back at the spot where they had been taken, their captors' only action was to loose their bonds, return their weapons, and dismiss them.

The suggestion to remove to Croatoan was met with such joy and relief, it hardly seemed worthy of deliberation. And with the decision swiftly made, all set immediately to work—some to stand guard with increased vigilance, some to return to Croatoan to prepare the new town site, and some to begin disassembling the houses, even down to post and hearth, for transport and rebuilding.

Elinor stayed behind to pack while Ananias accompanied the first load of materials. They'd argued whether to take women and children before all else, but at last it was decided at least a few houses should be ready beforehand. They wished to impose on the hospitality of the Croatoan people no more than necessary.

Their last days on Roanoac passed without event, aside from anticipation turning quickly to shortened tempers and squabbling over matters both great and small—including the question of whether the move should take place at all, when more expected attacks from Dasemonguepeuk never came. Then weather brought delays, and so it was January before the second voyage of the pinnace could set forth.

The wind kicked up a bit as they sailed southward, women and children and the older boys conscripted to help carry baggage. Overhead flew pelicans and geese and other water birds, outlined against a vivid blue sky and fluffy white clouds. The coastline on both sides gradually receded until either was but a smudge on the horizon, with the shore to starboard vanishing entirely as if they were once more on the open seas. This time, however, Elinor carried a babe in arms rather than in her belly.

"In the beginning was the sea," she murmured as the wind tugged at the edges of her coif and cloak. Ginny lay wrapped securely inside Elinor's cloak, against her chest. It had become her most favored way of carrying the babe, at least while she remained little.

"Ye'll not be able to stand at the rail the entire way, like your da," came the voice of Captain Stafford.

She bent a smile upon the man, who was nearer Papa's age than her own. "Nay, but I love the wind and the water. And as long as little Ginny is happy—" She peered down at the babe, still mostly covered by her cloak. "And how fares the wee one these days?"

She pulled the cloak back far enough to show Ginny's face, dewy with sleep and warmth. The closed eyes squinched more tightly shut against the sudden light.

Stafford chuckled. "Bonny she is. Gov'nor White must be missin' you all something fierce."

Her smile thinned. "And we miss him. I only hope he comes soon."

"Well, in the meantime—" He squinted and gazed out over the waves. "Ye'll have plenty to do on Croatoan, and the island affords much pleasantness. 'Tis good hap that we're removing there."

"I hope so," Elinor murmured.

A shout from the bow drew Captain Stafford's attention, and with a word of apology, he went to see to the matter at hand.

Ginny woke shortly after, and Elinor tucked herself into a corner of the deck on a coil of rope to tend her. Between the sun and wind and Ginny nursing, she found herself drowsing.

She'd not expected to find being back aboard ship so enjoyable. Perhaps it was the thought that they'd be taking sanctuary with the Croatoan, and she'd not have to be concerned with strange, threatening savage warriors stepping from the forest at odd moments. She and the others would be safe.

Who was that unknown warrior, and where was he now? Did he watch their actions from afar?

The sun had begun its descent into the west before the inlet and tip of Croatoan Island came into view. The pinnace dropped anchor then lowered a boat, and half the women were helped into it. Elinor waited while they were ferried to land and returned. Once more she made the babe fast upon her breast, then with help she climbed down the rope ladder to the boat.

There were already Croatoan women waiting when they reached the shore. "Wingapo! Wingapo!" they cried out, which Elinor knew as their greeting, wading out to the boat and holding out steadying hands as Elinor and the others stepped out and sloshed their way to dry land. The men came after with baggage before returning to the pinnace for the remainder of the cargo.

The Croatoan women embraced Elinor and her companions, cooed over baby Ginny, then helped carry their belongings, chattering the entire time. She could not help but laugh in response, their spirits were so bright and their manner so warm and open. Two in particular she recognized from their visit to Roanoac before Papa had gone, Wesnah and another whose name was Timqua, and both threw Elinor frequent smiles as they went. They passed through woods that appeared much as the flora on Roanoac, but with smaller, more gnarled trees, and down to the Croatoan town. Once again, the shapes of the houses and various other features were already made familiar by Papa's paintings. Still, how curious to see it all brought to life! The walls of woven reed, the thatched roofs, the dancing circle marked by its posts topped with carved faces. Wesnah, Timqua, and their companions beckoned to Elinor and the other Englishwomen, drawing them into one of the longhouses, where a fire burned and a delicious warmth enfolded them.

The women who had debarked before them were already seated around the fire. They scooted aside to make room for the newcomers, and while Elinor nursed Ginny, she and her companions were given cups of a drink both sweet and slightly bitter. Jane Mannering inquired, both with words and motions, what it was made of, and one of the Croatoan women showed her a leaf, stiff and glossy, and also by motions showed that such leaves were steeped in hot water. " 'Tis very refreshing," Jane assured Elinor and the others.

"What is it called?" Rose Payne asked, then remembered the phrase they were taught for such inquiries. *"Ka ka torwawirocs yowo?"*

"*Sacque*," responded one of the Croatoan women, smiling. She dipped her head and gestured to them all. "Wingapo!"

They all dipped their own heads in response and murmured their thanks.

Elinor vented a little sigh. The native women bustled about, bringing in pots of food and serving them in small vessels as well. Later would come the work of settling in their own town, but for now, the hospitality of this place could not be denied—and a sense of ease and comfort wrapped her about, such as she'd not felt for a long while.

Not since. . .before a certain strange warrior had stepped out of the woods.

The rest of the evening was something of a blur, as she found herself yielding to weariness. Native children kept running in and out of the longhouse to stare at them, doubtless amazed at their long gowns and layers of clothing. "Crenepo?" one young girl asked, wrinkling her nose, and an older woman gave her a light cuff on the shoulder and a string of words that Elinor could not differentiate enough to understand, though its tone seemed almost musical.

After a plentiful supper of oysters, sodden roots, and various squashes, they were made to bed down, both on pallets built against the walls of the house, and on the floor. Elinor was happy enough to lie down where she was, cuddling Ginny against her, pillowing her head on her bent arm. She fell asleep to the crackling of the fire and the murmurs of women's voices, in both English and native accents.

Ginny woke but a pair of times during the night and nursed immediately back to sleep, and Elinor came to full wakefulness when the sky was a pale grey. Others were stirring about her, and a lean feminine form draped in skins bent over the fire, prodding it back to life.

Elinor lay and simply watched her a moment, struck anew by the unconscious grace of these people. Their—aye, she could use the word—beauty, and generosity. What a grief were the wrongs done them, these gentle folk who had gathered them in yestereve as if they were long-lost family, fed and comforted and provided for.

She'd heard it whispered, between Papa and Master Harriot when he'd returned from the Lane expedition in '86, that these people showed more fruits of being true followers of God than those in England who attended church faithfully and quoted the scriptures. Such hypocrisy among those who claimed Christianity was partly what had driven many of them to the New World—they wished a place where they could worship and serve the Lord without church leaders purporting to dictate how it should be done. Every man could, within reason, read scripture for himself—as good William Tyndale had lived and given his life for—and follow the Gospel in its purity, as the German monk, Martin Luther, had preached and to which cause he had likewise dedicated his life.

Was part of God's purpose for this colony to spread the good news of Christ and His true and only sacrifice for sins to these people, so misled in their worship of, what was it, Kewás?

Gracious Lord, let it be so. Let us speak for You, and be heard, in this place!

She rose then, and while she was tending Ginny, the native women beckoned to her and her companions to follow them. A chattering crowd of children followed, girls of all ages and small boys.

The morning wind carried the scent of the sea and a hint of stink, doubtless from the shell middens they'd glimpsed on their way in, the evening before. But soon the freshness of the breeze off the water swept that away as they neared the sound.

They were led down to the edge of the gently lapping water, where the native women immediately doffed their fur-lined capes and what little additional clothing they had and walked into the sound. The children splashed ahead of them, shrieking and giggling. More beckoning, while Elinor and the other Englishwomen exchanged glances and laughed nervously.

She and Ginny could do with a washing, but—"Too cold!" she exclaimed, and made shivering motions. The Croatoan women responded to that with their own laughter, albeit good-natured.

Still, she'd not turn down the opportunity to wash out some of the baby's swaddlings. Handing Ginny off to Rose, she ran back and fetched the small bundle of soiled nappies, then hurried to wash them while the Croatoan women finished their ablutions. Margery Harvie had the same thought, apparently, as she stooped in the same task, a little down the shore.

Afterward, a morning meal was set to cook, with several of them attempting to help, but mostly only causing more amusement on the part of the Croatoan. The children swirled through their midst, and then Elinor looked up from her careful observation of the native women's methods to see—"Georgie!"

It was indeed he, in the company of young John Sampson and Thomas Humfrey. A pair of young girls—their bare, flat chests, adorned with a single strand of beads, attesting to the tenderness of their years—scampered in their wake, so clearly teasing the older boys that Elinor could not suppress a giggle.

Timqua came up beside Elinor and pointed. *"Manteo nutánuhs."*

Her mind tripped into comprehension. "Manteo—girl? Daughter?"

Papa had spoken of such, and Manteo as well, although in more general terms.

Timqua smiled. "Mushaniq." She tapped her own chest. "*Nutuduwins* Timqua." Then pointing again at one of the girls, dancing circles around the boys, " *'Tuduwins* Mushaniq."

John and Thomas grinned at the girls, likely at their nakedness, while Georgie assiduously ignored them. Both attitudes would need to be addressed.

For now, though, the presence of the boys brought a thrill to her heart, for surely Ananias was not far behind. And surely enough, presently he, Manteo, and some of the other men, both English and Croatoan, came striding into the town. Elinor rose and ran to greet Ananias. Such feeling she need not suppress here, at least, since the savages themselves were so open and warm.

Ananias caught her up in his arms, smelling of hard work and the sea winds. "I have missed you fiercely," he breathed into her hair, which was untidily escaping the coif.

"And I, you."

He set her down and, still holding her hand, looked about. "Where is little Ginny?"

"Agnes and Emme are looking after her while breakfast is being prepared. I was—well, I was attempting to help, although the women needed none." She laughed and led him toward the cooking fire.

"They are quite capable, are they not?"

Once they had all broken their fast, the women gathered their things for the trek over to the town site. The Croatoan women and a band of children came along, making for an even more festive party than expected.

At the outskirts of the Croatoan town, one tall house by itself drew her attention. The sides were covered in woven reed mats, but as she passed the doorway, she glimpsed a figure feeding a fire burning in the center of the ground floor, and an upper story where she could see. . .nothing. A faint smoky rottenness wafted from it as they walked past, and an unaccountable chill washed over her.

She edged closer to Ananias. "That place. Is it. . . ?"

"The charnel house, aye."

"I recognize it from Papa's paintings."

The chill returned. She knew already, from Papa and his paintings, that laid out on that upper floor were the bodies of the Croatoan deceased, with a carved wooden idol sitting watch, which they called Kewás. Such strange burial practices—to dry out the bodies, then remove flesh from bones before wrapping in a reed mat, and all were saved to inter at the same time—

Worst, though, was the thought of these beautiful, warm people not knowing the truth of their Creator God and His love for them. Of their thinking some cold idol was the best likeness available of Him.

The chill became a shudder that she could not suppress. *Gracious Lord, have mercy on them—and us!*

In the next moment it passed, and the sun was once again warm on her shoulders.

Part Three

Chapter Nine

May 6, 1588

John drew a deep lungful of the salty wind. The open seas at last, and a miracle it was that they'd gotten away—that he'd been granted even these two small ships, the 30-tonne *Brave*, accompanied by the 25-tonne *Roe*. The Queen's stay on travel was understandable, given the imminent threat of war, but most inconvenient. Though Ralegh, true to his word, had arranged for a fleet to sail as soon as winds were good, in the end all but these two pinnaces were diverted to the defense against Spain.

Six other men he had with him on this vessel, and four women, with all their necessary provisions, and nine sailed aboard the other. Yet even with this, John could not rest easy. Since dawn they'd watched the approach of a tall ship of 100 tonne, apparently friendly with a smaller French vessel they'd had conversation with the day before, and in deadly pursuit. The *Roe* was nowhere in sight. They were on their own, with no choice but to fight to help themselves.

Blast the captains and crew of the *Brave* and the *Roe*, these thieving mariners who had only their own gain in mind and were worse pirates these past two weeks at sea than even Simon Ferdinando. Four ships they'd given chase to on their very first full day at sea, and boarded them, conscripting three men but taking nothing else. Every second or third day since, they'd found another ship or two to similarly chase, regardless of flag or size—or that they themselves had passengers and cargo aboard, bound for a particular destination, which ought to be their first order of business and not the customary taking of prizes. And now, despite showing nothing but goodwill to the French ship yesterday, the *Brave* was about to have her foolhardy courage tested to the full.

He leaned over the rail as if by will alone he could force wind into the sails. With every breath nearly a prayer of its own, it might not be far from the truth. But as hap had it, he was the first to confirm that the approaching flag was decidedly not of England.

The first mate came to his side, squinting. " 'Tis also French," he muttered darkly after a moment. He turned and gave the command to ready their arms.

The *Brave* hailed the other ship, but no answer came. As it became obvious by the fitting of their sails that they intended to engage and board, the *Brave* gave them a whole side. The French ship took grave damage from the *Brave*'s guns at such close range, but throwing grappling hooks across, their crew came aboard anyway.

John gripped his rapier and met the fight as it came.

For an hour and a half the battle raged on, desperate and ugly. John took a strike to the head from a pike, whose owner he had dispatched speedily, and as he fought another French sailor, something hit him from behind. As he reeled, his opponent's blade glanced off his head, but John recovered himself and battled on, though a growing weakness in one leg greatly slowed him and eventually brought him to a panting halt by the mast.

And then, suddenly, it was over, the deck littered with the bleeding and fallen—the *Brave*'s master and mate among them. The French bickered over the fate of their captives, whether to put them all to the sword.

Oh God in heaven, merciful Father. If this is where You will it to end, then receive my soul in peace.

But at the last minute, the French captain commanded his men to plunder only. As they dispersed to carry out that task, John reached a hand to his hip and buttock, brought it away bloody, then pitched forward into darkness.

Elinor paused in her hoeing to swipe the sweat from her brow and peer over at the spread blanket tucked under a gnarled small oak where Ginny slept on while her mama and others labored to prepare the last bit of seed they'd be sowing before full summer. This was the middle sowing, after the way of the Croatoan, and already the first planting flourished and grew tall.

It was also the last day that Ananias and the other men went to Roanoac to fetch anything remaining of their town there. Stretching, she lifted her eyes to where their houses stood, some still being reassembled, just above the curve of the little bay, not dissimilar to where they had been on Roanoac but this time with no near land in sight beyond the scattered small islands. Nearby her in the field were half a dozen others, both men and women, taking their turn preparing the ground before returning to household duties. Behind her lay the gentle rise of the low hills comprising the middle of the island, and all around were the sweet breezes and birdsong of a new morning.

A last stretch of her back and hips, and she returned to the task of working the sandy loam. Though it was labor indeed, as her sore muscles bore witness, how lovely this island was, and how good to have neighbors whose only mind was for their benefit. And how glad they all were to be able to work the soil and begin laboring at their various trades without having to look over their shoulders. The forge was set up, and the blacksmith had already begun work, though his only materials were those they'd carried with them. A tanner was hard at his task on the other end of the island, the occasional whiffs when the wind was just so attesting to his diligence. The men were already talking of an expedition inland to find ores to smelt and clay for making more bricks. And the field next to where Elinor stood was already sown in flax, to supply more linen for clothing. A wry smile curved her lips as she worked. They, the planters from England, were not quite ready to give over their ways of dress for simple doeskin. Although by the time full summer arrived, she might reconsider.

By summer, however, Papa should return. He'd promised an absence of but six months, and such time had now passed and more. Ananias told her they'd already left a token of their move—the letters CRO carved into a tree at the edge of the shore, near the fort, and then CROATOAN carved into one of the town's palisade posts—so Papa was sure to understand and come as soon as he saw them.

"Ho, I've brought refreshment!"

Wenefrid Powell was striding up the slope, a basket over each arm. Her voice, however, startled little Ginny from her nap, and the child woke, sat up, and promptly began crying. Elinor crossed quickly to her, setting the hoe against the tree and brushing off her hands before lifting the babe into her arms. "There, sweetness. Mama is here."

The others crowded around Wenefrid, but Elinor held back until she could see whether Ginny needed to nurse right away or no. Each person took a portion from each basket—smoked fish and small cakes, probably of corn or the starchy roots the Croatoan had taught them were good for making a kind of bread—and moved away, drinking from their own canteens. At first Elinor thought Ginny was going to settle, but then the babe's brow wrinkled, her bottom lip curling out, and she set forth wailing in earnest. "I'll return if I can," she called to the others.

Master John Wright, more or less in charge of the planting effort, waved with a smile. "Go tend your little one and worry not about the field. We shall see to this!"

With a grateful smile in response, she shifted Ginny to her hip then headed for the town and her own house. The babe subsided into sniffles, resting her head on Elinor's shoulder. "What is it, sweetheart? Did you not get all the sleepies out?"

She'd been enjoying the sun and wind well enough, but it was good to come home, change her daughter's swaddling, then stretch out upon the bed to nurse the child and rest as well. As she suckled, Ginny's eyelashes fell, and soon she'd fallen back asleep. Closing her eyes, Elinor drowsed with her, until approaching voices somewhere outside startled her awake.

". . .see her traipsing about barefoot like a savage? Are we to lose our Englishness—all proper decency—here on this wretched shore, then? Already the men look at their women with open lust."

"Shh, before someone hears—"

"I care not. I am so weary of this place. I am sick unto death of roots and fish—I want bread again, and cheese."

Elinor's eyes burned. That she could well understand. But the rest? What was amiss with shedding one's shoes and going about with bare feet, when the sun was warm and the sand soft?

The wandering eye of the men was another matter. Papa had insisted they live as friends and brothers with the Croatoan—and other peoples if they were willing. Did that extend to marriage?

It was a matter that must needs be decided, and soon.

'Twas the last trip to Roanoac. Ananias would not be sorry. Accomplished was the labor of taking apart the houses, panels of daub and wattle and woven reed beneath, then thatch and beam, each dwelling carefully stacked and carried to Croatoan aboard the pinnace, with the longboats faithfully carrying bundles of smaller belongings. They'd needed to mind how heavily they'd laden the pinnace especially, because of the shoals and shallowness of the sound, and only with the most careful navigation did they make the journey south. Now they'd only to scout the fort and town sites to see if anything else could be safely brought.

The entire process had taken weeks, and with John White's soon return in mind, they'd carefully set markings on one of the palisade posts and on a nearby tree. It was agreed to do so early on, when the women and children and their needful furnitures were first transported. Thankfully there had been no reason to add the cross his father-in-law had specified if they had made the move under circumstances of distress.

They'd caught glimpses, while going back and forth, of savages paddling the sound in their canoes, usually by twos and threes but sometimes more. None approached to converse, but neither did any attack. And thus here they were, on the last trip.

They'd brought the pinnace for this one, thinking to bring aboard the remaining pieces of iron and bags of shot. At least two pigs of lead had also been left behind, by dint of sheer exhaustion after disassembling the houses and taking all necessary provisions and belongings.

And then there were the half dozen chests packed with assorted things that the planters had deemed unnecessary for the time being—three of which were Governor White's things. Ananias was determined to bring those as well.

He felt not entirely easy about this foray but knew not why. The waters were calm, the sky clear, and the air balmy. In all, a fine, fair spring day, and they'd finally agreed that some of them would go back to Roanoac while others would stay behind and prepare the first fields for planting.

Swinging round the east side of the island, they angled the pinnace toward the small bay and the mouth of the creek where in times past they'd anchored all their boats. "Ahoy!" Master Warner called out. "What manner of boat is that?"

"They are—canoes! And many of them," Stafford said. "Heel about! We must not land."

Ananias fair ground his teeth at being so close and having to turn back. "But we likely outmatch them!"

Stafford shook his head slowly. "Likely, but do we wish to risk more loss of life just as we are establishing the colony? And while I might by now know the tongue well enough to parlay—were they willing to do so—without Manteo here to advise us, I have little desire to go wading in where we are uncertain of our reception—or certain to meet with battle."

Wanchese's fury blew like a summer tempest. The very trees would have trembled had they known better, Sees Far was sure.

Not that he was of a calmer mind himself.

"They are gone—even down to houses. How can they so completely have taken everything, except a few items of wassador, too large and heavy to be of use to us?" Wanchese stomped about and gestured to the open space between the log walls.

Sees Far had no words for his old friend. The fire burned too deeply within him as well. They had prepared for this—made their oblations, painted their faces and bodies, smoked the uppowoc, drunk the sacque, then paddled across to the island, full expecting battle. But—nothing. Only the fort and town's palisade, both filled by naught but sunlight and birdsong and the chitter of squirrels.

"They must have gone to the Kurawoten." Wanchese turned a circle in the middle of the palisade, then stopped, shaking his fists to the sky. "Curse Manteo! Curse him for turning his back on the ways of our people. Curse him forever!"

Sees Far wanted to cringe, or to howl alongside Wanchese. The other men simply stood, watching, no doubt feeling the same.

"How can we make war against those who are no longer here? If Manteo had not helped them, we would be rid of them, as we were rid of the men left before. And now—now the Kurawoten will be puffed up in their own importance, and think they are stronger than us. All because they befriended these—these white skins." Wanchese spat to the side, then strode toward the opening of the enclosure. The rest of them filed after, silently.

"We will not rest," he muttered as Sees Far drew up beside him. "We will make war, and continue to do so, until they—or we—draw no more breath."

"I like it not," Ananias told Elinor later, once they'd returned to their new town on Croatoan. "To leave your father's things behind—be they ever so safely hidden—and the remaining iron and lead."

She soothed him with both hands on his shoulders, kneading away the stiffness there. "We will have other fair days, will we not? Other opportunities to return and fetch them all."

"Mayhap, mayhap not. We are in the planting season with little time to lose." He huffed, bending his head, for a moment merely savoring her touch and the easing of the ache in his neck. "Speaking of. I am sorry that you'll be subjected to such labor."

Elinor's hands stilled. "What? Why would you say such a thing? I knew when we sailed that this would be no life of ease, planting an English settlement in the New World."

"Aye, but I'd hoped you'd only have to give yourself to housewifely things—"

She laughed outright. "You are aware, are you not, that the women of Croatoan are the ones who work the fields? While the men fish and hunt and go a-ranging." Her fingers kneaded again, seeking the knotted places in his neck muscles. "I was not afraid of gardening, and tending fields is but a step beyond that."

"You are the bravest woman I know." Ananias sighed. "And your hands are pure bliss."

A deeper chuckle this time. "You do realize they are stronger now because of all the labor I've been doing?"

"Mm," was all he found himself capable of responding.

"And speaking of." Her hands went slack against his shoulders, and she leaned a little more fully against him. "While I was down here at the house yestermorn, tending Ginny, I heard talk outside."

He cracked an eyelid to look at her. A frown etched her fine brow.

"I think 'twas Wenefrid. Raising complaint first of all about my having bare feet. At least, I am sure it was me she referred to, since I was indeed going about without shoes."

Ananias snorted, half amusement and half derision against the woman who had proven herself quite the busybody over the past year, but Elinor forged on.

"And—there was complaint spoken about the way the men look at the savage women. Charging that it's lustful and will lead only to trouble."

"Hmm, aye. The council have already been discussing such things."

"Although—perhaps 'tis heresy to say so, but they seem less savage than they once did. And with so many attending church, however it may be from mere curiosity—" Elinor shrugged.

"The women's attire is less—ah, distracting—than it once was, but whether that continues once winter is full past and they've less need to cover for warmth, remains to be seen." Ananias angled her a wry smile. "But aye, it has been suggested that if they are willing to be baptized and follow Christ, then nothing hinders our men from taking wives of the Croatoan." Or, perhaps, the women from taking husbands of the same, though he'd not speak that aloud. It seemed less. . .fitting, somehow. He cleared his throat. "That said, many feel we should be patient until your father returns, since more wives and maids are sure to follow."

She nodded thoughtfully. "But at some point. . ." Hesitating again, she blew out a breath, then concluded, "I suppose we simply take each hap as it comes."

When Sunday came and 'twas time to ready themselves for meeting, Elinor made doubly sure to be completely dressed, from a smart black hat down to shoes and stockings. She wasn't entirely sure she remembered last week to do more than tuck a coif over her hair and throw a shawl about her shoulders.

Unfortunately, her efforts only had the effect of causing her to feel overdressed. This was, after all, not the Queen's court. Her Christian brothers and sisters might argue that coming to meeting was, indeed, attending the court of the highest King of all, but then, did God not see them everywhere, in whatever state of dress or undress they might be?

More thoughts of heresy. Even so, at the last minute she tossed the hat aside, then gave Ginny's cap a last tug and tuck of the string under her chin as Ananias fetched a stool for her to sit on as the service went long. They set off for the center area they used as their meeting-place until a church could be built.

'Twas another point of disagreement. Those who still leaned toward the old ways, or in sympathy with Her Majesty the Queen's church, which despite the name "Anglican" yet functioned as Catholic in most ways except insisting the clergy remain unmarried and holding to an unholy reverence of Mother Mary and the Pope, wanted a structure to reflect the grandeur of an English church. Those who were Separatists, as well as the handful Elinor suspected of being Puritan, argued for a simpler building. Either way, they needed a roof and walls, something to keep out the rain and wind. Today, however, was nothing short of glorious. 'Twould be a sore temptation later to not work in the fields or go fishing.

Another blasphemous thought to be crushed underfoot.

Half the town was already assembled there beneath the arching branches of half a dozen of the largest oaks the island had to offer. Most folk stood, but those who had need of seating were scattered here and there with the stools or chairs they had brought along. Ananias settled Elinor near the back, well under the tree branches for shade and out of the wind, then strode away to mingle with the other men.

Several of the Croatoan were already in attendance. Timqua caught Elinor's eye from across the clearing and, with a little wave, came toward her. 'Twas no surprise that Mushaniq and Kokon, Timqua's own daughter, scampered in her wake.

They knew enough of each other's tongue by now to greet each other and to ask after the other's welfare. Before long, all were assembled and the singing began, and Timqua and the girls went to sit under a nearby tree, swaying with the tune of the hymn. At one point, Elinor heard a high, sweet voice, and looked over to see Mushaniq singing along in fair imitation of the music, even if she understood not the words.

"God has brought us here and given us favor," Nicholas Johnson began, when the singing was done. "Such favor must not be taken for granted, nor wasted, but we must live with both truth and love in the presence of the people with whom He has given us favor."

Elinor shifted on her stool. Ginny had begun to stir, and she bounced the babe on her shoulder, patting her back.

Master Johnson lifted the open volume of the scripture in his hands. " 'I exhort therefore, that above all things, prayers, supplications, intercessions, and giving of thanks be had for all men. . .that we may live a quiet and peaceable life, with all Godliness and honesty. For that is good and accepted in the sight of God our Saviour, which will have all men to be saved, and to come unto the knowledge of the truth. For there is one God, and one mediator between God and man, even the man Christ Jesus, which gave himself a ransom for all men. . . . I will therefore that the men pray every where, lifting up pure hands without wrath, or doubting. Likewise also the women, that they array themselves in comely apparel with shamefacedness and discreet behavior, not with broided hair, either gold or pearls, or costly array, but as becometh women, that profess godliness through good works.' "

He turned to another passage and read again. " 'Furthermore, we beseech you, brethren, and exhort you by the Lord Jesus, that you increase more and more even as you have received of us, how ye ought to walk and to please God. . . . For this is the will of God, even your holiness, that you should abstain from fornication, and that every one of you should know how to keep his vessel in holiness and honor, and not in the lust of concupiscence as do the heathen which know not God, that no man oppress and defraud his brother in bargaining, because that the Lord is the avenger of all such things, as we told you before, and testified. For God hath not called us to uncleanness but unto holiness. . . . But as touching brotherly love, ye need not that I write unto you. For ye are taught of God, to love one another. . . . We beseech you brethren, that ye increase more and more, and that ye study to be quiet, and to meddle with your own business, and to work with your own hands, as we commanded you: that ye may behave yourselves honestly toward them that are without, and that nothing be lacking unto you.' "

Master Johnson set the Bible, still open, upon the table before him. "The Holy Scriptures exhort us each to possess his vessel in holiness and honor. Indeed, we each must guard our thoughts as well as our actions. Jesus taught that it is not enough to abstain from murder or adultery, that harboring anger or lust in our hearts brings guilt for such upon our souls already. By the same token, we cannot judge the thoughts and intents of the heart: that is God's alone to judge.

"Her Majesty the Queen may have had her own purpose for placing us here, as much for the glory of England as the glory of Christ, but we have our private purpose, that we demonstrate faith and love through our own conversation, in truth and simplicity. Let us not become divided over things that have no eternal weight. We have the freedom here to choose what to wear, what to eat, where to go, and how to live. Let us not abuse that, but let us also walk in love toward each other. Hebrews chapter twelve saith, 'Follow peace with all men and holiness: without the which no man shall see the Lord.' And in the next chapter, 'Let your conversation be without covetousness and be content with such things as ye have already. For he hath said: I will not fail thee, neither forsake thee:

so that we may boldly say: the Lord is my helper, and I will not fear what man may do unto me.' We lack for nothing when we look to the God who has promised to be with us always. He will care for us. He will provide for us. One need only to look at this lovely island and the richness of the New World, and the friends He has given us thus far, to see evidence of it."

He turned a page in the Bible and once more read, " 'Jesus Christ yesterday and today, and the same continueth for ever. Be not carried about with divers and strange learning. For it is a good thing that the heart be stablished with grace, and not with meats, which have not profited them that have had their pastime in them. . . . To do good and to distribute, forget not, for with such sacrifices God is pleased.' "

"Let us then be mindful how the people here of this island, though perhaps heathen themselves, have shared with us such things as they have, though we were not of their own, and may we never fail or forget to show them kindness in return. Let us forget not also, as I have preached before, that our God is rich to all who call upon Him, regardless of blood or station."

After meeting, everyone lingered, apparently struck too deeply by the sermon to move right away. With Ginny asleep in her arms, Elinor stayed put, watching people drift to and fro, discussing in low tones, gesturing with much feeling.

And over yon stood Edward and Wenefrid Powell, in deep discussion with Master Johnson after his impassioned words. Ananias stood nearby, watching them, arms folded and his mouth a hard line in the shadow of his hat brim.

Papa's words came back to her from not long after they had set sail—*"He is, I believe, Walsingham's man"*—and therefore an enemy of Ralegh, and a possible detractor of the whole venture. Wenefrid's constant ill temper and complaints were difficult enough to stomach on a good day. But to think that Edward—Master Powell—actively sought to undermine the colony—Elinor could not suppress a shudder.

Gracious God, let Papa return soon and set all to rights!

Papa had pleaded for them to have one heart, one mind, where planting this colony was concerned. And now, suddenly, they were divided—or at least Master Johnson had felt compelled to preach an entire sermon on the topic—over what? Elinor going barefoot while working the fields and hunting crabs? Or lonely, unmarried men noticing that the Croatoan women were comely?

If Papa was delayed, or not enough women came, then the men here would need wives. And while the idea seemed as strange to her as to anyone. . . Elinor took a long look at Timqua and the girls, who were talking to Manteo, no doubt receiving his explanation of all that had taken place. 'Twas not as alien as it had once been to think of them as sisters and kin.

Sees Far lay staring upward through the tree branches, watching the winking of starlight as the wind stirred the limbs above. How could a God who had lit such things in the sky and set the sun and moon in motion, who had shaped this world and placed man here, then neglect to be clear in what He expected of them? Did He delight in hiding and peeping out occasionally and forcing them to guess where He would be and what He wished?

Or was it as many priests insisted, that all goodness indeed flowed from Him, but He did not trouble Himself with human affairs? That He had set various other spirits over them, the Montóac, whose favor they must seek, or whose displeasure they must appease, lest trouble and misfortune steal all the good they could gather to themselves?

Or was He Himself Montóac?

Either way, what would Sees Far need to do to obtain the favor he sought? Defined in this moment, of course, as finding and prevailing over their enemies. The war party had returned from the island to find a messenger come with the word that the Powhatan were still considering the matter of the Inqutish, but their holy men cautioned them against rashness. Their enemies would be given over to their hand in due time, they were assured, but they must lie low and await their opportunity.

Sees Far's teeth clenched at the very memory. The most they had found to do while on the island was locate a few chests the white skins had buried and vent their frustration upon the contents, breaking frames of painted likenesses and tearing leaves from the books, then strewing all else about, to remain exposed to sun and rain. One thing Sees Far had longed to bring back was the strange Inqutish armor made of wassador, intended to cover the body and head and other parts, but he and others had tried it on only to find it painfully hard and ill fitting. So it too had been left behind, cast aside upon the sand.

But what wonder and dismay would have been in the visage of their enemies had he been able to come clothed in their own armor?

"We will make war," Wanchese avowed. Every nerve in Sees Far's body sang in assent, a deep, menacing song of fury.

Have patience they would, if necessary. Yet, however long it took, they would see the task done.

Chapter Ten

Summer 1588

Thunder crashed and the wind howled, rattling the roof thatch and yanking Elinor into full wakefulness.

Betimes she forgot they were living on an island and how very vulnerable they were to the summer tempests rolling in off the ocean. But then, in moments such as this—

Ananias sat up, steady and solid even in a moment of alarm. Between them, Ginny slept on. Raking a hand through his loosened hair, he cocked his head and listened.

The afternoon before, with clouds threatening and the wind rising, they had battened down everything loose, and Captain Stafford took a contingent out to the pinnace to ride out the storm. Now, however, all Elinor could feel was fear that they'd lose all. That their house would be washed away from beneath them.

Strongest of all, that Papa was somewhere out there in the storm, being blown off course.

Ananias rose and went to make certain the shutters were secure, and Elinor followed, drawing her shawl about her shoulders. As he went from one window to another, then peered up at the roof above them, she hovered, feeling largely useless. "Go back to bed," he murmured, but even when he padded downstairs, she stood in the middle of the floor, trying to pray and mostly failing at that as well.

Ananias returned presently and folded her into his arms. "All is well, love." When still she trembled, he tucked her closer and murmured a prayer over her head.

Sighing, she sank against him. "Thank you. 'Tis cowardly of me to fear, I know."

"I blame you not," he whispered.

And at that, inexplicably, the tears came. Spring had stretched into summer, and Papa had not come. Oh, all was well enough—the town had settled into an easy rhythm, and the second planting of their crops was coming ripe. But she feared, beyond reason, for Papa. For all of them. She could not articulate, much less explain, the heaviness that often swept over her in the dead of night, especially on nights such as this, with the storm raging relentlessly.

"It has been nearly a year since Papa left," she said.

"Aye."

"What if he never returns?"

"Ah, sweetheart." His strong hands smoothed across her back. "He'll return, never fear. You know his determination."

"Aye, but—" She blew out a breath. "The sea is so wild. This land as well."

"And we serve a good God who made them both."

Elinor huffed again, into his shoulder. "You are so wise."

He chuckled. "I know only the uselessness of dwelling on things beyond our power to change. Aside from our prayers, of course."

"Of course." She leaned deeper into his embrace.

They returned to the bed, tucking Ginny to the side so they could lie close while listening to the lashing of the wind and rain.

To their amazement, they slept, although fitfully. They woke early, with the sky still mostly dark, to standing water in the downstairs of their house, with a few shutters blown off and a few lower panels of the house crumbled and tattered. Not bothering to do more than throw a kirtle on over her shift, and her most worn at that, Elinor set Ginny on a step above the water and sternly bid her stay. Then with skirts tucked up above her knees, she joined Ananias in gathering floating bits of furniture and baskets and stacking them upon the table.

As morning dawned, they found the rest of the town fared no better—in fact, theirs was among the mildest damage. As they walked through the receding water, Ginny bundled to Elinor's back to keep her out of harm's way, and Ananias lending a hand where it was needed to move fallen limbs and trees, a cry came up from the other end of town. Elinor's entire body went cold, for it was too much like a similar cry a year ago, when Master Howe was found murdered.

With Ananias busy helping Henry Payne, Elinor and Rose hurried toward the commotion. This time—no mutilated body, but a sobbing Joyce Archard in the arms of Jane Mannering. "My boy," she wailed. "We cannot find our Thomas!"

Two of the other lads stood by, sad and a bit shamefaced—Georgie Howe and William Wythers. Apparently the boys had wandered away after helping Captain Stafford and his crew, and this morning only Georgie and William returned to the town. Both avowed most strenuously that when night fell they had taken refuge on high ground amongst the trees, but come morning, Thomas Archard was not to be found.

The crops, especially the corn, were well nigh ruined, especially where the tides had flooded fields and gardens. Flooding from sound-side was exacerbated by ocean-side surge, and Georgie and Thomas attested to "terrible high" waves breaking over the hills at least part of the night.

Over the next few days, they searched for but did not find Thomas Archard's body. Another was found, that of a grown man, unknown, of some native people, which the Croatoan took to administer their own burial honors.

Councils were also held, as folk from the Croatoan villages visited the English, and some from across the sound, the Cwareuuoc and Pomeiooc and others, came seeking each other's welfare. With the gardens and fields damaged, much talk was had about how to feed everyone through the winter. The Croatoan explained how the previous year, drought had much reduced their corn yield—thus the plea they'd offered Captain Stafford and John White when they'd first visited after Master Howe's death—and while they survived well enough on deer and what the sea had to offer, some grain and vegetables were still needful. A last planting at this time would not grow if the earth was drenched in seawater.

The suggestion was ventured, and discussed, that Manteo lead the men on an expedition to Dasemonguepeuk to see if any yet dwelt there, and if not, some might move to that place.

While some planting took place, testing whether the soil would continue to yield, negotiations were begun between the nearby towns for the Croatoan and English to move to the main. Manteo's expedition found Dasemonguepeuk largely uninhabited, with a promising site inland, surrounded by wetlands but still easily accessible by boat. The men had already begun calling it Beechland for the abundant supply of that tree growing there.

In the middle of it all, no English ships came. Sometime around Virginia's first birthday, a Spanish ship was sighted, moving slowly past Croatoan and on up by Hatorask, where it lingered off the coast. Orders were given for the dousing of fires.

And always, Elinor fretted for Papa's return. But the summer had worn away without any sign of him, and she knew too well how the season went for seafarers. Once they put out from England, customarily shipmasters followed the paths of the sea, southward along the coasts of Portugal and Africa, then on to the Caribbean before swinging northward along Florida. Depending upon weather, or if they stopped to take spoil from Spanish ships, it might indeed have been July or later before they arrived again off the shores of Virginia. Possibly they might even be delayed as long as September—but she recalled too well the dread with which the sailors spoke of this portion of the ocean during September and October. As even Simon Ferdinando had said—though he'd lingered some weeks to outfit his ship—all would want to be either back in the southern islands or headed home to England before the autumn sea-storm season was upon them.

Only the great explorers—and she could not recall whether it was Greenville or Sir Francis Drake or both—had dared sail straight across the ocean, from England to Virginia, and that with some difficulty.

So as August wore away into September, and Virginia took her first steps, to the delight of all, Elinor's hopes dwindled even as her prayers became more frantic.

Next year. Surely he would come next year.

It had been some time since John had stepped foot inside the hall of the Middle Temple, but he recalled most sharply that he'd best stay on Sir Walter Ralegh's heels or be lost in the raucous crush. The reek of too many bodies and spilled wine and ale already permeated the air, despite the spices being burned at the corners of the vast room.

Amid the laughter, shouts, and hooting all around them, men turned as Ralegh made his way through the crush, slapping his back and shoulders companionably and greeting him as if they were intimate friends. Ralegh met them all with nods and an unwavering smile. John did his best to smile as well as eyes fell upon him, the question open upon their countenances who he might be to merit following so closely behind the great courtier. In reality, his smile hid gritted teeth, and he ducked his head to bring a scented cloth to his nose in what he hoped was an unobtrusive effort to allay the stink of the hall.

At last they arrived at Ralegh's designated spot, reserved for himself and a guest, on the far side of the hall beneath the huge, round stained-glass window set high into the wall. Ralegh greeted those already standing about. "And you may remember my companion, Master John White, the good artist of the early expeditions to Virginia, and no less governor of the same."

John's turn to smile again, more genuinely this time, and accept and return their salutations. The conversation invariably turned back to Ralegh himself, and John stole the moment of relief to survey the hall. Lamplight glinted off jewels and polished tableware, in the midst of a sea of men who talked, argued, and gesticulated, in dangerously high spirits.

Cloth to his nose again, John drew a deep breath and raised his eyes to the intricately arched work of the ceiling. How stately the architecture of this place! His gaze traced the almost filigree effect of the double hammerbeam roof and the rows of great windows lining the upper walls, before lingering upon the finely worked carvings adorning the near corners and edges of the paneling. Artists from near and far had been employed in the workings—were still employed, if he recollected correctly—and their chosen themes from classical and national mythologies reflected each one's tastes. John had heard only praise of Her Majesty the Queen's boldness in allowing each artist to express his own unique vision of what would be beautiful and fitting on these walls.

Out of the press, a familiar face emerged—the angular, even bony features of none other than Thomas Harriot—lit by a glad grin. "John White! What a welcome sight you are. Ralegh told us you'd be here this night, and I had to come see for myself, though I scarce could get away!"

With a laugh, he seized John in a rough but warm embrace.

"And how fare you these past months?" John asked. The man looked hale, though clad in his customary garb of severe black.

"Well enough, I suppose. Still writing of our venture to the New World. Theodore de Bry is laboring over his woodcuts of your paintings—but perhaps you knew of this? Nay? Well then. You'll not want to look too closely at them, for in my opinion he has altered certain aspects that ought not have been." Harriot rolled his eyes.

John shook his head. Once a sketch or painting left his fingertips, he'd no oversight in the way it was presented to the world. Especially when others copied his work, or interpreted it for another medium besides ink and parchment.

"And you? How are you faring, after. . . ?" Harriot delicately let the question fall.

"Well enough, I suppose." John half smiled. "Ralegh has invited me tonight to give an account of all that's transpired in connection with the colony, so I'll not yet bore you with details."

"Ah." Harriot clapped him on the shoulder. "Patience shall be my most treasured virtue until then."

A wave of cheers heralded the arrival of platters of meats and various other victuals, borne by two men and an older woman who by long practice both pushed their way through the press and avoided the hands reaching to steal a morsel before they could even get to the tables. The three sailed all the way across the hall and deposited their burdens on the head table, where Ralegh and John stood. "My thanks!" Ralegh said, lifting his already-filled goblet in salute to their servers.

The headman dipped his chin in response, then bustled away to see which vessels of wine needed refilling.

Ralegh bid John and the others be seated, and as they filled their trenchers from the platters, John ignored the scuffle going on at lower tables for the food. The headman was now bellowing at a pair of fellows to cease shoving ahead of the others and for the love of God to remove their hats as well. Both men pawed their headgear from their heads but barely restrained themselves otherwise.

When Ralegh, John, and their companions had eaten and well drunk, Ralegh sat back and motioned to the others, then to John. "I bid you hear my good fellow Governor White and his adventures in returning to Virginia to relieve the planters there, earlier this year."

"Misadventures, more like," John said with a laugh.

Ralegh grinned and gestured with his goblet. "Do tell us, regardless. Spare not detail, for these men have power to aid us in our venture."

John took a sip of the watered ale and swallowed hard. He so despised moments such as this.

"Many of you are familiar with the bad hap of my return. I was compelled by the planters in Virginia—to the last man and woman, even my own beloved daughter, exhorting me to come back to England and ensure the effort of their relief. They were—you may also be privy to this—most foully made to settle upon Roanoac Island, a coastal place fair enough for temporary dwelling, but with little resource for a full-fledged town."

Nods accompanied the intent expressions gathered about him.

"So I left them, though not willingly. My every thought since has been of returning, to embrace again my daughter and granddaughter, and serve in the capacity for which our good sir here has enjoined me—that is, of Governor of the Colony of Virginia.

"Scarce had I returned, and that only by greatest hardship, with divers privations and even death stalking our ship, than I discovered Her Majesty the Queen has called a stay on all shipping ventures, under threat of war with Spain. I did, however, with Ralegh's most kind assistance, manage over the winter to procure two pinnaces, which I outfitted with necessary provisions and fifteen additional colonists besides, mostly near kin to those already in Virginia."

Ralegh offered to fill his cup, and John accepted, then turned his chair and settled in again, warming to his task.

"We were not able to set out until late April. All seemed well, except that the crew seemed determined to board every stray ship we passed, whether friend or foe. We passed Portugal without mishap, then off the coast of Morocco we were chased down by the French who boarded us by force. As we fought back, I was wounded, twice in the head by both sword and pike, then with shot in one buttock." He smiled ruefully, and the other men laughed, lifting their cups in toast. "As you see, I am much mended, thanks be to God. The French plundered us, including most of our sails and tackle, then let us go, and we limped back to England. Since then, however, I've labored without ceasing, but we've yet been unable to secure either permission or passage to once again attempt return."

Responses ranged from thoughtful nods to words of regret and sympathy.

"Thank you all for taking the time to listen. May you find it in your hearts to lend aid, whether with monies or by petitioning Her Majesty the Queen to clear the way for us."

As the men turned to other conversations, John blew out a breath and contemplated the shimmer of liquid in his cup. So much he had not said. Could not say. He swallowed back the sudden ache in his throat.

Oh God, please. . .let my words not fail. Move on their hearts—on the Queen's own heart—and make a way for me to go back. Please.

Would the Almighty regard a plea worded so familiarly?

Then again, did He not already know the burning of John's heart, where all was concerned?

Some days later, John welcomed Harriot to his own chambers, happily sharing a measure of watered ale and bread, freshly purchased from a nearby bakery. "So what response did you hear from the others at Middle Temple?" John asked as they settled in.

Harriot's brow ticked upward. "Some interest. Some scoffing. Naught different than at any other time regarding this venture." The clergyman took a bite and eyed him, chewing. "Do not lose heart. This matter is too weighty, even if they know it not."

John lifted a hand and dropped it again in a gesture of frustration and resignation.

"Nay." Harriot set aside his cup and reached for the folio at his feet. "Here. I wish you to read some of what I've written. Tell me if I may improve upon it."

John took the stack of vellum. *A Briefe and True Report of the New Found Land of Virginia*, the first page proclaimed. A smile curled his lips, despite his gloom. Oh, how he missed that new-found land!

In the pages of Harriot's script, he revisited both the land and the peoples, commenting here and there on things Harriot mentioned. One passage in particular brought him up short, and he read it again.

"This is wonderful. Your point that the English have much to learn from the savage way of life: 'Yet they are moderate in their eating, whereby they avoid sickness. I would to God we would follow their example. For we should be free from many kinds of diseases which we fall into by sumptuous and unreasonable banquets, continually devising new sauces, and provocation of gluttony to satisfy our unsatiable appetites.' And here: 'They are very sober in their eating, and drinking, and consequently very long lived because they do not oppress nature.' " He lowered the pages and fastened a look upon Harriot. "It is part of why I can hardly wait to return. The very air here in London—some days I can scarce breathe."

Harriot nodded. "I envy you, you know. Would that I too could return—converse again with these good people and teach them the way of the true God more completely. But"—and he shook his head—"God calls me here, to write these words and inform our own countrymen that the world is indeed wider than England, and other lands are worth more than mere opportunities for trade and material gain."

"Although there is plenty of that to be had," John said softly.

"Aye." Harriot sniffed. "And therein lies the rub. We may not take ourselves to other lands for the purpose of mere understanding and goodwill, nay. Always there must needs be profit in it, somewhere. Especially for those who lay out their own wealth for the venture." His eyes rose again to John's. "What think you? As Englishmen, we speak of treating with the savages better than the Spanish, but—have we a chance, after all that has transpired, to truly live as friends and brothers with them?"

John drew a deep breath. Harriot had seen the fruit of Lane's actions and, for that matter, of his own passage through the various towns of the New World, how even when not a hand was lifted in violence against them, waves of inexplicable sickness flowed in the wake of their visits. "I own that I know not."

Harriot nodded slowly. "And then there is the case of the slaughter of the Jesuits up on the Chesepiok, back in '72. Completely unprovoked, by all accounts. And yet one could argue the Spanish sent them merely to subdue the savages and so to better use them." He sipped his ale. "Are we guilty of the same, White? I know not. The Master commands us to go into all the earth and make disciples. Perhaps it is we who take advantage of those who go out for greed, in order that the Word of Christ may be made known to the nations."

John thought about that. "Are we then any better than they, in so doing?"

Chapter Eleven

February 1589

The wind blew as always, but the sun shone warm. Elinor could bear the confines of her house no longer, and leaving Ginny in the care of Mushaniq, under the watchful eye of Timqua, she took her cloak and went for a walk.

Six months and more it had been since the tempest that had all but wrecked their first settlement on Croatoan. As some had set their sights elsewhere—and with heavy heart, Elinor had said farewell to Rose Payne, Elizabeth Viccars, and the young Ann Coleman, who with their husbands packed home, hearth, and babies and removed to Beechland—Ananias and Elinor made the decision to move closer to Manteo's hometown on the northeast corner of Croatoan. There better to learn the ways and tongue of the Croatoan, they reasoned, and to give aid and comfort to each other through the coming winter, since foodstuffs had come into suddenly short supply.

She took the path along the shore, past houses both English and Croatoan, alternately watching where she set her feet and scanning the water. A handful of canoes floated out in the sound, mending weirs or gathering fish from them, and figures moved about on the far shoreline curving around to the left. Wind shushed in the trees behind her and in the tall seagrasses, still brown and grey with winter. The water of the sound lapped and foamed against the narrow strand. Elinor kicked off her shoes and edged into the wet sand, letting the waves wash over her feet and ankles, sucking in a quick breath at the initial shock of cold. Her flesh adjusted quickly, however, and the lingering coolness did much to soothe her fevered thoughts and heart.

Papa would surely return this year—surely. Not this early, of course, but—soon, perhaps? Certainly by the end of summer, within a few weeks of Ginny's second birthday?

Great, gracious Lord—our Father in heaven—hear our prayers. Hear. . . mine. Bring Papa safely back. Let us see each other's face again.

The tears surfaced in a violent wave, and she'd have fallen to her knees were it not for the cold water in which she stood. As it was, she could only stand there, clutching her skirts above the wetness, covering her face with a fold of her cloak.

Voices carried down the path. Ah, nay—she could not face anyone at this moment, much less make conversation as if nothing were amiss. Hopping back onto the dry sand, she snatched up her shoes and fairly fled into the brush. Under cover of the trees and bushes, she wiped the sand from her feet with the lower edge of her cloak hem, then replaced the shoes on her feet before setting off to higher ground.

Only the roar of the ocean itself would serve the tempest raging in her own breast. It was more of a walk than she'd first intended, but she knew well the path that angled first inland before cutting back toward the northern sea-side of the island.

Lingering grains of sand chafed inside her shoes. With a huff, she stopped to remove them again, then hurried on, the path worn smooth enough to accommodate her bare feet. The sounds of town life faded behind her as the roar of the ocean grew louder ahead.

Her passage startled a small herd of deer. With a brief smile at their inquisitive expressions and swift flight, she made her way through the last bit of maritime forest, with oaks wizened and gnarled by the constant sea winds. Those same winds caught her, buffeting, as she emerged onto the dunes, clothed in tall, rough grasses.

She stood for a moment, minding not the pull and chill of the wind for the grand vista of ocean waves, rolling, foaming, pounding against the shore. Then she picked her way across a band of loose, deep sand, scattered with dry bits of shells, clogs of reed and driftwood, and a half-buried dead cormorant. She floundered once, caught her balance, then trudged on until she reached the next strand, packed hard by the waves.

And then, a little closer, close enough for the fierce waves to overspill her feet on their final wash up the shore after breaking, but not close enough to sink where the ocean floor fell away with obvious and alarming depth.

How great and terrible it was. How vast, and how threatening, even on such a day with clear skies and bright sun.

"In the beginning was the sea," she murmured. The old phrase came to her lips without thought, but in the next moment, it dawned upon her—

"If the sea is this vast, this great and terrible—how much greater and more vast and terrible are You, oh God? And how is it that You deign to regard us at all? To dwell with us, as Scripture says You did when You took the form of a man so long ago?" Tears welled and were dried by the wind nearly as soon as they ran from her eyes. "Will You then not hear, and answer? Oh God—" And here at last she did fall to her knees, heedless of the soaking her cloak and skirts took, or of the way her coif blew away and her hair loosened from its moorings, for the weeping that took her once more.

How long she lingered, she had no sense for, but at last remembered she'd a child at home and best return. Still nursing, Ginny was, and Elinor had not yet conceived again. Soon, though, perhaps, gauging by the recent return of her menses.

The thought further wrung her heart. Would she have another child by the time Papa found them? He'd not know Ginny, so big a girl was she. Elinor's eyes stung again as she retraced her steps up the beach and over the dunes. Resolutely she blinked back the tears and kept on.

She'd hardly gotten back within earshot of the town before Georgie came running up to her, panting. "Oh—there ye be. Master Dare seeks you. We'd looked over on the sound-side, where someone last saw you, but you'd vanished. We'd—" He bent over, hands on knees, to catch his breath, then peered at her through a thick forelock of pale hair. "We'd feared the worst, we had."

"Gracious! 'Tisn't like I've never taken walks before." Nevertheless Elinor hurried on. She could hear Ginny's crying long before sighting her house. Inside, Mushaniq dandled the child on her hip, to no avail. Ginny's chubby, tear-streaked face broke into a weak smile at her mother's appearance. Elinor gathered her up. "There, my little one, I am here. Why then so sad? I was gone but a short moment."

Mushaniq chuckled. "She think you leave for always, like all baby do."

Elinor laughed as well, but weakly. How well she understood. First her own mama had perished just a handful of years before, and now—

Oh, Papa.

Merciful God, bring him soon!

It was foolish to worry so for her, when she'd only gone a-walking, but Ananias could not help it. The hollow ache in his chest when he'd returned briefly to their house merely to share a bit of news, only to find Ginny weeping inconsolably and a shrug from Mushaniq on which way Elinor might have gone, would not be denied.

And he could only fling the most inarticulate prayers at the heavens for her safety.

Down the sound-side path he ran, through the old town site and beyond. Of all he met coming or going, none had seen her. He stopped and stared out at the gently rippling waters of the sound. Had she succumbed to some dark thought and walked out into those waves, determined never to return? Or—his gaze eagerly traced the horizon for canoes—had she been stolen, or—worse? He dreaded as nothing else the finding of her lifeless body in the reeds, as they had found Master Howe. That afternoon ever haunted him.

He breathed in deeply, held it, then breathed out. God forbid any of those thoughts.

Another breath or two, and he felt an inner nudge to turn back.

Georgie met him halfway between the old town and the new, face flushed and sweating despite the chill breeze. "Found her! She's a' home now."

"Thank God," he exclaimed, and broke into a run.

Surely enough, she was there, seated and cuddling Ginny as the child nursed for comfort, the closed eyes and dewy cheek and hair testament to how long she'd wept. Elinor looked up with a smile as Ananias stopped, yanking off his hat and leaning in the doorway to regard them both. He huffed, part relief and part exertion. Her hair appeared mussed as from a stiff wind, but as comely as ever in its wildness.

Her smile faded a little. "I was but out for a walk," she murmured in a tone he was sure she meant as soothing. But distress clogged his throat, preventing any reply. He simply crossed the floor and took the hand she stretched out to him. Her blue-grey eyes shone in the dimness. "I would not willingly leave you, if that was your thought."

He shook his head. "Nay. But there are so many out there who wish us ill—" He swallowed and tried again. "I merely had a bit of news. We've been asked to join the Cora settlement. If not now, then later this year, p'raps."

Elinor tucked her chin and simply looked at him.

"I know how much you long for a permanent house. . . ."

"Aye. And I'd hoped this would be it." Gingerly she rose, Ginny having long since fallen full asleep, and carried the child to the cot standing against one wall. After settling Ginny onto the pallet and tucking a cover about her, she returned and slipped her arms about Ananias's waist. "I'd be happy enough here, with the Croatoan. But I'll follow where you lead. You know this."

"Aye." He pulled her close and laid his cheek against her hair, and she snugged in against his chest. "And thank you for that, Goodwife."

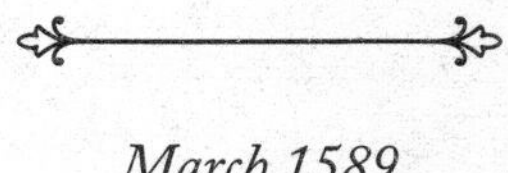

March 1589

"A toast to John White, governor of Virginia," Harriot declared, lifting his tankard, "and to a new assignment by Sir Walter Ralegh for the relief of our planters!"

"Hear, hear!" said Richard Hakluyt the Younger, lifting his cup as well.

John joined them, laughing, suffused with much joy for the recent turn of events. "Aye, and please God we may sail again soon."

The three men had gathered at a public house to celebrate Ralegh's latest writ. In truth, John found the company of the other two among the most comfortable of late. Both not only served as clergymen—and held that position with the utmost sincerity, unlike so many in the Church—but remained among the few who clung openly to hope for the fate of the colony of Virginia.

"I have been intending to ask you," Hakluyt said, after a generous swallow, "for a written account of your voyages. I earnestly desire to add them to my collection of such."

"Indeed?" John buried his nose in his cup. He ought not feel such pleasure at the request, but in this moment perhaps he was not so proof against flattery as he should be.

"Indeed." Hakluyt grinned. "I am very near to publishing my work of all the great voyages and discoveries thus far, and I wish, of course, to include yours among them."

Harriot lifted his cup again. "What exceedingly good hap!"

They were both entirely too merry. Laughing, John shook his head. In truth, it had been long overdue.

"So what say you?"

"I would be most honored."

The public house was noisy enough, but a nearby roar drew them all up. "Ho, what is this? The governor who could not keep his colony!"

All mirth collapsed into an all-too-familiar burn in John's belly.

Simon Ferdinando, the Swine.

The Portuguese navigator swaggered across the common room, weaving between the tables toward John and his party.

John had not moved, but Harriot put out a hand as if to motion him back. "Mind him not. He is but sotted."

Hakluyt likewise stiffened, and the three of them watched Ferdinando's approach.

"A painter should not presume to be governor," the Portuguese bawled, his accent even thicker than usual. "Nor to captain a ship."

" 'Twas you who made sure I failed at that task," John growled.

Harriot's hand slapped against his chest. "Answer him not. Do not deign to even look at him. He is not worthy of it."

Ferdinando's blue gaze, surely enough rheumy with drink, fastened upon John's companion. "Who is not worthy, churchman?"

Hakluyt leaned forward in his chair. "Leave off. We have done nothing to offend you this day."

"Nothing but breathe the air in this place," Ferdinando said.

The keeper of the public house edged closer. "If you break furniture, my good men, you shall not fail to pay."

John pushed slowly back from the table, scooping a pair of coins from his purse. "No need. We were but leaving."

Ferdinando's sneer deepened, but John turned resolutely away and did not look back. Even so, he felt the weight of that one's gaze like a dagger between the shoulders.

Late winter blossomed to spring, and spring to summer. This year's crops grew with less vigor than the year before, it was said by the Croatoan, not only because of last year's storm and flooding but also because of the lack of rain.

And still Papa had not come. The occasional ship sailed past the coast, all Spanish. As the summer built its unrelenting heat and clouds built in the east, and Ginny grew taller and began lisping words both English and Croatoan, the longing within Elinor stretched to unbearable lengths. It helped not that she sometimes sickened in the flesh, and thinking herself with child again, she rejoiced, only to find her menses starting once more.

They marked the end of Ginny's second year, and the wind blew fierce and strong, the clouds racing overhead from the northeast in a now-familiar pattern. And as before, the tide rose, over the strand and marshes, into the town, sending everyone scrambling for high ground. They'd little time to snatch even the most basic of provisions before fleeing inland and uphill.

At the top of the ridge they all stopped, many dropping where they'd halted and curling up in capes or blankets, others watching the coming storm to the east, and some venturing far enough past the ridge to observe the great waves already churning the ocean below. As night fell and rain began to lash at them, Elinor huddled, Ginny folded within her cloak, Ananias trying to shelter them both with his own body.

Not since they'd lain in the bowels of the *Lyon* could she recall such a long, miserable night. Squalls passed over them, the gnarled oaks tossing and bending before the wind, which grew more fearsome by the hour. Rain poured in sheets from the sky, lit now and then by lightning before even that ceased and it was just unrelenting darkness and the howling wind.

When the morning dawned at last, sodden and grey, the rain did not ease. Elinor rose, more to have something to do than aught else, and as she moved about, it was horrifying to catch glimpses of how high the water had come on both the ocean- and sound-sides. They could almost feel the spray from the waves breaking just a short distance away.

For a long stretch, she could only stand and watch those waves—in, out, in, out, coiling to the heavens in a column of spray, then collapsing back into the heaving grey waters, only to gather in a heap again—

In the beginning was the sea. And the earth was without form and void, and the Spirit of God hovered over the face of the waters.

It wasn't quite how the scripture went, of course. But it was how her own heart and mind's eye saw it.

There was blessedly no loss of life, but the crops were a complete loss this time. Houses wrecked, with little to salvage and rebuild. The pinnace and longboats were thankfully repairable, and Captain Stafford and others went immediately to work on those. The rest of them combed the island, collecting what they could of supplies and provisions and personal belongings the wind and tides had scattered about. A breeze blew, cooler now and from the west this time, and a few went crabbing while others paddled out to see if anything could be gotten from the weirs.

Elinor had never been so glad she still had milk to offer Ginny, at least.

"It is not often that the ground becomes so salted we cannot grow crops to feed ourselves," the weroances explained, "but when it does, we remove to the mainland, wait two, perhaps three or four years, and then all is well again. We shall do this. Our people will live on, however we must, and then we shall return to Kurawoten. Montóac will make a way for us, as he has kept us alive until now."

Elinor understood many of the words. *God. Make a way. Keep us alive.*

How could words from the mouth of a savage chieftain so convict her heart and yet give courage at the same time?

Although—not so savage any longer. Two years now they'd lived in this land, most of that time beside this people. Shared their own faith and seen it accepted gladly. Their ways were simpler, aye, and proper raiment was ever a matter for discussion, but were it not for their skill and cunning in making a living from both land and sea, Elinor knew the colony would have perished long since.

In fact—and it was an odd thing, one she'd overheard the weroances and priests arguing over not an hour before—in the storm, one of the casualties was one whole side of their house of the dead, including the Kewás idol that sat watch. The bodies themselves lay intact, and quite the stir it was what to do now. She'd heard mutterings that they should leave the bodies for now and return later for burial. Others suggested they carry out the burials now so there would be no need to come back, not until they were ready to rebuild the town.

Even more odd, it was the house of the dead that lay in her thoughts even more than her own, as she stood looking over the wreckage of it.

Ananias had already promised her a new one. *"And mayhap this time we'll not need to move from it. If it pleases you, that is."*

Ginny ran about with the older children, skirts rucked up, legs smeared with wet sand and mud up to her knees. She and little Henry Harvie kept pace with a handful of Croatoan children, their chatter a happy mix of English and Croatoan words.

If the future of the English city of Ralegh lay intertwined with these people, she would be at peace with such.

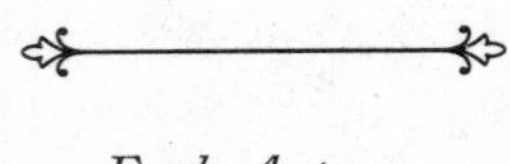

Early Autumn

They crouched in the brush, both Sees Far and Wanchese, watching the white skins as they bustled about the new town site not far from the Pumtico River, building houses, laying out spaces for growing crops.

"So they are back within our reach," Wanchese muttered.

Sees Far grunted his assent.

"I wonder if the Powhatan will be persuaded now to lend us their strength." Wanchese tilted his head, peering through the leaves, his countenance set in hard, brooding lines.

Sees Far flicked him a glance then hunkered more fully to watch. There—that woman at the edge of a new garden space, pausing between strokes of her hoe to call to the children scampering beyond. The sun glinted off of hair nearly the color and brightness of the sea strand of Hatorask and Kurawoten. Something about her seemed familiar—

His heart leaped. It was her—the lone woman in the forest of Roanoac Island. Two years past it had been, and that golden-haired child running about must be the babe she'd carried in her clothing that day. No covering did the woman wear now over her own head, but she'd braided and fastened it up.

"That woman," Wanchese whispered. "I know her."

Sees Far angled him a look. Wanchese only shook his head and motioned for patience, then with stealthy, backward-crawling steps, made his way out of the thicket. Sees Far followed, and at last, running swiftly, they retreated.

For now.

Once they were well away, Sees Far asked, "What mean you, that you know her?"

Wanchese lifted a shoulder, but his dark eyes glittered. "I know several of the men, from previous voyages. But this woman—she was but young when I met her, yet I recall. Her father held a strange but high position among the Inqutish. He is skilled in painting likenesses, and drew many pictures of our people, our ways of living, and of many plants and animals.

You remember, do you not? His work was much admired and wondered at in his land."

Sees Far did remember, and how that man was always sketching away with his strange implements. They had all viewed his work with amazement and admiration.

Wanchese looked away into the forest, appearing lost in his thoughts for a moment. "That woman is his daughter, I believe."

"Do not tell me you are thinking of taking her," Sees Far growled. "You have a woman now, already."

His old friend turned, every line of his form and countenance marked by haughtiness. "And that displeases you?"

Though he strove not to, Sees Far swallowed. "It was my thought that we had wholly given ourselves to making war on these people, until they had perished or were driven from our shores. That we would accept no home, no woman or hearth, until this was accomplished." He hardened his jaw, battling the urge to shift from one foot to another. "But perhaps I was mistaken."

Wanchese leaned in to peer at Sees Far more closely. His eyes crinkled. "Perhaps you wish this woman for yourself?" Then, just as Sees Far took a breath to deny it, he coughed a harsh laugh. "Before you spoke so rashly, little brother, I was about to say, it causes me to wonder if that man also is here, though I have never seen him. But since you have brought it up—" One eyebrow ticked upward.

Sees Far had to unclench his teeth to reply. "I am wholly given to the cause of war. I've no room for the tears of a woman."

"Nor for the softness and comfort of one?"

Toe to toe now, Sees Far held Wanchese's gaze. "Nor for that. Not yet. Perhaps not ever."

Several heartbeats, and Wanchese eased back, eyes widening slightly. "You are more dedicated than I thought. May your blood serve you well, then. We will see this done. But do not blame me, brother, for seeing to the continuance of my line. I have always desired children for which to fight."

"The soil here is different than either Roanoac or Croatoan," Elinor said. "Less sand, more loamy, although still very moist from the river and swamps."

Ananias nodded. He had taken a rest from another task on this crisp fall day to help her with plotting and planting a stand of flax, in the hopes it would flourish during the mild winter of this place. He tossed out the last handful of seed and surveyed their work. " 'Twill be interesting to see how the other crops do, come spring."

"Aye." Elinor blew out a breath. Spring. Once again, 'twas the soonest they could expect Papa to return. But 'twould do no good to brood, nor even to walk the shore watching as she once had. He would come when he would, in God's own good timing.

If only her heart listened to such reason.

"Since the day is yet young and we are finished here, might I take some of the other women out foraging?" She asked because being back on the mainland, they'd a need to be mindful of venturing too far alone.

"Aye, as long as you all stay together." He gave her a brief but pointed look. "The latest batch of brick is due to be pulled from the kiln, so I must needs go tend that anyway."

Elinor took Ginny and went in search of others who might be of a mind for the venture, then returned home briefly to prepare. She tied on a pair of *mahkusun* and a corresponding smaller pair on Ginny, as well as a cap and small cloak, before tossing her own about her shoulders and taking up a basket, a pair of gathering sacks stuffed inside.

By the time she made it to the edge of the town, word had spread and several had gathered to the foraging party—Margery and little Henry, Wenefrid with baby bundled to her, Agnes, Emme, and Margaret, as well as women from both the Croatoan and a neighboring town of the Coree. A couple of the boys were commandeered to go along with them as well, Thomas Humfrey, now a reedy young man of sixteen, and Georgie Howe, still gangly at fourteen but hinting at an impending transition to manhood as well.

Timqua fell into step with her as they set out. "There is a stand of nut trees nearby, and sassafras as well, a short distance from there. Mayhap we should choose which to gather first."

"Hmm." Sassafras was tempting, both for its aromatic sweetness and its goodness for nearly every ill known to man. Yet Elinor was most concerned about having adequate foodstuffs for winter. "Nuts first, methinks."

Timqua nodded and pointed the way.

Life on the main was different from that on the island in so many ways. Elinor missed the sea breezes, the pelicans, gulls, cranes, and sandpipers. Here, and the Croatoan had explained to them that it was mostly for the winter, the waterways burgeoned with ducks and geese, and the treetops often fluttered with bright green parrots. Walking through forests of impossibly tall trees, she could forget where she was and simply lose herself in the wonder of the place. Papa had talked of them moving to the main all along. Was this where they were meant to stay?

The town had grown up with astonishing quickness, once the decision was made to move, the mainland location being nearly due west across the sound from Croatoan. So far the place had afforded nothing but the peace and safety they all prayed for, but at odd times, Elinor felt a chill and the sense of being watched.

And she fretted at times that Papa would not be able to find them. The token carved into the tree and post at Roanoac Island was clear enough, but would he find the corresponding token on Croatoan, the letters CORA carved into a stout oak? Surely he would recall that they'd often referred to the Cwareuuoc as the Coree, and know to look for them in the region of that people.

She blew out a hard breath. It was, as every other thing, a matter she must leave in the hands of God.

"I remember," Menatonon said, speaking slowly, the smoke of his pipe curling from his nose and about his head, "when the Inqutish man, Rafe Lane, took my son captive and held him, not for ransom or to make him family, but in thought to force our people to his will, and to tell him what he wanted to know of us. I see how the Inqutish not only are bending the Kurawoten to their ways but have now come to live on this side of the sound where many of the Sukwoten once dwelt. Seek again the word of the priests. Pray to Montóac for a sign. If it is favorable, I will send with you warriors to make war upon them."

It was the word they had long awaited. Both Wanchese and Sees Far bent their heads in acquiescence and accepted the pipe, each in turn, before filing out into the night. Wanchese stood for a moment, shadows dancing across his features, cast by the fire in the middle of the town. "We will do as you bid."

They went next to the priest, who listened to their request and then, fixing both with a grave look, said that he would pray, offer uppowoc, and await the answer in a dream or vision. But the two of them should wait at hand.

So it was they spent a cold night upon the ground, wrapped in skins, with the town fire as their only comfort. A few others heard their purpose and kept them company. It was, after all, a decision to direct the course of all their lives.

Sees Far spent the wakeful and half-wakeful hours part in prayer, part in contemplation of the strangeness of these people they had set themselves against. Such ridiculous but fine clothing, and he longed to touch and examine it. And what had brought them here? Wanchese believed them hungry only for influence and goods. He insisted that Sees Far could not possibly imagine the heaps of things they hoarded over in England, especially the weroansqua that Wanchese called *queen*.

What Sees Far kept stumbling over in his mind, however, was this belief in a God who had been born a man, and who—dare he even think it?—had both died and been reborn. Their own stories told of deaths and rebirths, and he was well old enough to reflect on the turning of the seasons, to observe the continual dying and rebirth of the earth—but for a human man? No, there was not such a thing. It was madness even to consider. Not when even the priests could not agree whether Creator-God was Montóac, whom they must pray to, or whether he was as the Powhatan held, one called Ahoné, who did not even concern himself with the affairs of men.

Regardless, such madness should be scoured from the earth.

Although, truth be told, he sometimes found himself addressing the Creator-God, despite the priests' insistence that he was too lofty to be interested in the prayers of men. Yet he was always careful to word his plea in such a way that he might not offend.

Answer us, oh Great Creator, whether by your own mouth or lesser gods, or from mother earth. Let us not go forth except by your hand and will.

As the new day dawned, the priest came stumbling out of his house, scrubbing the sleep from his eyes and passing a hand over his close-shaven hair with its distinctive crest. Wanchese was on his feet before Sees Far, impatience written in every line of his taut body. "Yes? What does the spirit realm say?"

The priest's dark eyes shifted from him to Sees Far and back again. "Not all the words are good ones."

Wanchese gestured sharply. "Speak, regardless."

"This people. . .they are great. More like them will come, and fill the land in our place."

A huff. "This we have heard already."

The priest's gaze was severe. "Then listen, and take heed." He blew out a breath. "Despite that, if you bide your time until spring, you will find favor. As the trees put forth their first blossoms, stretch out your hand and bring war to these people." His gaze flicked then to Sees Far. "The woman you seek shall also be in your power."

Part Four

Chapter Twelve

February 1590

Another day, another missive. John wrote, tediously, the same words as the day before and the day before that. Begging, always begging, for Sir Walter Ralegh to intercede for him before the Queen, and to others, requesting favor and resources that John might go to the relief of the colonists in Virginia.

The fresh assignment the year before by Ralegh had fallen to nothing, whether by the machinations of his opponents prevailing upon Her Majesty the Queen to decree another stay on merchant shipping or otherwise, John knew not. All he knew was that yet another year of waiting and frustrations stretched between himself and the people on Virginia's shores with whom he longed to reunite. Of all John's friends, it seemed only Harriot and Hakluyt remained. To all others he had become as a plague, by reason of his frequent pleas for support.

And the accusations of Simon Ferdinando, echoed at divers times by others, still rang through his memory.

As he wrote, his eyes watered, as was their wont all too frequently. Elinor might be a mother again by this time. And little Virginia Thomasyn—why, his granddaughter would be two and then some. For the ten thousandth time, he put his head down, taking the tears into his sleeve and pouring them into most fervent prayer.

Please God—*please, oh holy God*—they were all well and prospering in the New World.

He was so weary of hoping. So weary of trusting and putting on a brave face. *I can bear it no longer, Lord, and yet I know I must. I will bear this sore trial as long as Thou deem it necessary. But please—I beseech Thee—*

He sat up, gave his face one last swipe with his forearm, and finished the note with a signature and flourish. He was folding it and preparing to seal it when his servant scratched at the door and entered. "A missive from Sir Ralegh!"

John pushed aside the newly written letter and reached for the folded and sealed parchment with a trembling hand.

I have obtained license by the Queene's Majestie, who in her grace hath granted dispensation to the venture, it read. *All preparations shall forthwith be made, as we discussed, in laying hold of 3 ships to be bound to me or my assignes, and that those 3 ships should take in, and transport, a convenient number of passengers, with their furnitures and necessaries to be landed in Virginia.*

The missive went on to name the owner of said ships, with directions for John to meet them at a particular time and place.

There was no time to waste. The owner and masters of the ships that Ralegh had engaged were very plain that the time neared for their readiness to put to sea, and they'd brook no delays.

He arranged for the transportation of his baggage and for Ananias's family to meet him at the quay with that one's young son, John. It would be a comfort to have the lad along, and Ananias would no doubt be glad of his presence as well.

Some twenty others were agreed to go along as planters, among them Robert, the strapping son of Thomas Coleman. A similar situation it was to Ananias's, only Robert was older and had begged to come along when his father had gone. Three years ago, John Dare had been too young to be allowed an opinion on the matter.

They were all to meet at a quayside inn, once John had spoken with the ship's owner and masters. The wharf was, as ever, noisy, crowded, and rank. The ship would be worse, especially once they put to sea. John's heart beat in his throat as he paid the dray driver, shouldered a satchel on each side, and beckoned to the hand carrying his chest to bring it to the inn. He would check in and stay the day or two until time to board and the ships weighed anchor.

The public room was nearly as busy as the quay, with less light and more fragrant smells. Over by the fire stood Master Dare with little John at his side. John let a smile curve his mouth. The irony, when two of the ships they were to sail with were named *Little John* and *John Evangelist*.

The boy caught sight of him and ran to his side with a bounce. John caught him in a quick embrace. "Ah, lad! So tall you've grown. Your papa will hardly know you!"

John Dare grinned, his blue eyes shining beneath a mop of pale hair, and so like his father it brought a pang to White's breast. *Soon, gracious God?*

His grandfather approached more slowly, a hand outstretched to greet White. "I will seek out the owner and shipmasters before aught else," John said, once the pleasantries had been exchanged.

"I would be pleased to accompany you," Master Dare said. "If you would not mind John tagging along? Others are here waiting but most are out at the moment."

White beamed at the boy. "His presence would be no trouble at all. Allow me to secure a room and receive refreshment; then we shall go forthwith."

He lingered barely long enough to take a bit of food and drink, impatient as he was to see to the next stage of this journey. At last—at long last he would be on his way back to Virginia.

Master Dare and little John in tow, he navigated the wharf with an ease born of several visits here, but still he had to inquire as to the offices of the ships' owner.

Upon his third try, he'd begun to feel anxious and out of sorts, but at last he spied the fine vessel with HOPEWELL freshly painted across the hull. Approaching a man in serviceable sea clothing only slightly better than those trucking up and down the gangway, he called out a greeting. "I seek the owner or master of this ship. Might you be able to tell me where I could find either?"

"You'd be able to find the owner in his office in yon warehouse, but I am Cooke, the *Hopewell*'s captain," he said gruffly.

"I am John White, governor of Virginia. I was told you and two other ships would be taken under bond of Sir Walter Ralegh, and well able to bear both myself and more colonists to that land."

As John spoke, the captain's brow knitted, and a slow wag of his head became a sharp shake. "We've received no such orders. Indeed, we're full up with men and provisions of our own, preparing to go ply our trade on the Spanish for the next few months."

Cold trickled down John's back as if he'd caught a sudden rivulet from an icy rain. Had Ralegh not assured him to the contrary?

"Might I speak with the owner?"

Cooke gestured for him to go ahead, and John hurried away, with a murmured apology to old Master Dare and his charge.

The owner greeted White with a firm lip. "There is no agreement with Ralegh. We have our voyages set and no plan to alter them. Nor have we room for you or your colonists, much less their furnitures."

White's throat tightened. "But Ralegh assured me such an agreement had been made—would be made."

The owner wagged his head with more persistence than the *Hopewell*'s master. "Nay. It has not."

No explanation, no brooking the possibility of negotiating otherwise. "When do they sail?" White asked.

"Two days hence."

No time, then, to return and address his complaint to Sir Walter Ralegh. "Might I myself gain passage, at least? Without the colonists and their baggage."

The owner's gaze remained flat and cold. "You may go apply yourself to the shipmasters and see if one of them has a corner you might occupy. But 'twould be only yourself and one chest, no more."

What followed in the next hour and more was akin to a nightmare, wherein John found himself pleading repeatedly with ship's captains who met his request with increasing crossness. At some point he sent Master Dare and little John back to the inn, and finally in desperation his last resort was to apply himself once more to the master of the *Hopewell*.

"Even if you regard the plight of our planters across the ocean so smally," he found himself near to babbling, "then have pity on me as governor of a neglected colony, and the grandfather of a child I've not laid eyes on in three years. My only daughter is there, and her husband. I must go—must know what became of them, and the hundred and more other souls which went besides. And 'tisn't as if you don't pass by there on your way back to England."

He was nearly weeping now. He did not care how much he abased himself—the need to be on one of those ships was all consuming.

The shipmaster heaved a great sigh, lifting his cap to rake a hand across his oily iron-grey locks. He squinted at the *Hopewell*, then swung his gaze back to White. "I suppose we could fit in one stop. And you'd have to agree to be of help, not get in the crew's way."

White nearly collapsed with relief.

With weary steps he returned to the inn, where he met the assemblage of his supposed colonists and delivered to them the sad news that they would not be sailing on the morrow, nor at any time very soon. To their downcast and, in a few cases, even angered visages, he could find no joy in the knowledge that he himself would yet be suffered to go.

There would be time enough for joy later, once he held Elinor and her sweet infant in his arms again.

The first blossoms were emerging. Sees Far had spent the winter anxiously waiting, and it was time.

Their contingent was ready. They would slip through the forest and wetlands and stage a mock attack upon the town the Inqutish had built in the middle of the thick forest west of Dasemonguepeuk, then swiftly make their way southward to where the other town had been built near the river of Pumtico. One of their party would pretend to ask for aid for the other town, and once the men had sent help—because they could not ignore the distress of their brothers—Wanchese would lead the attack on the town.

They were all on edge, strung tight as bowstrings. The night before, after painting faces and bodies in solemn preparation for war, they gathered in the dancing circle as the sun went down. Swaying slightly, waiting. Wanchese took up a gourd filled with dried beans and gave it a swirling shake that made the instrument sound like a low hiss, then a quick rattle. His voice followed, resonant and menacing, in words that called upon the spirits to aid them in their journey, to give strength to their bodies, to grant them victory over their enemies.

Sees Far took up the chant, and the rest followed, moving to the rhythm of the song, slow and deliberate at first but then with a driving beat, faster and faster until each of them dropped to sleep where they were. Even then, Wanchese stayed on his feet, humming, then crooning, his arms lifted to the sky as he turned slow circles. Sees Far fell asleep with the image of his friend's arms silhouetted against the stars.

They rose the next morning before dawn, gathered weapons and provisions, and set off into the swirling mist of the forest.

The brickwork was going well. They'd found good clay—how glad Ananias was to not have to carry it back across the water to the islands—and he'd set up a kiln near the blacksmith's forge. He and the other Assistants agreed that their town was coming together quite nicely, all things considered.

The women were gone out foraging. Even through the fall and winter, Ananias wasn't completely at ease with them doing so—the main afforded less protection than Croatoan Island had—but they'd no choice. Things had been quiet enough in the months since they'd removed from the island. Meat had been plentiful. They talked still of returning to the old town site at Roanoac to fetch at least the lead and iron to continue making shot for their muskets, but word had come from neighboring peoples that places abounded inland, as the ground grew rockier, where they might mine what they needed. Some of the Welshmen, experts in mining and smelting, were preparing an expedition for this very reason.

The town at Beechland sent word every week or two on their welfare.

A runner came toward them, from the river-side edge of the town. Ananias and the others set down their tools as the man approached—one of the savage peoples, with hair both cropped and tied back, his bare, patterned chest gleaming above deerskin kilt. Roger Prat greeted him in the Croatoan tongue.

He drew to a halt, head down for a moment, then straightened. "English—at Beechland—call for help. Attack."

A cry went round the group. Some reached for weapons, but Manteo and Chris Cooper both said, "Nay! We must talk."

Someone gave the call to fetch the women back from their foraging, and the rest of the townspeople were summoned to a meeting at the native longhouse they used for such purpose.

Speedily it was decided they would send a contingent. Manteo would lead about twenty men—a third of those who had removed from Croatoan to near the Cwareuuoc—and the rest would stay behind, on watch.

Manteo spoke first in his own tongue for the benefit of the Croatoan among them, then in English. "Please God we return in a few days. But it may be that we all must needs go to war, to make Dasemonguepeuk and Beechland secure at last."

Summer and fall foraging meant nuts and fruits at their sweetest, but Elinor loved the spring for the fresh reds and greens at the tips of the trees. She still missed the surge of the ocean and the sand beneath her feet, but oh, the trees!

If I take the wings of the dawn and dwell in the uttermost parts of the sea. . .

The familiar line from the Psalms flitted through her thoughts, and a smile curved her lips. The uttermost parts of the sea had led them, indeed, to Roanoac and Croatoan, and now to Cora Banks. The winter had been a pleasant one, mild and sweet, but oh, it was delightful to see color on the branches and flowers blooming on the forest floor.

The men were busy again building new houses, with Ananias

overseeing the brickmaking and other details. The flax had grown moderately well, and William Nicholes, the clothworker, gathered a handful of helpers to assist with harvesting and processing. Elinor looked forward to having fresh linen—her shifts and kirtles had become a bit threadbare, as were Ananias's garments. And if Papa brought sheep when he came, then they'd have wool as well.

She quickly turned aside that thought, but could not still the flutter of longing in her breast. It was spring. Only a few more months, and they'd hope of seeing another ship come. An English ship, and not Spanish.

The children ran ahead, loosely watched by a few older girls. Elinor wandered behind, seeking dandelion and other greens. They needed the tonic, despite the mild winter. Even so, the outing was more a stroll and less actual foraging, but all the women agreed they'd rather be out on such a lovely day than cooped up in the town.

A sound carried through the trees, and Elinor stopped, cocking her head to listen. A trumpet—their prearranged signal of distress, calling all to return.

It was the first time she could recall such a thing, at least while she herself was out.

Timqua straightened from examining a clump of greenery, her gaze meeting Elinor's. "We should go back?"

Elinor nodded and gathered up her skirts, calling for the children, who were nearly out of sight among the trees. Timqua did likewise, and only with the sorest reluctance did the group of them straggle out of the forest. As the Croatoan woman scolded them in her own tongue, Elinor bit back a smile at the wonder of being able to understand much of what was said.

They returned to the town to find the men in an uproar, making preparations for a party to go out to the aid of Beechland after the arrival of a native man requesting such. Elinor's heart sank. It was the first real trouble they'd encountered after leaving Croatoan last summer, and an unease settled low in her belly at the prospect of sending Ananias off—indeed, of any of the men leaving.

Did she speak, however, and make the task more difficult? The other women had the unknown man crouched by the fire of the longhouse, nursing a cup of the spiced tea they had learned to make from the Croatoan, and a handful of the Assistants sat by, questioning him. They were currently in the midst of discussing whether to wait the night or leave right away. The native man urged haste, but all were understandably hesitant. They still knew not the wild forests well enough to venture forth at night, especially in absence of a moon, and to Elinor's relief, their will prevailed in the matter.

Besides, Ananias argued, they'd work in progress that he simply could not abandon in the moment. Manteo frowned and shook his head.

They were no more at ease about this than she was.

Come morning, the men chosen to go prepared to set out. Elinor clung to Ananias, Ginny between them, wriggling to be let down. With a huff, Elinor set her on her feet and embraced him one more time. "Godspeed," she murmured. "Our love goes with you as well."

He kissed her once, twice, lingeringly. "Be safe. Do not stray far." Then with a crooked smile, he stepped away.

Elinor blinked back tears and, by habit, turned to look for Ginny, already bouncing about with little Henry Harvie and the others. When she again lifted her gaze, Ananias and the rest of the company were nearly out of sight through the trees, on their way to the riverbank where the longboats and pinnace lay. They judged it swifter to go by water, around land, and approach from the north, than to try to go overland. But how lonely the town already seemed without them.

The other men wandered away, talking in twos or threes as they planned the day's work. The women all stood and looked at each other. Margery Harvie, her features creased in worry, was again big with child, and Elinor shared her anxiousness that the babe would come before Dyonis's return. Wenefrid, clasping her babe, a girl already taking her first steps, looked downcast as well. Timqua glanced uncertainly from one to another, also torn by helping mind the children dashing about. And Jane Mannering, newly wed to Captain Stafford, appeared as lost as any of them.

"They have urged us to caution," Jane said, "but surely we must continue with our customary work."

Elinor and the others all agreed. The gardens and fields would not keep themselves.

Even so, when she ventured out a little while later to look at the progress of her various herbs and flowers—the iris leaves had grown tall and put forth stalks of buds already, and the mint flourished regardless of where she'd planted it—her sense of unease deepened, and she paused often to look around. Despite the fortlike palisade they'd built around the town on Roanoke Island, they'd not yet completed the task here. There were some who questioned whether they even needed one, but such were dismissed as foolish and naïve. The town had enemies, and even if those enemies had not yet struck here, it was bound to happen—as recent news from Beechland proved.

Still, life must go on, mouths must be fed, and surely there was no reason for fear on this particular day. Not here.

As the men continued the work in the town, with the most pressing talk being that of finishing the palisade, Elinor took Ginny and joined the other women preparing the ground for their first planting of corn, squash, and beans. One field already lay green with wheat, and Elinor's mouth watered at the thought of real bread, come a few months.

The children ran and chased with their usual abandon. Over at the side, Georgie Howe and John Sampson helped a pair of the Croatoan boys—oh, she could hardly call them such anymore, so tall had they suddenly grown—put up a three-sided booth on a platform for the purpose of guarding the fields after the seed was sown. Among the people of this land, this task was the work of the boys who had not yet passed into manhood. Timqua and the other women had told them of the ceremony the young men must endure to be accepted as fully grown members of their society, which included being sent out into the forest for days or even weeks, alone, to pray and search their own hearts for what sort of men they would be. Elinor and the other Englishwomen had shuddered at the harshness of it—but mostly at the thought that some of the boys did not even survive the ordeal.

With the first flowers just now emerging, it was not quite time to plant, and the Croatoan did not plow as the English did, since the ground was worked by hand, so for now they labored at clearing the area of fallen limbs and uprooting small bushes. Later would come the work of making each hill, where four seeds of the corn would be planted, and the squash and the beans sown around them. The Three Sisters, the Croatoan called the crops. The corn grew tall enough to support the beans, which climbed up the stalk as both grew, and the wide leaves of the squash kept the ground between cool and moist.

The thought of fresh produce made Elinor's mouth water. Apparently she had not broken her fast adequately enough that morning—but then she recalled what the morning had brought, and her appetite fled once again.

They'd read from scripture and prayed long over the men before they'd departed, but Elinor found her pleas winging heavenward time and again, regardless.

Did the Almighty ever tire of their prayers? Of their sundry troubles and complaints? For all that she adored little Ginny, the child's energy and needs wore upon her betimes.

The everlasting and almighty God does not sleep, neither grows weary. . . . Cast all your care upon Him, for He careth for you.

The words washed over her heart, soothing, calming. Whatever else happened—

A cry broke the sweetness of the morning. For a moment, Elinor thought it just the children squabbling—they were often a noisy, unruly lot—but something about the pitch, and its urgency, brought her straight upright from the task of digging out a large weed.

Across the clearing, through the woods, came a group of painted warriors brandishing weapons. Timqua and the others were already running, snatching children as they went, headed not for the town but the river. Elinor hesitated, torn between dropping her hoe and doing the same or lifting it and attempting—

Her hesitation cost her. One warrior angled directly toward her, seized the handle of the hoe, and wrenched it from her grasp. He cast the implement aside and gripped her upper arm, tilting his head. "*Pyas*," he said—*come*—and yanked her toward the trees.

Any comfort in prayer, any peace, dissolved now into an unrelenting litany. *God—oh God—please help us!*

She fought, but he was impossibly strong—and tall—and her

mahkusun gave her no purchase against the ground. Wildly she glanced about—where was Ginny? There, on the other side of the field plot, Georgie had plucked her into his arms and was backing in the direction the other women had gone, but with wide eyes fixed on Elinor.

"Go!" she cried. "Go, go, go! Protect her!"

Whether he heard her actual words or nay, he turned and fled, clutching her now-crying daughter to his chest.

Sees Far knew the woman's scream was directed at the boy, and saw his hesitation—was that her child? It was the woman he wanted, though, so he let the boy go.

Wanchese and the others had already run past him, toward the town. Sees Far let them go as well. His part of this venture had been fulfilled already—and far more quickly than he dreamed possible.

"The woman you seek will also be in your power."

He breathed a prayer of thankfulness and dragged her farther into the forest. At last he stopped and, forcing her to her knees, pulled a hide thong from his waistband. As he wrapped one end around her wrist, she grimaced but did not cry out, then surprised him by peering up into his eyes and speaking softly. He could not understand the words, but she was not out of her senses with fear, either.

Which impressed and pleased him in ways he did not want to contemplate.

She repeated the words, more urgently, added others to them. He seized her other wrist, and when with another grimace and a grunt she resisted him, he exerted his strength to bring her arm upward. Once again her eyes flew to his and held steady as he caught a loop of the thong around the other wrist and thus bound her hands before her.

He leaned down until their faces were very close. "Do not fight. It will go easier for you."

Uncertainty flickered in her gaze. How much did she understand, after—how long was it now? At least two years of living with the Kurawoten. She remained quiet this time. That was a help.

Before long, the other men came running back, most with captives in tow, mostly men but with a few women and children as well. Wanchese brought up the rear, glancing back, then with a word bid them all to make haste through the forest again.

Sees Far tugged the woman to her feet and nudged her ahead of him. With only the slightest hesitation, she turned and followed the others.

Screaming and crying and flinging herself about like an overwrought child would serve her nothing. But it was what she longed to do, with every fiber of her being.

And yet an unearthly calm held her, though her heart pounded in her breast and breaths came short and shallow. Her mind refused to wrap itself around the words he spoke—were they of the same tongue as the Croatoan, or was she simply unfamiliar with the particular meanings and the cadence?

Hurrying along in front of the warrior, she stumbled over a root and went down, painfully catching herself with her bound arms. A rough grip hauled her upward, and a hissed word doubtlessly admonished her to keep going. At last her thoughts broke free enough to send forth the simplest of prayers: *Oh God, help us!*

Pleas followed then for Ginny, for Georgie, for the other women. How many had the savages stolen? She'd no opportunity to look around yet and see, although the backs of several men from the town were visible through the trees ahead, herded as she was by their assailants—but running faster than she was able.

Her blood ran suddenly cold, and she nearly faltered again. How many had they left behind, slain?

God. . .oh God. . .

Was He listening? Could He even hear her?

Who is man, that thou art mindful of him?

For the first time, tears threatened.

Chapter Thirteen

Winds were favorable, and in less than a day they'd sailed round past Dasemonguepeuk and Roanoac, into the northern sound, and down the wide-mouthed river to the south, which provided the quickest path to Beechland. Leaving but a pair of men to keep the pinnace, they let down the ship's boat, intending to row farther up into a creek, until they could go no farther but on foot.

As they were in the process of climbing down into the boat, a splash came from the other side. "Man overboard!" the cry rang out.

Still on deck, Ananias ran to the opposite rail. Several lengths out from the pinnace, a cropped and crested head emerged, then lean arms working in strong, fast strokes. Swimming for the opposite bank.

"Hie there!"

"What in the name of all that's holy. . . ?"

"We've been cozened," Chris Cooper said, then swore.

Ananias clouted his shoulder but added, "Aye, 'twould appear he was no friend at all. 'Tis in question now whether Beechland was ever in peril, or if we were merely drawn out—"

He fell silent as the horror of the realization closed about him—indeed, about them all.

One man raised an arquebus and aimed at the fleeing savage. Before Ananias could stop him, he fired, then prepared another shot with swift movements. Another man likewise fired, but to no avail. The savage scrambled ashore then dived into the underbrush and scurried away. By the time the next shot was readied, he was long out of range.

"What do we now?"

Frozen in place, they stared at each other.

"We should make haste unto Beechland and be sure they've no need of our aid," Cooper said. "Then away home to Cora Banks."

Looking about to make sure no nasty surprises awaited them on either side of the river, they finished launching and loading the boat and rowed on as quickly as they could.

Scarce an hour, by boat and by foot, and they arrived at the town. Cooper called out a greeting, and Master Payne and others strode out to meet them. Inquiries revealed that there had been but the mildest attack—"But we strongly withstood them, and they soon fled," Payne said. "Nothing since. Why do you ask?"

Once again Ananias and the other men exchanged glances. "We must for home, and no delay," he said.

Wanchese called for a halt. Nearly all their captives dropped to the forest floor, exhausted and soaked by trudging along the bottom of a stream bed. Only one stayed upright, a lean man in whose eyes a fire yet burned, but even he found a large stone upon which to sit while he remained watchful.

Skico, the weroance's son who had once been a captive of the Inqutish on Roanoac, strode over to Wanchese. "They will pursue us, and they will not rest until they have recovered their people."

Wanchese smiled. "Let them try."

The expression chilled Sees Far, even as pride filled him that they had accomplished this.

Wanchese looked over at Sees Far then, and his smile widened. "I see you have found your preferred spoils."

"I have, well and truly."

Elinor could go no farther. After trudging through a stream bed for a good, long stretch, then being herded uphill and forced again to a run, when one of the savages called for a halt, she fell gratefully into the leaves, nearly facedown.

She faded in and out of sleep, in her weariness almost—not quite—making sense of the words they spoke. A heaviness pressed upon her, crushing until she could scarce breathe—

Save me, oh Lord! I am Thine!

The weight eased, and the forest air flowed into her lungs again, sweet and cool.

She lifted her head and looked around. Of the men, she could see Roger Prat, John Tydway, and two whose names escaped her in the moment—Martyn Sutton and John Bright? There were also three of the stripling boys—Robert Ellis, Thomas Humfrey, and William Wythers. And young Emme Merrimoth, with Elizabeth Glane.

A whimper escaped her, and she put her head back down. *God—oh God in heaven, hear and help us!*

A nudge to her shoulder drew her up again. The savage who had taken her offered a waterskin. "Drink."

She understood well enough, and would not refuse. In fact, she drank the skin nearly dry, and when she handed it back, he quirked a smile before slinging it across his body.

So he found amusement in that, did he? "What is your name?" she asked in Croatoan, but although his gaze flickered, he did not reply, only continued to watch her.

Another warrior, as tall as her captor, called out, "Get up! Keep moving."

She mostly understood that as well, but his next statement, by tone equally a command yet spoken more quietly, was lost to her. Though every nerve and muscle protested, she hauled herself to her feet and glanced about at the others, doing similarly. Emme and Elizabeth met her eyes across the space between them, stark fear written in the faces that were pale beneath the smudges of dirt. The men and boys were shoved into motion.

"We must keep moving," Wanchese said, "until we've returned to Okisco's town."

The woman had already risen, albeit slowly, and trudged away in the direction pointed out to her. Weariness stooped her shoulders and those of the other captives, but they all still walked on their own. Good. They needed strength if they hoped to survive.

Through the rest of the day, and a little into the night, they covered much ground before stopping to make a small fire. Most of the captives were asleep nearly as soon as they touched earth, but a few remained awake long enough to accept water and shreds of meat. The woman he'd taken did not stir when he nudged her.

Wanchese and the others debated whether the Inqutish would pursue right away, and if they did, whether they'd continue after nightfall. "They do not know our country," Skico said.

"But Manteo will remember." Wanchese grimaced. "That one—did anyone see him when we struck the town?"

"Is he even recognizable now as anything but an Inqutish?" A chuckle followed that remark.

"What a traitor he is to our people," Wanchese muttered. His gaze swept across the forms of their captives, all now slumbering or appearing to. "I'd as quickly spill the blood of these into the ground they seek to defile, but Okisco deserves to have a say in their fate. And I wish to see them answer for the wrongs of their people."

Sees Far was not of those chosen for the first watch, and leaving the fire now, he made his way to the woman's side. She lay curled, bound hands tucked under her head, with the hood of her cape pulled up over her hair. Would Okisco permit Sees Far to keep her? He'd no interest in her being the instead-of for his slain family and her who would have been his wife, but as a man without hearth and woman, was he justified in not releasing her to be used elsewhere, if Okisco judged her worthy of such? Or would she become a sacrifice, as they sometimes did? Doubtless the gods would be pleased with such a brave offering.

A part of him did not want her to become a sacrifice. But that was not his decision to make.

They sailed the entire night under a half moon and made it back to Cora Banks just before sunrise. The town was already stirring, a fire visible from what was likely the commons and men on guard outside the circle of houses.

"Ho, the town!" Cooper called out as they made their approach.

"Ah, the Lord be thanked!" Two ran out to greet them, William Berde and John Farre. "Are you all here and safe?"

"Aye, we are all well, but our savage friend turned out to be no friend at all, and abandoned us as soon as we reached the mouth of the last creek."

"No surprise." Berde shouldered his musket and scratched his bearded jaw. "You'd scarce been gone an hour before we came under attack."

The sourness of his gut had been worsening by the mile, but at this, he felt he'd been struck by a hard fist. "How badly did we fare?"

The two men exchanged a look. "Well," Farr said, "if you count lives lost, then not so badly. They set a house or two on fire, and Griffen Jones is wounded, along with a few others. But"—he also took to rubbing his jaw—"it seemed they were after captives. And several were taken." His gaze flicked away, then back. "Ananias. Wee Virginia is safe, but. . .they took Elinor."

The ground beneath him tipped, and the morning went black. *God—oh gracious God—*

Taken—into the vastness of this wilderness—

Hands were gripping his shoulders, shaking him. "Ananias—man, get ahold of yourself."

He sucked in a breath and opened his eyes, but still could scarce see the faces around him. Then Manteo's visage swam into view, so close he could see every line of the other man's face, the sternness etching his expression, and he was the one laying hold of Ananias's shoulders. "Taken is better than slain. Far better. Still hope this way. But you must not be foolish."

"Foolish?" he repeated. " 'Tis my wife, Manteo—stolen by savages."

Did the man's face harden even further for a moment, before smoothing? "I understand. But we all go together, or not at all. You will die otherwise."

He nodded once. "Where—where is Ginny?"

"Timqua kept her last night."

They continued on to the town, where their presence brought all who were awake out into the common. Ananias accepted the others' sympathy and condolences with but token thanks, pushing through the crowd until he reached the modest dwelling of posts and reeds that belonged to Timqua and her husband and family. The woman had risen already and beckoned him inside to where his daughter lay sleeping under a cover of skins, alongside Mushaniq. Heedless of waking her, he bent and scooped her into his arms, and as she roused enough to cry "Papa!" and fling her tiny arms about his neck, he buried his face against her downy hair and wept.

Ginny had not suckled very frequently of late, but it was often enough that after a day and night, Elinor's breasts ached with a fullness she had not suffered since her milk first came in after childbirth. Of course, all else ached as well, so what difference did it make? Still, as she trudged through the forest—and at least they were not made to run, as yesterday—she needed to keep her forearms pressed against herself, to ease the hurt.

Deeper was the hurt of her heart, in being snatched from husband and child and home. Yet she took a measure of comfort in their not being among her fellow captives. They could have been slain, true, but her thoughts clung stubbornly to hope. The memory lingered of Georgie's face as she cried out to him, even as the same prayer rippled through her on his behalf, and for Ginny and Ananias. Did Ginny weep in her absence? Was Ananias safe, after having gone to the aid of Beechland?

Oh, how she longed to be in her own house, child in arms and bedding down with her own husband and not—not being driven along like sheep or kine, with her bed the forest floor.

Furthermore, she and the others were given no opportunity to speak to each other, aside from a hurried whisper here and there. Two of the men this morning had attempted to break free, and the resulting scuffle left both with bloodied faces and only the Lord knew how many wounds, and yet they were made to march on, ahead of their captors. Those curious swords of polished wood were apparently far more effective than they appeared.

"Manteo! How long must we keep this pace?"

The Croatoan—once merely advisor, now lord in his own right, and war leader in the moment—favored Chris Cooper with an impassive look, even while they maintained the run through the forest. "Until night, when we can no longer see the signs of their passing. They will have gained an entire day on us. It is difficult enough tracking them, but we must be swift where the trail is clear."

It was almost more words than he ever spoke at once, except in his own tongue.

"Aye, and we ain't no bleedin' savages," came a mutter, too far behind Ananias to discern the identity of the speaker. He gritted his teeth and kept running, despite the sweat running down his face and beneath his armor.

He too was weary. He too felt tested far beyond what he could bear. 'Twas not merely this one event, but all the decisions, small and great, leading up to it. He had never for a moment questioned their choice to come sailing across the sea, until now. As he had averred to Elinor many a time, London was too crowded and filthy, and opportunities for making a good living too scarce. Here in this new-found land they would live or die. And if the Lord willed, the dying would come much later.

But now—in the face of losing Elinor—the one who by her very sweetness made the living all worthwhile—

He would not think of it. Could not. Megs had succumbed to fever not long after John's birth, though she was a hardy enough maid when first they'd met. Elinor more than matched her strength and courage—indeed, she'd become the very sun and moon to him. 'Twas more than unfair to have her fallen into savage hands.

And there was a difference between those who had become as brothers—not a few of the Croatoan ran with them—and the ones who still sought to dismay them at every hand.

They'd all agreed to set out straightaway. Most had already snatched a few hours' asleep aboard the pinnace, on the way back, and none would be able to rest now. They would sleep at full dark, of course, in turns, but until they could make some effort at recovering the ones taken—

He thought of little Ginny's tears as once again he'd left her in Timqua's care. Her tender, slight warmth against him—this child born of Elinor and himself, mayhap all that was left of her mother's sweetness.

God forbid such a thing, just yet.

I beseech Thee, oh Lord God. Let it not be! Protect Elinor and give her strength.

Near sunset the second day, they came to a stream where canoes were waiting, and Elinor and the others were put inside. Such relief it was, she could only curl up and let herself drowse. How long they paddled, she could not say, except that the stream became a river that grew ever wider, and at last they drew up on a shore where a native town stood, sleepy in the mist coming off the water. There they were nudged out of the boats and through the reeds toward the cluster of longhouses. Elinor and the other women were led one direction, the men and boys in another.

At least they would sleep indoors tonight. A greying older woman beckoned them into a longhouse, then pointed at the floor near the hearth. "*Nupes*," she said. *Sleep.*

Elinor did not need to be told twice. She was drifting nearly as soon as her body went prone.

"What is to become of us?" came Emme's whisper through the dimness.

"We shall doubtless see tomorrow," Elinor murmured through a yawn.

"How can you be so calm?"

"Weariness. And prayer." She yawned again. "Mostly weariness."

And then it was morning, and daylight filtered into the longhouse. Emme and Elizabeth were still sleeping. Elinor sat up slowly. Behind her a pot of something fragrant seethed in the middle of the fire. The old woman was nowhere in sight, but another was working at the far end of the longhouse. She turned, saw Elinor stirring, and approached with a hesitant smile. Elinor offered one in response.

The woman filled an earthenware dish and handed it to Elinor. With a word of thanks, Elinor ate, trying to take slow bites and not bolt it all. Meanwhile, her unknown keeper nudged the other two women awake and, filling two more bowls, fed them as well. After they ate, they were led outside and shown where they might relieve themselves and then to wash, where a sandy shoal edged the curve of the river. Mist still cloaked the surface of the water, and the not-too-distant calls of geese and ducks carried over the murmur of town life behind them. Elinor contemplated the gentle ripple of the current. 'Twould be too difficult to wade with hands still bound, even were the water shallow enough she'd need not swim. With a little sigh, she lifted her skirts as best as she could and crouched in the sandy mud.

The water lapped around her hands, cool and soothing. Heedless of the binding thong—it had already gotten wet many times—she plunged her arms in up to the elbow. Blessed relief of the burning around her wrists, at least for a few moments.

Elinor splashed water on her face, only to be nearly tipped off balance by a nudge to her shoulder. The woman who'd fed them pointed at the deeper water. "Go," she said, and gestured with more emphasis when Elinor hesitated.

With a huff, she rose, and again keeping her skirts raised in the front, she waded in, sucking in a breath between clenched teeth at the chill of the water. Even the sound on Croatoan was not this cold.

Behind her, Emme protested, offering an argument in Croatoan. The woman only laughed and urged her again.

Elinor went in up to her thighs, then submerged herself to her shoulders. "Come, Emme, 'tisn't so—oh, brr!"

They all laughed then, such incongruency in the situation. Elinor tipped back her head and wet her hair, running fingers along her scalp, smoothing the fraying braid that she could not mend until her hands were loosed, but the current tugged at her skirt, making it difficult to stay upright. In a moment, her feet were swept out from underneath her, and with a yelp, she went under.

Elinor thrashed, trying to get her bearings and find her footing once more, when a strong grip plucked her by the hair and clothing and hauled her upright. With a gasp, she planted her feet, water pouring from her, and batted her hair aside.

It was none other than her captor who drew her from the current and even now held her steady. Mingled annoyance and concern creased the strong features, his dark eyes flashing. He snarled a word and pushed her toward the shore.

Emme was sloshing back to dry ground as well, and Elizabeth had completely refused to go further than knee deep. The woman who had fed them was still laughing and bantering with Elinor's captor, although too fast for her to catch more than the occasional word. His expression remained stern, and his replies to her short and, to Elinor's ear, tense.

She'd no time to think upon the curiousness of it, however, because no sooner had she stepped back onto dry ground than he tugged her away with a sharp, "Come."

He beckoned to Emme and Elizabeth, then back through the town he led her, all the women trailing behind, including the older and younger ones who had tended them. The kirtle dragged at her shoulders with the weight of dripping skirts, and she shivered with the cool wetness. At the common fire, however, her captor brought her to a halt close enough to the flames to be well warmed. "Stay," he said with a nod.

Emme and Elizabeth sidled up to the blaze as well, slightly less sodden than she. Immediately the native women gathered closer, fingering their sleeves and skirts, then poking at their bodices as if to reassure themselves that they were indeed women. Elinor could not suppress a giggle—it had been a while since their presence had stirred such curiosity.

Across the fire, the men and boys were being herded along under guard, likewise surrounded by a gawking crowd.

Just when Elinor was sure they'd all actually be pushed into the fire, even if not by intention, a shout went up, and the press cleared to reveal an older man seating himself on a woven mat—clearly a weroance by the abundance of strands of copper beads and pearls adorning his neck and the number of men attending him.

A hush fell over the crowd, and the man spoke. Elinor thought she understood the gist of it at least, that she and her fellow captives were being discussed, which was confirmed when her captor drew her closer.

"Let me see them, these Inqutish," Okisco said, leaning forward.

Sees Far brought the woman he had taken, and she and her two companions reluctantly left the fire. He could not blame her, soaked as she was from head to toe, in such heavy garments. The men and boys likewise were prodded forward. The one with silver threading his dark beard started to speak, was cuffed by Wanchese, then turned, shoulders squared as if he would challenge Wanchese.

"Cease!" Okisco waved a hand, and Wanchese subsided. Okisco beckoned the Englishman closer. "What is your name?"

"Roger Prat. I speak for my people. Why have we been taken? We wish only peace with the people of this land."

A rude chuckle went around the gathered crowd.

"Peace," Okisco said, "when you take our sons hostage and attack our people at your slightest whim?"

The man's pale skin reddened. "Those were foul acts carried out by other men before us. We do not approve of them."

Okisco's face remained impassive. "Nevertheless, your people have declared themselves to be at war with us. It is our right to take captives and use them as we wish."

The man sputtered, but Okisco turned toward the others, examining them all. "They appear strong, for all their strange clothing."

"We should take them upriver and trade them to those who dig the wassador at Ritanoe."

"A worthy thought," Okisco said, and bent his regard upon the women. "Bring the crenepos closer. We should send one as a gift to the weroance of the Powhatan."

Sees Far nudged the woman closer. Should he speak? But no need—

Wanchese made a sound. "Sees Far will wish to keep this one for himself."

Heat washed through him, but he held himself still.

"Oh?" Okisco looked her up and down. "As your own woman, or for some other purpose?"

"I had not decided yet."

The weroance tipped his chin at the woman. "Are you spoken for?"

She drew herself up, flushing, confusion in her pale eyes. "Say—again?"

Her manner of speech was terrible. Okisco tried again. "Do you have a man?"

"Kupi." *Yes.* That she apparently understood.

Okisco gave a nod and looked at Sees Far. "It would be improper for you to take a woman who has a living husband." He posed the question to the other two women, who answered with a shake of the head. "Do you want either of the other two?" he asked Sees Far.

"No." The reply was out before he could even think about it.

Okisco regarded him, still impassive. Finally he waved a hand. "They shall all be taken to the place of trade, except for this one." He pointed at the slender, dark-haired girl, hardly old enough to be considered a woman. "She shall be sent to the Powhatan."

Fear jagged across the girl's face. The other two women huddled closer to her, speaking in soft voices, but she began to cry. The women of the town scattered to make preparations for them to leave right away.

Emme slumped against Elinor, sobbing. The best they could understand, the girl was to be separated from the rest of them, who were to be taken—where? They spoke so quickly, and with different enough inflections from the Croatoan, that the words themselves might be the same, but she could not force her weary mind to comprehend.

Most merciful God, help us!

She was beyond weary of the prayer, but it truly was all she had remaining.

They were allowed to stand there, embracing as best they could with hands still bound, until the women of the town came with bags of what Elinor presumed were provisions. And then the men who had taken them all drew them apart, two of them leading a weeping, wailing Emme away between them.

"God go with you!" Elizabeth called after, likewise tearful.

Elinor could not speak.

Her captor nudged her into motion, and her feet moved almost of their own accord. Where were they to be taken now? Would she ever see her husband and child again?

And why was the weroance asking after her husband?

The men were all attempting to ask questions and once again getting cuffed for their efforts. They were shoved and herded through the town, past the outermost houses and the edges of fields waiting to be planted, and back onto a narrow path leading into the woods beyond.

For much of the remaining morning they were hurried along, hardly given time to rest. At last, about midday, they stopped, with Elinor and Elizabeth pushed toward a clump of bushes. Once they'd seen to their needs, under the watchful presence of Elinor's captor and another warrior, they returned to the others and bits of dried fish were handed them.

Elinor did not want to be struck, but she still had to try. "What is your name?" she asked her captor, in Croatoan.

He flicked her a glance but otherwise did not respond. She was about to repeat the question, but one of the other warriors—the one who had struck Master Prat before the weroance—stalked across to her, his expression thunderous. Elinor shrank back, despite herself.

"So you wish to know his name," he said, in heavily accented but very good English. "What of my name, eh? Do you wish to know it?"

She stared at him, half in shock at his command of her tongue, half in fear. Was the man mad? And how did—?

"Do you know me?" he pressed. Elinor edged away but he stepped closer. "Behold my face. Do you not remember me?"

Should she remember? She blinked, searching for familiarity in the man's features despite the fearsomeness. Black, arching brows. Eyes of a deep brown, snapping with intensity. Black hair, glossy as a crow's wing, cut in a fringe above a bold forehead, and pulled back. The war paint still stark on his lean cheeks.

"I—"

And then it dawned upon her.

"Wanchese?" She could only speak his name in a whisper.

He laughed harshly. "Aye. 'Tis I, the one who came to his senses and returned to the land, unlike the traitor Manteo. Your people are but swine and have no regard for anything but yourselves. We will make of you food for the birds and beasts and fishes."

As he said these words, an arm came out and pushed Elinor back, and to her redoubled shock, her captor interposed himself between them. "Wanchese, *stop*."

An angry exchange ensued between them as they stood nose to nose. In a moment of silence, Wanchese twitched away and approached her again. "Your father helped the people who seek to take our land. He thought himself our friend, but he is simple and knows nothing. He is only a tool in the hand of your ugly weroansqua. Of the men who want only our wassador and game."

"He is not," Elinor said, very low, even though she knew it would only drive him further into anger.

But Wanchese did not strike her, only leaned down until their faces nearly touched. "Did he come as well, since you are here?"

"He—did." It could hurt nothing for her to speak the truth. "Sir Walter Ralegh appointed him our governor. But we were cast off in the wrong place, with fewer supplies than we supposed we would have, and so he sailed back to England to see to our relief."

Her heart clenched. This summer would mark three years. *Papa, where are you?*

Still sneering, Wanchese straightened. "In the wrong place? Where then were you to have gone?"

She blinked and slid a glance past him. Master Prat nodded slightly. "The Chesepiok," she said.

"Chesepiok." Wanchese coughed a laugh, then tossed a comment in his own tongue at his companions, who also laughed. He turned back to Elinor. "Fools, all. You would have perished straightaway. And for the better."

Elinor half expected him to fall upon her and accomplish the task himself, on the spot.

"God would have protected us," she murmured. "And did."

Wanchese spat to the side. "Your God. He is worthless. Only the gods of this land will avail you anything. You should consider serving them."

With that, he stalked away and gestured for them to be off again.

She hazarded a look at her captor. His face was, once again, as implacable and inscrutable as Wanchese.

And that one—they'd all thought never to see him again once he'd abandoned the expedition—what was it, five years ago?

Was he the reason behind all the attacks since they'd arrived on Roanoac Island?

Gracious Lord, protect my little one—and the others!

The day dragged on, and then the next. The ground became rougher and her heart grieved Ginny and Ananias's absence all the more.

Even in the face of Wanchese's wrath, she did not cry or run away. And it mattered not—she would be traded away, as any captive they'd taken but would not keep.

Even so, Sees Far seethed. He understood the anger Wanchese bore toward her people—that fire still burned in his own heart—but to single her out, as if the wrongs of the Inqutish were hers alone to answer for—

Still, she was a captive. There were no limits to the harshness allowed to be heaped upon either newly taken captives or slaves. Except that this one—this woman was Sees Far's own prize, not for Wanchese to use as he willed.

He must not show that he favored her, however, or things would go even worse for her.

Chapter Fourteen

Three days.

Three days they had combed the wilderness, to no avail.

Ananias and the other men waited, listening, while Manteo questioned passing natives. At last word came of a group of white-skinned captives that had been taken first to Weopomeioc and then upriver to a place where several different peoples came together to trade both news and goods.

"How do we get them back?"

"I know the place of which they speak," Manteo said. The Croatoan men with them all nodded. Manteo went on, "There will be many people. We must go only with much care, mayhap catch them before they reach the place." He fastened them all with a stern look. "Much care. Need I speak again?"

A murmur of assent was their only response. They pushed on, more quickly now that they had a more accurate idea of where to go. Ananias minded not the ache of his feet and body but thought only of having Elinor in his arms again. Even the cold spring rain could not dampen his spirits.

God in heaven, most merciful Father, preserve them all! And give us fleetness of foot and clearness of vision as we seek them. Let me hold my wife again!

Near evening on the fourth day, they came to a place where Manteo said they would withdraw from the path and keep watch. This was where parties traveling from Weopomeioc would most likely pass on their way to the place of trade. The trees grew tall, pines and oaks and other sorts that Ananias was not yet familiar with, and the ground was spongy but mostly dry. They'd no trouble finding a spot for all to camp, with a thicket behind which to build a small fire, to keep it unseen from the main path.

After a quick supper, most of the men, English and Croatoan, rolled up in cloaks and capes and stretched out on the ground, all weary enough to sleep wherever they lay. Ananias and two others, Henry Berrye and Anthony Cage, stood the first watch.

Dusk had fallen when they heard the muted sounds of a party's passage. The three of them crept through the forest, gripping their muskets, until they came to the edge of a rise. Peering over and through the bushes, they could see a large group of native warriors, accompanied by—aye, it was so! a small and very bedraggled company of English.

And there in the middle were two women. Even from a distance he recognized Elinor's bearing and mannerisms, and his heart leaped.

"I do not see one of the women, but the rest appear to be there, and—reasonably well," Berrye murmured.

Unable to tear his eyes from Elinor, Ananias drew himself into a crouch. As she stood beside a growing fire, weariness etched every line of her slim form. She swayed a little on her feet, then stretched both hands together—were they bound?—toward the flames. Someone spoke, and she tipped her head, affording Ananias a glimpse of her silhouetted features.

Heat poured through him, and anguish like prayer without words.

A hand came down on his shoulder. "Steady, man." It was Cage, whose previous experience as sheriff of Huntingdon made him an ideal member of their company. "Do not act rashly, now that we have them in our sight."

No promises. Ananias bit his lips together to keep the words unspoken.

"Shall I go back and let the others know?" Berrye asked.

"Aye, wake Manteo at least," Ananias said. He settled in more comfortably to watch.

The captives were fed. He could recognize most—he thought—Master Prat definitely for his dark beard with its streaks of silver. The other woman—Emme or Elizabeth? Both were young and more slender than Elinor, being but twelve or so when they'd sailed from England. It was almost as if the attacking warriors had selected their captives most carefully, the way they'd swooped in, snatched some of the colonists—and only those who were English—then gone again with little bloodshed.

What were they about?

Elinor ate and accepted a skin of water, but just as the warrior attending her—a tall, lean man with a single crest of hair from front to back and indeterminate markings upon his half-caped body—nudged her and pointed at a particular spot, another tall warrior darted forward and seized Elinor's other shoulder. He bent nearly eye-to-eye with her and began to shout. The tone of his voice carried even to where Ananias crouched.

A white-hot fury rose up in him. How long must he watch his own wife used so ill? His hand tightened about the musket—but shots were useless in such close quarters. He reached instead to his rapier hilt.

"We all go together, or not at all." Manteo's words came back to him.

Surely Manteo would not expect him to simply stand by at such evil hap as this.

There was a scuff and rustle of approaching men behind him. More were coming—they could then easily take the savages—

Next to the fire, the warrior took both of Elinor's shoulders and gave her a rough shake.

Nay. No more.

Dimly he heard Anthony speak his name, barely registered a hand upon his arm, but he cast off the man's grip, and with rapier in one hand and the musket in his other, he charged over the rise and toward the camp.

Weary—so weary. After the brief repast and bit of water, all Elinor wanted was to curl up on a patch of moss somewhere and fall into slumber. One moment she and Elizabeth had been murmuring to each other—*"Have faith,"* the younger girl whispered—and the next, Wanchese sharply reprimanded them for speaking. And then as her captor directed her to go lie down, Wanchese chose that moment to storm toward her.

She could hardly distinguish his words—was he speaking English this time or his own tongue? All she wanted was to crawl away and sleep. He seized her shoulders and shook them, then forced her to her knees, still snarling at her.

Closing her eyes, she tucked her head, but he grabbed her jaw and forced her face upward. For a moment, she could only blink into his eyes, narrowed to slits—

A shout broke across them, more an anguished battle cry than anything else, and chaos broke out in the camp. Elinor looked up—firelight glinted off of English armor and helm—and was that—

"Ananias!" His name broke from her lips.

Three native warriors converged upon him, and Wanchese swung away from her, wooden sword suddenly in hand. Nearby, Elizabeth screamed, and all the men and boys were in an uproar, but Elinor could not move. All she could see in the melee were the blue eyes of her husband, blazing in the firelight, fixed upon hers.

The commotion ceased with shocking suddenness. Ananias, too, knelt, his arms forced behind him, helm torn away and fair hair dark with sweat. He breathed hard through clenched teeth, glancing around him before fastening his gaze once more on Elinor.

She pressed both hands across her mouth, fearful of saying anything that might endanger his life.

"Elinor," he murmured, and Wanchese seized his hair. Ananias only grimaced. "Keep your bloody hands off my wife," he growled.

Wanchese yanked harder. "I shall do whatever I please with your wife. And you shall have nothing to say about it." An evil grin danced across his lips. "Shall I make you a captive as well? 'Twould be great sport to put you to forced labor for my people."

"Now you sound like Lane and his ilk," Ananias said.

Another jerk upon his hair, and Wanchese forced his head back. "The blood of Pemisapan cries out to be avenged."

"And so you slew one of ours when we first landed upon Roanoac." Ananias winced, then looked up at him again. "We want only friendship. We sent messengers out to noise that abroad, when first the killing took place, but none answered. And yet we would be willing to be at peace with you and your people, if you would but agree."

"Peace." Wanchese huffed. "Peace would be if you and your people, all wutahshuntas, would vanish from this land and more never come. I am a fool for believing that could even come to pass, yet it will not prevent me from trying."

And with that there was a flash in his hand, and a slash opened upon Ananias's throat, and a dark rush of fluid washed over the brightness of his armor. Ananias's eyes flew wide, his mouth opening—

"Elinor!"

His body slumped, lifeless, beside the fire. A thin wail tore from Elinor's own throat, and once again the camp burst into motion.

Someone seized her and hauled her to her feet, but her legs buckled beneath her. She was rudely lifted and slung over someone's shoulder and carried out into the darkness at a run. Others fled beside them, and more shouts came from the direction Ananias had come. Gunshots boomed, lighting up the dark forest with quick bursts.

Her captor ran faster. Shouts, more gunfire, and splashing just ahead. Elinor found herself dumped into a canoe, which tipped this way and that before hurtling off across the water. Hushed voices, speaking too quickly to comprehend.

She thought she had learned the Croatoan tongue so well by now—what then had made her an idiot these past days?

Ananias! My love! Oh God in heaven, they have slain my husband. Let me perish as well, if only it means my Virginia shall live. . .

Sunlight filtered through leaves above, playing across her face. The boat beneath moved with strong, steady strokes. Deep voices murmured against a chorus of birdsong and the occasional call of a loon.

And then she remembered.

Firelight. Shouting. A knife. Lifeblood, splashing down.

Oh God, they have slain my Ananias! I pray only that his soul winged its way directly to You.

Oh Lord, my Lord. I am utterly alone.

After paddling most of the night, only drawing up under a bower of overhanging trees for an hour or two of rest, they would soon run out of stream deep enough for easy navigation. Sees Far did not care. After the Inqutish man's death and the boom of his companions' weapons, they'd snatched their captives and fled out into the night, deciding to take the waterway as far as it would go for a quick escape, and then cross inland, later, to the place of trade. Word had already come of the company of Inqutish and Croatoan mixed, led by Manteo, and while Wanchese might have longed to engage them in battle, even he knew they were outmatched by the Inqutish weapons, especially while they had captives to transport.

And so they kept paddling, away from the wideness of the Chawanoac River and up one of its tributaries, lazily twisting its way through forest and swamp where great pines and cypress rose on either side like silent, ancient guardians. Sees Far loved the deep solitude of this place, yet not even its grandeur could completely soothe the restlessness of his spirit.

The woman lay in the bottom of the kanoe, a nearly shapeless heap of garments with golden hair dulled by its unkempt state. She'd hardly moved these past hours.

If Wanchese had wished to break her, he had succeeded. But who would have known her man would come charging down into the midst of their camp? Were the circumstances different, Sees Far would admire his courage.

Taking his life was the only thing they could have done. One such as him never would have submitted to forced labor.

And oh, the fire in the man's eyes when he looked at the woman. *Elinor.* Was that how she was called?

The sun stood high enough now to shine on the woman's face, and she stirred at last, only to angle an arm over her eyes.

Perhaps the man's death would reconcile her to staying with his people. It was often the way of captives, at least the ones who had been adopted young or taken as wives, that once they'd had time to learn the ways and tongue of their new family, acceptance and even affection flourished, as a green plant in the summer.

Not that it mattered. Okisco had spoken, and his word would hold regardless. The woman was not for him.

The crashing of ocean waves breaking onshore echoed through her dreams. Ananias, laughing and tossing Ginny into the air, who shrieked and begged for more.

Elinor came to wakefulness, the thunder of the sea fading under a chorus of birdsong and the lap of water against the side of the canoe. Sitting up, she blinked at brilliant daylight filtered through trees rising impossibly tall in the swamps around them, with various bushes and cypress knees scattered throughout. The air held a slight stench of decaying plants, not entirely unpleasant, but—

The memory slashed across her heart. *Ananias.*

How long before she could join him in that land beyond the sun?

She drew in a long breath, agony piercing all the way to her innermost heart. Could she even keep breathing, with him gone from her life?

Did she have a choice in the matter? Or would her traitorous body continue to take in air, her heart continue to beat, despite what she willed?

Another campsite, another fire. Elinor sat staring at her hands. Still bound. She could not blame them, with the way some of the men put up a row again that evening, until asked if they wished to perish as Ananias had.

She felt the glances of her fellow captives, full of care. Would that she could simply sink into the earth. Elizabeth alone had the bravery to sidle closer, pat her hands, and lean her head on Elinor's shoulder for a few precious moments before being dragged away and made to sit apart from Elinor and the others.

With a long sigh, she slumped to her side and curled up, not even waiting on supper.

There was a nudge to her foot, then another. Elinor peered past her fingers. The tall figure of her captor stood above her, holding out a portion of meat. "Sit up. Eat."

The words were understandable, if spoken with a different inflection than she was accustomed to.

She covered her face again, but the low voice of Master Prat came from nearby. "Please, Elinor, do as he says. Ananias would not want you to languish."

Her captor gave the man a long look, but seemed satisfied that he meant well and turned his attention back to Elinor. "Eat. Tomorrow we walk. You need strength."

Stuffing down a sob, she pushed herself upright again. He reached down a hand to assist, and she shot him a startled glance, but there was only calmness in his gaze and—was that a hint of pity? She accepted the hunk of roast venison, still hot to the touch. "Thank you," she answered in Croatoan.

Her captor bobbed a nod, then moved away.

The meat was savory and unexpectedly tender. Her eyes burned at how good it tasted. She glanced across to Master Prat, and he met her eyes with a firm nod, his mouth compressed.

They all did grieve, surely.

Sees Far waited until the woman finished eating before he approached again, beckoning. "Come. Wash now."

She hesitated, her pale gaze uncertain, and Wanchese loomed suddenly close, his hand falling upon Sees Far's shoulder. "Why are you coddling her? The women at Ritanoe will wash her."

"She stinks," he answered, keeping his voice level. "She has not washed properly since we left Weopomeioc. Besides, you know we will get a better price if she is not bedraggled."

Wanchese grunted and stepped back, looking the woman up and down. He gestured to the other girl. "Take them both."

Sees Far held out a hand to each and repeated the command. The women exchanged glances then slowly rose to their feet and followed him down to the water's edge. He pointed at the younger one. "You help each other wash. Do not run."

He waited until they both nodded, seeming to understand, then reached for the woman's hands and untied the thong binding them. When he'd loosed both, he looked at each in turn, again. "Wash, but do not run away."

They nodded, more eagerly this time, and while he withdrew to keep watch, they shed all but one thin garment and waded into the water, holding each other's hands. Feeling a sudden intruder upon their bath, Sees Far averted his eyes and instead surveyed the water and forest around them for possible threats. He was, after all, present as much to keep them safe as to ensure they did not escape.

He kept his place as they splashed and sloshed, murmuring to each other yet still more subdued than women usually were while they bathed. Yet they lingered, and he found himself content enough to let them do so.

He kept his gaze turned away when they returned to shore, dripping and wringing out their hair—ridiculously long it was, compared to the women of his people—and the skirts of their strange, thin undergarments. They helped each other with the outer clothing, and then the woman Elinor surprised him by approaching, hesitantly, while her hands were busy plaiting her hair. "Please, what is it you are called?"

The words were strangely spoken but clear enough.

"I am called 'Sees Far.' "

She mouthed the syllables.

"It means 'he who sees a long way.' "

A quick nod was her response; then she said, "I thank you, Sees Far."

When she had finished braiding her hair, he held up the thong he'd used as binding, and she lifted her hands for him to tie them again. The other woman followed suit, though reluctantly. That done, he gestured for them to go ahead of him back to the camp.

He would not ask her to speak her own name. It soured in his belly, somehow, that he should have learned it first from the lips of her man, whose blood now watered the earth.

It was bad enough she had presence of mind enough at such a time to offer thanks.

The sweet respite of a river bath and Elizabeth's company, with their hands free, was short-lived. With full darkness of night came a return of the heaviness and grief, and a resurgence of the memory of Ananias's final moments.

Wanchese sat nearby, sharpening the blade of his dagger against a stone, nestled in his palm. 'Twas a very English dagger—or Spanish, Elinor often could not tell—but by any account, of her former part of the world and not this one. The action he performed seemed so ordinary, so familiar, that though his deerskin apron and lean, bare limbs declared him every inch a warrior of this land, her eyes burned to think of all the times she'd watched Papa and Ananias absorbed in a similar task.

It was also the blade he'd used to take the life of Ananias in such a quick manner.

He finished, wiping the blade on his garment and lifting it to inspect the edge. She averted her eyes, but too late—he caught her turning away from watching him.

In a flash he was on his feet, crossing to her, crouching beside her, dagger in hand. She shrank away but he leaned closer.

He lifted the dagger, slowly turning it this way and that. "Your queen gave me this as a present. Is it not a thing of beauty?" He brushed a thumb across the edge of the blade. "And so sharp. Better than any weapon of my people, except for a shell." His sudden grin held more of an edge than the dagger. "You see, I do not withhold myself from saying when something is superior to what I have been taught to use. You English think you are all better than us, because you wear more clothing and use weapons that shoot far and do not break so easily. But you should agree that some things of ours are better. Like our gods."

She leaned away again, scooting along the ground to escape him, but he followed her.

"Where is your God? See, He cannot save you from my hand. Your man has fallen already—that was your man, aye?"

He grasped her jaw and forced her face toward his, but she half closed her eyes, keeping her gaze upon his shoulder. A lean, very muscled shoulder, but 'twas better than looking him in the eye.

He shook her a little. "What sort of God would give you and your husband and your people into our hand, if He had any power at all against our gods?"

'Twas too much like just before Ananias burst upon them. *Oh gracious God, too much—*

She squeezed her eyes shut, and words poured from her lips. " 'The Lord is my shepherd, therefore I can lack nothing.' "

His fingers gripped harder. "What is it you say?"

" 'He shall feed me in a green pasture, and lead me forth beside the waters of comfort. He shall convert my soul, and bring me forth in the paths of righteousness for his name's sake.' "

"What—nay!" He released her, only to cuff her on the side of her head.

Still the words came. " 'Yea, though I walk through the valley of the shadow of death, I will fear no evil, for thou art with me; thy rod and thy staff comfort me.' "

Another blow, this time against her shoulders, and she curled in on herself. " 'Thou shalt prepare a table before me against them that trouble me: thou hast anointed my head with oil, and my cup shall be full. But loving kindness and mercy shall follow me all the days of my life, and I will dwell in the house of the Lord for ever.' "

There were shouts, and a scuffle beside her, but no more blows fell. When she looked, her captor wrestled with Wanchese, forcing him away from her, yelling into his face. She wasted no time in scrambling farther away, and both Elizabeth and Master Prat came to huddle one on either side of her.

The two warriors faced each other in sudden silence, glaring, grimacing. Her captor spoke again, more quietly but no less forcibly. At last Wanchese spat a word and stalked away into the darkness.

What was it the woman had said to drive Wanchese to such fury? Sees Far waited until that one's footsteps faded into the forest, then he turned to his fellow warriors. "You wish to speak?"

Nearly as one, they shook their heads and turned away, although not without a smirk or two.

He walked to where the woman sat flanked by the other girl and the oldest of the male captives. "What is it that you spoke?"

She blinked, confusion in her eyes, but the older man cleared his throat and answered, "It is a prayer from our talking leaves."

Talking leaves—the thing they called a *book*. And—a prayer. Wanchese spent a year with their people. Had he heard this prayer, and recognized it?

"What was he saying to you?" Sees Far asked.

The woman only closed her eyes and pressed her face against the other woman's shoulder, but the man replied for her again. "He said our God has no power, that only your gods do in this place."

Anger rekindled in Sees Far's heart, along with a growing wonder. He had mocked her God, only to be infuriated when she spoke a prayer? "And what sort of prayer was it? Was she calling vengeance down upon him?"

The other man smiled—*smiled*—and shook his head. "*Mahta.* No. It speaks of our God caring for us, leading us through both good and bad, even if death threatens, and how one day we will live forever with Him."

And this was what had so enraged Wanchese? Why, if he knew Montóac to be superior?

He would not confront his old friend until his anger had cooled, but confront him he would.

Late into the night, Wanchese returned. Sees Far remained awake, at watch, having told the others to sleep while they could, and he rose at the other's approach.

Wanchese fetched his cape from the ground and wrapped it about his shoulders. "I will watch now, if you wish."

"I will stay awake a little longer," Sees Far said.

With a shrug, Wanchese settled next to the fire. Sees Far crouched nearby.

"We have been friends and brothers our entire lives, kupi?"

Wanchese's gaze flicked toward him, cold and stern. "Kupi."

"So I ask you now. What are the limits of vengeance?"

His eyes lifted again, searching. "The woman has made you weak toward her, I see."

Sees Far held himself still. “No more weak than you. Your anger has sorely infected you.”

He expected a resurgence of that anger, but Wanchese only snorted. “So you say.”

“It is so. To lose control over, what, a prayer?”

Wanchese drew his shoulders back, his eyes hard. “If you had seen what I have, you would not speak thus. These people do not believe in the God they profess to follow. They speak of love but their actions are driven by greed and selfishness. They do not even enjoy the wealth they possess. They have burned a town for a mere cup of silver. They took women and children captive, and cast the children into the river then shot them as they swam, for sport.”

“You have spoken truth. But what of Piemacum, and how he gave a feast and invited various men and women, and once they were merry with food and dance, he and his warriors slew all the men and took the women captive? Was that not a great wrong as well, and yet by one of the people of our own land? Did Pemisapan, in his day, not try to get the English to help them destroy the men of Pomeiooc?”

“We should have uppowoc for a talk such as this,” Wanchese grumbled, but there was no heat in his words. He sighed. “I believed, once, that we could live together peaceably with the English. When they first arrived upon Ossomocomuck—well, you remember. You were there.”

“There were good men among them.”

“Yes. But then they were corrupted either by their desire for wassador and pearls, or by their association with those who sought only gain. I speak of Harriot, who taught the English tongue more perfectly to Manteo and I, and learned our tongue. His curiosity was like a child’s, so perfect and pure was it—both his and John White’s.” He was silent a moment. “But what goodness they possess is at best a tool in the hands of those they serve.”

Sees Far watched as the moment of calm and reflection in Wanchese’s countenance was once again swept away by the hardness and anger.

“I will not deny that Wyngyno had it in his heart to use the Inqutish against our enemies as well. It is the way of life. But the treachery of the Inqutish, after all our peoples extended to them the hand of friendship and brotherhood, cannot go unanswered. If you deny this, you deny all that we are and are no better than Manteo."

Sees Far sniffed. "Manteo uses the Inqutish well, methinks. He is far more cunning than I'd have thought."

Wanchese nodded, a deep scowl carved into his features. "That he does. But I fear he swallows down too much of their poison."

Part Five

Chapter Fifteen

The trading town was busier than Sees Far could ever recall. The array of goods in the marketplace was rivaled only by the variety of people mingling amongst the booths and longhouses—Powhatan, Sukwoten, Tuscarora, Mandoag, Chesepiok, all walking side by side and trading as if they were friends and brothers, and not in some cases bitter enemies.

Wanchese strode at the head of their company, drawing stares and comments for the bedraggled group of wutahshuntas. Sees Far thought he glimpsed a Spanish through the crowd, similarly bound as their own prizes.

Fur capes of every shade and kind. Brightly colored feathers tucked into various styles of hair arranging, according to people. Bows and arrows, cudgels and wooden swords, and the rare blade from the strangers across the sea. Strands of beads, from either the bright wassador, white or black pearls, or bits of polished shell. Heads of black or silver, with the occasional chestnut. None carried the golden of the woman walking before him.

Elinor.

He had not yet spoken her name except in his own heart. This was the better way, to keep their association a matter of vengeance only.

He neither wanted nor needed a woman. Much of his conversation with Wanchese and the other men on this journey had been how to take more war back to these foolish English, once their captives were disposed of. Would they take more captives and sell those on the market here, if the first handful did well, or would they put the rest to death?

Sees Far thought of a particular light-haired girl child, even as his eyes traced the damp but tidy braid of her mother just ahead of him. She would fetch a good price and be gladly welcomed into some hearth.

Or would Wanchese, in his fury, slay her as well?

They found their way to the place where captives were brought for trade. While Wanchese went to speak with those in charge, one of the male captives, the oldest with the long beard, edged toward Sees Far. "What will happen to us here?"

He thought about how to reply. "You will be sold. Whether then you live or die, I cannot say."

The already-pale face went paler still. One man's face went red, and Sees Far held that one's gaze until he relented and looked away.

"If you fight, or run, you almost certainly will be killed," Sees Far added.

He resisted looking at the woman.

Wanchese returned with three men and a woman, who all proceeded to examine the captives, poking and prodding, peering inside their mouths, tugging at and stroking their hair and the men's beards, fingering their strange clothing, squeezing their limbs.

Indeed, a crowd had begun to gather, with questions of where they had come from, and what could be given in trade for them, and where they would go. Wanchese stood with his arms folded, face stern. At last he said, "I will decide where they will go. You who dig for wassador, they should go and beat wassador for you."

"It is good!" came the answer.

In the midst of their dickering on price, Sees Far spoke up. "I wish to take my portion in a share of the wassador, according to how they labor."

All fell silent with shock, staring at him.

"It is a slower way of payment," he said, "but eventually will yield more. Kupi?"

When the leader of those who dug the wassador could close his mouth, he was nodding. "Kupi. It is good as well. You come, help keep watch as they labor."

Wanchese gave only the slightest of smiles, his eyes glittering. "Very clever," he said.

Sees Far kept his own features impassive. He could no more explain the impulse to say what he had than he could capture the wind in the trees.

But Wanchese would not leave it alone. "No room for a woman, eh? Or merely hungry for more wassador than you can carry?" He lifted a deerskin pouch and shook it, clinking his share of the golden-red metal they'd traded the captives for.

"Neither. But none else will have such an interest in making sure they do not escape. Kupi?"

Wanchese laughed and turned away. Sees Far's heart burned within him. Perhaps he would indeed do better to follow his companions and vent that fire upon the rest of the strangers.

'Twas the first time since they were taken that all were allowed close enough for real conversation. Elinor thought she'd prefer the distance and silence to clinging embraces, repeated expressions of sorrow over Ananias's death, and questions about her well-being.

She missed the sea. She missed Timqua and the other women, their chatter and the squeals of the children, and the sounds of town life, men working and singing.

Most of all she missed little Ginny, and Ananias. Never again would she feel his strong arms about her, or his kiss, at once sweet and rough and full of life.

"Do not lose heart—God has not abandoned us," Master Prat said. The others leaned toward him as if to soak up every word of his exhortations, but Elinor sat loosely at the outer edge of the circle, watching their captors who talked and laughed beside the fire.

Except for Sees Far, who sat apart, against a tree. It seemed his wont of late. Wanchese threw him, and them, the occasional glance, but joined fully in the goodwill of his company. 'Twas strange how their new captors cared not if they conversed with each other. Perhaps with more of them to guard if trouble happened, they remained unconcerned, but whatever the reason for it, her fellow captives reveled in it, talking and even softly chuckling as if it were some festive occasion.

Elinor found a patch of mossy ground and curled up, eyes closed, as Master Prat led the others in a hymn. She'd no heart for any of it. At this moment, she felt as dead inside as her darling husband.

Strangely enough, 'twas her first glimpse of the mountains which stirred the first breath of life back to her soul.

They'd paddled upriver for three days, tucked the canoes up into a small stream, then set off on foot, over ground where boulders lay like scattered child's toys and the forest grew thick and tall. Their path took them uphill and down, and just as they were approaching the next rise, a break in the trees afforded a view of rounded bluish peaks, not a far distance away.

All of them gasped with amazement. " 'I will lift up mine eyes unto the hills,' " Master Prat said, very softly.

" 'From whence cometh my help?' " Elinor murmured. " 'My help cometh even from the Lord, which hath made heaven and earth.' "

He threw her a small smile. " 'He will not suffer thy foot to be moved, and he that keepeth thee, will not sleep.' "

"Ho, keep walking," one of their new keepers said.

Elinor recited the rest of it to herself. *"Behold, he that keepeth Israel, shall neither slumber nor sleep. The Lord himself is thy keeper, the Lord is thy defense upon thy right hand. So that the sunne shall not burn thee by day, neither the moone by night. The Lord shall preserve thee from all evil, yea it is even he that shall keep thy soul. The Lord shall preserve thy going out and thy coming in, from this time forth for ever more."*

Would He? Even in this, was God with them? Master Prat insisted so, but. . .Elinor's heart still lay, as it were, bleeding on a forest floor alongside Ananias.

Ginny yet lives, she reminded herself. And if even the slightest hope remained that Elinor could return to her daughter, she should not give up.

"Why do you suppose he stays?"

Master Prat's low voice carried across the sound of stones hammering together. The chunk of ore Elinor had been beating against a larger stone slab broke in her hands, scattering pieces and bruising knuckles for the hundredth time. She stared at the fresh blood welling on her fingers, then followed Roger Prat's gaze to where her captor Sees Far stood under a nearby oak, leaning against its trunk with apparent indolence. She knew, however, that he missed nothing. Even as she looked up, his dark eyes met hers, then flicked away.

With a sigh, she set to picking bits of copper, paler than that which they brought from England, from the crushed limestone and granite littering the ground around her. " 'Tis beyond me. Mayhap you should ask."

In truth, she wondered as well. Wanchese and the rest of their party had departed after seeing her and her fellow English captives delivered to the place where they mined for copper or other metals—which the native peoples called wassador—but even after spring bloomed suddenly to summer, Sees Far lingered.

She glanced up again and found Master Prat looking intently at her. "What is it?"

But he only shook his head, slowly.

Dumping the fragments of copper into an open deerskin pouch, she wearily took two more chunks of ore and set the smaller on the rock before her, then pounded it with the larger. Half a dozen others labored at the same task, stationed at various spots around the same outcropping.

Elinor knew more now about the process of working copper than she'd ever wished. Patches of dull green across the face of the rocky outcroppings—at first glance moss or lichen, but not either—marked where the copper could be dug. Open pits like hungry mouths took in shuffling laborers and spit them out again at odd intervals. She still shuddered at the memory of the only time she'd been made to enter one of those gaping maws to fetch baskets of ore, dug from God only knew how far below. Reduced to a screaming, sobbing heap, she still did not comprehend how it was they'd not instantly slain her. Instead, she'd been dragged back above, where her captor bickered with the others, and at last she was given the task of gathering from the piles of ore outside the mine pits and carrying such to those beating the fine, bright copper from the rock where it was imprisoned. Sometimes—such as now—she was made to take a turn at beating the copper as well.

Another glance up, and Master Prat was still watching her. "I suppose one might as well ask why Wanchese singled you out for such animosity," he said.

She stilled and faced him more directly. "What is it you are trying to say?"

"Sees Far favors you. Whether because of Wanchese and his cruelties or something else, but it is clear that he does."

Elinor resisted looking over at her captor, though a hot prickle swept across her skin. " 'Tis a ridiculous notion."

Master Prat shook his head again, very slowly. "He was asking after you at the council which decided our fate. That was why Wanchese asked whether you were a married woman."

She ducked her head, grimacing.

"Elinor." His voice took on a sudden urgency. " 'Tis too soon, we know—but any of us, except for Tydway of course, who left a wife behind—but Sutton, Bright, and myself, we'd gladly be husband to you in Ananias's place, if one of us suited you, once you feel ready for it again."

What she'd gladly do was sink into the very earth where she sat, and not have to face this man's earnest countenance.

"M–Master Prat," she began.

"Please. It is Roger. We need not such formality here, where we are all captives."

She kept her head bent, hiding her expression and the tears burning her eyes. "I am not unmindful of the honor you do me. But I cannot even think on that as of yet."

"Fair enough. But do keep it in mind, dear lady. We all hold much affection for you."

"For that, I am thankful."

She peeked long enough to catch his nod and smile, and to note that his face was as reddened as her own felt.

And Sees Far watched their exchange with an intentness she suddenly comprehended far too well, if what Master Prat had told her was true. She put her head down again, forehead upon her folded arms, and for a moment simply let the tears come.

Oh. . .Ananias. Oh, gracious Lord in heaven. What am I to even think of all this?

A touch upon her shoulder caused her to start. She looked up into Sees Far's countenance, creased in what she was sure was concern. "*Sá keyd winkan?*" he asked.

Are you well?

Concern, then, of a certainty. She gulped and jerked her chin downward in a quick nod. Then, swiping her face against her sleeve, she seized the chunk of ore and set to pounding again, half blinded by new tears and steadfastly determined not to look at either Sees Far or Roger Prat.

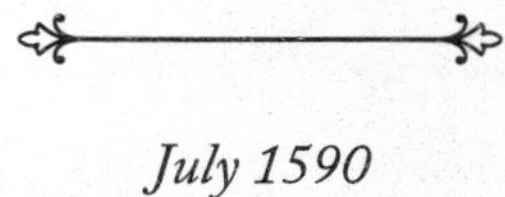

July 1590

The warmth of the sun poured across John's shoulders, easing the ache that perpetually resided there of late. In a moment of rare ease, he leaned on the ship's rail, his gaze tracing the forested rise, beyond turquoise waters, of Cuba. 'Twas not as striking as, say, the green-clothed cliffs of Dominica, but he found it still lovely. Always a wonder it was to see these far-flung lands, to bask in the heat of a tropic sun, and yet—

Please God this was the last time. That at the end of this voyage, he'd hold sweet Elinor and her wee daughter in his arms once more.

The longing remained so strong, so persistent, he was beyond weary of it. Of the details of their voyage, he kept careful account. Whether his perspective on the events thereof was of any weight, he knew not—but it helped pass the time.

Captain Cooke sidled up next to him on the rail. " 'Twas admirable work when we took the Spanish frigate. I believe we may make a privateer of you yet."

John gave a humorless chuckle. Pirate, more like. How far he had fallen.

Lord God, forgive me.

"Would that were my only purpose on this voyage," he said, "and not to burden you with my own aims."

The other man grinned, in apparent good humor after their success of the day before. "I own that would be preferred. But I shall not fail in accomplishing what you desire as well. Particularly when you have not withheld yourself from being of help when necessary."

John dipped his head to acknowledge the compliment.

"So, now that we have rid ourselves of the pestering Spaniards we rescued some weeks back, we will look to take on fresh water then press on past Florida and toward your Virginia."

He breathed out, a long exhale. "My most earnest thanks."

The buzz of insects filled the air as Elinor and the others made their way down the hillside from the copper mine to the town nestled below, beside the tumbling stream. The aroma of cooking venison wafted up with the smoke from the cooking fires. 'Twas a beautiful evening, with the cool leaves overarching and the forest floor veritably carpeted with wildflowers, their sweet fragrance added to the breeze.

Thankfully it had been a day of toting baskets of ore between the pits and the open area where they beat out the copper, and then taking full pouches of fragments to the fires where they finished separating copper from stone by melting it in earthen bowls. Long work with more walking, but Elinor preferred it of late to beating out the ore. It kept her in motion and not so subject to the discomfort of conversations she would prefer not to have.

Master Prat and the other men had not lessened their attentions. If anything, they were even more solicitous than before Master Prat's ungraceful confession. The favor of Sees Far was also unmistakable in recent days, if subtler. But how she wished she could escape altogether, even if only to tend the cook fires along with Elizabeth—who had been absent the last week but was now returned, Elinor could see ahead of her.

Too weary to run, she nevertheless walked a little faster. Elizabeth looked up and, with a smile, climbed to her feet to embrace Elinor.

"You are back from the women's house?"

"I am. And happy to be done for another moon or so." Elizabeth laughed a little. "As daft as it sounds." She settled back next to the fire, then eyed Elinor. "You still have not needed to go there, have you? While this was my third time since we've come to this place."

Elinor shrugged. " 'Tis been an unusual spring and summer."

"So you keep saying." Elizabeth turned back to the pot she was tending. "I think this is ready. Do you want a bowl?"

She leaned to peer inside the pot. "And what is it?"

"Peas and early squash," Elizabeth said, with not a little pride. "I have been helping the other women with the garden."

Elinor gladly accepted an earthenware dish and took a seat on a nearby rock. Others were gathering to sit at meat, in clusters, and she felt no surprise when Sees Far both took a bowl of the pottage from Elizabeth and brought Elinor a portion of roasted meat. She accepted it with a smile and nod, then tucked into the food.

How easily she had learned how to eat without spoon or knife, and nearly thought nothing of it now. In fact, were it not for the copper mine up the hill and the daily task of working the ore, this could be the town they shared with the Croatoan and yet another meal taken with them.

Her throat thickened without warning, but with a hard swallow, she forced down the bite she'd just chewed. Though her appetite fled, she kept eating, though slowly, avoiding the sharpness of Sees Far's gaze.

Full night fell, and though many of the other English drifted away to the fire for the customary evening song and dancing, she suddenly felt weary to her very bones. After helping Elizabeth clean the dishes and stack them again, she took herself off to the longhouse where she and her fellow captives slept. Ignoring the ever-lingering presence of Sees Far—in truth, his watchfulness was oddly comforting—she stretched out upon her mat and settled in to sleep.

A strange but not unfamiliar fluttering stirred deep in her belly.

Her eyes flew open, though the interior of the longhouse was darkened, its thatched roof obscuring even the sky.

The fluttering came again. Surely not. She slid one hand across her skirt, hesitantly pressing the garment against herself. There, beneath her fingertips, a small but definite, firm roundness could be discerned between the cradle of her hip bones.

Oh dear, merciful God. How can this be?

Her lungs pulled in a breath, deep and ragged. She half sat up, then rolled to her side, curling in on herself. She had no wish to solicit Sees Far's further attention, but the sobs would not be denied.

Mayhap he would think it a time of grieving, as many others before, and not bestir himself to inquire after her well-being.

Please God he would not inquire.

But—a babe—a last gift from Ananias to her. A last living piece of him. She'd half given up the hope of conceiving again. And after falling pregnant so quickly the first time, shortly after their wedding, amongst the squalor and commotion of London, who would have thought that here, in more healthful conditions, much more time was needful?

And yet—here she was.

She pulled up a fold of her skirt and, covering her face, gave herself more fully to the weeping.

Sees Far slipped outside and sat down, leaning against one of the posts making up the longhouse wall. He could not bear her weeping, but neither would he leave her completely alone. Not that there was any longer a reason for him to watch her so closely—none antagonized her here as Wanchese had, and she gave no indication of trying to escape.

If anything, she seemed resigned to the work of a slave, if not content. Perhaps she knew there was no sense in trying to escape, or perhaps Wanchese had truly broken her with the slaying of her man.

A breeze stirred the leaves of the trees above him, and he peered up through them at the stars. No recent word had come of Wanchese and the others. The last news had been of a company of mixed Kurawoten and Inqutish that had been opposed by a force gathered by Menatonan and the weroances under him. Reports of the outcome were less clear. It would explain how, after the initial surprise attack, their flight upriver and to the trading town had been unchallenged. Either they had given up retrieving their fellows taken captive, or else Menatonan had successfully beaten them back. Neither explanation sat easy with Sees Far. Rumors of war to the north had been noised about—the Mandoag were, after all, a quarrelsome people at best, especially in regard to the coastal peoples—but summer here in the hills remained quiet enough.

Though mountain views were splendid, he missed the sea. The heat here was well nigh oppressive, the air sticky even in the absence of accompanying mist. He missed the sea winds. The cool of the sound. The fish, so plentiful in the weirs.

He felt the familiar kick of resentment against the strangers who had pushed his people inland. Who robbed them of both life and laughter when the mysterious illness swept through, what was it, five turnings of the seasons now? He'd have taken Walks Softly as wife by now, and doubtless held at least one babe in his arms. Instead, here he was, exiled to the hills for the sake of—for the sake of this woman who still wept on the other side of the wall. A woman he could not bring himself to leave, no matter how fiercely his own anger burned.

He clasped the anger close to his heart. He should have left with Wanchese and the others. Could still leave. Come the rising of the sun, he would go to the ones in charge of the digging of wassador, ask for his share of the selling of the captives—

There was something the woman had done. A very small motion. But it held a significance, if he could but recall it.

One hand stealing across her middle, clutching her garments.

Cupping her belly.

Her lower belly.

Realization flared within him. Was she with child? Had she known?

She should have known. She'd not visited the women's house, as the other girl had done. But what if she'd not known, before that moment in the dark?

She belonged to those wicked strangers who had stolen their land

and life. She deserved to be desolate, as he was after the strange sickness stole his love and family.

Another child growing within her gave her more to lose. More ground for understanding just how her people had brought ruin upon his.

And yet. . .

As quickly as the fury had flared inside his heart, it collapsed to ashes.

Morning brought a gust of fresh hope, mingled with fresh fear.

Another child of her and Ananias! 'Twas no wonder the weariness plagued her both day and night, and that her appetite came and went at odd times. She'd not had the sickness of her first pregnancy, but by the roundness in her lower belly, the babe grew and thrived.

The men, however—once they knew of the child, they'd insist she choose one of them as husband. As if it mattered, captive as they were. Did such bonds even signify among those who used her and the others as slaves? Would she be allowed to keep the child, even if they allowed her to carry and birth it?

How long could she conceal the child's existence?

She went down to the stream with Elizabeth and the other women for their morning washing, but this time, as she entered the water and removed clothing, she did her best to keep her back to the others. They were well used to her and Elizabeth's more modest ways—although that had eased somewhat with the Croatoan—and no one made mention of it.

She sank into the deepest part of the stream up to her shoulders, shaking out her kirtle and shift underwater to allow the current to cleanse them. Then anchoring the garments with one arm, she touched her belly again, tracing the small but definite curve where the others could not see.

Another babe!

Oh gracious Lord. . .I can scarce believe it!

And oh. . .oh, how she craved holding Ginny in her arms. Every day, the worry and longing dogged her waking thoughts, and often her dreams as well.

As the other women were sloshing ashore, chattering, she followed, dragging the wet shift over her head, then pausing in the shallows to wring out the kirtle as best as she could before donning it as well. Her fingers fumbled with the laces, but she took a deep breath and forced herself to slow down. She had survived thus far, a day at a time. She would continue to look only at each day.

Braiding her still-dripping hair, she gathered with the other mine workers at the foot of the path they took up the hill. As he often did, Roger Prat edged closer to her and positioned himself behind her in line as they started out up the path. She threw him a glance. "Might we sing a hymn?"

His blue eyes widened, then crinkled in pleasure. "Of course."

He began, and she and others joined in.

She could not say she yet believed that God truly had all this in hand—that He had not abandoned them here—but she wanted this child to hear the songs of their faith, even if she wasn't sure where she stood within it.

Chapter Sixteen

For days, Sees Far merely watched and listened.

To anyone else, it would not appear that anything had changed with the woman. But he could see it—the new firmness to her shoulders, and clarity in her eyes. She kept her eyes as downcast as before, perhaps even more, and her movements as unobtrusive.

So she had decided not to reveal the pregnancy yet. With those large garments, she would perhaps be able to keep it hidden—except that the women often bathed together in the river, and she was too slim to hide such a thing for long.

Would they press her to drink a tea to be rid of the baby, or would they allow her to carry it to the fullness of time?

And did he even care—or should he—given that the child was her slain husband's?

Other thoughts swirled in his mind, things he dare not even begin to entertain.

Another change was in how she responded to the songs and prayers of her people. After Wanchese had expended his terrible rage upon her, she'd neither prayed aloud nor sung any of the songs, even as all the other captives joined in. But since that recent night she'd wept in the dark, she not only joined in but often instigated the singing or praying.

He could not decide how their songs and prayers made him feel. There was a strange beauty to them, and despite Wanchese's insistence that the Inqutish did not truly believe in their God, their reverence was clearly evident.

And regardless of whether that reverence was what set them apart from other slaves, something did, indeed. Mayhap it was simply their being of a people from across the ocean, of a tongue so different he could make no sense of it at all. But what if it was a deeper reason? What if their belief in their God was more genuine than those who had come before them?

Mayhap he would question them about it, particularly the oldest of the men, the one with silver in his beard.

Sees Far awoke with a start from a dream haunted by the song the woman had sung softly the day before while carrying baskets of ore from the pits where it was dug. In the dream, she had knelt before him, hands bound, while he was the one bending to scold her as Wanchese had done. Her only reply was to open her mouth in song—one that he could strangely understand.

"You are He-who-sees-far. Rise up and be what your name says."

Even as the words echoed in his thoughts, the only sound that met his ears was the soughing of breaths from the other sleepers inside the longhouse, and the heavy chirr of cicadas outside. In the distance, an owl hooted. He sat up, swiping a hand across his face, and rose from the sleeping platform, then picked his way across to the doorway.

The woman slept back to back with the other girl, neither stirring as he passed. The very thought that he would treat her as Wanchese had, unsettled him. Even more, the prospect of her responding in either song or prayer. His gods were stronger than hers, were they not? After all, they had delivered her into his hands. No matter her faith, her God had not withstood such a thing.

So why did her plight so tug at him?

He went off into the trees to relieve himself, then returned to the longhouse, but with the night air so close and hot, he could not bear the prospect of entering and lying down again. A sigh escaped him as he lowered himself to the ground outside, back to the wall.

He'd just tipped his head back and closed his eyes when a shuffling brought him to alertness. It was the older Inqutish man who emerged and stopped in the doorway to regard him for a moment before coming to settle at his side.

"You also not sleep?" the man asked, in the tongue of the People.

Sees Far grunted.

They sat for a little while in silence then, as Sees Far knew would happen, because the Inqutish could not keep silent for long, the man stirred. "Perhaps I speak amiss, but I see your interest in Elinor."

"You do indeed speak amiss." Sees Far put his gruffest tone behind the words.

The man kept his voice very soft. "Why then do you stay?"

Why indeed? Sees Far pushed the persistent question aside. "Such talk should take place only with a pipe of uppowoc."

The man breathed a chuckle. He hesitated, then ventured, "I do not know your people's customs concerning captives. Would one of us be allowed to take her as wife?"

Sees Far met the other man's gaze in the dusk. This one thought such thoughts, even in his position?

"She and Elizabeth, they deserve—protection." He obviously had to search for the right words, but his command of the tongue was impressive.

"Our people do not use slaves in such a way," Sees Far answered haughtily. "But one who wishes to take a captive female to wife would go to the one who holds her and inquire. The price of her worth must be paid, however, and I do not think you hold wealth enough for that."

Another silence, but the man did not flinch from Sees Far's gaze. "Would you perhaps ask for her, then?"

A fist to his belly would have struck the breath from him with less force.

"You speak amiss," he said again.

But once lodged beneath his skin, the idea sank deeper and would not be easily plucked out.

It was as good a time as any, though, to ask the man the other thing burning upon his heart. "Tell me of your God."

"My—God?"

"The Creator, for so we believe Him to be as well. Tell me what your people teach of Him."

With much fumbling, the man communicated that it was as Wanchese claimed—they believed their God, who was high above everything on the earth, somehow had decided to come be born as a man, from a woman—and that without benefit of begetting by a human father. While Sees Far was tumbling that about in his mind, the Inqutish went on to explain that this God-man had been killed by others—but somehow He had planned that death, to rid the world of its sins, and then came back alive again from the dead.

Sees Far sat in silence. Surely he could not have understood properly.

"Are you sure that is the way the story is told?" he demanded at last.

"Story it is not, but truth."

Sees Far waved a hand. "All is story, and truth is in all, if we only have ears to listen." Or so the elders and priests always said.

"It *is* true," the Inqutish said. "God became man in our *Je-sus-kryst.*" Sees Far was not even sure he heard the sounds properly. "Then Je-sus-kryst died, was buried, then was—resurrected—came alive again. Breathed. Ate food. Appeared to—"

"Ate food? You are telling me a God-man with an undying body partook of earthly food after He came alive from the dead? No." Sees Far made a hard gesture with his hand. "That is too much to believe."

To his surprise, the man beside him laughed softly. "God becomes man, dies, and lives again—and that is the part you find difficult?" He laughed again. Strangely enough, the sound lacked the ring of mockery.

When he spoke again, it was in their strange tongue, and then he fell silent.

"What is it you say?"

The man cleared his throat. "It is—hard to translate. The people of whom Kryst was born always looked for a sign—wonders that only God could do, through the hands of Kryst—and those of the peoples outside looked for wisdom. But His own people found Him an offense, while others outside thought it all foolishness. And yet—God chooses to make use of such foolishness to draw men's hearts to Him."

Sees Far grunted again. Foolery it all surely was.

After another while, the man rose and, stepping away, dusted off his backside.

"What are you called?" Sees Far asked.

The man stopped, peering at him as if he had not heard properly. "I am called Roger Prat."

Such strange sounds their tongue had. "Rah-jer-prat."

He nodded, his mouth quirking, and took himself back indoors. "Winkan nupes."

"Winkan nupes."

But despite the exhortation that he sleep well, Sees Far slept not at all the rest of the night. When the sky was grown light enough to see his way clearly, he took himself down to the river for a wash—and to pray and toss a handful of uppowoc over the water in hopes Montóac was in a listening frame of mind.

And if not the spirit-gods, then the Creator, or Rah-jer-prat and Elinor's God. Or were they one and the same, and it was only their understanding—or his—that was lacking?

He waited until the slaves were all set to work before approaching the chief over the mine.

"The strangers work harder than we expected," the man said, after exchanging pleasantries with Sees Far.

"Yes, a surprise it is."

The man beamed. "We are pleased."

Sees Far jerked his chin toward Elinor. "What will be the fate of the women?"

The other man's gaze went sly. "The usual. One of the young warriors is talking to me about the younger, who has been helping at the cooking fires."

"I wish to purchase the other."

He considered Sees Far for a moment. "The younger has been to the women's house three times since coming here. The older, not at all. She may be with child."

He shrugged. "This matters not at all to me."

One eyebrow rose.

"It would complete my vengeance against her people. And she will be of less use to you as the child grows, if so."

"There is also the matter of the value of another captive, if so."

Sees Far held his gaze steady. "I have accrued a stack of deerskins from my hunting, both here and on our journey. And there is the matter of my share of the wassador, which I have not yet asked of you."

The other's face creased with a wide, slow smile. "I see you have thought well on this."

"I have."

He angled his head. "Come to the fire this evening, and let us talk over the uppowoc. Kupi?"

"Kupi."

A week had passed, and either none had taken notice, or they noted it not to her. Elinor durst not breathe easy over the matter, however. Now that the child had made his—or her—presence known, she felt the flutters and even kicks nearly every time she was still enough to do so.

She drew a deep breath. One day at a time, only.

They had finished their morning washing and been handed still-warm rounds of *apon*, the bread they made from dried *pegatawah*. She nibbled gratefully at hers, and found herself thinking suddenly of butter, and how good it would taste with this—

"Elinor." Roger Prat nudged her elbow, then pointed.

Sees Far walked toward them with a look like thunder upon his face. Elinor's fingers fumbled the flat cake and she nearly dropped it. What on earth had she done?

He stopped in front of her, glance barely flicking to Master Prat, and lifted that old, hated leather thong. Nay—not the old, but one new and unstretched. Her heart pounded.

"*Micis*. When you are finished, we will leave."

She could only gape, the apon still cupped in her hand.

"*Mehci* micis!" *Eat now!*

She looked around. "What is happening?" she asked Master Prat, forgetting her Croatoan.

Roger Prat looked stricken. The master of the mine stepped up beside Sees Far, whose countenance was still hard as stone. "Sees Far has purchased you. You will go with him."

Mouth still open, she turned and surveyed the others. John Bright and Martyn Sutton both protested and moved forward, as if to prevent such a thing, but they were held back. Elizabeth stood to one side, hands over her mouth.

Then Roger Prat spoke so softly she had to strain to hear. "Go with him, Elinor."

She was sure she misheard. "Pardon?"

A sheen stood in his eyes. "Go. Recall that there is yet hope." His gaze did not leave hers. " 'Put thy trust in God, for I will yet give Him thanks, for the help of His countenance.' "

She could still make no sense of it. But Sees Far stood before her, his mouth firm and the thong clenched in one fist.

With a deep breath, she brought the apon to her mouth and applied herself to finishing it. Slowly, she chewed. She would need the strength.

After, she wiped her hands on her skirt and held them out before her.

Sees Far watched every flicker of the woman's features as she was informed of his intention, comprehended the situation, then obviously and deliberately chose courage. The small flame that had been flickering within his chest now burst into a full blaze. He cared not that whatever Rah-jer-prat had said seemed to help. Even so, she was nothing short of wondrous, her bravery more than a match not only for that man who had dashed into their midst to challenge them, only to be slain by Wanchese, but also for. . .a warrior of the Sukwoten.

More than a match for him.

Satisfaction surged with the fire inside him, thickening his throat. He wrapped and tied the thong with quick, sure movements, but less tightly than he had before. She would indeed complete his vengeance. Not as he had first foreseen, but—

He would accept this new way without complaint.

After making sure her hands were securely bound, he allowed the others to say their farewells, then lifted one of the bags of provisions—dried meat from a deer he had himself brought in—and tied it across her back. A second he slung across his own shoulders, and with a crisp "Pyas!" and a wave to the others, he led her away.

He'd not even thought overlong on where they'd go. He'd no desire to stay near the mines, as welcoming as the people there had been, but neither could they return immediately to the lowlands, and certainly not to his own people. It was too close, too soon after her being taken—she would find an opportunity to escape and be gone. And he would not yet put her back within Wanchese's reach.

Not that his old friend would disrespect the customs of taking and keeping captives. Sees Far had paid for her, and she would be regarded as his.

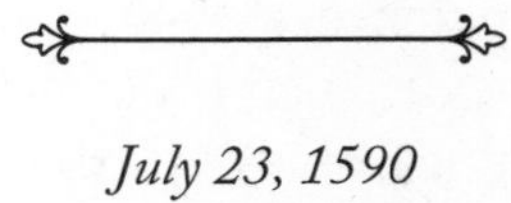

July 23, 1590

Three ships, small pinnaces all, on the horizon. "Think it be Captain Harpe's pinnace and prizes?" Captain Cooke asked.

"They look heavily laden," John said.

"Aye." He turned to the crew and called out, "Hoist the flag!"

To their dismay, the three ships became a flurry of activity, all sails being hoisted, and they heeled about, changing course for shallower waters. Captain Cooke swore softly. "Give chase!" he commanded.

For the next hours, they pursued, expending shot and powder with the occasional firing of the ship's guns, but the pinnaces stayed in waters too shallow for their own larger ship to safely enter. At last, they had gone as far as leeward from Havana and seen none of their own ships, and they decided to turn back.

They put over again to the Cape of Florida and followed the coast northward, then, striking out into deeper waters to catch the ocean current, lost sight of the coast.

Falling in again with the *Moonelight* and their prize frigate, they continued on for another day, as the weather changed from fair to threatening. The seas rose, the clouds gathered, and thunder rolled as lightning struck. Most terrifying were the great waterspouts that fell round about them, nigh unto their ships. How they escaped, John was not sure, except by the very grace of God.

Very shortly now, and mayhap he would hold his daughter and grandchild in his arms once more.

Through a day, and a night, and another day, Elinor followed Sees Far. They kept, if not a leisurely pace, then one she would not have termed brisk either, but the country itself had remained rough, with many hills, large rocky outcroppings, and trees so great she'd not have been able to span half of a trunk with her arms. The best she could tell, by the angle of the sun, they were traveling west. She asked but once, early on the first day, where they were going, and his manner so discouraged further inquiry that she did not try again until late that second evening. Bringing her a pair of rabbits he'd shot with his bow and dressed, he kindled a fire and told her to set the meat to cook, while at the same time helping her complete the task.

"Will you unbind my hands so I may work?" she asked.

A single shake of his head. "I do not wish you to run."

"I would not."

"I do not know that for sure."

He handed her a sharpened stick and assisted with threading the carcasses upon it, then set it between two forked sticks placed into the ground pointing upward. That done, he remained crouched by the fire, looking everywhere but into the flames.

"Where are you taking me?" she asked.

His eyes shifted to hers. The shadows played across his face, but even in firelight the marks across his forehead and cheeks seemed less strange than before.

"Are you with child?" he asked, with one hand miming a roundness of the belly.

Though she tried to remain as impassive as he, she could not help the widening of her eyes.

"You have not been to the women's house at all. And I saw the other night how you touched your body, then wept."

Her hands knotted into her skirts, just over her belly, but—there was nothing she could say, nothing she could do, if his will was to do her harm.

"What. . .do you plan to do with me?" she asked at last, fumbling through the Croatoan words. The order of their speech was still so strange at times.

His eyes glittered, and his chin came up. For the breath of a moment, she was minded of Wanchese. Yet when he leaned toward her, seeming to test her mettle, she did not feel the need to shrink away.

"Whatever I wish," he said.

Again, an echo of Wanchese, however unwittingly—for she did not think Sees Far knew English, or at least not as well.

"You are my slave," he went on. "My crenepo."

She tipped her head. "Which is it? Because is not a slave more like a dog at heel, than a woman?"

Did his lips twitch? Somehow it heartened her to think she tempted him to smile. But rather than answer, he turned back to the fire and turned the rabbits on the spit.

She was more than happy to pull up her knees, loop her arms around them, and rest her head, eyes closed.

What seemed only a moment later, a nudge awakened her. She straightened, breathing in. Where was this place, again? Oh—she had been dreaming of Ananias, walking on the seashore as the waves pounded, with Ginny on his shoulders, laughing.

Sees Far handed her a haunch of rabbit, still sizzling from the fire. She thanked him and set to, managing most of the portion before her stomach decided abruptly that it had had enough. She offered him the rest, then rose and took herself down to the stream to wash. Presently he joined her.

Back at the fire, he reached for a rolled-up deerskin and tossed it to her. "Nupes."

Sleep. Too weary for anything else, she pulled the cover over her and curled into the moss.

Her last waking thought was the memory of her wedding to Ananias, and the feel of his kiss when they were alone together at long last, after.

He knew he ought not sleep the first night, but sleep took him anyway. And with sleep came the dream again.

Mother Ocean was not playful this time, but roared in her full glory, waves crashing over the sea strand all the way up to the foot of the dunes and sending spray high into the air, though the sun shone beneath a blue sky. And still the Man walked, face shrouded as one of the poles of the dancing circle, but he was not alone. A woman accompanied him, tucked to his side, her golden hair streaming bright in the sunlight.

He recognized her immediately.

So, so very far away they were. Sees Far called out, but they could not hear over the roar of the waves—or did not heed him. He tried to run, but his feet could not get good purchase in the sand, and the more he scrambled to follow, the farther away they went.

He woke, startled and shaken, to great trees arching over him and, beyond, a sky at its most vivid before the rising of the sun. The woman slumbered on, wrapped in the deerskin he'd given her.

Rising, Sees Far went to the stream and washed himself. Even with the water's chill, the dream was still there, the ocean's roar pressing upon his inner ear, nearly as loud as the early-morning birdsong and rustle of the trees, no small noise themselves. And the Man, his arm around Elinor—

How had she found her way into his dreams, even before ever she had come to his country? And his suspicion about the One who walked with her, now that he knew what they believed of their God—but how could he have known that, before meeting her people?

Unless his name truly did refer to seeing a long way not only in actual distance, but also in terms of time?

The priests had said, when he chose his name, that he might at some point be compelled into service as one of their own. But he had no interest in burning the uppowoc, in tending the dead, in searching the stars and imploring the spirits on behalf of those around him.

But this. . .why this?

The very idea of a God becoming man—of their Creator not only taking notice of them but bending close enough to touch—ensnarled his thoughts like nothing else.

Why would He do such a thing?

And why, if it were true, did His people not better live their faith in Him, if He had such power as to bring a Man back from the dead?

Why would He deliver them over to the will of their enemies? Allow them to suffer starvation and loss?

Would that he had asked Rah-jer-prat about this while he'd still opportunity. He did not want to admit to the woman that he entertained such thoughts.

Returning to the fire, now but ashes, he nudged her awake and sent her to wash while he scattered what was left of the fire and made sure there were no live coals to carelessly ignite the forest around them. When the woman had trudged back up the hill, he handed her one of the last apon. She ate, and he rolled up their deerskins, then took up the length of cord from the tether on her wrists and bid her come along.

The sun had barely begun to show on the horizon, not at their backs but a little over their left shoulders. Deer and rabbits and other game lifted their heads and watched their passage with curious eyes, then, finding no apparent threat, returned to their foraging.

Elinor suppressed a yawn. Sees Far set a brisker pace this morn, following a faint path beside the stream above which they had camped the night before. 'Twas beautiful country, all green and yet cool, with scattered flowers of blue even this late in summer. Great, craggy outcroppings of granite broke up the forest floor, clothed in bushes with glossy green leaves, and clear, cold streams spilled down the creases in the hills, often forming waterfalls where she longed to linger.

And Sees Far navigated it all with his usual lithe grace, while she tripped and stumbled ever so often, compelled to go faster than she otherwise might by her bindings.

How she wished to ask again where they were going. His brooding silence made such a thing more unpleasant, however, than if she simply pretended to already know, and follow him accordingly. And so she did her best to keep up, while noting small details of moss and blade and leaf and bark. Papa would have loved to see this part of the country, and to paint it—

A gust of longing, sharp as winter wind, swept across her. In a moment she was choking on the tears. *Gracious God, preserve him! I know not now whether to even pray he finds his way back to us safely—but Your will be done, and keep him safe, regardless! And Ginny—oh, my dear child, if she lives, keep her and the remaining townspeople safe as well. May they not sorrow. May they know Your comfort and presence—may we all know Your comfort and presence—*

The wind swirling about her turned warm and soft, and she shut her eyes, forgetting to watch where she was going. The bindings on her wrists yanked her forward, and her foot caught on a stone and she fell, a cry escaping her lips.

Mayhap she should save prayers for nighttime, when she was ready for sleep, and not ranging a rough hillside.

Sees Far was instantly at her side. *"Sá keyd winkan?"*

Are you well? She bit her lips, sucking in a breath against the sharp pain in hands and knees, but nodded once. He would expect an affirmative response. The dark eyes shone with skepticism as he helped her to her feet.

"You are slow."

She swallowed and sorted through her words for a reply. "I would be less so if my hands were free." When he stared balefully at her, she lifted her arms then let them drop. "I will not run."

A huff, and he seized one hand, turning it outward to examine the abrasions on both palms. "You are also clumsy," he said, but more softly this time, and began to work the knot free.

He would truly trust her to walk free? What madness was this?

The knot came loose, and as if he'd heard her thoughts, he glanced up, unwinding the cord. "I cannot have you hurting yourself. The ground will grow steeper yet."

She gave the burbling water a glance, and he motioned toward it with a nod. She wasted no more time but clambered over the rocks to the water's edge, where she stooped and let the water flow over her hands and wrists. Lifting her skirts, she examined the similar scrapes to her knee and washed those as well.

"Come," Sees Far called at last, and with a regretful sigh, she left the stream and returned to the path. He was already in motion.

What a difference it made to be able to lift her skirts with both hands, or to use one to help with balance as she navigated the uneven track. She might even take pleasure in such a jaunt, were it not—

Sees Far's voice startled her. "What is the meaning of your name?"

She'd have gawped at him were it not for the need to mind her path. "Say again?"

He waved a hand. "You are called *El-in-or*. What does it mean, in your tongue?"

Like the Croatoan when they first met, he had trouble with the *l*, but got it nearly right. "I—I know not."

He gave a snort and flashed her a sharp-edged smile. "You do not even know what your own name means? How was it chosen, then?"

"My father and my mother chose it when I was born. It is the name of some of our country's weroansquas." A memory tickled, and she added, "My father often said it means 'light,' but I know not whether that is so. I think it may be a mere fancy, but perhaps not."

He stopped and swung toward her, his eyes wide and expression rather stricken.

"What is it?" she asked.

But he shook his head and turned away again, running nimbly up a portion of the hill, then pausing at the top to watch her ascent.

"Is that your people's way? To choose the name of a baby before they are old enough to choose for themselves? What if you wished to be named something else?"

She shrugged. "We. . .are pleased. . .to keep the names our parents have given us. It is our honor to them."

She'd had a similar conversation with Timqua and the other women over the curiosity of the changing of names among the Croatoan and other native peoples.

"A woman does take the name of her husband when they are married," she said. "It is also an honor we do. Thus my father's name was John White, and mine before I wed, Elinor White, but now I am Elinor Dare."

Oh, Ananias. . .

Sees Far's eyes were sharp upon her again. Did he not comprehend her words, or did he merely find their customs strange when compared with his own people's way?

She gained the hillock where he stood, and without comment he led on, then abruptly stopped at a rocky outcropping that overlooked the forest beyond—

And wave after wave of far blue mountaintops. Breathless, she leaned against a sapling and simply drank in the view.

"This is the sight I had desired to see," he murmured beside her, so softly she was not sure she'd caught the words aright. "I miss the sea, but all my life I have heard stories of the far blue mountains. And now I behold them for myself, standing among them."

"They are—" She struggled to find proper descriptors in his tongue. *Beautiful. Magnificent. Awe-inspiring.*

Gazing out over the view, he said a word. She tried to mimic it, and he repeated it, more slowly, and she tried again. She'd no idea which exact meaning it took, of course, but—

Then he was not looking at the landscape at all, but his eyes were on her, skimming her features and hair. He whispered the word this time, almost with awe.

There was something in his expression that minded her strongly of tender moments with Ananias, yet surely she misunderstood. Heat swept through her, and she turned back to the astonishing vista before her—but barely saw it now.

When she peeked at Sees Far again, he gave a little smile and likewise turned away, setting off again along the path.

He should not engage in such playfulness with her, and yet he'd seemed not to be able to keep silent, when the sun and wind so caught her hair and drew the golden fire from it, and the sky had been reflected in her eyes.

Beautiful she was, whether she accepted or even understood the compliment. Perhaps the Kurawoten, backward people that they were, had no such word as he'd offered her. Yet in that moment he could not hold back from declaring it.

Did she still cling to the shadow of her slain husband? It was possible. He'd seen those who loved so deeply that when loss overtook them, they could not move past the grieving for a long while. Had her Inqutish husband kept her well?

If so, then she would not welcome his advances—if he decided even to offer such, after she had given birth and finished nursing the child. For all his lofty words to Wanchese, he found that her question—*a slave, or a woman?*—stung him. Vengeance demanded she remain a slave—and nothing changed that she was his captive, even if she did offer willing submission in her promise not to run away, and he let her walk unbound.

And yet. . .yet. She could not have known how the declaration of her name's meaning would strike so deeply. Did she even recall it was him she had met upon Roanoac Island that day, in the mist? He was certain not, or she would have spoken so.

Did he wish her to know?

The sound of ocean waves from his dream once again pressed upon him, and the image of her in the sheltering embrace of the unknown Man. A sudden longing gripped his throat.

Was it jealousy that another would hold her so, or. . .the wish that he was the one being so sheltered?

Chapter Seventeen

August 17, 1590

In the two ships' boats they approached the inlet, the water shifting from deep blue to grey-green as it boiled with the tide. The other men were rowing too slowly—why were they rowing so slowly? At the same time, while they complained and cursed at the wind and waves, John recognized that caution was needful.

A man in the bow to navigate, Captain Cooke at the tiller, the boat pitched and bobbed its way through the inlet as the sea surged with what seemed a life of its own, as if protesting their passage. A wave washed up over the side, drenching them all and half filling the boat.

John helped in the frantic effort to bail seawater from the craft, while those plying the oars labored to bring them safe to shore, not upon the island where he so longed to set foot, but on the nearer strand of Hatorask. Drawn up on the sand, they all piled out, unloading goods and supplies, finding much soaked and spoiled.

And then a cry drew them all around to watch, helplessly, as the second boat entered the fuming, frothing inlet.

"They left her mast up, the fools," the captain said.

John could not breathe. Prayers and curses broke out anew around him as for a few moments, it seemed the boat would succeed in its passage, but one wave then another swamped it, and the boat tipped over. A collective moan and cry went up from the sailors on the beach.

The captain shouted for any who could swim strongly to shed as much clothing as possible and go to the aid of those in the water.

When all was done, only four of the eleven souls in that other boat were brought to safety.

A heated debate followed, wherein most of the other men wished only to return to the ship and quit this place. The words *cursed* and *foolhardy* were bandied about, but John held firm. They'd come too far now, he insisted. Let the deaths of those seven not be wasted.

Let no more lives be squandered on this wretched venture, someone countered.

Captain Cooke made a sharp gesture. They'd come thus far, he said, and they'd go at least to the settlement site to find whatsoever they might.

Having retrieved the other ship's boat, they fitted everything and set out once more—now a party of nineteen rather than twenty-six. John's heart felt keenly the loss of all, but especially of his friend Captain Spicer and the young Robert Coleman, whose father was with the expedition three years before.

How heavy the news would weigh on Thomas, once word reached him.

By the time they gained the shore nearest the town, it was so dark that they overshot the place by a quarter mile, but as they were making their way back, the hot flicker of a great fire came into sight over on the north side of the island. Cooke gave the command to row that way, and when they had come opposite the fire, they threw down the grapnel, then one of the soldiers drew out a trumpet and, in hopes of raising the attention of whoever might be there, played a merry tune.

The notes fell into silence. John began to sing, and others joined him, one song after another, calling out in between, "Ho, the land!"

No answer.

John's throat squeezed more tightly. Nothing for it at last but to bundle into his cloak and curl up where they were in the boats. Long he lay, staring up at the stars.

Lord God. . .Almighty One. . .how many times have I asked You to keep them safe, and let me see their faces again? Yet I ask once more. Tomorrow our sweet Virginia Thomasyn Dare shall be three, and a comely maid she must be. Let me—let me just once again—

The words faltered. God had brought him thus far. He could carry John yet further.

Morning dawned, the water pearlescent in the sunrise, with the merest sliver of a waning moon overhead. The waves roughened anew as they neared the island. Gripping the side of the boat, the moment John felt the keel catch on sand, he leaped over the side, heedless of the captain's command for him to wait.

He already had waited, far too long.

A moment of alarm hit him as his boots found purchase in the surf and he slogged ashore. A memory—George Howe's half-clad body, shredded and full of arrows, lying at the edge of the marsh.

He stopped, a wave catching him from behind, slapping the back of his legs and causing him to sway. Squinting, he scanned the shore and the dunes beyond. Naught within sight, but—were those footprints? He went up the beach more slowly. Definite footprints, with indentations of bare toes.

Another survey of the shoreline, and then he pressed on, up the dune and into the forest of pine and oak.

Under cover of the trees, he stopped again to gain his bearings. The other sailors had followed him up from the beach, and beyond the crackle and scuffle of their passage, there was no sound, only birdsong and the deep drone of insects.

They pressed on, through forest of pine and oak, until they came to the fire—but only burning grass and sundry rotten trees greeted their sight.

John huffed. "Well. We are close to the place where I left Lane's colony the year before I was appointed governor. Let us go see what may be seen there."

Back to the shore and farther north. "Look," Captain Cooke said, "more footprints. I judge two, perhaps three? And bare feet, so—savages?"

John lifted his cap and raked his fingers through sweat-dampened hair, separating the strands to better catch the coolness from the breeze. "Aye." Impatience was near to choking him at the moment, but there was nothing for it but to keep going.

At last they came even to where the town was situated. There was the path, as he'd recalled—and there, upon a great tree at the brow of the sandy bank, the bark had been stripped and three Roman letters inscribed:

C R O

John stopped, a shock sweeping from toes to scalp, lifting every hair upon his body.

There. The token he had bid them leave, giving sign to where they might have gone. And without the cross that he'd instructed them to use if their departure had been under circumstances of distress.

CRO. *Croatoan*. Signifying the place where they'd gone.

John fell to his knees. "Thanks be to God!"

The edge of the town came into view. Or what he presumed was the edge—a palisade, comprised of stout logs, complete with fortlike spurs on the corners. No other tracks marred the sandy earth. No sign of life greeted them.

They circled the palisade until they reached the opening, one end lapped over the other with room for two men to walk abreast between.

And there, on a main post over on the right side, was a section with the bark cleared and in large letters carved:

CROATOAN

John's breath left him in a rush. "No cross or other sign of distress! Thanks be to God—again! They went safe to Croatoan Island, then, as I suspected when we saw the tree on the shore."

He turned to go inside the palisade. Three of the other men reached it before him, took several strides inside, and halted. Heart thudding, he entered, slipping past them to look. And there—

Was naught.

No inhabitants, nor houses, nor anything at all.

'Twas not unexpected, but when the moment had come, he found himself wholly unprepared.

They all scattered about the space, overgrown with weeds and grass—whenever they had departed, it would have been a year or more ago.

"Look, the iron fowlers are still installed at the corners—from the former fort, do you think? And a pig of lead, and sacker shot. They could not have taken those as well?"

"Mayhap they were judged too heavy for their boats."

"Mayhap. But 'tis passing strange."

"Another pig of lead here, and several iron bars."

"And yet they took down the houses, to a post, and carried them off?"

John walked about, letting the other men's talk eddy about him like the water of the inlets. The past night and day had already held too much heartache.

He turned a slow circle, inhaling the rich smell of pine, and closed his eyes. Here his own granddaughter breathed her first breaths. Oh, the irony of walking this ground on the third anniversary of her birth! So close, and yet—too far away.

Gracious God. . .

The prayer blew away even in the forming of it, the longing pressing yet more heavily on his heart.

Oh—Elinor. Oh, my child, and child's child. Will I yet hold you in my arms, this side of heaven?

The others had begun to file out of the palisade. He followed, feet dragging. 'Twould do no good to linger, however, if they had gone elsewhere.

Captain Cooke fell into step beside him. "Croatoan Island, then? Back to the south?"

"Aye. 'Tis our best hope. But we should go back along the water, to the point of the creek, where they had left their boats and the pinnace."

Cooke agreed, sending half of the men back the way they had come. But the place where the boats had formerly been anchored was likewise bare. There was no longer even any sign of them, nor of the ordnance which had been set up. "At least they took some of the ship's guns," Cooke muttered.

John nodded, distracted. "Well, I suppose we should rejoin the others."

They were not yet halfway back before some of the sailors met them. "Sir, we have found a place where divers chests were hidden in the sand, but long since dug up again and ransacked. Much of the goods therein are spoiled and scattered about, with nothing the savages thought of use left undefaced."

They pressed on and presently came to the place. And here John stared about, not a word of intelligent speech on his tongue, nor any rational thought in his mind.

His feet took him of their own accord. Five chests in all, judging by the fragments left. The planters had hidden them most carefully, 'twas certain, but to no avail. Three of the chests had been his own—that much was clear by the markings on the fragments of the lids. He picked up a book, its covers torn away and ink blurred by rain. Many more lay scattered about. Maps and pictures in frames, all rotten and spoiled—here was one, not framed, the drawing of Manteo's daughter, utterly ruined. And—was that his armor lying about, nearly eaten through by rust?

"I am sure," he said slowly, near to choking upon the words, "this must be the work of our enemies from Dasemonguepeuk. Doubtless they came over after they saw our planters leave, and dug anyplace they thought something of value might be buried."

How he'd quarreled with the men over the necessity of leaving his goods behind. What foolishness—and yet, facing now the utter ruin of it all, though it much grieved him, he could not deny the joy at Elinor and Ananias and the others being away safe on Croatoan.

"Yet you are confident of the planters being now upon the island named by the token they left?"

"Aye, it is where Manteo was born, and his people are our friends."

"If friends savages can ever truly be," one of the sailors muttered, and John turned upon him.

"You know not of what you speak. They are verily friends and brothers, better indeed than many English I have known."

The sailors only looked at him in shock, then turned away. Captain

Cooke scrubbed at his beard and squinted. "Well. Let us look about a bit more, then haste back to our boats. I like not the look of that sky."

By the time they took to the boats again and were on their way back toward the inlet, the wind and seas had begun to rise, and the scudding clouds promised a foul and stormy night. They made passage through the inlet—and John was sure the channel had shifted even since the day before, with how wild were the waves. Past the inlet, facing open seas, it was hard labor rowing back toward the ships.

"We're glad to have you back aboard, and no mistake," the mate said to Captain Cooke as they gained the deck of the admiral. "But we still have six men ashore on Hatorask, filling our casks with fresh water."

The captain grimaced. "Let us choose five strong men, well able to swim, and send out the boat again to fetch them back."

While that was being accomplished, John helped as best he could, but felt largely useless while the ship was being prepared for a stormy night. He was about to turn in when the ship's boat returned with all eleven men safe—yet all the casks, freshly filled, had to be left behind. "Please God we may be able to retrieve them, if we are not blown too far off course," the captain said.

It proved a terrible night, and all agreed that the cables and anchors would scarcely hold until morning. John himself slept but little, praying much for both the ship's well-being and that of his daughter and family and all the planters. Yet morning came, and here they still were.

The captain summoned John to his cabin, along with the shipmaster and several others. "What think you, then? Shall we weigh anchor and set for Croatoan? The wind is favorable to sail that way."

John swallowed past what felt like his heart, beating right up in his throat. "I am most desirous of that."

He felt the eyes of the others upon him, but none made comment.

" 'Twill be but a quick foray, but 'tis ridiculous to have come so far and not at least attempt it," the shipmaster said at last.

The others added their assent, and John drew his first easy breath that morning.

"We will leave our fresh casks upon shore, then, until our return. Let us go out and see to the weighing of anchors."

Four anchors in all must needs be drawn up. John held back, watching and praying, as the wind whipped at men and sails alike, and the crew began to turn the capstan on the first anchor. The anchor itself was nearly cleared of water and to home on the ship's hull, when a loud report sounded, loud as cannon shot, and the ship lurched. A great cry arose. "The cable, she has snapped! We've lost the anchor!"

The ship shuddered and heaved, and a second report followed. "Another anchor lost!" came a shout.

John clutched the rail, trying to see while not being flung into the dark waves.

"God above have mercy! We are driving too hard toward shore. Heel about!"

But there was no controlling the bucking, heaving beast of a vessel beneath them. John hooked an arm through the rail, hunkering down against the ship's side to pray with inner moanings that had no words.

"Let fall another anchor!"

Yet another surge, and more shouts and cries of the crew. It looked as though they were able to secure the fourth and last anchor. Peering through the rail, still bracing for the impact of the ship driving aground, John recognized the outline of Kenrick's Mount. Moving southward, then, but still north of Croatoan. And by the angle, they were yet headed straight for shore—

The ship canted and abruptly heeled. The wind-driven strand lay parallel now to the ship's rail. The ship rose and fell in a more normal motion, and held course. John got his feet beneath him and rose, still trembling, still praying.

"We've chanced upon a channel, close to shore, that will accommodate the ship," the captain said, still standing at the tiller, the wind whipping his hair straight out to the side. The grimness had not yet left his expression. "If it remains so, until we can reach deeper water—"

Remain it did, and deeper water they did gain, but the weather grew fouler and fouler. John's heart sank, for they'd begun to lack both water and victuals and talk was now of returning to St. John or some other southward island for resupply.

He crowded again with the shipmaster and other officers in Captain Cooke's cabin. "Things are dire and no mistake," the captain said. "The storm buffets us still, and we are soon to be out of water and food. What say you all of this?"

He had presented the inquiry to the room as a whole, but his gaze lingered on John.

"I would implore you most earnestly," John said, stammering, comprehending too well the danger of presenting the plea so often, "not to forget our countrymen who wait for us upon these shores."

"I am endeavoring not to," the captain answered evenly. "Has anyone any proposal for accomplishing that and yet keeping ourselves alive?"

"If we could"—John thought fast, spoke faster—"by any means supply our want of victuals and other necessaries, either at Hispaniola, Saint John, or Trynidad, then we could continue in the Indies all the winter following"—*oh, my dear Elinor, forgive me!*—"with hope to make two rich voyages of one, and at our return, visit our countrymen at Virginia."

The captain and company looked thoughtful, if not a little surprised, at his bold suggestion. "It is a good plan," the master said, and the others agreed.

"It rests only to know what the master of our consort the *Moonelight* will do in this plan," the captain said.

The wind quieted enough by evening for them to draw close enough to the *Moonelight* to inquire of her, but the other ship had suffered badly in the tempest. The master insisted they could not continue, between the leaks and other damage done their ship and the sore loss of Captain Spicer—which wrung at John's own heart as well, in addition to the disappointment of being so close to Elinor and little Virginia and yet not able to reach the shore.

And so the *Moonelight* went directly for England, while they themselves set course for Trynidad.

They kept course two days before the wind again changed. This time it was west and northwest, and blew so forcibly the ship could not bear sail at all except the forecourse half-mast high, which enabled them to run upon the wind—and due course for England. For the Azores, then, they stood, rather than their first determination of Trynidad. Perhaps there they could supply their wants.

John knew he dared not hope for more than this. In all things he gave himself to the details of the voyage and only allowed private mourning at night, wrapped in his blanket, under cover of dark.

The end of August. Three years ago he had left Virginia—his country, his granddaughter. Would he ever see either again, or his daughter and countrymen?

Deep in his heart, he suspected not. And he had neither spirit within him even to hope, nor, for now, any more prayers.

He was not sure there would ever be prayer enough either to move the seas or to soothe his aching soul.

"We are no longer going toward the mountains?"

Elinor had not been sure of their direction the first day or two, but now the country they traveled through was decidedly less rough than it had been.

Sees Far glanced back. "I have seen the mountains. That is enough. Now I wish to see the ocean once more."

They were headed back to the coastlands? She dared not entertain the tendril of hope that sprang up in her heart at the possibility.

Of course, to what purpose remained to be seen. But out here in the open forest, anything seemed possible.

Oh, my darling Virginia Thomasyn. To hold you again. . . !

Sees Far had spoken but little as they walked. Elinor relished the freedom, however, of her hands being unbound, and though their victuals might be lean, neither did she go hungry. In fact, Sees Far had brought down a deer a few days ago and then set up a lean-to so they might stay long enough not only to roast it but smoke the rest into jerky. He saved the hide, of course, but carried the bones and other offal away into the forest, so as not to draw bears or wildcats. Elinor shivered at the thought of encountering either, but Sees Far shrugged and said the fire would keep them away. But it was best to take precautions, though he hated the waste of throwing away good bones and various innards.

They'd caught a glimpse of bears yesterday—a mother and two cubs. Sees Far kept walking, so Elinor did the same, and though the bears stopped to look, they did not approach. They also saw deer, skunk, opossum, and raccoon aplenty, along with more birds and insects than Elinor had words for. Many she knew already from Papa's drawings and paintings. Sees Far answered all her inquiries about names and habits with much patience, though by the little smile at the corner of his mouth, she suspected he found amusement in her childlike curiosity.

Ginny would have been wild with delight—and never quiet. Elinor's heart panged. The questions Sees Far could not answer, by his own admission, were those concerning the intended actions of Wanchese and the other warriors, and by extension of course the fate of her fellow English and the Croatoan.

For the thousandth time, she sent up a prayer for their safety.

That was another matter. Out here, at odd moments she felt utterly lost in the wildness of the country. At others, she sensed the nearness of God as nowhere else—not even in the church back in England.

"I will love thee, O Lord, my strength. The Lord is my stony rock, and my defense, my saviour, my God, and my might, in whom I will trust: my buckler, the horn also of my salvation, and my refuge. . . ."

Somehow those words were more vivid after seeing the wild mountains and all the rocky hills.

And then she would remember where she was, and whose company she kept—and that Ananias was sundered from her, if not forever, then until her natural life was ended as well, and their daughter, if she yet lived, was without comfort of either father or mother.

"I will say unto the God of my strength, why hast thou forgotten me: why go I thus heavily, while the enemy oppresseth me? My bones are smitten asunder, while mine enemies. . .say daily unto me: where is now thy God?"

Indeed. . .where was He? Had He forgotten her? Roger Prat did not think so, and even suggested that Sees Far's taking her away again was evidence of hope.

Yet here they were, still wandering the wilderness as if he'd no plan to rejoin human company again, while his fellow warriors continued wreaking vengeance upon the English planters.

Elinor could not breathe. She stopped, her eyes snapping shut, and let the sounds of the deep forest surround her in the moment.

God in heaven. . .if You hear me. . .protect my daughter. Protect those who care for her. And, if it please You, myself as well, for the sake of this new life I carry.

The pang of her heart did not ease. Was Ginny now taken captive, or did she lay slain as well?

"Pyas! Why do you linger?"

She did not reply to Sees Far's urgent command and question.

Lord of heaven and earth, where are You? Why have You brought me to this situation?

The slightest rustling gave her to know that Sees Far approached. "*Sá keyd winkan?*" he said, more quietly but still sharp.

She did not want to look at him. She did not want to see the concern in his dark eyes. Did not want to be reminded again that it was his company she now kept, whether or not she willed it—that she would never again in this life see love or concern or any other feeling from her own dear husband, and instead her every move was at the whim of this man—

He was so close, she could feel his breath.

She opened her eyes to see him standing before her, head tipped, brow creased, gaze searching her face.

"I miss my husband and child," she whispered, in English.

His expression flickered, the frown deepening, but he did not move otherwise. She should be grateful he was not as other captors and prone to striking at the slightest provocation, whether that be speaking in the wrong tongue or anything else they deemed impertinence. She should not further presume upon his goodwill and continued kindness. But something inside made her cast caution aside and ask.

"Where are Wanchese and the others? Where is my daughter?"

She repeated the questions in his tongue. Would he even be able to give answer?

Did his body stiffen, ever so slightly? His gaze spark? His eyes held hers for an unaccountably long time; then he shook his head. "Pyas. We will talk."

With that, he turned and retraced his steps down the rocky, forest-clothed ridge. A gust of breeze shook the leaves overhead, and swallowing, she followed.

He glanced back at her. "Why would your God abandon you to us? If He has power to come alive again after He is dead?"

She was not sure of all the words he used, but thought she understood the question as a whole.

And what a question. How to answer at all, much less explain concepts of belief and faith and trust with her own still-growing knowledge of his language? She did not know the proper words.

Oh God. . .are You here? Present even in the questions of this man? Is this why You have put me here, that he may hear of You? Or. . .am I merely a bit of flotsam, caught on the waves of this life?

She thought of Papa, years before, his expression both tender and earnest, leaning close to answer her objection to wading through long recitations of the Psalms and other scripture. *"Read it now, Daughter, while there is yet time and opportunity. You know not when you may need it, laid up like treasure in your heart, when there is not the written Word to come to."*

Her eyes burned. She was so weary of the tears. So weary of the grieving.

So weary of her own endless questions.

"I do not know how to say it," she began. "But it is like—you give me food, and lead me to where I may drink and wash. In return, I—follow. I—"

She huffed. What were terms for *accept* and *not doubt*?

"I come with. You do not always talk. I do not know where we are going. But still I come with you."

He'd halted, eyeing her. Did he understand what she was trying to convey?

"You give me food and water. Help me when I fall. Not strike me. You are good—more good than Wanchese, at least."

His mouth quirked briefly.

"And so I follow. I do not run away. Because—" Memory of a particular word surfaced, which, if she properly comprehended it, was an approximation of *hope*. "I hope that you will keep giving me food and water."

"But if I did not give you food, if I struck you and was bad?"

She spread her hands. "I am your slave. You bought me. If you feel, here"—she tapped her breast—"that it is good. . ." Another huff. "Our God is good. No bad at all. I—*hope*—in Him for food and clothing and help when I fall. And if not, He knows why. But He is good."

Meanwhile the panic still beat inside her breast. *What if He is not?* the doubt whispered.

Sees Far looked at her a moment more. "Mm," he said. Turning, he continued walking.

At least it spared her having to struggle further for the right words. For now.

Such matters begged an evening fire, and a pipe of uppowoc with a cup of something sweet and spiced. Sees Far thought he knew what it was she wished to express but had not the right word for, but it was impossible to untangle the full meaning while walking.

Although something she had said confirmed to him that his chosen direction was indeed the right one and sparked a new purpose within him. Besides, of course, his desire to avoid the Spanish, whose scattered forts stretched from the southern coastline to the mountains near the place he had taken Elinor before turning eastward again. Others might dare trade with or ally themselves with those bearded ones, but they were by all accounts worse even than the Inqutish.

All morning, the stream they followed widened to a creek, big enough for a kanoe. When the sun stood straight overhead, he bid Elinor sit and handed her a bit of jerky.

Taking his own, he settled on his haunches facing her. "I think I know the word you wish. *Trust.* You trust me to feed you and tend your needs. And I allow you to walk unbound, trusting that you will not run."

Her eyes lit with understanding. "Yes. So it is, that I trust God to do what is good for me, even if it is hard in the moment." She looked at the jerky. "I also remember He says He will make even the bad turn out for good for me. I do not know how He will do this. But I trust that He will."

"How does He say this?"

"In His book—His Holy Scriptures—" She waved a hand in apparent frustration at her lack of words again.

"I know of which you speak," he said slowly. "The man Lane and his company brought that bound bundle of flat leaves, with what they called writing. They said it was sacred, that it told them things of God no one else could know."

Elinor nodded, and appeared to understand so far.

He tore off a bite of dried meat and waved a hand. "Many of our people held the book and rubbed it on their bodies, as well as kneeling with Lane and his men in prayer. It did not protect us from the sickness after. Many died."

She frowned. "It. . .is not like that. The book itself does nothing, only the words therein. It is not so much what you do. It is what you think, here." Her fingers went to the side of her head. "And what you feel, here." As before, she touched her chest.

"So it is more a matter of belief and not ritual?"

Confusion clouded her face this time.

He shook his head. "It does not matter. Finish eating."

He rose and went to the stream to wash. She joined him shortly, and Sees Far waited until she finished before pulling her old tether from the pouch at his waist. "We are going to a town. I must bind you again."

She rose, wiping her hands upon her skirt, but avoided his eyes as she lifted her arms, sighing as the bonds settled about her wrists, though he did his best not to tie her as tightly as even the last time.

He took the cord length, tipped his head toward the path, and led off.

It was not long before the sounds of life carried through the trees, and as they passed a field, ripe with pegatawah and *mahkahq*, houses came into view beyond. Sees Far called out a greeting, and several came out in response, mostly women and children who, after their first look, ran to crowd about him and Elinor. Hands reached out to touch her hair and garments, to pinch and pat her skin. A babel of voices questioned and marveled. “She is my slave,” Sees Far announced, taking care to put the right amount of pride in his voice. “She is of the strangers to the east, from across the ocean.”

There were exclamations and not a few who recoiled. “Do you come to bring us war?” one woman demanded.

“No,” Sees Far said sternly. “Why do you speak thus?”

The women all exchanged glances. “The weroance and his men are out hunting, but come, eat, and we will talk.”

His mouth was already watering, but he knew to be courteous and show no emotion until he was seated outside one of the longhouses. A pair of aged men hobbled out to greet him, and sat with him as the women brought him a dish of mahkahq and *apohominas*. As custom demanded, he also must ignore Elinor, except to motion her down beside him.

“It is hard to say whether she is handsome or not,” one of the older men said.

The other lifted strands of pearls and wassador hanging about his neck. “I will buy her from you.”

“I do not wish to sell her,” Sees Far said impassively.

The man cackled. “I do not blame you.”

“The women said there was news of the strangers?”

One of the women set a cup on the ground next to him, then handed Elinor a cake of apon. She peered at the back of Sees Far’s shoulder. “What town are you of?”

He lifted the cup and sipped. It was a warm sassafras. “I am Sukwoten, formerly of Wyngyno’s men. I last followed Wanchese and the others to raid the English.”

She gave a brisk nod. “I thought it was so.” She turned to the elders. “Tell them what has been happening in the lower country.”

The other two men accepted cups as well. “Wanchese has not fared well,” one began. “He returned, he said from selling the captives they had taken, and went back to carry out their vengeance upon the strangers who came from over the sea. But the Kurawoten have added their strength to these strangers, and after one of their men was slain, they rose up and made war against Wanchese and his men." The elder sipped his drink. "The Sukwoten are being pushed farther inland."

Sees Far set his cup down and brought the dish back to his chest, eating with more thoughtful movements. He did not look at Elinor.

"They have stirred up a nest of bees," the other elder said. "Who would have thought it of the mild Kurawoten?"

"They have become bold because of the weapons brought by the strangers," Sees Far said, but even he thought his voice lacked the edge it needed.

"And yet you have taken one of their women," the first man said. He laughed again. "I will give you for her twice what I am wearing in wassador and pearls."

Sees Far laughed, though he felt no humor in the man's offer. "No, but I will keep her. She completes my own vengeance against the strangers for the sickness they brought."

Eyes widening in understanding and sympathy, both elders nodded. "It was a terrible sickness indeed. Many said the strangers must be gods, and not men, for all they said and did."

"No, they are men, who bleed and die as we do. One must only find their weakness." He resisted the urge to glance sidelong at Elinor. How much of their conversation did she follow? "But they are also more cunning than they first appeared."

The other men returned from hunting, handing off what they had taken to the women for preparation.

The weroance led the others to Sees Far, gathering round him as the women had to examine him, the token on his back of following Wyngyno, and not least of all Elinor. Several of them clamored to buy her, but the weroance silenced them all and fastened Sees Far with a stern look. "We hold no love for the Kurawoten and the strangers, but neither do we wish for war. You should leave, and soon."

"Do Wanchese and his company yet live?"

"We do not know, only that there was a bitter battle many suns ago."

One of the women approached Elinor and poked at her shoulder, directing her to come help with cooking. When Elinor appealed to Sees Far, he nodded and gestured for her to go.

"We will allow you the hospitality of our fire for this night," the weroance said. "Upon the morrow, you should go."

"I thank you for your food and hospitality this day," Sees Far said. "I will pray that no war is brought to you for it."

Chapter Eighteen

Elinor was apparently not grinding the corn fast—or well—enough. The woman who had tasked her with it cuffed her on the shoulder and scolded, pointing at the grains beneath her grinding stone. And her own exhaustion frayed the edges of her understanding, which had not happened in a while.

"I—do better," she stammered, and was cuffed again.

"Do not speak! Only work," the woman said.

Elinor blinked and swallowed back the tears, and leaned harder into the grinding stone. It wasn't that she'd not done this particular work before. And it definitely wasn't due to weakness of the body. She suspected the woman wished simply to find fault.

Whatever the bend of conversation surrounding Sees Far, he looked none too happy about it either. Oh, the folly of longing for the solitude of the forest with him! She should be glad to be with other women. But then again, her status as a slave made her no better than a beast of burden, and they seemed glad to remind her of that fact.

Even so, the work was no more difficult than pounding copper ore. She shifted on her knees, turned the grinding stone about, and tried a different angle.

At last she'd produced enough to satisfy them, and then they set her to turning the spit on which a brace of fowl roasted. She was also the last to be fed, along with half a dozen others who apparently shared the same status as she. They eyed her, but none tried speaking, at least not directly to her. Elinor was too weary to care and had to force herself to eat.

About sunset, singing and dancing broke out around the main town fire. Elinor had forgotten how raucous it could be, and yet soothing as well. Sees Far approached directly for the first time since she had been sent off to work, and made her sit outside one of the nearby houses while he went off to talk again with the other men.

Presently a young woman approached and took her by the hand. "Come, sing for us!"

At first Elinor shook her head, but then suffered herself to be led toward the fire. The others fell silent, waiting. What should she sing?

A particularly mournful song came to mind, of a hawk carrying away the singer's beloved, and of a hall with a wounded knight being wept over by a maiden. And at the end, a sign proclaiming the Body of Christ over all. . .

She closed her eyes and gave herself to the song—to all the longing and loss.

He bare him up, he bare him down
He bare him into an
orchard brown

Lullee, lullay, lullee, lullay
The falcon hath borne my
mate away

And in that orchard there
was an hall
That was hanged with purple
and pall

And in that hall there was a bed
And it was hanged with gold so red

Lullee, lullay, lullee, lullay
The falcon hath borne my
mate away

And in that bed there lieth a knight
His wounds bleeding day and night

By that bedside kneeleth a maid
And she weepeth both night
and day

Lullee, lullay, lullee, lullay
The falcon hath borne my
mate away

And by his bedside standeth a stone
"Corpus Christi" written thereon

She let the last note fade from her lips, and her eyes fluttered open. The entire town stood staring at her.

In the next moment, all was noise and commotion. Several of the men surrounded Sees Far, clapping him on the shoulders and, if she was not mistaken, dickering with each other for who could offer the best price for her.

The women crowded about her again, touching her hair and clothing. Elinor held still, hardly daring to breathe, much less move. She was yet very much a captive, and the reminder of such came when one of the little girls asked, "What are you called?" only to be yanked away by one of the older women and reprimanded.

It did not matter how well she might entertain. In their eyes she was less than a human.

Several of the women asked Sees Far how much he would sell her for, but he refused them all, laughing—although she thought it was less comfortably than he might previously have. But his dark eyes flashed across to her, holding her gaze with not a little pride at possessing such a prize.

How dare he—*how dare he!* And yet she understood. From what she knew of the people of this country from dwelling among them these past three years, pride and position and honor were all. And she represented his superiority over the English, despite what she had heard of the Secotan being pushed back from the coastlands.

As the women continued to poke and prod at her as if she were a sheep being judged for its fleece and fatness, one made discovery of her ever-rounding belly. "Oh ho! She is with child! Is it of Sees Far's begetting?"

She could not stop the blush rising into her face. "No. It is the child of my husband, who was slain by Wanchese."

That simple statement sent them all a-crowing again, with many more congratulatory cries offered to Sees Far for such an exploit.

"No wonder you are not willing to leave her," one said.

Elinor's face veritably burned now, as Sees Far, smirking, tossed back a cup of spiced juice.

On any other night, he'd leave her to bed down with the other women or captives, but after having half the town or more ply him with very tempting offers for her purchase, Sees Far would not. And though she was not his woman, not in the sense of being his wife, none would gainsay him leading her off by her tether and lying down next to her for the night.

He'd not risk having her stolen from him while he slept.

Taking the length of cording from her tether, he wrapped it about his own wrist until only a span remained between his hand and hers; then he lay facing her, his bound hand down, his bow, quiver, and wooden sword in the small space between them.

Not entirely comfortable, but less chance in this arrangement of being caught by surprise.

She watched through half-lidded eyes while he set everything just so.

"Did you hear what he said of Wanchese and the others?" he murmured, for her ears only.

Her eyes opened further; then she gave the barest of nods. "Mayhap my daughter is not also a captive, or slain?" she whispered. Her pale eyes glinted in the dark.

"Is that your wish?"

"Very much my dearest wish."

How is it she knew how to convey the nuances of that and yet had to be taught the word for *trust*?

"Do you not care for your own person?" he asked.

Her gaze held steady for a few breaths. "Inasmuch as the life of this child I carry depends upon it—yes. Otherwise, no. I know I will be in the presence of my God the moment I leave this life."

He felt a frown gather on his brow. "You do not fear dying?"

Her eyelids fluttered, then steadied. "Dying, of course. Who does not? But after? I do not."

Would she never cease to surprise him? True enough, he had watched her sing—and listened to her high, almost unearthly voice—with the feeling that he did not understand what sort of creature he had captured that day, moons ago—but this. Who did not fear death?

"Because of your God? Or because you wish to be with your slain husband?"

A tiny smile curved her lips, and her eyes fell closed. "Both, I suppose."

He could not blame her for the latter. Had he not felt the desperation of the sundering between himself and the girl who was to have been his wife?

It gave him cause, though, to be glad she had a babe in her belly to tie her to life.

She woke from troubled sleep filled with dreams of Ananias, always present but never noticing her, to the awareness of a muscled arm beneath her neck, a lean body against her back, and a hand extended across her waist, fingers cupping the curve of her belly.

The babe within kicked and danced, as if seized with the need to remind her of its presence.

Her next fleeting thought was one of obscure comfort—how secure she felt in such a strong, warm embrace—

Which was not the embrace of Ananias.

"Do not move," her captor breathed, just behind her ear.

The binding on her wrists reminded her of the folly of attempting escape, but—there was something else, a tension in his body signaling more than the mutual strangeness of a shared embrace.

Voices, hushed, carried across the night air.

"Be ready to rise when I say," Sees Far whispered again. Slowly, stealthily, his hand lifted from her belly and reached across to his weapons, lying just in front of her. His grasp closed around them, shifted, then stilled.

"Now."

In one motion, they rose as one, his arms bringing her upright more than her own effort, and dragging her along as they dived into the darkness of the forest beyond the longhouse where they had lain.

Shouts behind them gave witness to the discovery of their absence. Already rushing them away, Sees Far gave more speed to their flight, half carrying Elinor when her feet tangled in foliage and her own skirts. “Toward the stream,” he murmured into her ear. “We will take a canoe and try to be away before they know we have gone that direction.”

She did not know how he managed to keep them both from falling headlong as they dashed downhill, but manage it he did, and though she could hardly breathe for the tightness of his embrace, neither could she protest being whisked out of imminent peril.

They reached the stream, and Sees Far hesitated but a moment to unwrap the tether from his own wrist. After lifting her into one of the canoes, he seized the paddle, shoved the vessel into the water, and leaped inside in nearly the same movement. “Lie down,” he said, setting them down the current.

She flattened herself against the rough canoe bottom, peering over the edge. Starlight and the sliver of a moon gave them just enough illumination—and she already knew that Sees Far’s vision, true to his name, was sharper than her own, if not many others as well.

“What happened?” she ventured to ask presently.

“*Ehqutonahas*,” he said. *Be quiet.* But then he added, “Sleep now. We will talk later.”

She did as he told her, no less and no more. Thankfully.

He thought through what had taken place. He’d slept but a short time, coming half awake when Elinor’s restlessness disturbed his own slumber, and somehow when she’d turned over, it seemed the most natural thing to move his weapons and simply tuck her against him. She’d settled instantly, with a little sigh that sent a squirming through his middle like eels. And then the slight but definite movements of the child inside her, tiny flutterings like a bird in his hand. For a long time he lay there simply lost in wonder.

But the voices came—which at first he thought merely the wind, until words were understandable—*woman* and *captive* and a muttered phrase about catching them asleep.

They meant to either kill him or make him captive as well, and take Elinor.

Whether his own pride or stubbornness or something else entirely, every drop of his being rebelled at the thought. She was his, and he would not see her given to another, or allow himself to be caught as well.

He could hardly believe they had gotten away. Would they pursue, and if so, how far?

It reminded him of the night they'd escaped after the slaying of Elinor's husband—except that it was the two of them alone, and he paddled downstream rather than up. But now, just as then, he kept paddling, swiftly and surely, around fallen trees and beneath overhanging branches, some of which lashed his face and body in his haste and in the dark.

At last the sky began to lighten and the birds awakened with their usual morning chorus. He saw nothing, heard nothing besides the sounds of making their way in the night, or of human life within the handful of towns they passed, as silently as he could manage. He would not stop. If the very sight of this golden-haired woman drove an otherwise peaceful town to thoughts of capture and thievery—

Not that he blamed them. She had captured his attention from the very moment he'd seen her in the mist.

An echo of laughter rippled through his thoughts, of Walks Softly, his intended, indulging in merriment over some foolery he'd performed for her. Her round face, creased in a smile and lovely in its youth, with her own distinctive pattern marking her cheeks, and her sweet, lithe body, sharpening his hunger for the time he might make her fully his own. Then her form, still and lifeless, hardly recognizable as the girl he'd desired.

His throat ached at the memory. He thought then of Elinor's words the night before. Would he join his own lost love in the afterlife, if he could? No, life here was too sharply sweet, and the shadow of death itself too dark and uncertain. What would it be, though, to have trust in God so sure, so strong, that death held no fear?

Could it be because of their very belief in a God who had overcome both human weakness and death?

He thought again of her husband, his hair bright in the firelight, his eyes full only of love for his woman.

No fear there either.

Then Elinor and the prayer that had driven Wanchese to fury.

And beyond all, the brilliance of a sunlit seashore that had haunted him since first he dreamt it during huskanaw. The Man, wrapped in his cape, from whom all the light seem to radiate. The woman and the man, walking behind him, both with hair the color of the sand.

The woman, turning to look back at him, with the cloud-filled sky reflected in her eyes.

It was indeed Elinor he had dreamed of, before ever she had come to this land. Of that he now had no doubt.

How could that be? Yet even as he wondered, he accepted it. The ways of the spirit were unexplainable and unfathomable. Did not their priests and elders say that it was so?

And if the Creator-God had pointed him to this woman since his earliest awakening in the spirit, who was he to refuse the path laid before him?

Elinor awakened to early-morning mist on the water and birdsong filling the trees, herself curled in the bottom of a narrow hewn canoe, with Sees Far, hair loose around his shoulders, paddling not as furiously as he had when she'd fallen asleep. They were alone, as far as she could tell, both on stream and on shore.

As she sat up, he laid the paddle across his knees and beckoned with curled fingers, reaching for her bound hands. She leaned closer so he could more easily loosen the knots.

Scratches crisscrossed his arms and shoulders and face, some merely red and angry but others deep enough to draw blood. The marks of their flight during the night? If he'd been unable to avoid branches and brush, no wonder.

Before she could make comment upon it, however, her hands were suddenly free, and he took her forearms in his own lean, rough grip and turned them this way and that, examining her wrists. Then his hands covered the marks the cords had left, and he looked up into her eyes.

Her heartbeat stuttered, and to distract from the flush stealing across her cheeks, she asked, "Will they pursue?"

"I do not know. We must be prepared for it."

"What took place back there?"

His dark gaze did not waver. "They wanted you. I would not part with you, no matter how high their price, and I overheard them talking of either slaying me or making me a slave as well." His shoulder lifted. "I judged it best to escape."

She offered a hesitant smile. "I am glad."

One eyebrow lifted. "Are you?" His hands still encircled her wrists, his touch stinging the raw skin a little, yet warm and not overtight. "What makes me better than any other captor?"

Why did his question tease another burst of nervous laughter from her throat? Was she a callow maid, to blush and giggle as if he were a suitor? Nay, she was a wife bereaved and a mother robbed of her child. A sober woman of mean estate, and a Christian in the company of the heathen. . . .

Except that she was not sure any longer whether he was so hardened in his pagan faith as she once thought.

She cleared her throat. "I trust that in your heart you are good and not bad, and will continue doing me good."

Would he understand that it was God Himself she nudged him toward?

Please let his eyes be opened to the truth. . . .

Silence wrapped them about, a single drop of a moment in time, as the canoe drifted down the current and the wild forest surrounded them, and Sees Far gazed deep into her eyes. How long and black were his lashes, and how a part of him were the markings upon his cheeks—

Abruptly he released her, sat back, and took up the paddle again. "We are without deerskins to sleep upon, or much food. There will be little enough comfort until we are in a place where I may hunt again without worry of pursuit."

For lack of better employ, she reached for the fallen tether and absently coiled it. "Have you decided where to go next?"

He gave a sharp shake of his head and did not meet her eyes this time.

'Twas best to preserve silence and let him think. And she would not admonish him about washing the scratches—'twas too intimate, in the moment.

But she could pray, and would. *With all else, God, grant him wisdom. Thank You for preserving us safe thus far.*

What magic this woman cast over him. He was her captor, she his slave. Nothing more.

Even as he avowed it in his heart, he knew it to be untrue. Slave she might have been at the start, but no longer.

Lying so close to her last night had been a mistake. It was one thing while they lay facing each other, but when she'd turned over, so near that her hair tickled his nose, and he could breathe in the fragrance of her—

It was more than the dreams now. It was her own living presence.

But where to go next—where indeed? Returning to his own people would put her within reach once again of Wanchese, and speaking of trust. . . He did not trust his old friend any longer to respect the bounds of her as Sees Far's own.

Sees Far had once accused Wanchese of obsession with the woman, but was he himself not guilty of the same now?

If they left the river and went west again, or farther south, they would likely encounter the same situation they had just left, and run into the Spanish beside. And though alone he might be able to provide for her, he was not able, without the benefit of a community, to protect her and her child.

That left but one choice, if he valued at least her life.

His greatest fear at this moment, however, was who they might meet on their way downriver. The passage itself would be easy—keep paddling until they found the sea. It was the countless towns they'd pass on the way, or men out fishing or hunting.

There was also the matter of direction. He knew from others who had ranged farther that while all rivers flowed eventually into the ocean, some went more eastward while others turned south. Leaving the river, then, and walking overland toward the rising sun would be surer—and safer.

The creek they now navigated joined with a wider one. Sees Far turned the kanoe upstream and chose the next easternmost waterway. Slower going, but it would put them closer to their intended destination. Elinor remained watchful and quiet, loosening and rebraiding her hair but making no comment.

Finally, when the stream was barely deep enough for the kanoe, Sees Far let it glide to a stop and, stepping out onto the bank, pulled it ashore. He hated to leave it, but it was no longer of use to them.

He helped Elinor out, then laid aside his weapons and gear and waded into a clear part of the stream to wash, head to toe. Not only had he no occasion yet to clean the many scratches from their flight, but his entire body was sticky with sweat and grime.

When he returned to the bank, wrapping his deerhide kilt so it draped around the front, adjusting the otterskin where it fell in back, Elinor had returned from tending her own needs and stood guard over his gear, facing the other way. To preserve his modesty, or her own? It did not matter. He set to tying up his hair—feathers were among the things left behind during their escape—and slinging bow and quiver and carrying pouch across his body.

He looked at Elinor. Her dress hung nearly in tatters. Would she wear deerskin if he provided it? Her mahkusun had life enough left, though perhaps they could use stitching or another layer of hide over the sole before long. He would at least take a deer and dry it, as before, as they went.

For a moment, their gazes met. Hers was clear and calm. *"I trust you,"* she had said. How far did that extend?

And more, could he indeed make good upon it?

Walking was the more tedious mode of travel, but noting the angle of the sun as they went, Elinor understood without being told why it was necessary. She'd already realized the stream they'd taken for escape tended in a more southerly direction than they likely wished.

Well, that is, if Sees Far was leading her where she suspected, which was still very much in question, but he had the manner now of a particular destination in mind, unlike their previous and much more leisurely wandering.

He led now, near as she could tell, due east. The usual hazards slowed them—bears and large cats, and snakes that Sees Far pointed out as poisonous. Not all were harmful, he explained, and any would slither quickly away once people made their presence known and did not provoke the creature. But better peril of beasts than of men.

As before, he shot a deer and they stopped long enough to cook and dry the meat while he worked the hide. Often she would catch him looking at her, but always without making comment, except what was absolutely necessary. Her discomfort was now even greater than when they had first left the copper mine.

She missed Ginny. She missed the chatter of the women—even the women of the mining town. She missed being able to hum or sing, for he was continually hushing her, on the lookout for their possible discovery.

It was, truly, tedious and very wearing.

To keep her mind busy, she recited all the scripture she knew, both silently and under her breath, as Sees Far allowed.

While they were waiting for the meat to finish drying, Elinor explored within sight of the camp, marveling over plants and flowers, insects and birds. As over on the coast, flocks of brightly colored parrots flew about, and other songbirds of various and less brilliant kinds. Water birds both great and small populated a nearby pond, with one great white heron taking flight to the other side. She tried to engage Sees Far in conversation, asking him what divers things were called, but he only frowned and shook his head, keeping his attention to whatever task he had at hand.

She felt no end of relief when at last he pronounced the meat ready, and they continued their journey.

Four or five days along, however, he surprised her by asking what things were called in English. At first his curiosity pleased her, but his persistence wearied even as it amused. He was like a tall child.

His ability to learn both shocked and impressed her, however. And if nothing else, it helped pass the days.

He knew at last precisely where they were. This was the swamp he had wandered during huskanaw. A short distance away lay the hummocky island where, curled up in fear for his life, he'd first dreamed of the distant ocean's shore, the walking Man, and the figures of Elinor and her husband.

Should he tell her? That question had pressed more and more upon him these past few days. He'd already broken his recent resolve not to make conversation with her, in seeking to learn her tongue. But the process of asking her for various words, and repeating them until she was satisfied with how he said them, did at least distract him from weightier matters.

Which included, the farther east they went, the increasing likelihood that they'd encounter people he knew, who knew him, who would question him on just why he had wandered so far from former home and hearth, in the company of a woman from the strangers. And they would not be satisfied with evasions or refusals to answer.

The sun sank nearly to the horizon before they reached that bit of high ground he recalled. The swamp around him was alive, just as he remembered it, with the calls and cries of birds and frogs and various other creatures. The island itself was smaller than he remembered.

Elinor watched him as he gathered wood for a fire. "Do you know this place?"

He nodded but did not otherwise respond until he'd gotten the flames going well enough to sit back on his haunches and watch them. She settled on the other side. He pulled a chunk of dried meat from his carrying pouch, then handed the pouch over to her to do the same.

"Do you know of huskanaw, which boys endure when they are of a certain age?" he asked.

Her eyes caught the light of the setting sun. "Kupi."

"I found this place on that journey. It was here I dreamed the dream from which I chose my name."

She nodded, still watching him.

He told her what exactly he had seen. How he had recognized her as one of the figures in the dream the first time he had seen her.

"And that was—when?"

He fixed her with a look. Yes, it was time to admit that.

"There was a day at the turning of autumn to winter, when your people first came to Roanoac, and mist covered all. You and the women had gone out with your baskets to forage. You carried a child inside your clothing, and a youth was with you."

Her eyes went wide and her mouth dropped open as all color fled from her cheeks. Her hands covered the lower part of her face. "That was—you?"

Sees Far nodded slowly.

"You—came and went so silently. I was afraid—" Tears flooded her eyes and poured down her cheeks, as her skin went from pale to reddened. "Were you of those who killed one of our men very soon after we came to the island?"

"Kupi." He kept his voice impassive.

A sob escaped her, and this time she bent her face into her hands.

"I am a son of Granganimeo, who died of the sickness brought by your people, before you. When they first came, my people welcomed them as friends. We fed them and gave them hospitality. Our women—led by my mother—even chased us away upon our return from a hunt to find them there, when they showed fear of us. But then they burned a town of Aquascogoc over a wassador cup, without trying first to resolve the matter by talk. Your Captain Lane chose cunning over friendship, and betrayed us before the other towns. Throughout all, the sickness spread, and some of my family died. Wanchese had already set his heart against your people, from all he had seen on his voyage to your country, but it was the killing of Pemisapan—the one your people knew as Wyngyno—that set me against them at the last."

He blew out a breath. Elinor had returned to watching him, her tears yet flowing though she brushed them away every so often.

"I took you, yes, to satisfy my desire for vengeance against your people for the dying of my own family. But—I no longer burn with that vengeance, even though Wanchese likely does."

Elinor wiped her face and firmed her lips. "And—why not?"

"I do not know," he admitted softly.

Her eyes squeezed shut again. After a few more moments of weeping, she tucked her unfinished piece of dried meat back in his bag and, pushing it away, curled up on the ground, head on her arms, her entire body shaking with quiet sobs.

It was a less tumultuous response than he had anticipated.

She had no response. No words. Not even any prayers.

God—oh gracious, merciful God—

And where was He, this God who had indeed suffered her to fall into the hands of an enemy far more treacherous than she had guessed?

How could You do this? Allow me—all of us—to be taken, and then for Ananias to risk himself and be slain—what purpose could You possibly have in it all? What good can there ever be in such a thing?

The babe inside kicked and squirmed as if to remind her there was yet reason for living, but she only wept harder, remembering an unforgiving ship's deck and stifling heat, night after night, on their journey from England, through the West Indies, and finally to Virginia. The brilliant sunlight abovedecks and onshore, through the West Indies.

Before they had landed here, and the darkness swallowed her entirely.

Did Sees Far truly lead her back to the Croatoan and English, or was it his intent to return to his own people, with nothing but more captivity for her—perhaps within reach of Wanchese again and thus subject to that one's ill use?

If the latter, she did not want to take another step. She might as well lie here until her body expired from want of water. 'Twas better to take this child, unborn, straightaway with her into heaven rather than inflict any more misery upon it.

Chapter Nineteen

Only after her husband was slain had he seen her so completely broken. And it broke something inside him as well.

Any hope he'd had of an alliance between them—of even a truce—died.

It was no more than he deserved. It was his people's way—war and vengeance and the taking of captives. They did their best to exact justice but then were duty bound to accept what Montóac handed them. Whatever that looked like.

He fully deserved this woman's hatred. But—he longed for something else.

Before, he'd have seen her distress as the natural end of his taking her captive, and all else that had befallen her. And before, he'd have rejoiced at her having been humbled.

What had changed him so?

She did not move the rest of that evening. The next morning, at daybreak, she was up, seeing to her needs in the brush but otherwise refusing to eat, drink, or look at him. But when he bid her come and set off again across the swamp, she followed. He was forced to stop several times to allow her to catch up—out here, he dared not let her get too far behind.

He reminded himself he should not care, except that he had expended time and goods in keeping her alive and securing her for himself. He should feel a sense of satisfaction that she was finally, fully abased.

All he felt, instead, was a hollowness inside.

Montóac—gods and spirits of the earth and sky, what is this? Have I not served you by striking a blow at those who have dealt treacherously with my people and brought only ruin and sickness? Is it not the way of life to make war on our enemies and bring them hurt and sorrow when we can?

And how long could she last without food or water? Especially being with child? Would she do harm to the child by her refusal to eat or drink?

Once again she lagged behind. He looked back to see her staggering from one tree to another, sloshing through shallow water, at last stumbling and falling to her knees. Shaking his head, he hurried back toward her and reached her just as she pitched face-first into the murky water.

He pulled her upward, coughing and spluttering, but otherwise limp, and lifted her into his arms. She weighed almost no more than a child herself—but he'd not be able to carry her the entire way, in this manner.

Her head lolled against his shoulder as he settled her more firmly against himself and set off again.

If You are listening, Creator-God, whether You are called Montóac or Ahoné—or God of Elinor, if You and our Creator as I understand Him are not the same—I need a kanoe. And cover under which to steal it.

A very short time later, the clouds gathered overhead and a soaking rain fell, driven by a suddenly cool wind. Sees Far trudged on, still carrying her in his arms.

Then, in the downpour, he saw the stream. And drawn up on the near bank, a kanoe, unattended.

Oh Great Creator-God. Can it be?

He looked about. Was there a town near? Hunters who had left it?

Lightning crackled a short distance away, and thunder rumbled overhead. He hesitated but a breath longer before dashing for the kanoe.

Still expecting at any moment for his skin to be pierced by arrows, he settled Elinor in the bow, took up one of the two paddles, and slid the kanoe into the water and hopped inside.

The rain continued for the better part of the day. Elinor remained unresponsive, even when he stopped for a rest in between showers and, propping her in his arms, washed her face and trickled water into her mouth. She swallowed what little he managed to get in, but when he attempted to tip her head enough to take more, she gagged and choked. Her eyes fluttered open and closed again, then she sagged against him.

What if he could not induce her to take enough water—or food—to stay alive?

He pushed back her hair with one hand, then cradled her close and bent to whisper into her ear. "Elinor. You must live. Your children need you to live."

She did stir at that, sucking in a deep breath and coming upright to blink at the forest around them, then into his face. "What—did you say?"

His hand still cupping her head, he gazed into her eyes. Mingled light and dark grey they were, like storm clouds. "Your children need you to live. Eat and drink. Gather your strength again."

She collapsed into weeping, but softly.

"At least drink more water."

He brought the opening of the gourd to her lips. At first she resisted, but he kept trying, and at last she put her hand over his and tipped the vessel for a long drink.

He didn't even mind that some splashed over the edges and onto them both.

When her thirst was slaked and she lowered the vessel, her eyes were clearer. She swiped at her mouth with the back of her hand, and he brushed away an errant drop with his thumb.

Her brows drew together, but though he expected her to pull away from him, she did not.

"Why do you say such a thing?" she asked after a moment. "Why would you do all you have, and then insist I should live? Unless you intend only to torment me further."

"I have no wish to torment you," he said.

Frowning, she shook her head and turned her face away.

There was nothing more he could say for now.

How bitter the betrayal of her own bodily need to answer her thirst, and thus needlessly arouse strength and hope.

She could not accept his avowal that he intended not to cause her more suffering. He had already used her so roughly, and nothing could end her torment of knowing how greatly his actions were responsible for bringing about such ill hap. He claimed to have somehow seen her in a dream, long before there was ever an effort to plant an English colony here—what rubbish.

And then there was the matter of his being party to George Howe's murder.

Curled in the bottom of the canoe, beneath the untanned deer's hide Sees Far had covered her with, she'd wept all the tears her eyes were able to give. Now only a curious stillness remained.

Did Wanchese have it aright, that the gods of this land were stronger than her own? Somehow, she could not accept that either, and yet the memory of his taunts echoed still within her mind.

"Who shall separate us from the love of God?"

She curled up more tightly, ignoring the protests of the child within, as the scripture came to her unbidden.

"Shall tribulation? Or anguish? Or persecution? . . .hunger? . . .nakedness? . . .peril? . . .sword? As it is written: for thy sake we are killed all the day long, and are counted as sheep appointed to be slain. Nevertheless, in all these things we overcome—"

How could that be? Verily, she did feel like nothing more than a sheep going to slaughter.

"—in all these things we overcome through him that loved us. For I am sure, that neither death, neither life, neither angels, nor rule, neither power, neither things present, neither things to come, neither height, neither depth, neither any other creature shall be able to depart us from the love of God, which is in Christ Jesus our Lord."

Dry sobs shook her again, more a shiver than anything else.

Could she accept this, at least? That no matter what assailed her—death, life itself, the peril that she and little Ginny and others suffered—the taunts of Wanchese or the inscrutable actions of Sees Far—nothing indeed separated her from the love of God.

This God, who against all reason or sense or understanding, as Sees

Far had protested, had indeed become a Man and submitted Himself to being not only bound and captive but taunted and beaten and then slain as a sheep, the final sacrifice for their sins.

And was not His taking on flesh—He, the limitless Divine Creator of all that was seen and unseen—a kind of captivity as well?

She had heard these things countless times throughout her life, but never before understood, as she suddenly did in this moment, to her marrow.

Christ our Lord lived this captivity in His own flesh. Indeed, He bore our very griefs and sorrows.

What then was the answer to her dilemma of living with the man who had taken her captive and who bore on his hands, if not directly the blood of her husband, then at least that of her countryman?

". . .and of such were some of you."

What book and chapter was that from?

"Bless them which persecute you. Bless, I say, and do not curse."

"Love your enemies. . . Do good to them that hate you. Pray for them which hurt you. . . ."

She did indeed pray for Sees Far, once. Before she knew his part in Master Howe's death. Before he'd claimed to have dreamed of her, when still a youth.

In time past, God spoke to men in dreams and visions. But did He still?

And more, would He to one yet unregenerate, steeped in doctrines of demons? Although she was not, as others, convinced that these people were nothing more than savages, completely ignorant, completely wicked in their ways. The Croatoan had long since swept any notion of that away—indeed, Manteo himself, before ever she met his people.

But who was she to say how God could or should speak to the hearts of men? What if, as she had wondered before, God had used her to draw Sees Far to Him?

Because surely the people of this country were, indeed, as dear to God as any of the English. How arrogant they were to think they alone had obtained His favor.

She sat up. Behind Sees Far, beyond the forest to the west, the sun was setting, pouring colors across the sky with such brilliance she could only stare and gape.

He looked over his shoulder, then turned back and met her eyes with a half smile.

It completely transformed his visage. Or was it her heart that was changed?

He pushed his carrying sack toward her. "Will you eat?"

She dug inside and pulled out a piece of dried meat. He nudged the drinking gourd toward her as well.

She did not suppose he would answer, but—she would ask anyway. "Where are we going?"

His gaze swept the creek banks and surrounding forest as he paddled. Just as she gave up on a reply, he said, very softly, "I am returning you to your people."

She almost dropped the dried meat she was nibbling. "What—why?"

The look on his face now was so mournful, it brought an ache to her throat. "That is where you should be."

"But—what about the others still captive?"

His eyes were suddenly sharp upon her. "I can do nothing for them. But you—for you I can do this."

She found herself quite dumb with amazement.

"We will paddle through the night," he went on. "I wish you to sleep while you can, and I cannot say how long it will take us—"

He stiffened, looking past her, and with an abrupt turn of his paddle, drew the canoe to a halt in the current and turned it partly about. "Get down," he said.

"What—?" She glanced, but he repeated the command more urgently.

"Cover yourself with the hide," he added. "And—say that prayer which made Wanchese so angry."

"What?" Her jaw fell open again.

His eyes flashed to hers, dark and intense. "That prayer which made Wanchese angry. Cover yourself, and pray it now."

Just in time she dived under the deerskin. He'd seen the flicker of firelight, heard the voices, and despite his efforts to hold the kanoe still, the current pulled them around the bend of the river. A little farther, the corner of a longhouse roof came into view. Several figures stood on the bank, talking and laughing.

They saw him almost immediately and called out greetings, lifting their hands. "Come, friend! Join us for the evening's dance!"

He waved back. "You are kind, but no, but I am expected downriver before full dark."

"Ah! From where do you come?"

"I have been to view the mountains and now I return to the sea."

"That is a story we wish to hear!"

He was sure they would.

A pair of men entered a kanoe and paddled out to meet him. "Will you not at least share a meal?"

"I have provisions and wish not to deplete yours."

"Our harvest has been plentiful! Stay and share with us."

The other kanoe drew closer. Could they see the edge of Elinor's skirt, peeping out from beneath the deerskin?

God, make her unseen to them!

Elinor heard the voices and suddenly understood. *Oh gracious Lord. . .*

"The Lord is my shepherd, therefore I can lack nothing. . . ."

It was so difficult to focus on the psalm while Sees Far conversed. She wanted to hear what they were saying. But with such a reception as they had met with before, prayer was too needful to ignore.

And the fact that Sees Far had specifically asked her to pray—

"Yea, though I walk through the valley of the shadow of death, I will fear no evil, for thou art with me. . . ."

With that psalm ended, she flailed and settled upon the Lord's Prayer.

"Our Father which art in heaven, hallowed be thy name. Let thy kingdom come. Thy will be fulfilled, as well in earth, as it is in heaven. Give us this day our daily bread. And forgive us our debts, as we forgive our debtors. And lead

us not into temptation, but deliver us from evil. For thine is the kingdom and the power, and the glory for ever. Amen."

Thine is the kingdom. Thine is the power.

"Who shall separate us from the love of God? . . . In all these things we overcome."

We overcome. . . .

Oh God above, Almighty One, to You be the kingdom and the power and the glory forever!

". . .the kingdom and the power, and the glory. . ."

At last the voices fell silent, but she remained huddled, praying more with feeling than words.

"It is safe now," Sees Far said.

"Forgive us our debts, as we forgive our debtors."

She pushed the deerskin aside and peered around. Distant firelight was still visible behind Sees Far, in the trees, but nothing else could she discern around them.

"I will let no one take you from me," he said, still watching the twilit forest. "And I will let no harm come to you, if it is within my power."

This time, her heart believed him.

Two days later, they stood upon a riverbank in a place she thought she recognized.

Sees Far had indeed paddled through the night, then drawn the canoe up into thick brush to hide during the daylight hours, snatching sleep while she kept watch, and then paddled through a second night and continued well after dawn.

The sun was halfway up the sky when he maneuvered the canoe into a tiny stream off of the wide river and, after hopping out, pulled it far enough onshore to make it secure. And as so many times before, he helped her out.

This time, he did not immediately release her hand but rather, with his thumb brushing across her wrist and knuckles, gazed at her for an unaccountably long time.

He looked wearier than she had ever seen him. And she noticed details she previously had not. The very sparse beard emerging from chin and upper lip, the previously shaved hair on the right side of his head now grown out to fingertip length—both small signs of neglect of his own appearance. The glossy black hair shining in the morning light. His strong features, as if carved from polished wood—cheekbone and forehead, nose and chin and jawline.

"Your town is that way, through these woods. I will follow from a little distance to make sure you do not meet with any trouble."

Ginny! She would know at last what befell her daughter, perhaps even hold her sweet body in her arms—

"Wait. You are not coming too?"

He gave a quick shake of his head. "I am not of the Kurawoten. They would slay me, and rightfully so."

She curled her fingers more firmly around his. "It is not so. You. . .do not know them. Once they have heard your story, and how you have labored so to bring me home—"

"Elinor."

The sound of her name on his lips nearly undid her.

His other hand came up to cup her head—she remembered a similar motion, days or was it weeks before? Then he bent and pressed his lips to her forehead for a long moment.

He smelled like cedar, and wood smoke, and the wild forest.

"Elinor," he whispered again. "Were things different, I would stay, and gladly. I would—I would even ask to be the man who hunts for you, who stands in as father to your children. But—with all I have done, I am not the one to do this service for you."

"Sees Far—"

"No. Hear me. Go to your people, to your daughter. Finish the grieving for your husband, but then live, and be happy. I can give you nothing else, but that I can give."

Tears poured down her cheeks, unchecked. "Oh, Sees Far. Do not—do not say so."

Both his arms came around her, strong and warm, comforting in ways she could not explain and likely should not even feel. Then he released her and set her back from him. "Go."

Even then she lingered. Where were the words when she needed them?

"I forgive you," she said at last.

His eyes widened a little.

"Because of my God, and what He has done for us, I forgive you. His Son died for the sins of all of us, the big as well as the small. You can know Him, truly—and you no longer need to do sacrifice to gain His favor—or that of anyone else."

He made no reply—not that she expected it—but wonder filled his face.

"Come with me, and you can learn more of Him. Manteo could explain where I cannot, for he too has become a follower of Christ."

Sees Far drew a long breath. "*Kuwumádas*," he murmured, then, "Go."

Had he just told her he loved her? A ragged sob escaped her.

"Please say you will come," she said, then turned and walked in the direction he had pointed

Her heart pounded with every step. She knew now where she was—just a short distance upriver from Cora Banks. Was the town still there? Had they moved elsewhere? Were—

She heard voices—women chattering, children laughing and singing. Somewhere farther, a man's call, in English.

Her feet carried her forward, running now.

Sees Far followed behind, as he had promised, but silently. Oh, he was weary—but this task at least was nearly done. He had navigated past villages and hunting parties, mostly by traveling these last two nights, and brought her safe at last to her people.

Fool that he was, for allowing her to soften him so—both to her own person, and to her God. He let out a silent laugh.

Ahead of him, she broke into a run and emerged from the forest to the edge of the field where he had first taken her. She called out, drawing first the attention of those at work and play, then shouts and glad cries as they recognized her and ran to surround her. One small, slight figure in particular made her way through the crowd, crying, *"Ma-ma!"*

Sees Far watched, unable to move, as Elinor fell to her knees and gathered the child in, weeping loudly. Something had gripped his own throat as well and would not permit easy breath.

After several moments, Elinor rose, lifting the child into her arms and speaking in urgent tones to those around her. Many still pressed in to embrace her, the women and men alike, some in the strange apparel of the foreigners but others in the familiar tunics and kilts of the Kurawoten. Among them he recognized Manteo.

Then, as she spoke, they drew back as if considering something weighty. She turned to Manteo, questioning. He rubbed his chin, eyes scanning the forest which still concealed Sees Far—or did he mark his presence among the trees? But at last he turned back to Elinor and murmured something with a nod.

Her daughter still on her hip, she took a few steps back toward the forest, also gazing in his direction. "Sees Far! Come! They are willing to hear you, and receive you, because you have brought me back."

Silence hung in the late summer heat for a breath, then two, then three.

"Please come," she said, and he could hear in her voice that she was very near again to tears.

Did he dare?

Creator-God, and God of Elinor. Preserve me. I trust You.

He stepped out from cover of the forest, lingering in the shadows. A ripple went through the watching crowd, yet no one launched toward him in attack, and no bows were drawn.

But Elinor smiled and held out a hand to him.

He walked out into the sunlight, crossing the space to her, and took her hand.

Epilogue

Late Winter 1593

> *. . . The 2. of October [1590] in the Morning we saw S. Michaels Iland on our Starre board quarter.*
>
> *The 23. at 10. of the clocke afore noon, we saw Ushant in Britaigne.*
>
> *On Saturday the 24 we came in safetie, God be thanked, to an anchor at Plymmouth.*

It was done at last.

John set the stack of parchment, every page filled with his hand as neatly as he could make it, into a tidy pile at the upper corner of his small desk. The entirety of his account of that ill-fated voyage, set out with as much detail as he was able. Strange how these days he was reduced to fleshing out a picture with words and not with sketches and watercolors.

With a little sigh, he reached for a fresh page, dipped his quill in the ink, and began again.

> *To the Worshipful and my very friend Master Richard Hakluyt, much happinesse in the Lord.*
>
> *Sir, as well as for the satisfying of your earnest request, as the performance of my promise made unto you at my last being with*

> *you in England, I have sent you (although in a homely style, especially for the contentation of a delicate care) the true discourse of my last voyage into the West Indies, and the parts of America called Virginia, taken in hand about the end of Februarie, in the year of our redemption 1590. And what events happened unto us in this our journey, you shall plainly perceive by the sequel of my discourse. There were at the time aforesaid three ships absolutely determined to go for the West Indies. . . .*
>
> *. . .summer was spent before we arrived at Virginia. And when were come thither, the season was so unfit, and weather so foul, that we were constrained of force to forsake that coast, having not seen any of our planters, with loss of one of our ship-boats, and 7 of our chiefest men, and also with loss of 3 of our anchors and cables, and most of our casks with fresh water left on shore, not possible to be had aboard. Which evils and unfortunate events (as well to their own loss as to the hindrance of the planters in Virginia) had not chance, if the order set down by Sir Walter Ralegh had been observed, or if my daily and continual petitions for the performance of the same might have taken any place. Thus may you plainly perceive the success of my fifth and last voyage to Virginia, which was no less unfortunately ended than frowardly begun, and as luckless to many, as sinister to myself. But I would to God it had been as prosperous to all, as noisome to the planters, and as joyful to me, as discomfortable to them. Yet seeing it is not my first crossed voyage, I remain contented.*

Did he indeed remain contented? John set the quill inside the inkwell and, sliding the parchment aside, rested his forehead on his fists. *God in heaven, verily only Thou knowest all my heart. Only Thou knowest where Elinor and Virginia—and the others—are, yea, even at this very moment. I have none other upon earth, no other hope besides Thine own.*

The words from a single verse in the scriptural book of Hebrews flitted across his memory. "For here have we no continuing city: but we seek one to come."

Though the dream of the City of Ralegh may have come to nothing, they were indeed promised a city to come, one not made of human hands. And though he might never again in this life hold his daughter and grandchild, verily they would meet again someday in that place.

As he straightened, scrubbing the tears away with his sleeve, a woman entered, bearing a tray of meat and fresh bread. "John, will you not eat?" Her Irish lilt held a tone of admonition.

The smell drew a growl from his middle. "Aye, and gladly."

He waited until she set the tray down before sliding an arm about her middle. She leaned into his embrace, rounded belly firm against him, and met him halfway for a kiss. The babe inside her thumped as if in protest, and he drew back to smooth a hand across the curve, rippling with the new life beneath. "My dear Bridget," he murmured. "And sweet little one. What would I do without you?"

Nut-brown hair glistening in the candlelight, only the crinkle at the corners of her eyes betraying that she was not but a fresh maid, she smiled and kissed him again. "Starve, I expect. How did you ever remember to feed yourself before?"

With a last caress, his new wife sailed from the room and left him to his work.

He took up the quill again. Aye. He would choose contentment, along with continued prayer.

> *And wanting my wishes, I leave off from prosecuting that whereunto I would to God my wealth were answerable to my will. Thus committing the relief of my discomfortable company the planters in Virginia, to the merciful help of the Almighty, whom I most humbly beseech to help and comfort them, according to His most holy will and their good desire, I take my leave: from my house at Newtowne in Kylmore the 4 of February, 1593.*
>
> *Your most well-wishing friend,*
> *John White*

THE END

Acknowledgments

As always, I am indebted to so many, and no less for this story than others:

Becky and her crew at Barbour—a quietly amazing editor and publishing house who so graciously worked with me despite a concussion, COVID, my daughter's knee surgery, and holidays and homeschooling and all the other obligations and drama that go with being mother to a large family—including the birth of a miracle grandbaby;

Ellen, for your incredible patience in slogging through this hot mess;

Tamela, agent extraordinaire, for all of your comfort and encouragement when I was sure I'd be in actual breach of contract with this one;

Lee, Jen, Beth, and Jenelle, for always being there even while working on your own projects;

Lee McMaster, for pointing us to some of the most amazing food in Nag's Head, and providing very unexpected connections;

Scott Dawson and Warren McMaster, Outer Banks residents, for being willing to answer questions about your expertise and research. All mistakes in the subject matter are my own.

Shirley Wicker of the Hatteras Island Ocean Center, for lending an enthusiastic ear to my research and teaching me the proper local pronunciation for Chicamacomico;

Allen Arnold, for always encouraging and challenging writers to partner with God by taking risks and choosing the hard thing;

Dallas Jenkins, for sharing so much of your own process, both the "Red Sea" moments and reminding me that I don't have to feed the five thousand, only bring my humble loaves and fishes;

My family—for simply being who you are, and always being down for a research trip;

And a long-overdue THANK YOU to all those in years past who encouraged me in my writing, from my third-grade teacher, Mrs. Williams, to my own mother; from school friends (Brenda, Kelly, Karen, just to name a very few) to friends of my mother (Beckie Knowles and Michael Case); and then those who mentored and helped me early on and later (Leisha, Donita, Brandilyn)—and countless others! I may not remember all the names, but every one of you played a part in this lifelong journey, and I am so grateful.

Last but foremost, my Creator-God who has carried me through it all, even when I barely believed.

Historical Note

How does one write about real historical figures and do them justice?

Elinor Dare was just nineteen when she took a giant leap of faith and followed her husband Ananias in his late twenties, and her father, John White, nearly fifty, to the New World. White was of an old age to be starting over in a brand-new land—but try he did.

A vast difference there is between writing a historical account and writing a novel. With the former, the expectation of historical accuracy (as much as possible) is a given. A novel is something else entirely—even here, accuracy is usually appreciated, but the taking of artistic license is allowed.

It's also a tricky thing dealing with actual historical figures as opposed to fictional ones, because somewhere I'm going to get it wrong. How much artistic license do I get to take when portraying, say, Sir Walter Raleigh on-screen? (Which was actually a lot of fun.) In the end, I am not writing a textbook, but a novel, meant to entertain more than it informs—and yet I cannot let go of my own need to "get it right" as much as possible.

With a story such as this one, where certain things are known and then beyond that it seems anyone's guess, there are still different takes on the information available.

I'm indebted to several authors who did write what amounted to textbooks, and most excellently in their own way. Each had their own firm interpretation of the evidence. Lee Miller made for an intimidating introduction to the entirety of Lost Colony events with a rendering so vivid, it made my early attempts at dramatization seem redundant. She also suggests that John White and the colonists were Separatists, and thus considered disposable for such a venture, which I found an interesting theory. Brandon Fullam is sure that John White was unfair and petulant, and that Simon Fernandez (Ferdinando in this novel) was merely misunderstood, not the villain he's often painted to be. (He also explores the timing and effects of hurricanes in a way no one else does, which I found very helpful.) Scott Dawson brings to bear several generations of local Hatteras Island history, as well as personal archaeological research, to show that the Lost Colony was never really lost, only abandoned by England. Philip McMullan was convinced not only that they were never lost, but that

Raleigh maintained contact and for years secretly imported sassafras, thought to be a remedy for syphilis. David Beers Quinn's exhaustive work, which I nearly missed because I somehow thought I wouldn't need "one more resource," also characterizes White as something of a whiner, but otherwise offers an absolute wealth of information I couldn't find elsewhere.

My thoughts about John White, after reading (and re-reading, and re-re-reading) his accounts and poring over his amazing artwork? Here we have, I believe, a brilliant and sensitive man, who despite his use of the term *savage* (which, as I've already explained, was a colloquial term of the time) did see the indigenous peoples of America as beautiful, intelligent, and worthy in their own right, not merely as objects of conquest or conversion—or at least, to a lesser degree than others of his time. That same sensitivity made him vulnerable to the opinions and agendas of others, and thus some have charged him with weakness in leadership. I understand that vulnerability all too well—and many things Fullam found incomprehensible, I felt were instead consistent with White being a man of faith—that is, of true faith, not one who paid mere lip service to Christianity but whose actions were driven by pride or ambition. (Contrast with, say, the actions of Ralph Lane.) And so I have endeavored to portray him.

Of White's fate after 1590, we know nothing, only that he wrote to Hakluyt from Ireland, which itself had suffered recent subjugation to England. (Another story entirely!) There is some slight evidence he had heirs on that side of the pond, which means he possibly remarried at some point, and a notation exists in legal documents of a Bridget White in connection with his estate. One writer refers to her as a possible sister, but I've posited her as a second wife, who could very well have brought him some measure of comfort and contentment after his failure to return to the New World.

For Ananias and Elinor Dare: there is a bit of discrepancy on what year they married. Some accounts go with the earlier date, positing that John Dare, the "natural" or illegitimate son who is recorded as being awarded in 1597 whatever estate Ananias left behind, and a Thomasyn Dare were Elinor's children as well, and left behind in England. Evidence for that is scant, however (especially for the existence of Thomasyn Dare), and for the purpose of this story I went with a later date of marriage, with Virginia being their first child, and John Dare having been born to Ananias of an earlier relationship. The occupation of Ananias, we also know. Many of the men on this venture possessed skill sets crucial to the running of an independent community—clothwork, metalwork, mining, even a former sheriff. I've mentioned a few as I could. There were also a few who had been part of previous expeditions. Two who apparently had been in prison together. Many family associations we can at least guess at, while likely many more we don't know. (My thanks to William Powell for his genealogical work many years ago, as shared by Roberta Estes.) Some men were unmarried; some left wives and children behind. Of the women, we know very little about those who were unmarried, although there are shreds of possibilities for some. I used local Hatteras Island tradition and stories about the vanished community of Beechland as a guide for which men and families might have moved or stayed.

To completely understand the brouhaha over why the settlers did or did not want to settle on Roanoke Island—and why the colony was being established at all—one must understand that England and Spain were bitter enemies at this time. Spain held most of South America and ruthlessly exploited its resources, taking slaves, using native labor to mine for gold and other resources. Spain made her riches from the New World. England made much of her riches in taking prizes of Spanish ships returning through the West Indies. The struggle between these nations was not just political but religious as well, since Queen Elizabeth, being Protestant like her father, King Henry VIII, before her, refused to submit to the Catholic Church. Elizabeth's own cousin, Mary Stuart, ascribed to Catholicism and used religious differences to foment rebellion against Elizabeth—and was executed for the same, earlier in 1587 (a fact I somehow neglect to mention anywhere), so it wasn't just a struggle across the water, but on the very soil of England. The Catholic Church by definition ("catholic" meaning "universal") believed itself to be the only valid expression of God's people, while Protestants viewed the Pope as "the Spanish Antichrist." Other permutations of Christianity were also viewed with disdain, if not outright hostility. One Spanish account refers to Simon Fernandez (at least we think it's him) as "the Lutheran Portuguese," but then White views him as vulgar and vile and pretty much heathen.

(Modern Christians tend to be much more accepting of fellow believers across denominations, thankfully!) Whether Lost Colonists were Separatists or Puritans or otherwise is unknown, but the topic definitely remains rich ground for speculation.

Speaking of such—some will be disappointed that I didn't incorporate the Dare Stone. Some will be ever so relieved that I didn't. I confess: I did, for about five minutes, plan to use it, and even shaped some of the story around the tale hinted at on the first stone—and that one only! All the rest were firmly and clearly proved to be fakes. Some research seems to lend credence to the possibility of the first one being legit—a mineral assessment showed the rock as being similar in composition to stone found inland, around the state line between Virginia and North Carolina, where the legendary "Chawnis Temoatan" was possibly located. Also, it's plausible that Elinor might have had the tools and the knowledge to accomplish the carving. Local opinion of the Dare Stone, however, is emphatically negative—because apparently the man who claimed to find the stone spent quite a bit of time and effort trying to get the community to buy it from him before taking it to Emory University. To me, that smacked of forgery—but I still feel a lingering awe of the stone and the message chiseled there. Maybe that's just a normal human reaction to the unknown—much like the Carolina Algonquian response to all the instruments and gadgets and weapons the English showed off.

Another thing pushing me toward disregarding the Dare Stone is the oral tradition of Native peoples that Virginia Dare was adopted into the Croatoan tribe. Call it sentimentality, but I would honestly like to give Native oral history the most weight.

The CORA Tree, still standing today on Hatteras Island, is an object of similar speculation and legend. It gave me much delight to actually locate the tree on one of my visits to the island and see with my own eyes the letters that are indeed still distinguishable on its trunk. Was this one of the clues the colonists left John White in an attempt to communicate where they might have gone? That makes far more sense to me than a legend about a witch, the popular explanation for those letters carved into an ancient oak.

Other issues with interpreting events: Did White return to England with the Greenville expedition in 1585 or with Lane in 1586? This matters because it would determine whether White could have been present during Lane's attack on Dasemonguepeuk (and thus Wyngyno's murder). Again, some writers thought he would have returned to England earlier, but Quinn makes a pretty good case for White's having stayed in the New World through winter (and accompanying Thomas Harriot on his scientific explorations), so that's what I went with.

Similarly, some writers do not credit White as accompanying Captain Edward Stafford to Croatoan in August 1587 after George Howe's death. I couldn't see why he wouldn't—he'd be eager to renew contact with Manteo's people. Then I noticed his comment, buried in his arguments on why he shouldn't leave the colony and expressing concern about his belongings, that being gone from them three days already proved nobody would be able to keep track of his stuff for him. (Which also indicates that the expedition to the Croatoan lasted three days and not merely two—thus solving a particular dilemma I found regarding dates.)

Nautical terms can be difficult—more so when dealing with period terms that aren't fully explained in the context of a primary account. John White wrote that his 1587 fleet consisted of an admiral (a flagship between 120 and 160 tonnes), a flyboat, and a pinnace. I later learned that the term *pinnace* can apply to the ship's longboats, a single-masted vessel capable of carrying up to twenty men, but in this case meant a full-masted small ship with a deck, of anywhere between 25 and 50 tonnes. Tonnage as it relates to ships is a description of how much cargo can be carried, and it was explained to me that a ship could accommodate roughly one person per ton. (Adjusting of course for crew members and whatever additional cargo is being carried.) We presume that of John White's colonists, some were carried over on the flyboat, but we don't know who or how many, or if the flyboat carried mostly cargo. Also, while we know the name of the admiral/flagship in the 1587 voyage (spelled either as the *Lyon* or the *Lion*, and of course I went with the one that seems most unique), we don't know the names of either the flyboat or pinnace. For the latter, I borrowed the name *Sunne*, the name of the first English pinnace built, according to Wikipedia, at the Chatham Dockyard in 1586. Wiki also says that most such vessels were around 100 tonnes, but whatever the size of the pinnace left at Roanoke Island, it would have to be small enough and of shallow enough draught (sit high enough in the water) to sail the Outer Banks sounds and navigate the ever-changing inlets.

The colony roster from John White's account includes not only Manteo, returning to his homeland, but another Native by the name of Towaye. Nothing is known of him, although we do know there was a Native man in England, probably a captive of Sir Richard Grenville's 1585 expedition, christened on March 27, 1588, taking the name Raleigh, and who died of influenza April 2, 1589, in Grenville's house. One source suggests that Raleigh was actually Towaye, but that seemed unlikely if White includes him on the roster of colonists. It made sense to me that if Towaye was Croatoan, Manteo might release him to return to their people sooner rather than later, and I have him doing so in this story.

Another exceedingly sticky thing was trying to portray Carolina Algonquian, a language and culture that vanished more than two hundred years ago, with the authenticity I wanted. John White's accounts and drawings, and the writings of Thomas Harriot, were invaluable. Harriot is reported to have compiled a dictionary of the language, but it did not survive. We have some knowledge of the Powhatan tongue, which is very similar, from William Strachey and John Smith, contemporary to the settlement at Jamestown, Virginia, but most of what I use here I owe to both Scott Dawson and the late Dr. Blair Rudes. I decided, however, it would be easier to render various words phonetically rather than strictly use their spellings. Carolina Algonquian contains one or two strange consonant forms—some *r*'s are more a flip of the tongue, so they get rendered as a *t* or a *d*, phonetically, and the language lacks an *l* entirely, thus the problem of their saying words like *English* or *Elinor*. For *English* I've borrowed what Dr. Rudes developed for the Powhatan speakers in the film *The New World*. Also, after studying the various spellings of names, and Dr. Rudes's article on pronunciation, I decided to go with John White's own spelling of Wyngyno rather than the otherwise-common Wingina, because I felt it easier to point the reader to what seems the more historically authentic pronunciation of ween-GEEN-ah/oh (hard *g* as in *gate*) than the usual modern win-JEAN-a.

Finding names for fictional characters nearly undid me. I hated using what amounted to cool-sounding groups of syllables with no known meaning, although I did resort to that in a few cases—and one account I ran across states that some Native peoples did actually employ such methods, so we English speakers aren't the only ones who don't always pay attention to meaning when we name our children. Also, for adult names, it seems Algonquian-speaking peoples didn't tend to use words referring to animals or various objects (which would have made choosing fictional names so much easier), but rather words referring to personal traits or attributes. We do know that young children were often given a "milk name," which later changed, thus my choice of Owlet in one scene for a young boy and Mushaniq ("squirrel") for Manteo's fictional daughter. I wish I could have done better!

The same limitations applied to Carolina Algonquian culture. Again, John White's paintings and Thomas Harriot's writings were my mainstay, but Ralph Lane's account was also helpful even if his perspective is severely biased. For wider study of Native culture, the volumes by James Axtell and then Brett Rushforth's *Bonds of Alliance* were very helpful. There is so much we do not know—for instance, I spent an entire afternoon trying to track down an answer to the burning anthropological question of whether kissing is universal to all human cultures as an expression of affection. (The answer: yes and no, as it applies to parental affection and erotic expression, respectively.) But there is also much we do know, such as the fact that indigenous tribes did indeed freely take captives and practice slavery among themselves, largely as prizes of war—and I was fascinated to find it was so much a cultural fixture that highly decorated and ruthlessly effective slave halters were used by various Native peoples, with a few surviving examples. I considered incorporating the use of such a device and decided against it, but the fact remains that slavery was a fixture of Native culture. Native peoples seemed to see no inconsistency in taking some captives to replace deceased family members, while essentially treating others as beasts of burden or using them as potential sacrifices. (We moderns have similar inconsistencies, if you think about it.)

Pinning down the nuances of Native belief about God and the spirit realm was also difficult. Scott Dawson's glossary includes a brief description of *Montóac* as the Great Spirit or God, but further research suggests that this term refers, as my glossary states, to the collective guardian spirits or spiritual force of all living things—of whom *Kewás* may or may not have been one. It's probable that Kewás refers only to the actual idol, not the spirit/s represented thereby. Among the Powhatan (whose language is very similar), the Creator-God was referred to as *Ahoné*, above and separate from all other gods and generally detached from His creation after setting everything in motion. The evil god, analogous to Satan, was referred to as *Oki* (oh-KEE). After a discussion with Dawson about the exact meaning of Montóac, wherein he reminded me how fluid things were because the Native peoples had no written language, I decided to leave room for doubt either way—and thus Sees Far's own questions and struggles.

In the historical notes accompanying my previous title *The Rebel Bride*, I discuss the difficulty of writing across history and across cultures. Much is made these days of telling stories in one's own voice—only writing characters whose ethnic and/or cultural experience matches the author's, and to a certain extent, I see their point. But the reader should consider that any story that isn't autobiography borrows from the perspective and experiences of others, and not every such borrowing qualifies as cultural appropriation. (Think about *Hamilton* or *Bridgerton* for what I consider loose examples of cultural appropriation that no one questions.) I would point again to the precedent set by *Uncle Tom's Cabin*, a nineteenth-century novel of enslaved people written by a white woman, yet cited as the most significant influence in moving people's hearts and minds toward the American Civil War and the ending of slavery. Every writer must research to learn things we previously did not know.

Lastly, I'm painfully aware that even with more than a year's study, there are holes in my research. I'm sure I've gotten at least a few things wrong. I continue to study and fully expect that by the time this book comes to print, I'll be thumping my head against the nearest wall over some mistake or another that will be obvious to an informed reader. I beg grace and hope I can do better with the next book, but. . .perfectionism never sleeps.

Bibliography

Axtell, James, ed. *The Indian Peoples of Eastern America: A Documentary History of the Sexes*. Oxford University Press, 1981.

Dawson, Scott. *Croatoan: Birthplace of America*. Infinity, 2009.

Dawson, Scott. *The Lost Colony and Hatteras Island*. History Press, 2020.

Fullam, Brandon. *The Lost Colony of Roanoke: New Perspectives*. McFarland & Company, 2017.

Harriot, Thomas. *A Briefe and True Report of the New Found Land of Virginia: The Complete 1590 Edition with 28 Engravings by Theodor de Bry after the Drawings of John White and Other Illustrations*. Dover, 1972.

Hakluyt, Richard. *The Principal Navigations, Voyages, Traffiques, and Discoveries of the English Nation*. Google Books. Abridged edition, *Voyages and Discoveries*. Penguin Books, 1972.

Horn, James. *A Kingdom Strange: The Brief and Tragic History of the Lost Colony of Roanoke*. Basic Books, 2010.

Humber, John L. *Backgrounds and Preparations for the Roanoke Voyages, 1584–1590*. North Carolina Department of Cultural Resources, 1986.

Lawler, Andrew. *The Secret Token*. Anchor Books, 2018.

Lawson, John. *A New Voyage to Carolina*. Google Books, 1709.

McMullan, Philip S., Jr. *Beechland and the Lost Colony*. Pamlico & Albemarle, 2010 (as a master's thesis), 2014.

Miller, Lee. *Roanoke: Solving the Mystery of the Lost Colony*. Arcade, 2000, 2012.

Milton, Giles. *Big Chief Elizabeth: The Adventures and Fate of the First English Colonists in America*. Farrar, Strauss and Giroux, 2000.

Oberg, Michael Leroy. *The Head in Edward Nugent's Hand: Roanoke's Forgotten Indians*. University of Pennsylvania Press, 2008.

Quinn, David Beers, ed. *The Roanoke Voyages 1584–1590*. 2 vols. Dover, 1991.

Rushforth, Brett. *Bonds of Alliance: Indigenous and Atlantic Slaveries in New France*. University of North Carolina Press, 2012.

Sloan, Kim. *A New World: England's First View of America*. University of North Carolina Press, 2007.

Strachey, William. *A Historie of Travaile into Virginia Britannia*. Hakluyt Society, 1612, 1849.

A handful of online sites were absolutely crucial to my research as well:

Coastal Carolina Indian Center: CoastalCarolinaIndians.com

Virtual Jamestown: virtualjamestown.org

The Other Jamestown: virtual-jamestown.com

Roberta Estes, scientist and genealogical researcher, particularly this page: https://dna-explained.com/2018/06/28/the-lost-colony-of-roanoke-did-they-survive-national-geographic-archaeology-historical-records-and-dna/

The British Museum online, for their collection of John White's drawings and paintings: https://www.britishmuseum.org/collection/term/BIOG50964

Cast of Characters

Roster of the 1587 voyage to Virginia

*Denotes Assistant

**Denotes married woman

***Denotes boy without parent or other known attachment

Men:

1. John White
2. *Roger Bailie
3. *Ananias Dare [wife Elinor, below]
4. *Christopher Cooper [possibly related to Thomasyn Cooper White]
5. *Thomas Stevens
6. *John Sampson [probable son John, below]
7. *Dyonis Harvie [wife Margery Harvye, below]
8. *Roger Prat [possible son John, below]
9. *George Howe [son George, below]
10. *Simon Fernando
11. Nicholas Johnson
12. Thomas Warner [possible wife Joan Warren, below]
13. Anthony Cage
14. John Jones [possible wife Jane, below]
15. William Willes [Wylles?]
16. John Brooke
17. Cutbert White [possibly related to John]
18. John Bright
19. Clement Tayler
20. William Sole
21. John Cotsmur
22. Humfrey Newton
23. Thomas Colman [possible wife, below—fictional name Anne]
24. Thomas Gramme
25. Marke Bennet
26. John Gibbes
27. John Stilman
28. Robert Wilkinson
29. John Tydway
30. Ambrose Viccars [wife Elizabeth and son Ambrose, below]
31. Edmond English
32. Thomas Topan [possible wife Audry Tappan, below]
33. Henry Berrye
34. Richard Berrye
35. John Spendlove
36. John Hemmington
37. Thomas Butler
38. Edward Powell [wife Wenefrid, below]
39. John Burden
40. James Hynde
41. Thomas Ellis [son or brother Robert, below]
42. William Browne
43. Michael Myllet
44. Thomas Smith

45. Richard Kemme
46. Thomas Harris
47. Richard Taverner
48. John Earnest
49. Henry Johnson
50. John Starte
51. Richard Darige
52. William Lucas
53. Arnold Archard [wife Joyce and son Thomas, below]
54. John Wright
55. William Dutton
56. Mauris Allen
57. William Waters
58. Richard Arthur
59. John Chapman [wife Alis, below]
60. William Clement
61. Robert Little
62. Hugh Tayler
63. Richard Wildye
64. Lewes Wotton
65. Michael Bishop
66. Henry Browne
67. Henry Rufoote
68. Richard Tomkins
69. Henry Dorrell
70. Charles Florrie
71. Henry Mylton
72. Henry Paine [possible wife Rose Payne, below]
73. Thomas Harris
74. William Nicholes [possible connection to John Nicholes, an Assistant who remained in England]
75. Thomas Phevens
76. John Borden
77. Thomas Scot
78. Peter Little
79. John Wyles [Wylles?] —twin to William?
80. Brian Wyles [Wylles?] —related to William/John?
81. George Martyn
82. Hugh Pattenson
83. Martin Sutton
84. John Farre
85. John Bridger
86. Griffen Jones [possible wife Jane, below]
87. Richard Shabedge
88. James Lasie
89. John Cheven
90. Thomas Hewet
91. William Berde

Women:

1. **Elinor Dare
2. **Margery Harvye
3. Agnes Wood
4. **Wenefrid Powell
5. **Joyce Archard
6. **Jane Jones
7. Elizabeth Glane
8. Jane Pierce
9. **Audry Tappan [Topan?]
10. **Alis Chapman
11. Emme Merrimoth

12. **Colman [fictional name Anne]
13. Margaret Lawrence
14. **Joan Warren
15. Jane Mannering [Mainwaring?]
16. **Rose Payne
17. **Elizabeth Viccars

Children:

1. John Sampson
2. Robert Ellis
3. Ambrose Viccars [b. 1583?]
4. Thomas Archard [b. 1575?]
5. ***Thomas Humfrey [b. Oct 1573?]
6. ***Thomas Smart
7. George Howe
8. John Prat
9. ***William Wythers [b. Mar 1574?]

Children born at the colony before White's departure:

1. Virginia Dare [b. Aug 18, 1587]
2. Harvie [fictional name Henry]

Native American repatriates:

1. Manteo
2. Towaye

Others:

Coleman, Robert: probable relative (possibly son) of Thomas Coleman, accompanied 1590 voyage but perished at Hatorask inlet

Cooke (Cocke in some sources): captain of the admiral in 1590 voyage

Dare, John: "natural" or illegitimate son of Ananias, left in England

Drake, Sir Francis: English explorer

Ferdinando, Simon: Simon Fernandez (or Fernandes), navigator of Portuguese birth, originally taken captive as a privateer but pardoned by Queen Elizabeth, presumably for his seafaring knowledge and in exchange for his service. Last name recorded variously as Fernando or Ferdinando but mostly as the latter by John White.

Gland, Darby: crew member of the *Lyon*, originally an Irish prisoner but escaped in the Caribbean during the 1587 voyage (or released by Simon Fernandez ostensibly as a spy to the Spanish)

Greenville, Sir Richard: English explorer, spelled variously Grenville, Greinvile

Kendryck, Sir: fictional name of English gentleman accompanying 1587 voyage, actual name unknown, who threw his political weight behind Simon Fernandez's insistence the colonists remain at Roanoke Island

Lane, Rafe (Ralph): English explorer, in charge of the 1585–86 expedition

Spicer, Edward: captain of flyboat on 1587 voyage and captain of the Moonelight during 1590 voyage but perished at Hatorask Inlet

Stafford, Edward: captain of pinnace in 1587 voyage

Thomasyn: John White's first wife, maiden name Cooper, probably a relation of colonist Christopher Cooper, and deceased before 1587

Walsingham, Sir Francis: spymaster to Queen Elizabeth

Croatoan

Kokon: Timqua's daughter, companion of Mushaniq (fictional)

Manteo: Native man, a Croatoan warrior, who accompanied Amadas and Barlowe back to England in 1584; returned in 1585 with Lane's expedition and stayed to support the English; returned to England in 1586, and part of White's colony in 1587; "to snatch" [modern pronunciation MAN-ee-oh; historical probably mahn-TAY-oh]

Menatoan: Croatoan man, sometimes confused with Menatonon

Mushaniq: Manteo's daughter (fictional) [MUSH-ah-neek]

Timqua: Manteo's sister, who helped rear Mushaniq (fictional)

Towaye: Native man who accompanied the 1587 expedition back from England; nothing is known about him besides his name being recorded on the roster alongside Manteo [toh-WAH-yay]

Wesnah: fictional name of Menatoan's wife

Secotan

Granganimeo: weroance and brother-in-law of Wyngyno; "he who is serious" [possible pronunciation grahn-gah-nee-may-oh]

Owlet: Secotan boy (fictional)

Sees Far: Secotan warrior, son of Granganimeo and friend to Wanchese (fictional)

Wanchese: Native man, probably a Secotan warrior, who accompanied Amadas and Barlowe back to England in 1584; returned in 1585 and disappeared into the wilderness; "to take flight from water" [modern pronunciation WAHN-cheese; historical probably wahn-CHAY-zay]

Wingina/Wingyno—weroance of Secota, Dasemonguepeuk, and Roanoac; gifted Roanoke Island to the English; changed name to Pemispan ("he who watches") when suspicious of Lane's motives. John White spells it as Wyngyno [modern pronunciation win-JEAN-a; historical probably ween-GEEN-oh, with hard *g* as in *gate*]

Other Natives

Menatonon: weroance of Chawanoac; "he who listens well"

Okisco: weroance of Weopomeioc, region north of Chowan River [oh-KEE-sko]

Piemacum: weroance of Pomeiooc, enemy of Wyngyno [possible pronunciation pee-AY-mah-kum]

Skico/Skyco: son of Menatonan [SKEE-coh]

Regions and People Groups

Aquascogoc (sometimes Aguascogoc) [ah-kwah-skoh-gock]: a mainland region and people adjacent to Dasemonguepeuk

Chawanoac [chah-wah-noh-ock]: Chowan River

Chawnis Temoatan: region where copper is mined

Chesepiok (or Chesepioc) [chay-say-pee-ock]: Chesapeake, both the people and the region

Cora Banks: fictional town on the Pamlico River, named after the Coree/Cwareuuoc people

Coree, Cwareuuoc [kwah-ray-yuh-wock]: a people located between the Neuse and Pamlico Rivers; probable derivation of the word "CORA" carved into a tree on Hatteras Island

Croatoan: present-day lower Hatteras Island; in Algonquian, Kurawoten [kuh-ra-WOH-tain]

Dasemonguepeuk: the mainland peninsula nearest Roanoke Island. Spelled variously Dasemongwepeok, Dasemonquepeu, Dasemunkepeuc, etc. [possible historical pronunciation dass-ay-mong-kway-pay-uhk]

Hatorask: present-day upper Hatteras Island; also referred to inlet adjacent to the southern end of Roanoke Island and/or Port Ferdinando

Jacán: originally planned as the site for the "Cittie of Ralegh," located at or near the site of Jamestown, Virginia; named after the Spanish mission of Ajacán, site of a massacre of Jesuit priests in 1571 by the Powhatan

Kenrick's Mount: highest point on Hatorask

Mangoac: a people of the mainland

Ossomocomuck: present-day Outer Banks of North Carolina

Pomeiooc (Pomeyooc): mainland region just south of Dasemonguepeuk, north of the Pamlico River

Powhatan: a people group in possession of present-day Virginia

Pumtico/Pomtico/Pumitukew: Pamlico River

Ritanoe: inland Native town where copper was mined

Roanoac: present-day Roanoke Island

Secota/Secotan: a people group residing mostly upon the mainland but also apparently in possession of Roanoke Island at the time of the first English voyage in 1585; in Algonquian, Sukwoten [suh-KWOH-tain]

Weopomeioc/Weapemeoc: mainland region just north and east of the Chowan River [way-oh-pom-ay-oc or way-ah-pem-ay-oc]

Historical Terms

arquebus: a type of matchlock gun commonly used in the sixteenth century; also *harquebus*

coif: a plain cap that lay across the head, worn by both men and women, more snug than a hood, less ornamented than eighteenth-century women's caps

doublet: a man's garment for the upper body, a type of fitted vest, worn over a shirt, with or without detachable sleeves

fowler: a type of small cannon, used either at the fort or on board ships

"give a side": a nautical term referring to cannon or artillery fire; to "give a whole side" means to fire from all the guns along one side of a vessel

grapnel: a hooked anchor for use with ship's boats

kirtle: a woman's gown, worn over a shift, having a moderately boned bodice and full skirts, with or without detachable sleeves

planters: those sent for the establishment of plantations, i.e., the colonists or settlers

shift: a woman's loose garment of linen, worn as an underdress or nightdress

slops: a man's garment, like trunkhose but not fitted to the leg, often worn by sailors or laborers

trunkhose: a loose-fitting man's garment for the lower body, rather like poofy shorts, tied at the waist and gathered around the thigh; forerunner of breeches

Glossary of Carolina Algonquian Words

ahoné [ah-HONE-ay]: Creator-God in Powhatan culture, and likely among other coastal Algonquian peoples

apohominas [ah-poe-HOE-muh-nahs]: hominy

apon [ah-PONE]: corn bread

crenepo [cray-nay-poh]: woman

ehqutonahas! [eh-kwuh-TONE-ah-hahs] Stop talking! Hush! or Be quiet!

Inqutish [ink-uh-teesh]: English [from Blair Rudes's transliteration of the Powhatan pronunciation / England: Inkurut/Inku(d)und]

Ka ka torwawirocs yowo: How is this called?

kanoe [kah-noh-ay]: canoe, dugout style from trunks of various types of trees, mostly cedar

Kewás [kay-WASS]: an idol representing a god of the Algonquian pantheon; Kewasowoc, plural

kupi [kuh-PEA]: yes

Kuwumádas [kuh-wuh-MAH-dahs]: I love you

Kurawoten [kuh-ra-WOH-tain]: "the talking town" or "the council town"; see "Croatoan" under "Regions and People Groups"

mahkahq [MAH-kahk]: squash

mahkusun [mah-KUH-sun]: shoe (origin of the word *moccasin*)

mahta [MAH-tah]: no

Mehci micis [MEH-chee MEE-cheese]: Now eat!

Montóac: gods, spirits, or the collective spiritual force of all living things; the name attributed by some to the Creator-God or Great Spirit

mushaniq: squirrel

nunutanuhs [nuh-nuh-tah-nuhs]: my daughter; since the prefix appears to be a personal possessive, I've supposed that the root *nutanuhs* may be simply *daughter*, and I've used it so

Nutuduhwins: I am called

nupes [nuh-pace]: sleep

pegatawah [pek-ah-TAH-wah]: corn, maize

pyas [pyahs]: Come!

Sá keyd winkan: Are you well?

sacquenummener: yaupon berries—"nummener" seems to refer to the berries, "sacque" might refer to the plant as a whole

Sukwoten [probably suh-KWOE-tain]: see "Secotan" under "Regions and People Groups"

Tunapewak [t/dun-ah-PAY-wahk]: the People ("the true, real, or genuine people")

uppowoc: tobacco

wassador: precious metals, specifically copper

weroance/weroansqua: leader or chieftain over a town or towns ("one who is rich")

Wingapo: How are you? or Hello!

Winkan nupes [WINK-on nuh-pace]: Sleep well!

wutahshuntas [wuh-TAH-shun-tahs]: foreigners, strangers

Transplanted to North Dakota after more than two decades in Charleston, South Carolina, **Shannon McNear** loves losing herself in local history. She's a military wife, mom of eight, mother-in-law of three, grammie of four, and a member of ACFW and RWA. Her first novella, *Defending Truth* in *A Pioneer Christmas Collection,* was a 2014 RITA finalist. When she's not sewing, researching, or leaking story from her fingertips, she enjoys being outdoors, basking in the beauty of the northern prairies. Connect with her at www.shannonmcnear.com, or on Facebook and Goodreads.

Other books by Shannon McNear

The Blue Cloak

Rachel Taylor lives a rather mundane existence at the way station her family runs along the Wilderness Road in Tennessee. She attends her friend's wedding only to watch it dissolve in horror has the groom, Wiley Harpe, and his cousin become murderers on the run, who drag their families along. Declaring a "war on all humanity" in 1797, the Harpes won't be stopped, and Ben Langford is on their trail to see if his own cousin was one of their latest victims. How many will die before peace can return to the frontier?

Paperback / 978-1-64352-314-9 / $12.99

The Cumberland Bride

In 1794, when Kate Gruener's father is ready to move the family farther west into the wilderness to farm untouched land, Kate is eager to live out her own story of adventure like he did during the War for Independence and to see untamed lands. And she sets her sights on learning more about their scout, Thomas Bledsoe. Thomas's job is to get settlers safely across the Kentucky Wilderness Road to their destination while keeping an ear open for news of Shawnee unrest. But naïve Kate's inquisitive nature could put them both in the middle of a rising tide of conflict. Is there more to Thomas's story than he is willing to tell? Is there an untapped courage in Kate that can thwart a coming disaster?

Paperback / 978-1-68322-691-8 / $12.99